Elliott Murphy, sir  n
Paris for over twen.., ..., ...g .....y-
five albums of original music since his debut album
AQUASHOW in 1973. He continues to perform
concerts in Europe, Japan, Canada and the USA.

He is also a prolific author of fiction and poetry and
has published numerous collections of short stories,
most recently CAFÉ NOTES (Hachette), as well as
the neo-western novel POETIC JUSTICE (Hachette).
His writing has appeared in Rolling Stone (U.S.),
Vanity Fair (France) and other publications.

Born in 1949 to a show business family in New
York, Elliott began his career with a troubadour like
odyssey in Europe in 1971, which included a bit
part in Federico Fellini's film *Roma*. Returning to the
USA he quickly secured a recording contract and
international media attention. His 1996 album
SELLING THE GOLD featured an extraordinary
duet with Bruce Springsteen who often invites
Elliott on stage to perform with him during his
European tours.

In 2015 Elliott Murphy was awarded the Chevalier
des Arts et des Lettres by the French Minister of
Culture.

www.elliottmurphy.com

By The Same Author

Poetic Justice (Novel)

Café Notes (Short Stories)

Where the Women are Naked

  and the Men are Rich (Short Stories)

The Lion Sleeps Tonight (Short Stories)

Forty Poems in Forty Nights (Poetry)

Marty May

ELLIOTT MURPHY

MURPHYLAND

BOOKS

ISBN: 1541240545
ISBN-13: 978-1541240544

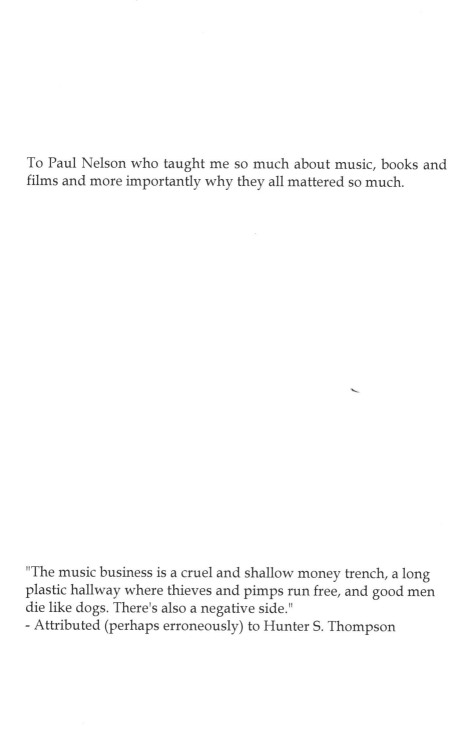

To Paul Nelson who taught me so much about music, books and films and more importantly why they all mattered so much.

"The music business is a cruel and shallow money trench, a long plastic hallway where thieves and pimps run free, and good men die like dogs. There's also a negative side."
- Attributed (perhaps erroneously) to Hunter S. Thompson

Author's Note:

Marty May began as a short story written in my mother's kitchen on York Avenue in NYC in 1978. I remember having dinner with Paul Nelson, the legendary rock critic, at *Jackson Hole,* a burger joint he favored and telling him I wanted to write something about the music business, something real. Not about the glamor and stardom and drugs - not the usual story - but what its like for most working rock musicians who sometimes get their shot at the big time and most often blow it for one reason or another. Paul took a few drags from his ever-present *Nat Sherman* cigarette and told me to go back to F. Scott Fitzgerald's *Pat Hobby Stories* to find my prototype, which I did. Pat Hobby was a Hollywood screenwriter on the skids in much the same way as Marty May is a rock star trying to crawl back on top to a mythical place he really never even knew.

Some time after finishing the story I ran into Jann Wenner, publisher of *Rolling Stone*, on 57th Street and 5th Avenue. Jann and I knew each other since the early days of my recording career and when *Rolling Stone* moved to New York in 1979 I wrote a piece for him titled *Elliott Murphy's Big Beat,* a photo journey through New York's legendary rock landmarks with anecdotes by yours truly. Jann asked what I was up to and I told him I was writing short stories. He seemed interested and so I sent him *Cold and Electric,* which at the time was just that, a short story, and later to be the central movement of *Marty May.* Good to his word, Jann published *Cold and Electric* in *Rolling Stone* in January 1979 and I believe it was the first short story ever published in the magazine. Although I didn't have my photo on the *Rolling Stone* cover (which is the holy grail of every rock star) I did have my name there, as an author of fiction and that was something.

Jann encouraged me to expand the story into a novel and so I did. He was a fine editor himself and we worked closely together and Patty Romanowsky, a *Rolling Stone* editor, came on board as well. Literary agent Sarah Lazin who was managing *Rolling Stone Books* at the time shopped the finished novel around but could never find the necessary co-publisher we needed. I'm sure I didn't hear all the criticisms of my novel but I do remember one publisher saying that people who were interested in rock 'n roll just didn't read books.

Some years after, Jann Wenner sent me a note to cheer me up. He said he was sure that Marty May would find his audience someday but not now. And he was right because a few years later I found a publisher in France who published a very condensed version of the novel called *Cold and Electric* and similar editions were published in Germany and Spain shortly afterwards. Now, a quarter century later, I took a new look at the complete version of the novel, dusted it off, and decided to call it *Marty May.* Slight edits were made but essentially I left my early writing style in tact including the switch between third and first person narrative which I still think is essential to the landscape of the story. And ironically, I think *Marty May* is more timely today then ever: the search for the American dream, the loss of credit both in economic and spiritual terms and the continuing drama of white and black America coming to terms with each other.

Part One
Reunion
New York City
New Jersey
1982

Chapter 1

MAY, MARTY (b. 1949, Pocahontas Heights, N.J.) virtually plucked from a high school dance by Blind Red Rose, May spent five years with the legendary blues singer before beginning a solo rock & roll career. He achieved sporadic success but was unable to

Dave Simmons stared at what he had just typed, shook his head and then slowly pulled the paper out of his typewriter. He gracefully threw it into the trash bin next to his desk, and lit a long brown Nat Sherman's cigarette; staring now at the paperless typewriter. His desk was nothing but a rectangular plank of thick raw plywood supported by metal file cabinets. Stacked underneath it were piles of rock magazines and novels by Raymond Chandler, Philip K. Dick and F. Scott Fitzgerald. The large IBM Selectric *typewriter sat in the center of the desk icon-like with a half dozen packs of Sherman's around it. Behind him was a wall covered with nothing but vinyl records; albums and albums stacked floor to ceiling, some in shelves, some on the floor, some leaning against the wall. There was nothing on any of the walls of his apartment, no photos, no art of any kind but in one particular spot low to the ground was the distinct outline of the soles of two feet. This was where Dave Simmons braced himself to do his one hundred sit-ups each morning.*

He picked up the black rotary dial phone from his desk and quickly dialed a number from memory.

"Windsor Records."

"Publicity department please," he said. His voice was gentler than he looked. You might expect something rough and Runyonesque to come punching out from behind the Sherman's and the shades and the Irish tweed cap pulled low and worn regardless of the season but instead he spoke with a medium high Midwestern drawl and a slight hesitation before he spoke. He was a naturally shy man in an unnatural and un-shy business: the music business.

"Windsor Publicity. Can I help you?"

"Uh ...yep, hope so, I'm Dave Simmons and I'm writing a book about blues and the connection to rock and ... "

"Simmons?" interrupted the nasal voice of the female publicist. "Aren't you a record reviewer?"

"Yeah, well, sometimes for Rolling Stone ... I have done that." He had hoped that this wouldn't happen, not having been too kind to some of

Windsor Record's latest releases in his widely read reviews. "But now I'm working on this book about the influence of blues on rock & roll, mostly white rock & roll, and I need some information about Marty May."

"Marty May? Is he one of our artists? Doesn't sound familiar."

"Well, he may not be one of your artists anymore, but I believe he was a few years ago. Recorded a few great albums for Windsor. I should know," he let out the slightest laugh. "I reviewed them."

"I'm sorry, I can only help you with artists on our current roster but thanks for the reviews. Would you like me to send you a few great recent releases? I know you'd love them if you liked Martha May so much."

"Marty, not Martha - he's a guy." He had expected as much. "Well, do you know how I could maybe get directly in touch with him? Just an address or a phone number would do? Or a manager at least?"

"Let me switch you to the A&R - I think they go back a little further than we do."

The A&R department did go back just far enough to help Dave Simmons out and they had a phone number for Marty May still on file but little more then that, they apologized, because his albums were all 'cutouts[1]' now. When Dave Simmons asked exactly what that meant the A&R man didn't know.

"Uh.... I guess it means nobody buys them so we get rid of them any way we can."

"Too bad," said Dave Simmons. "They were great records."

"There's a lot of great records," said the A&R man. "And most of them are cutouts."

The address on West Seventy Second Street, a pre-war building with a doorman, was more luxurious than Dave Simmons imagined he would find Marty May living in. In fact, it was probably more than he himself could afford and he was surprised that a rock star without a record contract could. The doorman announced him over the intercom and Dave walked into the carpeted elevator. Meanwhile, upstairs in his apartment, Marty May was trying to look casual and elegant at the same time, wildly brushing than messing up his long hair and trying on whatever clean shirts he could find. He had even tidied up his place although not so much that it would look like he cared what some rock

---

[1] In the recording industry, a **cut-out** refers to a deeply-discounted or remaindered copy of an LP, cassette tape, Compact Disc, or other item.

critic would think of his pad. But he felt a cold sweat appear on his forehead when he answered the door.

The two men faced each other having never met before. Dave Simmons was taller than Marty, something Marty's rock star slouch exaggerated even more.

"Hi. I'm Dave Simmons." They shook hands.

"Hi Dave. Welcome to my digs - have a seat." He'd almost replied, I'm Marty May but had caught himself just in time.

But in fact the apartment was not as nice as Dave had expected judging from the ritzy appearance of the building: there was an old couch with a faded Mexican blanket thrown over it, some chairs that once belonged to a suburban kitchen set and a beat up wooden coffee table covered with enough cigarette burns. But there was a gold record award on the wall over the couch and the recently sprayed glass cleaner was running down the side of the frame. That was something he could write about at least.

"Nice place, he said. "Been here long?"

"Oh ... long enough," said Marty. "I'm planning on moving but I just can't find the time. I may go to the west coast - join the crowd. Most of my good furniture and stuff is in storage." He lied.

"Is this one or two bedrooms?"

"One," said Marty. "Who needs more? You want something to drink?"

"A coke would be great," said Dave.

Marty went to the refrigerator and opened it before he said that he was out of coke.

"How about coffee?" asked Dave.

"Well ... I'm kind of out of coffee, too," said Marty. They both laughed self-consciously. "I usually go out for breakfast," said Marty. "Kind of a habit from all those years on the road, I guess."

"You spent a lot of time on the road?"

"Enough," said Marty defensively.

"Sure, listen, I'll have anything you have."

"How about a beer?" asked Marty. He reached for a six-pack of Beck's.

"Great,"

"So what's this book you're working on?" He handed Dave his beer. "Some kind of rock & roll dictionary? Don't tell me Webster's is doing it."

"No, no. I don't think that Webster's even has the word rock and roll listed."

"You know, I never looked." In just a few gulps Marty had almost finished his beer. He burped.

"Actually its a book about blues and rock & roll," said Dave. "Kind of like an encyclopedia, you know, everything in alphabetical order."

"I get it," said Marty. "Make it all legitimate, like jazz or something," He was still unsure how to act with this guy; it had been a few years since he'd done an interview but he remembered being burned a few times when he came on too friendly and the interviewer then went and made him look like a clown.

"So when was your last album out?" asked Dave abruptly.

"Oh ... let me see ... I guess a little over a year ago."

"You mean there was another one after This Time I Mean It?"

"No ... that was the last one, I guess."

"I thought that was out about three years ago? Seventy-Eight or Seventy-Nine wasn't it?"

"Right, somewhere around there. Here ... I was thinking of the European release or something." At once Marty knew it was stupid to lie; of course this guy would know the release dates of his albums, he would come prepared if nothing else.

"That long ago? Three years? Man, time flies." He stood up and went into the kitchen to get another beer and Dave Simmons set up a cassette recorder.

"Looks like we're getting down to business here," said Marty when he returned. "Better watch what I say."

"Yeah, well, I know you got things to do."

Marty said nothing, sipped his beer.

"What I'd like to begin with is your time with Blind Red Rose. Its true that you met him at a high school dance?"

"Actually a college dance," said Marty

"How old were you?"

"About seventeen, I guess."

"You went to this college?"

"It was a college dance, I didn't go there, was just playing in the band - still in high school and was gonna graduate that June. Must have been some time in the winter. But I think one of the guys in my band did go to the college and his girlfriend was on the social committee or something so we got the gig." The memory grabbed Marty and he suddenly remembered that bass player's face and his brand new Chevy

Camaro that he refused to carry equipment in because he was afraid it would damage the interior. Marty knew, even back then, that a guy like that would never make it.

"So what happened?" asked Dave.

"Well, let me see...it was nineteen-sixty-eight, I think, and we were a blues band ... or at least a 'white blues band', you know, we played a lot of Cream and Hendrix but we also played a lot of Chicago stuff, Muddy Waters, Howling Wolf, John Lee Hooker...no, he was from Detroit wasn't he? Well anyway, it was all Chicago blues to me. Kind of like Paul Butterfield – you know who he was?"

"Sure, Mike Bloomfield, incredible guitarist, went on to play with Dylan.

"Right. So we were there to play our own set and then to back up Blind Red Rose, who never carried a backup band, just came to the show and made do with whatever he could find, kind of like Chuck Berry. You know he never carries a band either."

"He should," said Dave. "Whenever you see him these days the show always depends on how good the back up band is and what kind of a mood Chuck is in.

"Well I suppose its a little more complicated than that," said Marty defensively. "It's expensive to carry a band." He didn't like hearing a rock writer criticizing Chuck Berry. If it wasn't for Chuck Berry there might not be any rock & roll at all. And certainly not any rock writers.

"Blind Red Rose just traveled with his daughter, Ruby Rose. She was like his manager, his agent ... in fact, she took care of everything," said Marty.

"I know," said Dave Simmons. " I spoke to her. They live outside of Detroit now."

"Wow! Really? You spoke to Ruby?" Marty's voice got animated. "She's great. Ruby is one of the great ones. Do you have her number? I'd like to call her. I haven't spoken to either one of them in years. They lived in Brooklyn when I was playing with Red. By that time, Red did carry a band of mostly white guys from New York except for the drummer who was black, of course. Red didn't like white drummers - said he didn't believe in them. Always accused them of speeding up on him although the truth was that he was always slowing down around the last verse." Marty shook his head and laughed. "What a character. That man has got his own sense of time for sure. Taught me most of my own bad habits. They should have stayed in New York, you know? But after I left ... well, *they just didn't keep it together here for that much longer. And I kind of...lost touch, you know what I mean."*

"Yeah, were there any hard feelings about you going out on your own?"

"Of course not!" said Marty defensively. "Why would there be hard feelings? A gig's a gig." He got up to get another beer.

"Stupid question," said Dave though he didn't really think so. "I can give you Ruby's number of course. They're supposed to come to New York soon for a gig at Tramps. And I'm gonna interview Red when they get here."

"Ruby's the one you should interview," said Marty. "She knows more about the blues than her father. I remember once she told me that BB King was..."

"But ... uh ... what happened at the dance?" interrupted Dave.

"Oh ... they asked me to join them on the road. Or at least Ruby asked me to join them. So I said, uh, sure and I think I left the next day or the day after that."

"So you never finished high school?"

"No...I didn't really have time. So what? Diploma doesn't mean much in my business."

"'Course not - probably would have been surprised if you did. Most good musicians barely get through school," Dave smiled.

"I don't know about that either, I heard that Mick Jagger went to The London School Of Economics," said Marty. "'Maybe there's a lesson to be learned there somewhere. He does pretty well."

"Yeah ... maybe. But those were great records you did with Blind Red Rose," Dave wanted to get back on the track before Marty popped another beer. "But they're really hard to find now and expensive, too. Kind of collector items."

"Oh yeah? Then I wish I had a few copies to sell," said Marty carelessly. Quickly he added: "I wouldn't really sell them, you know, but I do wish I had a few copies. I don't know what happened to mine."

"How many records did you do with Rose?"

"Two...maybe three."

"Three? All I know of is "Red Rose And Blues" and "Night Blooms A Red Rose."

"Well, there was a live album somewhere over in Europe. The one time we went there we played a blues festival in Germany and somebody recorded it and put out an album when my own stuff started doing well.

14

It was called something like "Early Days Marty May With Blind Red Rose". Creative title, huh?

"Yeah, really."

"I never got paid for it. I don't think Red Rose did either. But he's more used to that kind of thing than I am. I get pissed off when I get ripped off and he gets surprised when he doesn't.

"So, how long did you play with Red Rose?"

"Oh man...I don't know..." Marty counted on his fingers. '67, '68, '69 ... about five years, I guess. In the beginning it was just Red and Ruby and me and we'd pick up the rest of the band wherever we'd be playing. I was kind of the musical director, if there is such a thing in blues."

"He was big there during the Blues craze of the late sixties."

"Yeah, I mean he was always 'big' as far as I was concerned. But he did well during those years, probably the only time he really worked steady. That's when we had a full band and an agent who booked the dates. We played a lot of festivals and stuff."

"So what happened?"

"Well...you want another beer?" Marty walked into the kitchenette but kept talking. "I just split. The Blues thing was kind of dying and I had an offer to do my own album, which is what I always really wanted to do anyway. Hey, Ruby and Red understood - they know you gotta go for it in this business if you want to get anywhere." He came back with another beer and sat down. "So I guess you could say that's what happened - I went for it."

"And how many solo albums have there been?"

"Five, although the first one was a kind of group thing, Marty May And The May Men. I wasn't sure if I wanted to be both lead guitar and lead singer so I had another guy who sang most of the songs. But finally I didn't like being part of a group. I never really believed in democracy when it comes to rock & roll."

"What do you mean?"

"Well, I don't know ... the whole band thing, it seems to work better for the English, you know? They manage to keep bands together for years and years like The Stones, or The Who, or The Kinks. As long as they're all taking tea at three or whatever. But for Americans it's different. Maybe we're a little too independent. We come up with individual guys like Elvis, Dylan, and Buddy Holly. We're just not team players. At least I know I'm not. Anyway, I figured it was my career and I wanted to call the shots. So I did."

"*Which record was that?*" *Dave pointed to the gold album over the couch.*

"*That was* **Burnin'** *it was a live album. The one before that, Mayday, it went gold too.*" *Marty added proudly.* "*I lost the award somewhere. I think I left it at one of my managers' offices.*

"*Were those the only two that went gold?*"

"*What, isn't two enough?*"

"*I didn't mean...*"

"*Who knows? I never trust the way record companies count anyway It seems either you sell twenty thousand or you sell five hundred thousand - never anything in-between*"

"*So what happened?*" *asked Dave.*

"*What happened to what?*"

"*To you. To your recording career.*"

"*What do you mean?*" *asked Marty.* "*I'm still here.*" *He looked away and finished his fourth beer. He had a bad feeling; he'd been too nice to this guy. There was a silence and then finally he said* "*You know, this seems to be getting less and less like an interview and more and more like an obituary.*" *Suddenly, he felt mad and drunk.* "*You can do that on your own time, OK?*"

"*Well...I didn't mean it to be that way. I'm just trying to get the facts, Marty. So what are you working on now?*"   "*This interview, I guess.*" *Marty looked at his watch.* "*Listen I got to go. Let's finish up on the phone sometime, okay?*"

"*Yeah, fine...whatever you want. I'll call you and give you Ruby Rose's number anyway.*" *Dave Simmons packed up his tape recorder and at the door said:* "*I hope I didn't offend you in some way. I   certainly didn't intend to.*"

"*Don't worry about it,*" *said Marty. He tried to smile.* "*I'm not throwing you out or anything. It's just that I got to get ready for a rehearsal.*"

Of course, there was no rehearsal though Marty did pick up his electric guitar and play for a while. Then he sat in bed and watched TV. The beer had made him drowsy, but before he would let himself fall asleep he got up and removed his Fender Telecaster guitar from where he had placed it at the foot of the bed. He didn't want to kick it off in his sleep and so he placed it out on the couch where Dave Simmons had been sitting.

He looked at his guitar sitting there and he held an empty beer bottle like a microphone, "So tell me," he said in a nasal mid-west accent to his guitar, "What the fuck happened?"

The phone rang just when Marty was dozing off and he hesitated picking it up. Too much blues coming his way lately...

Chapter 2

"It was only a figure of speech.

"Goodbye, Mr. May."

"Hey don't hang up on me again! Come on, I had the decency to call you back, OK? I'm trying to be nice - just don't hang up on me okay? Let me explain what I meant."

A long pause, which I imagined, was timed for effect.

"Proceed, Mr. May."

Finally, the voice of *American Express* had spoken.

"All right ... now when I said that I don't have a pot to piss in - it was just a figure of speech. You know? So there was really no reason for you to get so upset. I wasn't trying to insult you or *American Express* or anyone for that matter. Believe me, I have the deepest respect for *American Express*. As far as I'm concerned, the whole concept of traveler's checks is just brilliant fucking brilliant! I mean you're out there on the road partying and who wants wads of cash in their pockets when some..."

"Watch your language, Mr. May. I will not be abused by you even if you are - at least for the moment - a cardholder."

"Now that's what I mean, what we have here is a communication problem like in Cool Hand Luke when Paul..."

"I don't go to movies, Mr. May."

"All right ... its just part of my vocabulary that's all. You know, in the music business don't care about things like that. You see where I'm coming from? I think if we could just try to relate to each other on a more personal..."

"Personally, I have no interest in where you're coming from," he interrupted. "But I can tell you that if something isn't done about this account very soon you'll be going to court in the very near future."

"But I'm broke!" I pleaded. "Can't you understand? The bottom fell out, the rainy day came, and my ship has definitely not come in! That's what I was trying to tell you when I said I don't have a pot to ... you know what in!" "Mr. May, I've had about enough of this conversation. And besides, if you're telling me now that you don't have a 'pot to... well, let me say that whatever you have or don't have is certainly not the fault or concern of *The American Express Company*. We issued you a credit card in good faith."

I tried to remember what the good faith of American Express had gotten me. Maybe a few pairs of snakeskin cowboy boots, a couple of *Sony* portable cassette players, a Warhol lithograph ... no I already sold that months ago. Anyway, nothing to add up to the ridiculous sum of five thousand dollars! I mean there are people out there in the third world who don't make that much money their whole lives. And fuck if I haven't spent it and I can't even remember what on.

I checked the time. Oh yeah, I guess my *Cartier Tank watch* was somewhere on that Amex bill too. But I didn't feel guilty - I felt like another victim of the system. Like I was tricked into becoming a consumer, like my success was guaranteed and maxing out my credit cards was part of the deal. Not my fault if I take things literally when *Cartier* advertised its newest status watch as part of its 'Le Must' collection.

"Well ... even your own commercials say that I shouldn't leave home without it," I retorted.

That brought out a slight laugh. "Well, in your case you obviously should never have left home with it. But what I don't understand, Mr. May, is how you let it get this far. For years you had a good credit history with us. You spent a lot but you paid on time, you and your wife..."

"Ex-wife."

"Oh ... well the point is that you should realize we never would have let you overextend yourself if you hadn't proved trustworthy in the past. We considered you a good risk." Then he added nastily. "Up to now, that is."

"You know, you're overlooking a very important factor here." I swallowed hard and lowered my voice. I tried to sound like Gregory Peck. "I am a celebrity,"

"Mr. May, even celebrities have to pay their bills. Not that it matters but what kind of a celebrity are you?"

"I'm a rock star," I said almost sheepishly.

"I never heard of you." (Truly the cruelest cut.)

"But that's the point. Why don't I do a Television spot for American Express? You know, one of those where the semi-famous person says, *You may not know me but ...,* It would be great!"

"I don't get it, Mr. May."

"Well ... I mean... there's a whole baby boom generation of consumers just starting to work, and I am ... or at least I use to be... quite a hero to a lot of them. Don't you think that you need someone these kids look up to for the front man of your commercials? Why not someone like me? And I'd be willing to apply ... part of my fee toward my debt.

"I think you should see a psychiatrist, Mr. May. First of all, like I said, I never heard of you and secondly, you are hardly a role model for the type of customer we're trying to attract. The American Express Card is a symbol of success not failure."

"Hey! I'm NOT a failure!"

"Well then, what are you?" he said calmly.

"I'm between peaks in my career. Its normal in my business." Not sure of that myself though.

"Mr. May, like I said if it weren't for your past credit history I would have handed your account over to our attorneys right away but I've gone out of my way to work with you on a personal basis."

Personal, I thought. This is personal? Personal would be more like lending me the money to pay the bill, no?

"And do you appreciate this special attention?"

I didn't answer.

"Hardly," he whined on. "Let me check the record here ... first, you refer us to an accountant to whom it seems you owe more money to than to us. He even offered me a fee if I could help him collect! And then you made me go over each and every individual charge while you denied any knowledge of most of them and then..."His voice was getting higher and louder.

"Then you invent a totally ludicrous story about a Marty May impostor who goes around the country using your cards!"

"Well ... someone did that to Alice Cooper."

"Mr. May! The point is that there is no one out there who would want to impersonate you."

"Ok, ok ... I did finally admit that it must have been me who made all those charges."

"But only after I mentioned words like fraud and lawyers. And we've been through the 'check's in the mail' routine for over three months. Remember, Mr. May, when I sent over a messenger to personally pick it up when you said that you were too sick with the flu to get out of bed? And what do you do? You didn't even have the decency to answer your own door. And then today, you pretend you're some kind of servant with a ridiculous accent and tell me that your 'master' has gone on an extended tour for six months to the Far East. Are you kidding me? Extended tour to far east!"

I cringed as he mimicked my Asian houseboy accent. I got it from a Peter Sellers movie I had seen the night before and it wasn't as good as his.

"Well, I'm speaking to you now."

"Yes, you are. But you wouldn't be if my secretary hadn't called you back posing as a writer from Rolling Stone!"

"You know now that you mention that, I want to say that I just can't believe that a prestigious firm such as yours would stoop to such ... trickery ... to collect this relatively ... insubstantial and hardly overdue debt."

"How much longer Mr. May?" said the voice of doom.

"Give me a couple of weeks? I'll figure something out, I promise you."

What was I doing here? Hardly pleading for the lives of Sacco and Vanzetti? But my Amex card had played such a large part in my own life's little melodrama that to save it was to save myself in some symbolic fashion. What would I be without it? People don't write letters anymore so what else do we have as proof of our existence? Phone bills and credit card receipts, that's all. If my card were taken away they would also be taking away that sunny afternoon I strolled into Tiffany and charged my ex-wife's wedding ring. And they'd be taking away the rainy three days I spent in Haiti getting our divorce. Good or bad memories – it didn't really matter now - it was all part of me - it was all my history. And if I believe in anything, I believe in history.

Once, in L.A., I charged cocaine from a dealer who took all major credit cards. I don't know how he worked this scam but the receipt had Expensive Habits Inc. written on it. Get a corporation and you can do anything. Afterwards, I'd probably used my same Amex card to chop the coke up.

Mainly my card had been for nighttime activities. I hadn't so much bought things as I had done things. I'd need the right front fender of a Lincoln Continental stretch limousine as proof of purchase. I mean, who's to say that a two-hour cruise through Central Park at three in the morning isn't worth a hundred and fifty dollars? (Including tip.) This is the stuff rock dreams are made of and I felt a responsibility to do my part, to keep those rock dreams going.

I once read an interview with Johnny Carson, and he talked about something called 'fuck-you' money. He said that was the best thing about making tons of dough. Well, the closest I ever came to having 'fuck-you money' was my gold American Express Card. And if I ended up with 'fuck-me debts' well ... so be it. At least I face these alone. You know, for all those years I had that Amex card in my pocket and knowing that I could walk into any restaurant I cared to and any chic boutique that caught my eye and call for a limo any time day or night ... well, it was worth it. For me, it was as close as I came to making it.

Finally Mr. Moore spoke: "I'll tell you what I'm going to do for you, Mr. May: I'm going to give you a final extension of thirty days. If you promise that at that time you will personally come down to the American Express office and pay this bill in full. But if you try to use this card at any time before this account is settled it will be taken away from you for good and probably cut in half right before your eyes!"

A castrated credit card! Just the thought grossed me out.

"And this is the absolute last extension, Mr. May. There will be no more phone calls from me because if you fail to pay in thirty days then its all over between us and our lawyers will see you in court."

"Oh ... that's great. Believe me, you won't ever see me in court."

"What...?

"I just mean ... you can depend on me. I give you my word."

"It's not your word we want. Its your money."

That was the most honest thing this man had said to me. Then I heard an unusually loud click. Was our conversation going down on tape somewhere? Well, at least someone was still interested in recording Marty May.

Chapter 3

'Or it's all over between us!' I'm sure my ex-wife Barbara had said that same thing to me shortly before she left me although I couldn't remember exactly what her ultimatum had been about. Had she had enough of the rock star life? Waking up at four in the afternoon, running out for dinner and then coke-propelled club-hopping the rest of the night and into the wee hours? Or was it just to hang up my wet towels after my shower?

On the floor of my closet was a large box that had once held a stereo receiver and I dragged it out. Inside were clippings from magazines and newspapers and some fan letters. There were pictures and press releases from record companies and some folded up posters. It was all Marty May stuff - it was all about me. I dug deep into the box and pulled out a newspaper article. It was a little torn in the folds but it wasn't ancient. It just looked that way from being over-handled at moments such as this. It was from nineteen seventy-five: a good year. It had appeared in *The Los Angeles Times*, written by a famous rock writer and it was about a soon to be famous rock star. It was about me and it began like this:

Rock's next generation has arrived!

And it went on…

For those of us fortunate to have witnessed Marty May's performance last night at The Roxy the wait for the next big thing is over. After years of uninspired offerings from the leftover dinosaurs of the Sixties we finally have something to raise the prospect that rock is not yet dead. If I told you that Marty May has all the rebellion of Dylan combined with the musicianship of Jimi Hendrix and the sexiness (though far more subtle) of Mick Jagger and I swore that I wasn't working for his record company would you believe me? You should.

After playing with various congregations over the past couple of years (as well as paying his dues by backing up blues legend Blind Red Rose when fresh out of high school) Marty May has finally stepped into the limelight.

His first solo album MAYDAY, is a collection of rock anthems that range from his Hendrix-like "Feather Pillow Fortunes" to what can only be described as 'Like A Rolling Stone Part Two' "Now What Loretta." He sings with the shy confidence of Van Morrison in the shower and just when you think that every possible lead guitar note has been played to death Marty comes off with some innovative and authentic licks, which tastily reveal his blues background.

Marty May - MAYbe he's the one to watch.

I looked around and no one was watching me except the cockroaches. And they were actually scurrying away from me. Getting out my old press was worse than trying to call an old girlfriend. That brief moment of rekindled romance is soon replaced by the cold leftovers of what little is actually left of the relationship. But what else did I have to do? I dug deeper into my graveyard scrapbook.

Nothing looked as dated as the trade magazines like *Billboard* and as I leafed through it I couldn't help but be amazed at all the full-page, full-color ads for albums and groups that were never heard from again. And those ads cost something like Ten thousand dollars each. Man, I could live on that for a year today. And when I came to the page with my dumber but younger picture on it I really *did* wish I had the ten big ones today instead of this box full of career hangovers. But actually it wouldn't even be that much because Windsor Records had cheaped out and only gone for a black and white ad:

MARTY MAY
Just the Man
And his Music

Because that's enough
The new album From Rock's Great Hope
(And then a picture of me holding my guitar wearing some ridiculous sheepskin vest standing in front of some tough looking bar in downtown L.A. looking totally out of place.)

THE USUAL PLACE (That was the name of the album)

I laughed out loud. But then it only hurts when you laugh doesn't it? Hauling out the old press in times of crisis is a fast fix but the comedown is long and treacherous when the initial euphoria so easily turns into another hopeless attempt at figuring out my fall from grace. What was it? Bad promotion? Bad management? Born under a bad sign? I opted for the last: it's the only one that a bluesman could live with. But the truth is that the blame falls hardest on that select group of five hundred thousand Americans who chose not to buy my last two albums and nothing sounds worse than a failed album. But it was still early and my evening was still free - I could get depressed all night long if I wanted. So I turned on the TV, watched a game show, and went to sleep.

When I awoke it was twilight. There was still an hour to kill before the news so I went down to my lobby to check my mail. And today, among my junk mail, a torn copy of Billboard magazine and overdue bills was a handwritten envelope addressed to Marvin May. No one had called me that since high school and now they were calling me again. It was an invitation to my Fifteenth high school reunion. Strangely, the first thing I did was go into my bathroom, look in the mirror and see if I had aged. But mainly, I had not cleaned so I grabbed the Windex and cleaned the mirror.

And had I aged? How could I tell? Since I didn't graduate from high school I didn't even have a yearbook photo to compare to. Missing out on the yearbook photo shoot was one thing I really regretted about dropping out: my biographer wouldn't like it. What I saw in my reflection still had a touch of innocence, I suppose, and a slight gesture of surprise and even a little more character than I had suspected. Someone once told me that every bad dream gives you a wrinkle. I should look like a mummy by now.

Of course they're inviting me to their reunion now that I'm almost famous, I thought. They laughed me out of the school, out of the town and out of the state, and now they want me to come back, well ... And I did think these words even while knowing they were far from original. They were the words of Janis Joplin but in my case, the truth was that three months or so before my upcoming graduation I had dropped out of school to go on the road with a truly legendary, black and blind blues singer. And now, fifteen years later, I guess I was a rock 'n roll star of similar legendary dimensions: broke, in debt, and technically a high school dropout. All I needed was a catchier name. Something like *Bo Lightning May* could work...

But you know, I'm not sorry I dropped out of school although I must say that at the time I didn't realize the stigma that went with it in society and back then I certainly didn't want to be a member of *society* at all. Things like medical insurance, pension plans, or social security didn't mean much to me. And that's the problem: they still don't. But now I know that someday they will; and that's where they get you - in the long run. Rock 'n roll is a race for sprinters, no one really expects you to make it to the finish line alive.

I wish I had a picture of myself back in my high school days. My band was a *Young Rascals* clone and we used to wear knickers just like they did and we had that big Hammond B3 organ sound that was so popular then. My hair was down to my ass but I don't think I had even heard the word *hippie* yet. There was a blues craze going on back in sixty-seven. I don't know why. The blues comes and goes; must have something to do with the general mood of society. And let me tell you the days of flower power weren't all incense and peppermint. I guess I had started smoking pot; I didn't take LSD till much later, until it was almost out of fashion.

I remember when Blind Red Rose showed up at the dance. Our job was to play a set and then back him up when he did his own show. He didn't rehearse with us at all but all his songs were mostly standard twelve bar blues so we could follow along alright although he does occasionally stretch it out a little and he definitely makes the chord change when he feels it and you least expect it. My band was already on stage and I remember him being led through the crowd by a black woman who looked half his age, and I remember thinking that blind or not he was doing all right with the babes. She looked sexy and strong and it wasn't until after the show that she introduced herself as Red's daughter. Ruby was taller than me and real solid; the kind of, woman you'd like to fuck but not fight because she'd probably kick your ass. She had wonderful dark, crimson hair, and later I found out that that's why they called her Ruby. It could have been her real hair color because they did call her father Red although by the time I met him he didn't have a hair on his head. I remember thinking that Ruby looked like a female Malcolm X; same ready grin but something very serious going on behind that smile.

Ruby's daddy was long past the age of caring much about his backup band or his lead guitarist or all those other things us young musicians took so seriously. When we were on the road he wouldn't even change his guitar strings until he got down to three and that was only at her insistence. Ruby had been taking care of all Red's business since Red had shown up at her mother's old house in Detroit thirty years after going out for a newspaper. Ruby's mother had passed on from cancer but the people who were living in the house accompanied Red down to the corner Bar-B-Que where Ruby was then working as a waitress. When they met, Ruby looked her father over and repeated her mother's favorite line concerning his disappearance: "And just what newspaper were you looking for? *The HONG KONG PRESS?*" Red just shrugged and mumbled something about being a rolling stone and reached out to hug his daughter and Ruby put her arms around him too, just glad that she had some real family again.

And that was it. Ruby and Red had been together ever since. She needed a father and he needed a manager not to mention someone who would make sure that he didn't get hit by a car returning from gigs half drunk and still blind. It didn't take long for Ruby to get hip to the fact that young white boys with long hair who played loud and distorted blues riffs copied from old Chicago blues men were making a lot of money at the time. She'd seen what The Rolling Stones had done for Muddy Waters career and she knew that with a kid like me leading a backup band and supplying a little *white bread respectability* (as she was so fond of calling it) Blind Red Rose could play the big rock festivals that were the rage then and start earning the big time money that had always eluded him.

Her approach to me was ... original. She just stood at the side of the stage like she always did and watched her daddy's show while pouring him some bourbon into a Coke and passing it onstage when needed. Man, I was just thrilled to be playing with him, he was so damn real, so if I played exceptionally well that night I don't remember. But after the show and after she had gotten paid Ruby came over to me as I was putting my guitar in its case.

"What's your name?" she asked sternly.

"Marvin...Marvin May," I replied meekly.

"I'm Ruby Rose." she said proudly and squinted her eyes just like Malcolm X used to do.

"Oh ... Are you his wife?" I gestured to Red.

"Hell no! I'm his daughter! How old you think I am?" This shook me up. I didn't know what to say and was afraid she was going to take out a knife or something. My hometown of Pocahontas Heights had not offered much experience in the interaction between whites and blacks.

"How long have you been playing that thing?" She pointed to my guitar.

"I don't know...since I'm about twelve or thirteen."

"Well how long is that?" She leered at me. "A year or two?"

"No, no. About five years, I guess. I'm seventeen. Why?"

She looked me up and down and then stuck out her chin and smiled: "I bet you never been laid."

I was terrified. Was this a proposition? Or was she doing some side business of her own?

"What do you mean," I stuttered.

"You don't know what I mean?" She laughed. "Well, than you're in worse trouble than I thought boy!"

"Well, sure I've been laid. With a girl if that's what you mean," I said meekly, more embarrassed then anything else. But thank god that I had been laid...once.

"What the hell else do you think I was asking? Of course with a girl." She laughed at me. Her father was sitting some distance away and had to be out of hearing range but I swear he was smiling too. Maybe this was their routine to intimidate young white boys like me.

"What's this all about?" I asked.

"How'd you like to go on the road with Red Rose? And have all the women you want?" I looked at Red Rose. He hardly seemed to be the sexual magnet Ruby was hinting at.

"Will I get paid?"

"Course you'll get paid," she replied as if this was a secondary consideration. Maybe Ruby had some notion that only black people got laid. No sex for us white bread. As I look back now I'm truly amazed that I had the balls to take her up on that offer. I didn't have a lot of reasons to stay in Pocahontas Heights. It was just like thousands of other scared white suburbs across America and it was so non-rock 'n roll. Besides, my father had died a little over a year before, leaving my mother, my sister and I to try and fill in the gap somehow and I wasn't much good at this. For some reason his death affected me in an opposite fashion from what they show you in the movies. The standard, "I guess you're the head of the family now, son," spoken by the doctor to the crying widow and her only male child just didn't catch on with me. My family was over and I just wanted to move on.   And   they couldn't kid me. Once the old man was gone the whole setup was shot to hell, life insurance or not. And I had this vision that wouldn't go away of my father sitting on the couch, with the TV on, with his mouth open and his eyes turned upwards; his elbows turned outward in some strange way. This was how I had found him, dead of a heart attack when I came in after a band practice one night.

I knew he was dead, way too late for any kind of resuscitation. The worst thing was waking up my mother and telling her and seeing her face. And that's a vision I wanted to get away from, too. And I even have this terrible memory of my older sister Lee up at college in Massachusetts being awakened with the news of her father's death. And I wasn't even there to see it, but I still have that vision in my head too. Anyway, I can't honestly say if I was really ever thinking about any of this when Ruby Rose came up with her offer. I think it was more the way she asked me if I had ever been laid.

My mother reluctantly accepted my decision but she didn't have the strength to fight it. I did promise her that I would finish school eventually. I suppose I still could. I certainly have the time now.

But the moment I hit the highway with Red and Ruby, it was the beginning of a new life, and that's what every death calls for. And it was the kind of life I had dreamed about since I had first picked up the guitar. By the time we were cruising down the Pennsylvania Turnpike I didn't care if I ever saw Pocahontas Heights, New Jersey again. The only thing I had gotten out of that place was enough 'blues' to relate to Red Rose's music. The monotony of the rows of cotton fields from Red's childhood couldn't have been that much different from the suburban ennui and the rows of development housing out in Pocahontas Heights.

Sure, he had things like the Ku Klux Klan to think about but I had the New Jersey Highway Patrol.

I was about to try another hook shot into the garbage with my high school reunion invitation when I noticed a handwritten note on the back:

Dear Marvin,

Although you were not an official graduate of the class of 1967, you are one of our more illustrious classmates, and we're all looking forward to seeing Pocahontas Heights' very own Rock Star again! I hope you can take some time from your busy schedule to 'jam' with your old friends. (And to say hello to someone who still has a special space in her heart for you.)
Yours Truly,
Betty Reed (Social chairman)
P.S. Hey handsome it's me Betty Klein!

Holy Shit! Betty fucking Klein! This very cute and popular cheerleader who I had carnal knowledge of on the football field after a bonfire rally for a big game no less. It was my first time, a one-shot only deal and Betty was drunk as hell and I don't even know if she remembered it the next day but I sure did. Still do, those cheerleader skirts were very short and accessible and I remember every detail. But what I don't remember is what the hell I was doing at a pep rally. I hated sports, still do. Maybe, I just knew instinctively that something would happen, I was drawn to a 'scent' like a wild animal. You see I was walking around the woods next to the football field drinking beer when I heard someone giggle and I saw Betty Klein trying to take a pee but having trouble standing up. Or squatting. Not sure which direction she was going. And I was drunk enough myself to go over to her and ask her if she needed any help. But she didn't say anything, she just put her arms around me and the next thing I knew my zipper was down and we were leaning up against a tree fucking standing up which was not easy and probably a lot better as an erotic memory than as the reality of birch bark scraping her back as I pulled off her cheerleader sweater. Man it didn't take me long - I had been waiting about five years.

Then we heard some voices and we quickly separated in every sense of the word and went off in different directions. The strange thing was that we never mentioned it to anyone as far as I knew or each other for that matter and when she would pass me in the hall she would just politely say *Hi Marty* like she had for years, though I always thought I detected a slight blush. But come on, she was a *jock* and I was a musician, which was almost like a hood. But still, I knew that she knew that I knew too. And that was something.

We use to call her "Betty Boobs" for two obvious reasons and after our personal pep rally this took on new firsthand meaning to me. The few times I thought about Betty since I imagined she became something like an exec in a makeup company or a sexy TV anchorwoman. But how could I attend this reunion now all these years later, Betty Boobs notwithstanding. And on the other hand how could I not attend this fiasco when it seemed like a necessary chapter in *The Marty May Story* - a someday soon to be (I'm sure) major motion picture starring ... never mind.

So I kept turning the invitation over and over like there'd be something more but there was nothing of course. And when Ruby Rose asked me if I ever had been laid and I said, "Yes" that "YES" was Betty Klein. And now here she was writing to me. Ain't life strange?

I didn't make up my mind one way or another but I did call the RSVP number inscribed on the invitation on the offhand chance that Betty might be on the other end. Maybe some lusty high school memories would brighten my spirits.

"Dr. Gross's residence."

"Dr. Gross's residence?" I repeated. I looked at the card. "Is Dr. Gross a woman?" I asked.

"No ... he isn't sir."

"Well...then is Dr. Gross's wife a woman?"

"Of course she is. May I ask who's calling?"

So this is what happens to good looking, smart, and sexy girls who don't become newswomen. They marry doctors, of course.

"I'm sorry. Could you please tell Mrs. Gross that Marty, I mean Marvin, May is on the phone. A blast from her past."

I'm sure that the maid must have figured this was some kind of an obscene phone call.

"Please hold on, sir," she said stiffly.

I pictured Betty coming to the phone in a slinky negligee. No, that was silly, it was six o'clock at night. But maybe she had a phone in her bedroom. And she was changing for a big dinner party with other doctors and other doctor's wives. Maybe she was naked. Maybe I should get naked...

"Why, hello Marvin," she purred.

"Uh ... hello Betty." I was actually getting nervous. I felt like I was calling her the day after the pep rally. What's happening?" I asked inanely like a 60's relic.

"Why, you're what's happening Marvin. You're the famous one." Even with her New Jersey accent I felt like I was speaking to a young Liz Taylor.

"Well, I don't know about that, I mean..." I stuttered somewhat honestly.

"Now before you say one more word, just please tell me that you're ... coming," she said provocatively.

Oh God! "Well, Betty, I'm not really sure of my plans for that evening at all yet. It's a Friday, isn't it? I...uh... might have to..." I didn't know what to say.

"I bet you have a big concert that night?" she asked cautiously.

Well, not exactly." In fact, my last concert big or otherwise was six months ago in some dive in Brooklyn. I brought only a drummer and a bass player with me to maximize the profits. I made nearly a thousand bucks but was traumatized when the place filled up with bikers in the middle of my set. *Gimme Shelter* Part Two.

"Well, no, I don't have a concert that night," I said. "Lately, I've basically been writing new material." Like bouncing checks, I thought. "It's a lonely life Betty, just me, my guitar, and my rhyming dictionary."

"Oh Marvin! You were always so funny," Really? I thought. How would she know? "Oh!" she said suddenly, "I forgot that you're not Marvin anymore are you? It's Marty now, isn't it? I'm sorry." She was actually apologizing to me. This was getting good.

"Yeah, it's been Marty for quite a while, Betty. Blind Red Rose couldn't pronounce Marvin on account of he had only a couple of teeth so he called me Marty or at least that's what it sounded like. And I guess it just stuck, you know. Besides, Marvin's a little too stiff for rock 'n roll, don't you think?"

There was a pause. "What's a Blind Red Rose?" she asked innocently.

"Oh ... it's a long story, Betty." And suddenly I felt as distant from Betty as I did the day after our affair. "You see, I was playing this dance and..."

"And I know it's a fabulously interesting story too, Marty," she broke in, "And that's why you simply must come to our reunion so I can hear all your wonderful stories."

"Well ... I'm sure it will be a lot of fun but..."

"Of course it will be fun, Marty! Fun, Fun, Fun!" She sounded just like the cheerleader she once was. I fantasized her naked shaking pompoms and everything else. Then she lowered her voice: "And we never really talked about that night, you know."

I swallowed hard. "Oh…"

"Don't tell me you've forgotten?" she said with a teasing giggle.

"No, I haven't forgotten, Betty."

"You know we're not encouraging non-alumni husbands or wives to attend," she said softly.

"That's not a problem as far as I'm concerned," I said. "I've been divorced quite a while…"

"Oh, believe me, Marty, you're not alone. I'm one of the few who are holding on, God help me. But what can I do? You know how it is the kids and the house…"

"The kids?" Cheerleaders aren't supposed to have kids. I instantly modified my fantasy. After all Betty was thirty-two like me. But then again, that's far from over the hill.

"Oh yes, three of them - two boys and a girl. But enough chitchat. Say that you'll make it please Marty."

Did she really say that? "I don't know, Betty, I'd really love to but I..."

"I bet you're afraid that you'll feel funny being the only rich and famous one there," she said. "That everyone will make to big a fuss over you asking for autographs and stuff."

"Rich and famous?" I was dumbstruck. No one had ever called me that before.

"I know all about you rock stars, Marty. The kind of life you lead, the groupettes…"

"Groupies," I corrected her. "Although I don't…"

"You can't fool me," she purred.

"Oh believe me, Betty, I don't want to fool anyone." Or did I?

"Now, you might be the only famous one there, Marty, but there will be plenty of rich ones too. We turned into quite an affluent bunch, you know. A lot of doctors, dentists, stockbrokers and lawyers and girls that were smart enough to marry them." She giggled. "Believe me, the parking lot will look like a Mercedes dealership. Did you hear about Timmy Carver?"

"Timmy Carver?" I couldn't place the name. "Was he big or something? Football player?"

"He sure was, Marty. Now he's a pro football player can you believe it? He's going to be there, and Alexander White tool He's coming all the way up from Washington DC."

"Alexander White? Who was he?"

"Well, he wasn't much in high school," said Betty. "He was a real bookworm; kind of a late bloomer but now he's an important man. I think he sells guns and stuff to governments all over the world."

"Guns?" I asked. "What kind of guns?"

"Big guns. Like for wars and stuff," she said cutely. "He's a ... what do you call it? Munitions! That's it! He's a munitions dealer. My husband Harry told me all about him when there was a big article in Newsweek. Don't you remember? Something to do with the Libyans? Anyway, he's just made millions! And he's coming tool"

"Oh great."

"And the funny thing, Marty, is that I had to convince him to come just like I'm doing with you. Except that I was telling him about *you*. Isn't that funny?"

"About me? What would he care about me?" I immediately got paranoid.

"Oh he knew all about you, Marty. Or at least he said that he did. Said he loves rock music and listens to it all day long while he's selling fighter jets."

"Now that is amazing." Fighter jets? "You know, I never really thought about what happened to anybody I went to high school with except you, of course, Betty."

"Well, since I'm social chairman, I get to keep up with everyone. And I can tell you that no one is quite as famous as Alex White or Timmy Carver. Or especially you, Marty," Betty was a diplomat too. "But it is just wonderful how good everyone is doing. It's too bad you missed the tenth anniversary."

"I never heard about it. I guess I was out of town probably on tour." I was even beginning to feel left out.

"It was great, Marty. And the really exciting thing is how productive these get-togethers can be, too."

"Productive? In what way?"

"Oh, in lots of different ways. Like for instance our class president, John Gatling, he lives in California now and he's one of the first real pioneers in solar energy. When he started his newest company, what do you think he did?"

"I can't possibly imagine."

"Why, he gave everyone in the class an opportunity to invest. Unfortunately, my husband Harry's malpractice insurance had just about tripled that year so we were in no position to get involved but I hear that those who did made a killing. A real killing. But I'm sure at this reunion there will be even more interesting opportunities ... including renewing, our friendship, Marty."

Betty was really putting out like the head cheerleader she'll always be, I guess. And she was pretty damn convincing. I got to admit that my first thoughts were concerned with how I might maneuver her back out onto the football field (or just behind it) but then I started thinking about a whole other side of this reunion that had eluded me. Betty had said that even Al White had heard of me and he must have fortunes by now. With just a little dough behind me I could start my own production company, pay to record my own album and then get some label to distribute it. They all preferred 'finished product' these days anyway. I could see my future in a full-page full color ad in *Billboard*.

MARTY MAY INTERNATIONAL VENTURES (AN ENTERTAINMENT GROUP) IS PROUD TO PRESENT THE FINEST ACHIEVEMENT BY ANY ARTIST IN OUR TIME. THE ALBUM: MARTY MAY REUNION.

But there was more to it than this: maybe this reunion would lift my spirits and be some kind of watermark to measure my own little struggle. A chance to take stock and see how I was running compared to the rest of the pack. Shit, instead of an invitation for this shindig, Betty should have sent out portfolios outlining all the opportunities awaiting the alumni. There was business, romance, and sociology. And in my case if I handled my cards right a huge ego boost.

"Well, now that you mention it, Betty, this may be a lot of fun after all. I've missed ... all of you ... so much, you know. Okay, you win. But, if they ask me to sing or play the guitar, I'm leaving. I'm there for a good time not for work."

"Don't you worry, Marty," she purred emphatically. "I'll take good care of you." She whispered: "I can guarantee you a good time. Bye, for now."

Sexual fantasy was taking hold of me like two lines of strong coke although I must admit that the investment opportunities were as enticing as getting it on with Betty for the moment. Man, how a loan of five or ten grand could put me right on my feet again, give me some headroom. And that's not a lot of money, is it? I mean, to someone who has money; that's nothing. Surely one of my successful, rich, dear old friends would be interested in helping me out. Perhaps there might even be a way to turn me into a tax shelter. It might even be to someone's advantage to lose money on me. And that I was good at - ask any of my record labels.

You see, for all these years I had felt like a willing pawn in the funny money music business game because it seemed that in every record contract there were five or ten clauses that allowed the label not to pay any royalties to the artist. I remember sitting in my lawyer's office going over the recently arrived contract of what proved to be my last big deal and I was sitting there trying to get through this horrendous weighty document that would decide my fate for five years or more and the only thing that I could think about was that it was costing me $125 an hour just to sit in this guy's office and *read*. And he kept getting phone calls all the time that clock was running. But the one clause that did strike me as funny was about "cut-outs" so I asked my lawyer exactly what that meant.

"Supermarket sales," he answered between calls.

"What?"

"You know, all those records that you see in supermarkets or Woolworth's that are selling for ninety-nine cents or a dollar ninety-eight?"

"Sure I've seen them." I'd even bought a few in my time.

"Well, those are cut-outs," he said. "They've been cut out of the catalogue and so they sell for a lower price."

"So what does that have to do with me?"

"Nothing," he said, "It's got absolutely nothing to do with you. Because you don't get paid for cutouts. You receive no royalties once a record has been declared a cut-out."

"What? And who decides if a record is a cutout?"

"The record company," he said. "But don't worry, they only make cut-outs from records they've already printed and are sitting in a warehouse taking up space."

"Oh, I see… but who makes sure that they aren't just printing up records and than calling them cut-outs?" I asked.

"They do," he replied matter-of-factly.

"Well, I don't think I like this. I don't want this cutout thing in my contract."

"Sorry Marty. It's got to be there. Even I can't fight it."

"Why?"

"Well," he shrugged his shoulders. "Just call it another *standard of the industry*," he said as he pressed another blinking button on his phone.

Now I can't tell you how many times I've heard that fucking term: *standard of the industry*. If I didn't understand what the hell it meant back then I sure do now. It means that the standard of the industry is to try and find as many ways as possible not to pay artists their royalties. Like, there's also a thing in recording contracts that you don't get paid royalties on 100% of your record sales, you get paid on 90%. So if you have a royalty rate of, let's say, 10% of 90%, it's really only 10% of 90%. I remember asking my lawyer about this too.

"It's because of breakage," he said. "We allow them ten percent for breakage." he smiled.

"Oh, I see." I said as I went on reading my contract. Yeah, that sounded reasonable. Records break right? Wrong! Vinyl records don't break. Records bend in half and you can use them to play Frisbee with if they're bad enough.

"I know they don't break," my lawyer answered me. "But they used to break when they were seventy-eights back in the 1920's. It was a different material." He looked at his watch discreetly. No one watches the time as closely as lawyers and psychiatrists.

"Seventy-eights? I'm not making seventy-eights, am I?" Weren't these like my grandmother's records?

"Of course not," he said calmly. "You're going to record an album. A few albums as a matter of fact." He smiled in a fatherly fashion.

"So why are they allowing ten percent for breakage?"

"Standard of the industry." And then I guess my time was up because he stood up, opened the door, and said "Good luck to you, Marty."

And these were just the aboveground standards of the industry. I had heard horror stories about how a record company won't promote an artist because they've been designated as tax write-offs! But I never really believed that because failure comes easily enough in this business. You don't have to invent it.

But the point that was raging in my mind was that it was about time that I started getting a few of the benefits of all this knowledge. Why did I always have to be the victim in these schemes? Maybe I could turn this around at my high school reunion. Let the executive in me take over for a little while ... if there was one. And then, there certainly was the romantic angle to consider, too. My one-night stand (literally) with Betty was surely the shortest fling in my love life's history. And amazingly enough, it was one of my most erotic memories. Did she still have that cheerleader outfit? And it couldn't have been my imagination; she was definitely still interested. I wondered, had it been that good for her too?

Chapter 4

My fifteenth high school reunion was a week from this Friday night and I felt good, I felt ready, I felt like I had a paying gig or something. I didn't need rehearsals but I did need to prepare.

So what would I wear to impress the shit out of them? Opportunity had knocked, rang, whatever ... and I would make the most of it. I'd go back to Pocahontas Heights in style. Everyone knows it takes money to make money so maybe I could finally make all the cash I had dropped on my rock star couture pay off. I started rummaging through my closets, everything looked so out of styles but strangely enough my older clothes looked more up to date. Yippee, even the fashion cycle was turning my way. Didn't I recently read something about New Romanticism, new classicism and Blitz - some kind of music fashion thing happening in London lately? Man, lately in England it was more a matter of what a band looked like than what they sounded like. Most of the New Romanticism groups reminded me of that great 60's band Paul Revere and the Raiders or early pre-Las Vegas Tom Jones. Rock fashion moved fast these days: From the slums of punk to the manor born in just a few short years.

So I found a black velvet suit that was so wrinkled it had naturally evolved to the crushed velvet stage and along with that some high snakeskin boots that I bought in London ten years ago and a white ruffled *I got to be me* Sammy Davis shirt, stolen from the wardrobe room of "The Midnight Special." It had a ridiculously long pointed collar but I could cut that off like a tux shirt and wear lots of scarves.

And scarves I had. Lots of them because I considered them good luck. There was almost something religious about them; aren't they used for praying somewhere? And if you look carefully you'll notice that all the greats used to wear scarves. Dylan used long wool ones for blowing in the windy streets of early 60's Greenwich Village and Elvis would literally give them out at his concerts like he had a never-ending supply. Now that I think of it, I've never seen Keith Richards without one; maybe that was how he had survived, they were his good luck too. Next to the electric guitar scarves might be the most important accessories in rock 'n roll so I picked out no less then three to garnish my outfit: two around my neck and one around my waist. I tried tying one around my forehead, like an Indian, but enough was enough. Even with luck.

I had a dress rehearsal and was charming to my mirror. I pictured myself strolling up to Betty. She'd be dressed in one of those little silky dresses that fasten in the front. You can get them off in a second. "Hi yaw, sweetheart," I'd say. She'd turn around. There would be Hollywood star-filters glistening on her eyes. Fifteen years had only made her more attractive; she would be just like a younger Mary Tyler Moore. "Marty," she'd say, "I've waited so long." She'd press her large perfectly formed breasts against me as we kissed, she'd toss me an envelope containing the keys to her Mercedes along with her divorce papers. "Take me, anywhere, I'm yours." And presto we'd be on the beach, in Acapulco and I'm strumming an acoustic guitar, singing an old Hank Williams song, wondering how my stock is doing and...

The ringing of the phone broke my reverie.

"Marty May?"

"Maybe ... who's this?" I was paranoid

"Marty, it's Ruby! Ruby Rose!"

"Ruby! I don't believe it! How the hell are you?"

"Why, I'm just rollin, and tumblin, all night long," she said in mock blues fashion. "I got your number from this writer Dave Simmons; he said he'd spoken to you just last week I believe. Said you was doin' fine"

"Yeah, he was supposed to call me and give me your number too. How's Red? And where are you?"

"Red's okay but listen, I'm in New York baby."

"New York? No!"

"Sure as hell! You think I'd spend my daddy's hard earned cash calling a low down guitar hustler like you long distance?" She laughed. "How's about this? Why don't you meet me down at Tramps in an hour for a drink? You know that joint? Down on Fifteenth Street somewhere?"

"Sure, I know the place."

"Well then, get moving boy! I got a big surprise for you!"

"I got out of my 'rock star' gear and into something more presentable for Ruby, like jeans and a t-shirt."

Tramps was a cabaret that had changed into a blues club. It was the only place in New York where you could still listen to the likes of Lightnin' Hopkins or Willie Dixon on a Saturday night.

Jerry, the owner, was a straight-shooting Irishman who still had a bit of a brogue and a passion for the blues. He'd bought me many a Guinness Stout while telling me how he'd have to search these blues legends out down in Mississippi or Texas or Chicago where they'd be living in semi-retirement and often in poverty. Sometimes they'd be just too old or too sick to make it up to New York to play his club. But more often than not they were ready, willing and able to make the trip. Jerry had a good house band that could back them up and was the only club owner I ever met who was dedicated to making sure these legends of American music kept playing. It would take an Irishman to appreciate the blues.

Tramps was a late-night club so when I arrived in the early evening to meet Ruby it wasn't crowded at all. There was a long oak bar right when you walked in where the locals drank and then a room in the back with tables and finally, a low stage. An underground railroad shaped club made sense for the blues, too. Jerry wasn't even there yet so I sat at the bar and had a Guinness in his honor. Ruby was right on time like always.

She caught me by surprise, grabbing me from behind and giving me a powerful bear hug. I turned around and she was standing there smiling and laughing. She hadn't really aged very much at all since the last time I saw her, about five years ago and just like then she was dressed in red, her favorite color. Her hair looked even more red and brilliant than I remembered it and her teeth more white and her face more black. Guess I'd been living in the white man's world too long. The only real change that I did notice was that one of her front teeth was now solid gold.

"Ruby! Baby, you look good. What's your secret? Are you practicing voodoo again?" I pointed a finger at her accusingly.

"Now don't you mention that damn black magic to me, Marty May. Just last year I had to sit with my feet in chicken blood for an hour cause some fool slapped a mojo on my ass."

We both laughed. Only Ruby could get away with saying that and having me believe it, too.

"You don't look too worse for wear yourself, Marty. As a matter of fact ... She leaned close and squinted her eyes and rubbed my cheek. "As a matter of fact ... you're getting darker. You're not so white anymore!"

"I just can't afford soap," I said. "Where's Red? Did he come with you?"

"No, Red's back at the hotel. We're staying at the *Chelsea* with all the other *artistes*. Come on, let's go sit down at a table and be civilized. A lady like me can't stand at a bar like some floozy! Has that rock 'n roll spoiled all your good manners, boy?" She said only half-kidding. We moved to a table near the stage. Ruby always like to sit near the stage even when there was no show going on. I had another beer and she had some Jack Daniels on the rocks *with a sprinkle.*

"So where you been at, Marty?" she asked. "Ain't heard nothing from you since that time we just happened to run into you in St. Louis which musta been a decade ago. God knows I tried to call you but it seems that Mr. Marty May, international star of stage, screen, and motel rooms, has a very 'unlisted' number. Made me feel guilty just asking for it!"

"What can I say, Ruby, I think that must have been my record company's idea." I lied.

"And speaking of your record company, when I used to call them ... how many was there, by the way?" she asked accusingly. "Seems like you got more record companies then BB King's got wives."

"Three ... but never two at the same time," I said.

"BB neither! Anyway, I think I must have left plenty of messages at all three and each time they assured me that you would most certainly get the message pronto. So what do you got to say for yourself now, boy?" She wasn't really mad but she knew I deserved this and I knew it too.

And I remember getting those messages too and thinking I should call and then never doing so. And I would have loved to see them, too, but I always thought I'd be too busy. But that's bullshit and I know it. Because the real reason, the real feeling I had gotten when I heard that Ruby and Red were trying to get in touch with me was fear: I was afraid they wanted something from me and even now I'm ashamed to admit it. But it's true. When I first went solo Ruby had called me asking if I might consider doing one or two of Red's songs and I had said, yeah, great idea but then when I mentioned it to my record company they said the blues didn't sell anymore and they had that very persuasive way of convincing me to do things their way, like saying they wouldn't know how to market a Marty May Blues album. Of course, what they meant was that if I did a blues album there would be no ads in Rolling Stone or Billboards down Sunset Strip in Hollywood. Typical, because here I'm discovered and noticed because of my reputation as a blues guitarist and then they don't want me to record any blues. So, I think I told Ruby that I'd try recording some of Red's songs and send her the demos, which of course I never did. I thought I was putting my career first but now it seems just too shameful to think about.

"I plead guilty, your honor," I said and bowed my head. "I've been a bad boy, ain't no getting around it. But I've done my time believe me ... so how's about I buy the drinks and we call it even."

She considered this for a moment and than she said: "It's a deal. You're forgiven. I got to remember that you white bread just suffer from a tremendous lack of soul. It can be a real disadvantage." And than she smiled widely and her gold tooth glimmered and I knew there were no hard feelings.

"How's Red? I haven't heard too much about him for a while."

"Well, I guess you and my daddy both better hire new press agents because he ain't heard too much about you either lately, Marty! You both need to come out of the shadows. Ah, to tell you the truth, Marty, Red ain't been doing all that great. You knew he had a stroke last year, didn't you?"

"No, I hadn't heard anything about that." And then I really felt lousy about not seeing them in all this time. "How is he? Can he still play?"

"Yeah, he can play and he survived but it kind of slowed him down real bad, you know. He's still spending a lot of time at the doctor and they're still sending a lot of medical bills our way. I should call up the Library of Congress where they got all my daddy's early *field recordings* and ask them about his 'blues pension', he sure could use it! I mean, those congressmen got pensions so why not my Daddy? He's been plowing their fields for quite a while now." She laughed. "But they'd probably tell me blues pension was called welfare," she added bitterly.

"Are you still working? Still on the road?"

"Well, I guess you could say that we got a little bit too much vacation time lately, if you know what I mean, Marty." But she *could* laugh about that.

"Believe me, I know. I could have written a small encyclopedia between gigs lately," There was no point in trying to hype Ruby about the state of my own career. She was still a good-looking woman. I suspected that she was somewhere in her early forties, though she would never tell her real age. Whenever I used to ask her, she'd just say *I'm old enough to know better, and that's not old enough to tell.* And she was capable too. I remember watching her deal with club owners and agents and you better believe that no one no one ever got the best of her. She was just as crafty as any $125 an hour lawyer I ever knew. So I wondered what her life was like during these slow years and why she never married.

But what about you, Ruby? What have you been doing? Are you married?" I asked.

"Hell, no! You think after hanging around with musicians all these years that I'd be crazy enough to get seriously involved with a *man*? I got my hands full with Red. And he ain't no bundle of joy either"

"But there are other men besides musicians, Ruby. I mean look at you; you still turn me on." I think she blushed at this though I really couldn't tell.

"Now you just stop jiving me, Marty May! Asking me all these personal questions. I ain't got time for any man and that's the end of it. I knew what I was doing when I left that Bar-B-Que with my daddy and I ain't never regretted it either." So maybe it was as simple as that. She was a woman of her word. And leaving that waitress job to join her daddy on the road was the same as putting her signature on a contract although I didn't envy her future. Red was really getting old and now after his stroke I was sure he would need a lot of looking-after.

"And you know how it goes, Marty," she went on. "The blues just ain't as popular these days as it use to be. Those five years that you played with Red were the good years. I mean, when I picked you up, we were just starting to do some steady business and I could feel what was coming with all these white kids 'cause it was in the air and on the streets. With the war in Vietnam and with the drugs and all, they was beginning to feel oppressed. And I knew the kind of music oppressed people want is the blues. So we rode that blues tidal wave for all it was worth. What do you thinks been getting us by these past years?" She leaned close and whispered though there was no one near us to overhear. "And you know how I feel about getting paid in cash. Save Uncle Sam from having to do all that figuring' with taxes and all." She winked. "I bet you don't even remember how good those days was, Marty, do ya?"

"Oh, but I do remember, Ruby. That's where I learned most of what I still know today about playing the blues and what I should have stuck to. It's like what you said about getting married; that the road ain't no home..."

"... And a marriage needs a roof over its head," she finished. It was one of her most famous sayings if I recall.

And then I remembered how Barbara had made a face when I suggested that we invite them to our, wedding and said that they would feel out of place and uncomfortable and like a schmuck I went along with her. I guess it was because her parents were footing the bill. Man, that was enough bad karma right there to jinx our marriage.

"Man, things took off fast during that time, Ruby. When I first hooked up with you, it was just you and me and Red, of course, and we'd pick up a backup band. And I remember we were playing about half white clubs and about half black clubs. I was always a little uptight in the black ones, if you want to know the truth."

"I always told you just to mind your own business and nobody's gonna bother you. But you always insisted upon calling everyone 'boy' if I remember right. Got you into quite a lot of trouble you young honky."

"I did not. I never called anyone *boy* in my life. That was one of the first things you told me!" We both laughed out loud which brought the waiter over so we ordered another round.

"But then things really started to take off and we were playing bigger shows and opening for Eric Clapton and every star you can imagine. Some of those festivals we did right before I left were gigantic." And they were. I never played concerts like that when I went out on my own. "That show in England, the three day blues festival, when there was over a hundred thousand people. And Red was just magic. He can still play that National guitar when he wants to." I was filled with the excitement of the old days.

"Well, he *used to* be able to play that steel guitar. His hands don't move quite so fast any more, Marty."

Then Jerry Ryan, the owner of Tramps, came over. Dark haired handsome Irishman, tall and always in a suit and hat with James Joyce glasses. It was about eight o'clock in the evening and his working day was just beginning. My kind of guy.

"Marty May! As I live and breathe! How are you, Marty?" He yelled up at the bar. "Can I get a couple of Stouts over here, God willing?"

"Hi ya, Jerry. You know Ruby Rose?"

"Do I know Ruby? Are you kidding me? Ruby and I go way back."

"Too far back for both of us to speak of in public," Ruby interjected.

"Are you ready for the big night?" asked Jerry as he pulled a chair in next to us. I didn't know if he was talking to Ruby or to me or to both of

"Now you hush up, Jerry!" waved Ruby. "You're letting the cat out of the bag here. Loose lips sink ships."

"But they're great for oral sex," said Jerry almost spitting out his beer.

"What's going on here?" I looked from one to the other. "Are you two hiding something from me?"

"Ruby and Jerry looked at each other. "Aw, go ahead and tell him," said Jerry.

"Well, as I was about to get into, Marty..." Ruby gave Jerry the evil eye. "Red ain't no spring chicken no more. His performing days are limited, severely limited if you know what I mean. As a matter of fact he's doing one more show, probably be his last one before he goes out to pasture. And Mr. Jerry Ryan here has agreed to let Red have his final night under the spotlight here at Tramps so we're gonna try and make it a little special and, well ... I was wondering if you might come down and play a few numbers with Red. For old times sake and all."

"Are you kidding?" I said excitedly. "Of course I'll come down and play. It would be my pleasure."

"Great!" said Jerry. "I'll put that in the advertisements in next week's Voice."

"That ought to bring down at least three or four people," I said.

"Get out of here, Marty," said Jerry. "You're still a respected name in this town."

Ruby was visibly excited. "Marty, it will be fantastic! I knew I could count on you. And Red will be so pleased. Listen, the gig is next Friday, so maybe you and Red should get together a little before and rehearse some of the..."

"Next Friday? Oh, no it would have to be that. Ruby,
I'm supposed to go to my high school reunion out in New Jersey that night. I ... uh...kind of committed myself there." What was I saying? What was I doing?

"Your high school reunion?" Ruby was shocked. "Are you jiving me, Marty? I know for a fact that you dropped right out of high school to come on the road with us. You always used to blame me for your lack of education." What a memory.

"Well, you're right Ruby. It's true that I never *officially* graduated, but I was a member of the class. And they're kind of depending on me." I knew it would take more than that, "You see, Ruby, it's kind of in my honor, you know what I'm saying? I'm really the only reason that they're having such a big party. Its all for me ... like a grand homecoming or something."

"But this is in Red's honor," said Jerry Ryan. "And believe me, I'm not making a bloody cent on the deal. I'm giving it all to Red." I could see he didn't buy the way I was weaseling out of this.

"Now you lay off of him, Jerry," said Ruby. I could hear the disappointment in her voice. Why wasn't she mad at me too? Did she have that much insight? "I understand, Marty. I didn't realize it was something special like that. Could we move the show Jerry?"

"I'm sorry, Ruby, but I'm all booked up for over a month. That Friday is the only possible night.

"Maybe I can do both," I said halfheartedly. "Maybe I can come down after my reunion." But I didn't really believe this. If my reunion was what I wanted it to be, the last thing in the world I would want to do is leave early.

"Well, Marty, you see Red's gotta play kind of early, around nine or ten o'clock or so because of his health, said Ruby.

"I don't know what to do," I said, lying again. "As I said, I kind of committed myself."

"Well, you just do what you got to do," said Ruby. "Red will understand, believe me." She smiled faintly. "You go on and have a good time. And don't you go breaking the hearts of your old girlfriends any more than you already have." I had a suspicion that Ruby understood my motivations better than I did.

"It's a shame," said Jerry. "It would have been a night to remember all the rest of our freaking' lives." He got up and left. I don't think he was too happy. I think my days of free Guinness Stouts a Tramps had come to an abrupt end.

Ruby kept up a good face. "Don't you worry about Jerry," she said. "We'll get by without you just fine. Less than a week is not much notice for someone like you ... I understand." But I heard a sad sense of resignation in her voice and felt a cold distance between us like I wasn't the first white man to let her down. I don't think she would be able to overlook all these years I didn't get in touch with her, now. We left soon after. I told her to give my best to Red and that I would try to make it down after the reunion. But neither of us really believed this.

I was a schmuck. But if I didn't go to my reunion maybe I'd be an even bigger schmuck. I just had a feeling that I could make something happen out there. That it was a new beginning that by going back in time I could fix things up. And maybe I just wanted to show off and kiss the girls and make them cry. I don't know what the fuck I wanted to do. If I played with Red Rose, I'd wake up the next morning to my same goddamn miserable situation. And maybe worse: what if nobody came to Red's show even *with* my name on the bill? And there'd still be the phone calls from all the people I owed money to. I had already sold all of my spare guitars and amplifiers that I possibly could and if I kept playing these gigs in the kind of dives that I had lately I was sure to ruin whatever name I still had left in this business. I needed some new blood in my career and as much as I loved Ruby and Red there was just no new blood there. None that I could see. And just maybe out in Pocahontas Heights there might be something. I didn't know quite what, but I'd be on top looking down and that was better than where I was. I had to think of my future ... I'd think about my soul some other time.

But I sure didn't like hearing about Red's stroke and it was painful to think of him sitting in his black suit and buttoned up white shirt with no tie in the Chelsea hotel when Ruby would tell him that I couldn't make it to his farewell performance. I didn't want to think about what he would be thinking behind those sunglasses, behind those sightless eyes.

You meet a lot of guys in the music business. I knew this one drug dealer named Freddy who was a pretty decent guy. He was always telling people not to snort too much coke at once or they'd get too jittery. When he finally cut me off it was because I owed him about three thousand dollars and he knew that I didn't have it, nor would I have it in the near future. He just told me to forget about it and go out and get healthy for a while which is what I reluctantly did.

And Freddy, as soon as he had raised a little capital he bought himself a Cadillac limousine and started driving it for paying customers at night while dealing coke and stuff at the same time. It was a winning combination and soon he bought another limo and then another and then he stopped dealing coke completely. Of course, he would still give a little to his good customers.

Freddy used to call me for advice, he'd ask me what musicians would be good clients and who would be a stiff and who he should let have credit and who he should make pay in advance and what management companies he should try to get close to - all of that. Imagine me, a credit-rating service. But I did my best to spread the word about him and his ever-increasing fleet of cars and soon he was the rock star's choice for a set of classy wheels in NYC. Maybe Freddy was the only guy in New York who owed me a favor. I called Freddy and explained that I wanted a chauffeured limousine to take me out to my reunion and of course he had to stick it to me about wanting to show off but then he said he'd give me one of his older stretch Cadillacs for the night and an older driver who couldn't take the pace of the Rolling Stones, who were then in town.

Chapter 5

Ruby, in a red dress with a short furry coat, wire-rimmed aviator shades and a large black leather pocketbook that spelled business walked briskly down Twenty-Third Street. Two teenage Puerto Rican boys in counterfeit designer jeans, said something to her in Spanish as they passed but when she looked back at them straight in the eye and told them to go back to their Mamas in Spanish they imagined a razor or a gun (which there wasn't) in her bag and they didn't say anything more. Then Ruby walked into a donut shop on the corner and got a dozen - half jelly-filled, half honey-glazed - freshly baked donuts and picked up a wad of napkins and a New York Post from the rack by the door. You were supposed to put a quarter in the slot for the paper. She didn't. It was half a block to the Chelsea Hotel and when she entered she noticed the brass plaques next to the front door about Dylan Thomas. She knew the name, knew he was some kind of poet and she knew that he had lived a little or died a lot in the Chelsea Hotel but she had never read his poetry nor did she care to. And she imagined someday a plaque by the entrance to the Chelsea Hotel, right next to this famous poet's name, for William J. Rose AKA Blind Red Rose and this made her laugh for she knew it would never be. No way.

There was modern art and sculptures lining the lobby of the hotel and she didn't care about this either. She didn't stay at the Chelsea for the counter-culture glamour; she stayed there for the price of the room and the location near the blues clubs downtown where her father played when he was in New York City. She knew a hotel in the Village that she could stay in for about the same money and be even a little closer to her daddy's gigs but she didn't trust the Village or the people in it. Their motives weren't clear to her; everyone was so hip and liberal but you couldn't squeeze an extra taxi fare out of them. She was not afraid in The Chelsea Hotel on West Twenty-Third Street, nor was she afraid any place else except the Deep South where she didn't like to be on the road at night if she could help it.

She let herself into the room with the key she had taken with her. Red wasn't going anywhere without her and she didn't want to disturb her father if he was sleeping. He wasn't. He was sitting in front of the television. A fairly intellectual summary of the news was on channel thirteen, the public station. He always turned to the public station whenever he could, wherever he was, regardless of what was on. Years ago, Ruby had asked him why and he said it was because of the commercials, he didn't like them, there were too many, and they reminded him of everything he would never have, never own or possess. There were no commercials on public television, though sometimes they would have fundraising drives. Red found these very, very funny and he would sit in his chair and howl with laughter when they begged whoever might be watching to send in money. Sometimes he would talk back to the TV and say things like "Oh yeah? And what if I don't? What cha gonna do then? Turn off my set?" And this would make him laugh even more. He was an old black man in a black suit and a white shirt buttoned to the collar with no tie. He traveled with two suits and three or four shirts and a few changes of underwear and a National Steel Guitar in a battered case that was heavy as hell and which Ruby ended up carrying most of the time. He used to travel with a flask of bourbon - Wild Turkey or Jack Daniels - but after he lost that flask he just carried the bottle wrapped in a towel stuffed in his bag. Since his stroke last year he didn't travel with any liquor at all which made him a little ornery in his daughter's opinion. Ruby never understood how a blind man could watch television. Her father always wore very dark sunglasses with thick black plastic frames and sometimes he took them off to go to sleep and sometimes he didn't. He wasn't totally blind and Ruby knew this although he would never admit it himself and the more she'd question him about it, the more blind he would act. She suspected that one eye was totally useless, no vision at all, and the story was that he had been kicked by a mule or hit by a white sheriffs baton sometime when he was a child near Tupelo, Mississippi where he grew up. The only time she ever heard her daddy talk about his blindness was to a young German TV interviewer who was doing a documentary on the blues and who had come to film him outside of Detroit where they were staying with Ruby's half-sister's place.

It was the German interviewer's first question: "How did you lose your eyesight?" Ruby couldn't remember anyone ever asking her father that directly before. In fact, she herself had never asked him that directly. But to the German filmmaker, although filled with respect and admiration for her father, Red Rose was a relic of America much like the Mayan ruins of Mexico were to that country and he was not afraid to explore this old black man in just such a way and to ask him anything he wanted to.

"Well, ya see, ma eyez was in luv wit' each other. They did every lil' thang together, ya know, whatever da one was lookin' at, well, than that's wha da other one wanted to see, ya know, they was jus' like Romeo

In Juliet, ya know, and when the one died, well, than the other jus' died too. Ya understan dat son?"

But the German interviewer with the expensive Swiss tape recorder was not there to understand. He was there to get the facts, write the history, and enter the data. Ruby just thought that whatever it was that her daddy last saw, and she doubted it was the hindquarters of a mule, had made him decide at that early age that if this was what there was to see out there that he would just as well save his other eye the misery of being exposed to it. And apparently his good eye had agreed with him because now it was covered with a milky cataract which Red Rose had no desire to have removed. But she also knew her father well and she knew that once he was blind he no longer had to work out in the fields and could play the guitar all day long.

"Hey Daddy, it's me," she said as she entered the room.

"I know," said Red. "I know it's you."

"You want a donut?" asked Ruby. She was eating a jelly filled one herself.

"Umm hmmm," her father drawled and she handed him the one he would like the best, honey glazed.

"What's the news?" she asked.

"Not much," said Red Rose. "De caw some poltishan stealin' agin. Dat's all."

"Some what?" asked Ruby. Sometimes she herself couldn't understand her father's deep southern drawl. Especially when he didn't have his false teeth in like now.

"POLITISHANN!" Her father repeated emphatically. "Ya know, some sinatour ... some ol dem congreshionel men... de caugh dem all stealing again!" This made her father laugh out loud and Ruby laughed with him as she got up and spread a napkin on his lap to catch the crumbs. "I don't unnerstan' why de so surprized at all deez ... shenanigans," said her father. "I coulda toll dem 'bout dese politishions ... (He picked up his guitar which was usually close enough for him to grab.)

"Likka theef in da night..." (He sang)
"Widda gun or a knife
"You stealing ma heart
"Leaving me crying
"Likka theef in da night
"You don' never come back

"You stealing ma heart 'cause... (He paused)
"You got none of your own."

He strummed a final chord and then he put his guitar down and was through with the subject. He'd said his piece.

"I just saw Marty May. "

"He was da best damn guitar player I ever had," said Red Rose. "Even better than D.C. Jones, gawd res' his soul."

"Who?" asked Ruby. "You don't mean the D.C. Jones who played with Sonny Boy Williamson? Do ya?"

"Sure do," said her daddy. "Daz da man. And Marty May was a better guitar man than D.C. Dat I know, dat you can be sure of." He nodded his head up and down in agreement with himself.

"But you never played with D.C. Jones," protested his daughter. "He died back in the thirties. He was dead before I was even born." She smiled and shook he head. "Someone just told you about D.C. Jones once didn't they?"

"Now ya hush up girl and have a lil' respect for your daddy and don go telling me who I was playing wid when an, where an' how cuz I sure as hell played with D.C. many and many a time. Ya think ya know everything there is to know about me don' ya? Well ya all got another thang coming if dats wha you think. Now give me another donut and stop sassin' or I go get me a drink!"

She handed him another donut and wiped some of the honey glaze off of his chin but she knew that he had never played with D.C. Jones because those two stayed about three states away from each other. Her father grew up in Mississippi and Texas and didn't even get to Chicago until the late Forties. She had even overheard him tell people that he used to go whoring and drinking with Robert Johnson the biggest, baddest, bluest legend of them all. But she knew that this wasn't true either because anyone who she ever talked to who actually knew Robert Johnson described him as a mean and possessed man and she couldn't imagine him dragging around some blind kid from the backwoods of Mississippi, which was what her father would have been back then. She knew Red was getting senile; too much Jack Daniels and way too much hard traveling had taken its toll. His confusion about people and places and times amused her on occasion but it frightened her too for it was as if the knot that bound her to him and his life to hers was becoming undone.

"*Well anyway, Marty May can't play with you this Friday night. He's got to go to some testimonial dinner or something,*" *she said disgustedly.*

"*Well, what the hell would make you believe dat boy would wanna play wit me dis Friday night or any Friday night?*" *said Red Rose.* "*He's some kinda star now. Didn't you tell me dat once? How I done made dat boy a big star?*" *This amused him.* "*I'm da starmaker!*"

"*That's right, Daddy. You made him a big star. But I don't think he's so big a star anymore. You know how it is with these white boys and their rock 'n roll. It don't last forever.*"

"*Umm hmm.*" *He nodded his head up and down.* "*He shoulda stuck with da blues. Dats what I toll him once. Stick wid da blues an folks will never forget ya,*" *said Red Rose.*

"*That's right, Daddy,*" *said Ruby as she surveyed the meager contents of their hotel room.* "*They'll never forget you,*" *she laughed.*

"*Well, me an' Marty will get together some other time, honey,*" *said Red Rose with confidence.* "*Some time when I'm playing one of dem big festivals or theater concerts. He'll wanna play wid me then. Maybe me an' Marty will make another record sometime. Those were good records we made cause that boy's gotta good dose o' da blues. You can't never tell what's gonna happen. The Man's gotta plan, ya know. He's got a plan.*"

"*I wish he'd let me in on it,*" *said Ruby.*

"*Now don't ya worry bout nothin' baby,*" *said Red tenderly.* "*You jus, stop tellin' me who I played with and where and when an' everything's gonna be jus' fine. Now give yo daddy one of those jelly donuts: dat you been hoarding' for yourself.*"

And when Ruby said, "*Sheeet Daddy! You about as blind as a hawk!*" *This made him really smile*

"*If only I cud fly,*" *Red Rose replied.* "*If only I cud fly.*"

Chapter 6

If you could avoid the rush hour, Pocahontas Heights was about an hour's ride from Manhattan once you were freed from the city traffic by the appropriately named Lincoln Tunnel and although the reunion was scheduled to begin at eight, I didn't have the limo pick me up till after seven-thirty wanting to be fashionably late and all that crap. Honestly, it was a beautiful night for a ride with the sun setting in glittery gold in the west. I took this as a portent of a gold record in my future. We shot free of the confines of the Lincoln tunnel and headed for the New Jersey Turnpike, past Newark Airport, and into gasoline alley where across the Hudson, the oil refineries lay with high flaming smokestacks in the no-man's land of the Jersey swamps. These huge steel spider-like structures were truly awesome and mysterious - an industrial lunar landscape and the lights flooding the complex shone through the grimy air as indiscriminate particles of a molecular rainbow. When I was a child and my father would take the family into the city for a Sunday dinner or to see a parade I always mistook the oil refineries for some kind of great amusement park and this would make my father laugh when I asked him if we could stop and go on the rides. He was ahead of his time in not being a big fan of oil companies when he replied, "Sure, those guys love to take you for a ride." Looking back, it's hard to see what he was complaining about; gas was only about forty cents a gallon in those days.

So I sat in the back seat of the limo and fiddled with the dials of the FM radio. I found a soothing female DJ and it felt so perfect; she was playing a slow tune from a Steely Dan album. Their L.A. transplanted New York soul was romantic and sad, the cry of strangers in a strange land, New Yorkers on Hollywood Mars, looking up at Palm trees sprung from a younger galaxy. We left the superhighways for the smaller roads where an abundance of fast food places flew past the tinted glass; everything neon and disposable seemed to have found a home here. There was even a surprising and somewhat frightening new chain of health food drive-ins.

The Pocahontas Heights High School class of nineteen sixty-seven reunited in the cafeteria of our old school and I only hoped they would be serving better food than what I remembered being grossed out by at lunch way back then when I stool in line with my tray. As the limo pulled into the Parking lot adjacent to the cafeteria, I gave some last thought to Ruby and Red Rose and the choice I had made and my heart sunk a bit. But I wouldn't think about them tonight if I could help it. The part I was playing was going to be difficult enough without thinking too much about who I really was.

The parking lot looked full and, just as Betty had predicted, there was quite a smattering of Mercedes and Cadillacs but mostly there were small cars, Japanese and otherwise, gas efficient, good for shopping center runs and picking the kids up at soccer matches. My plan was to time my entrance so that it would be most noticeable to those already inside; I remembered that the cafeteria had large plate glass windows facing onto the parking lot. I had the radio up loud, too loud, and after the driver had pulled up next to the curb closest to the entrance I just sat there for a few minutes with the windows down and the music blaring. After all, what rock star would leave his limo while a favorite song was still blasting. Wearing sunglasses had been an early consideration but I knew from past experience that tripping on the dark pavement was not worth the points I would gain in image.

Now I'm telling you, Howard Hughes, at his most debilitated, probably could get out of a limousine faster and with more agility than I did that dark night. I even thought of a reason to get back again in once I had already gotten out so I could exit all over again. But I'd like to think my plan worked because I thought I saw heads turning inside the large plate-glass box of the cafeteria. The driver asked me what time he should return to pick me up and as coolly as I could I asked him to keep the limo, in plain sight. He seemed to understand, but was kind enough not to seem too understanding. He just nodded with the slightest of grins.

"Yes sir, Mr. May, anything you say."

Reentering my alma mater resulted in the déjà I was already expecting and also a little unexpected anxiety. Once again I was reminded of the panic I had felt upon my first day of public school when my mother had left me in kindergarten. In fact, nothing had changed, they were still painting the walls with the same puke green color and the institutional smell was an instant reminder of just what a drag my school days had been. Schools may look pretty inviting from the outside, usually a nice democratic red brick, maybe a little white tower with a fake bell or a flag flying and massive sets of doors welcoming the youth of America. Inviting as a gingerbread house in the forest. And than once inside wham bang, the doors shut and its jailhouse time because inside its another story. Why do they do this? Why are the colors they use so ugly? The chairs so uncomfortable? The books so boring? It must be society's way of screening its kids; marking the troublemakers and non-conformists early on so they can be segregated to go to prison, become streetwalkers, leave the country, play electric guitar in a blues band...but indeed I was getting a bit carried away even if I did feel like a fugitive from a chain gang walking back into the arms of the law after already serving a twelve year sentence.

Surveying the group of adults who used to be my classmates I saw that quite a large number had showed up for this reunion and I wondered what for. Certainly, their motives couldn't be as base as my own. Betty had told me that most had stayed in the area and even I was within driving distance. As I looked them over I they all looked older than I or maybe it was just the way they dressed, relatively conservatively, guys in khaki pants and button down shirts their wives in pants suits. After all, I was the only one with a 'crushed' velvet suit and three scarves. But then again, rock 'n roll ages you from the inside out, leaving the grace on your face but the toll on your soul. Now that rhymes and I swear it's original - better to remember to jot it down when I got home. My immediate animal instinct was to find the watering hole - the bar, which consisted of some cafeteria tables put end to end in a corner spot. Could be the same grey haired Eastern European ladies in their white uniforms that used to cook those awful lunches that were now serving the drinks? Not taking a chance, I ordered a beer and it was domestic, of course. I drank fast and had another in my hand before I knew it. I was self-conscious and quickly became aware of a guy staring at me. He had a beard and was tall enough to stoop, dressed in a baggy tan Brooks Brothers suit with that distinctive extra buttonhole on the lapel. When I smiled at him he didn't smile back so I kept on drinking my beer just trying not to notice him. The cafeteria itself had not changed, still smelled the same – not too appetizing and there were posters on the walls for student's activities: A talk on nuclear reactors, a meeting of the future nurses club, student elections and a monthly meeting of the free sex league ... just kidding.

Seriously, the only group I ever joined had been the High School *folksong club*. Of course, they were interested in Peter Paul And Mary, The Kingston Trio, and The New Christy Minstrel while I was more into Bob Dylan, Phil Ochs and Leadbelly so I quit after a few meetings. But this was in my sophomore year, nineteen sixty-five, I guess. Now, I wondered if there even was such a thing as a *folksong* club in this high school anymore. Had it evolved into a *disco song club*? Did they sit in circles singing Donna Summer songs?

Finally the guy in the Brooks Brothers suit did approach me walking fast in my direction and I felt threatened though I knew that was foolish. Perhaps he could be security, they had checked the records, they had found out I hadn't really graduated, my invitation was a mistake and they would throw me out on my ass with my dreams and schemes all in vain.

"Are you with the band?" he asked tightlipped.

"What do you mean? What band?" I replied defensively.

"The band that was hired for this party; they're late, you know." He seemed to be blaming me.

"Oh ... I didn't know...no, no, I'm not with the band." For some reason I felt guilty.

"Well, you know what they're like," He smiled with stained bad teeth.

"What who's like?" I asked.

"Musicians," he said. "I thought you were a musician I'm sorry."

What was he sorry for? Should I have been insulted?

"I'm not with the band but actually I happen to be a musician myself. I'm Marty May class of sixty-seven," this seemed the proper introduction, how Harvard alumni might introduce themselves to one another. But everyone was 'sixty-seven' here. "How do you do?" I held out my hand.

He did not immediately shake my hand but snapped his fingers first. "Marty May! You're the local rock star aren't you?" Then he shook my hand enthusiastically.

"Last time I looked anyway." I smiled the appropriate, understated kind of smile that I used to have to use a lot. A smile of fame and humility that the public appreciates on those they choose to make famous. But honestly, I liked his immediate recognition; it felt good. I felt like I knew who I was and hoped it was an omen of things to come.

"Well, it's great to see you again, Marty. I don't know if you'll remember me but I'm Bill Harding; actually Doctor Bill Harding now."

"Sure, I remember you. Weren't we in gym class together? So you're a doctor! Congratulations. Listen," I said smiling, "Maybe you can take a look at my sore throat later? Its been bothering me since..."

"Only if it's psychosomatic. I'm a doctor of psychology." He replied in a laugh-choked voice, "You're the local rock star and I'm the local 'shrink'!" What a punch line. He'd almost doubled over laughing. I didn't get it but I could have laughed myself because Bill Harding a shrink was the last thing I imagined this guy to do! I should have recognized him earlier but his full beard covered his features. Now, I remembered him as an unfortunate teenager who one day in the showers after gym had the misfortune to get an erection and as might be expected for the rest of his high-school days the jocks used to call him Bill *HardOn* instead of Harding. From then on \even the gym teacher sounded like he was saying *HardOn* when he called the roll and came to Bill's name. And now he was a psychologist and maybe that wasn't so unusual an outcome after all for a guy whose sexual impulses had marked his adolescent days. It was the kind of thing that I imagined could have happened to Freud in Vienna High.

But more then that I couldn't believe my luck! I'm not in the place for two minutes and I run into a rich suburban shrink. Or at least I figured he must be rich. Aren't all shrinks rich? But then again, aren't all rock stars supposed to be rich too? Like the captain of a U-boat I began to stalk my prey with my hand on the torpedo launcher. "Tell me, Bill, how's business?" I anticipated a few moments of bragging before I launched my sting.

"Lousy," was all he said.

"Lousy?" I repeated in surprise, "I thought the suburbs were full of alcoholics, frigid housewives and their cheating husbands all in need of your kind of services? I mean, isn't it like what you see on soap operas?"

"Sure," he said nonchalantly. "It's as fucked up as it ever was. But the real problem in my *business* is that hardly anyone wants to go the conventional route of psychoanalysis anymore. They take self improvement courses or they become Scientologists or Moonies or they're born-again for the umpteenth time and the cheap ones spend two ninety eight on the paperback version of *How to Be Your Own Best Friend* thinking that's gonna fixed their fucked up lives." He seemed angry with the neurotics of the world for not doing what was expected of them. "You tell me, who's gonna lie on my couch and tell me their problems for a hundred bucks an hour? For that kind of money you could go down to Club Med twice a year. And I'll telling you the honest truth, Marty, what am I gonna tell them? That there's nothing to be anxious about? That there is no economic crisis? That there is no threat of nuclear war? That there's nothing to be nervous about? Shit, I wake up in a cold sweat myself sometimes. Its scary out there."

"Really ... Bill ... I'm surprised to hear that. But his talk was making me nervous. I kept putting my hands in and out of my pockets.

"But the biggest problem," he continued, "Is that
Neurosis, whatever the hell that means, is so damn popular these days! No one wants to be normal. God forbid! It's very chic to have a problem. Don't you read People magazine?" He lit his pipe.

I was looking around the room and I noticed a lot of people looking at me. I began to feel uncomfortable in my clothes, dressed unlike everyone else. In fact, unlike all of Bill Harding's neurotics I wanted to be normal - it was my dream. So I considered taking off the scarf around my waist before I remembered that it was covering a broken zipper. Were people looking at me because of how I looked or who I was? I would try to believe it was the latter.

Doctor Bill had finally gotten his damn pipe lit. "But enough of my tale of woe, Marty. Tell me about yourself. You know, I think it's really great that you got to where you are and I remember you always playing the guitar in bands at dances. You got real perseverance and that's a rare quality these days when everyone is looking for the quick fix." His sincerity embarrassed me. "So tell me about the music business. How do you feel about it?" he asked with a penetrating stare putting me on the couch so to speak.

"The music business, Bill? Oh ... well, couldn't be better." I tried to imitate the language of all the record company executives who had screwed me the most. "It's a gold mine out there, Bill. We may be selling saucer like pieces of plastic, true..." I held up one finger, "But what we're really providing society, and especially young people, is culture, unique American culture, and I'm proud to be a part of that. Its an honor to serve." But Bill Harding's face registered no reaction at all. Jeez, the guy was a real pro.

Fearlessly, I moved to my next stage: "And I honestly believe, Bill, that music will never go out of style because today young people, teenagers would rather go without food then their favorite albums. I mean, it's like what you were saying yourself, rock 'n roll is like therapy for a lot of people. And we don't charge by the hour." I gave him a conspiratorial grin but no reaction back. "And our generation, the generation of Woodstock, of peace marches, of ... uh ... commitment to higher beliefs, we'll never give up rock music ... 'till the day we die. It will be the dominant soundtrack of our lives. We will always..."

"I gave it up easily enough," he interrupted. "I haven't bought a record in years. It's all such crap, nowadays. One good song on an album and the rest is just filler. And the crap they play on the radio? I mean, if I ever hear *Tie a Yellow Ribbon round the old Oak Tree* again I'm gonna hang myself. Figuratively speaking, of course."

"Well, I admit the quality has gone down somewhat in the past couple of years, and the music market, so to speak, is in need of a cultural correction," Where did I come up with this shit? "But the important thing to remember, Bill, is that we, as an industry, have kept going in the face of adversity. Many of us are still fighting the good fight. Quality over quantity is our motto and it's really beginning to turn around. There's some great new ... talent out there if you're willing to look for it." God help me if he asks me to name names.

"But I keep reading how bad record sales are today," he said surprised. "Why just a month or so ago there was a report in The *Wall Street Journal* that albums are selling maybe one quarter of what they used to, and that concert tickets are way off too. And that kids copy albums onto cassettes for their friends and cheat the record labels out of a sale."

"Oh that? Well, I think they just leak these kind of reports out for tax reasons. You see, let me tell you what went down," I lowered my voice. "There was so much money being made in the last decade or so that all of a sudden the IRS was buzzing around the major labels like flies. And you know what I mean when I say this is a cash business." I whistled and made a gesture to my pocket. "What Uncle Sam didn't know wouldn't hurt him, right? So lately those of us in the ... uh ... artistic core of the industry, we've been forced to 'defuse' the issue a little by underestimating ... growth. But believe me, there's still millions to be made by those in the know." I winked at him even though I knew I was winking far too often and Dr. Harding was gonna diagnose my twitch soon enough.

"Is that so?" He was beginning to seem interested.

"Absolutely!" I said with authority. "As a matter of fact," I stopped and shifted my position closer to him. "As a matter of fact, Bill, I'm starting a new ... uh ... production company right now. A few of my associates and myself, of course, are looking very seriously into the Asian market. Teenage consumerism is an untapped vein there, you know. As a matter of fact, the Chinese kids are just dying for rock music."

"Who are your associates?" he asked. "You mean your band?"

"No, no ... I mean business minds. Wall Street ... Washington think tanks. It's all in the planning stage, Bill, but if I give you a piece of inside info can you keep it to yourself?"

"You can trust me, Marty," he said, "Secrets are my business."

"Well, let me say this," I took a long, look around the room to make sure that no one was listening in on us and then I whispered: "A certain large banking concern who specializes in travelers checks has shown a great deal of interest in being involved in whatever projects I might foresee, forthwith..." I knew I had used too many *for* words. "For...whatever." I laughed.

"You mean American Express?" He said wide-eyed. "That's a big one."

I put a finger to my lips.

"Oh! Really?"

I nodded my head coyly.

"Well that sounds promising indeed. Good luck with it Marty." He smiled.

"And by the way, Bill, we're interested in finding a few outside investors too, good for public relations, you know. Real members of the community, the kind of people you could show on a TV ad, investors with ... uh ... vision. Somewhere in the five to ten thousand dollar range. You know, I'd be willing to take a chance on you if you were interested and submit your name to the board. They might go for a psychological aspect in figuring out what consumers we should focus our..." I was getting lost.

"Well, that is very nice of you Marty, after all these years and everything to just meet me and give me an inside shot. Tell me, what's your long-term capital gains situation, tax-wise? Could I write this off?"

Now this I was unprepared for.

"Well, I think its...good, yeah its very good, and a write-off could be in the cards that's for sure but that's all I can tell you, Bill, because I had to sign a confidentiality agreement myself. If the rest of the board even knew that I had mentioned any of this to you they'd be furious with me. But maybe we could set up a meeting sometime after my own ink is dry so to speak." I realized perhaps this was not as simple as it looked; it wasn't like trying to sell The Brooklyn Bridge to some farmer from Nebraska. Not that I was totally trying to *con* him. I mean, I *could* start a production company, I *could* try and make some foreign licensing deals...well, maybe China is a bit of a stretch but I *would* be entitled to a certain large percentage as artist and producer wouldn't I?

"I really don't think that meeting would be necessary, Marty."

"Well, hey ... if you just want to work this thing on a handshake type of basis, Bill, that would be fine with me," I said optimistically. "We are alumni, after all, and if you want to keep your investment more anonymous."

"Handshake? You're misunderstanding me, Marty. Listen, I appreciate you extending this offer to me, but I'm just not interested." He made a face like he had just tasted something bad. But I wouldn't let go that easily.

"I understand completely, Bill, and it makes absolutely no difference to me because I'm sure we'll be *turning down* more partners than we can accept... but I'd love to see an opportunity like this go to someone with the same... roots. Someone I could really ... relate to." I gave him a slight pat on the shoulder but I don't think he liked being touched.

"Let's walk around a little, Marty." He said, "I want to tell you a story." And so we did, away from the bar and through the crowd. We both spotted faces that we vaguely knew, and waved hesitantly. "We're a good looking bunch, don't you agree?" He asked me.

"Sure, great looking bunch." I didn't know what he was getting at. "And trustworthy, too. Wouldn't you say?" He looked down at me; he was almost a head taller.

"Absolutely!" I agreed. "Good solid middle-class American stock."

"Were you at our tenth year reunion, Marty?"

"No, I'm sorry to say, Bill ... I couldn't make it even as much as I wanted to. I think it was at the time of The Grammy Awards. I was probably accepting an award or something."

He stopped walking and looked at me seriously. "Well, let me tell you what happened at our tenth reunion. I met an old classmate of mine, of ours, who had been living in California. It was when the energy crunch was news and this guy said he was a solar energy expert. As a matter of fact he had started a little business for solar heating and was looking for investors, kind of like what you're doing here tonight I suppose." I started to cringe. "I remembered him from high school like I remember you; he was one of those scientific kids, quiet, good student and, to make a long story short I invested what little savings I had with him. I had only been in practice a couple of years."

"And you made a killing?" I asked hopefully.

"The only killing I've made is the one I've fantasized doing to him in my mind. I never saw him or my money again and company soon ceased to exist. It was all a total scam, in my opinion. He came to that reunion just to bilk his old high school buddies out of their cash. Oldest story in the world." He said very seriously, like he was almost accusing me. "I'm amazed I fell for it but I did."

"Really? A fellow classmate? Well, this is completely different. We're much too public to try any scam like that." I laughed reassuringly.

"Oh, don't take it personally, Marty. Your deal sounds very interesting indeed - it really does. But after that last fiasco I decided that I would never mix business with pleasure ever again and especially with old schoolmates. But I honestly do want to wish you and American Express the best of luck and I'm sure you'll be topping the charts in Shanghai before you know it."

"Thanks a lot. I'll keep you informed of our progress..."

"But listen, Marty, if you ever find that you're having a little trouble with the *you know what*," he made a slight pelvic gesture. "With the groupies and all, give me a call. Impotence is my specialty." He handed me a card.

"I'm more interested in raising cash than raising..." I mimicked his gesture with my own pelvis, "*That*, right now."

"Sometimes one may have more to do with the other than you might think." He winked slyly and walked away. Maybe he had a point there. And where was Betty *Boobs* anyway?

Returning to *GO*, not collecting anything at all, I went back to the bar that had become quite crowded and loud by now. This was a hard drinking bunch. From outward appearances, I'd say that my ex-classmates had made the now standard evolution common among my generation from marijuana to martinis. And I was with them all the way. While trying to shout my order over the heads or rather under the armpits of too many men in large sports coats, a gray haired man in a tweed jacket, a red vest, and a rep tie smiled at me. He too was trying to get some service at the bar although he seemed not as impatient as the rest of us *social drinkers*.

"Hello son," he said. "Enjoying yourself?"

"Why ... yes, I am." Had he called me son? "If I could only get a drink, everything would be honky-dory." Then I realized that far from talking to a fellow alumni, I was talking to a teacher and I was sure I remembered him.

"Aren't you Mr. ...?" I tried to look like I had his name on the tip of my tongue.

"Mr. Gridley," he added mercifully. "And yes, I'm a teacher."

"I thought so," I said. "I'm Marty May, class of ... well, class of sixty-seven like everyone else here, I guess."

"That's nice," he said condescendingly. "Hope you're having swell time."

"Why, yes, it is nice, I guess. I wonder if I was in any of your classes? Were you teaching here back when I was a struggling student?

"Sure was, and still am. I teach English Lit. Did you take it?"

"I think so. Didn't everybody?"

"You never know," he said. "I think some kids get by just studying shop, gym and home-economics!" An in-joke apparently, but I laughed all the same.

"So tell me, have things changed drastically around here since I left? I asked.

"Not really although kids grow up a little faster these days - at least the girls." Did I really detect a slight twinkle in his eye? "I've been here since sixty-one. Things go full circle, you know, I'd say that around the time you graduated and for a few years afterwards things got a little wild all that pot, you know, but now I'd say that it's pretty much like when I first arrived. Except for the girls, they just keep getting sexier! I can hardly keep my hands off of them," He laughed. "And that would mean my job! But its not easy, let me tell you." So is this what went on in the faculty lounge?

" I'll tell you what the biggest change is Marty, Jack Kerouac is finally on the curriculum. You can't imagine how I had to fight for that."

"Oh? I'm surprised it was a problem. Kerouac is an icon, isn't he?"

"Well, the conservatives don't like him because he was a beatnik and the liberals don't like him because he ended up a drunk who disavowed the hippies and supported the Vietnam War. Quite a character old Jack. But the powers that be on the school board are always a problem. Now, they won't let me teach Nabokov anymore, or at least not *Lolita.* And I love that book. Its my bible." I imagined it would be. "I tell them that there isn't anything in there that these kids don't already know. But they don't listen; they don't want to hear that. In their minds everyone is a virgin until they graduate from high school. Especially their daughters. Oh what I could tell them. Sometimes these girls who sit in the front row with those short skirts - Jeez, its like a peep show!"

"Who's they?" I asked.

"The school board, the parents, even some of the teachers if you can believe that. If it was up the head of the English department they'd still be reading *The Good Earth* and *My Antonia.* If there was every a way to turn kids off to reading for the rest of their lives those books are it. But I don't push it. I've got my tenure and I like it here. It's their kids, I'll teach them anything they like," he said dryly. Finally, we managed to get our drinks - more beer for me and a Scotch for him. We moved out of harms way and stood by one of the windows. I looked out and saw my limo shining bright, still in its parking place. My driver was standing next to it, watching the late arrivals and smoking a cigarette.

"So, what brings you here? What's so special about the class of sixty-seven that you wouldn't rather be home watching TV?" I asked him as we drank.

"Nothing's special about this class," he said matter-of-factly. "They're all basically the same but I go to all the reunions, whenever I can.

"You do? Why? Not too exciting." I felt I could be honest with him. He certainly couldn't afford to be one of my *investors*, not on a teacher's salary.

"Oh, I don't know about that. Maybe for you but for me it's actually quite exciting. You see, you're my students and I made an investment in all of you back when I was teaching you so I'm always curious to see how it panned out. And I love to see how the girls turned out. To see who ended up with the best boobs!" He laughed. "There are a couple of real babes here tonight."

Boobs and Babes? From the mouth of my English teacher, no less.

"Listen, no offense to you, Mr. uh ... " He went to shake my hand.

"May." I said, "Marty May." Strange to be called Mister by a teacher.

"Right – May. No offense but I'm going to circulate a bit if you don't mind. Some of those little girls who used to turn me on are all grown up now and one-hundred percent legal!" He winked at me. "No more *jail bait* if you know what I mean."

"Sure ... Mr. Gridley, I know what you mean." And he skirted off into the crowd like Groucho Marx. I could hardly blame him. Judging from the age of groupies I've known I'd probably be worse in his position. Ironically, he'd probably lose his job for doing the same thing that's almost expected of a rock star on the road. I circulated myself and I bumped into a few people I remembered and quite a few I didn't. But I couldn't seem to find my real close friends, my ex-girlfriends; maybe I didn't have any. The little chats that I would have with different people were all similar and fairly rehearsed, even my own was becoming somewhat polished. I was holding off on my investment scheme trying to figure out exactly what my *capital gains* situation was in case anybody asked again. Could have used an economics dictionary.

As I made the rounds and talked it appeared we all had condensed our lives into tidy three-minute recitations for the occasion: college, career, marriage, kids, divorce (lots of them) a little travel. And one guy who I used to share a locker with talked of nothing else but his yearly vacations to Mexico. Was he working for a travel agency? I had come to this ritual sure that I was so different from everyone else and my appearance was drastically different. But in so many other ways we were all the same; same generation, each in our own cultural and working place within that framework. I was always a bit of an oddball, I guess, and I still was but I was still accepted as this too. No one seemed surprised that I had turned out as I had even if I had taken for granted that my fifteen years of professional rock 'n roll had taken me far away from all of this suburban New Jersey life and to a different and much cooler world. Not true. The major difference was that I looked like I played electric guitar and most of these people looked like they played golf.

A handsome couple passed by and smiled to me and nodded to me as they smiled and nodded to everyone else they passed. But wasn't that...? I quickly walked up behind them.

"Uh ... Gail?" I said loudly cupping my hands to my mouth." Is that you Gail?"

The couple turned around. He was good looking, athletic, in an Izod shirt with a casual sports jacket. She had on slacks, some kind of expensive sweatshirt and jogging shoes.

"Yes?" She looked at me.

"Gail? Gail Rosano?" I said.

"Well, you're half right. I'm Gail, but not Rosano anymore. This is my husband Greg Small, so that makes me Gail Small." Both she and her husband seemed to find this hilarious.

"Gail! It's me, Marty! I mean ... Marvin! How are you? I can't believe its you." She was the only girlfriend I ever really had in high school. We even went steady, I think.

"Do you mind?" I said smilingly to her husband and gave her a little kiss on the cheek. She didn't reciprocate.

"Do I have a choice," he muttered under his breath.

"Oh ... Marvin, yes. Hi. How are you?" she said formally.

"I'm fine and Gail, you look just great - fantastic. It's so good to see you here. In fact, you're the first person I really know here. I'd forgotten you'd be here. It's really great you came."

"Oh ... yes, uh ... me too," she said unemotionally. Her husband stood there awkwardly, looking from her to me. He was not amused.

"Greg, I'd like you to meet...uh ... Marvin... " Gail put on a grotesque embarrassed grin. "I'm so sorry, I forgot your last name."

"May!" I said, horrified. How could she forget?

"Nice to meet you, Marvin" said her husband with faint enthusiasm. "We better get moving." He turned her around by the shoulders.

"Did you believe that outfit?" I heard him say as they walked away. "Who was that? The class clown?" And Gail laughed.

I slunk back to the bar, leaving my half-filled beer on a window ledge. "Could I have a vodka martini?" Moving on to the harder stuff, as Dylan would say.

"I don't think we have any more vermouth. That would need vermouth in it wouldn't it?" asked the women in the white uniform tending bar.

"Straight Vodka will do, then. Make it a double and save me a trip. Just throw in a twist of lemon - we'll disguise it." She didn't get it. I quickly finished half my drink; I was feeling better. From this point on I decided, I'd let people approach me. And just then a dead ringer for a very big Sylvester Stallone towered over me and stuck out his hand.

"Are you the famous Marty May?" he asked. Did I unknowingly make a pass at his wife? "Uh...well, yeah." I cringed.

"Well, it's great to see you again, Marty.' He shook my hand vigorously, squeezing a little too hard. He smiled like a grizzly bear; he looked as if his nose had been broken once or twice but he wasn't a bad looking guy. His suit was straining at all the muscular points and he was uncomfortable in it, always shrugging his shoulders and sticking his finger under his collar.

"Tim Carver here and I've been looking for you!" Tim Carver had been the high school football hero. Betty had mentioned that he'd gone on to play pro. I remembered once hearing that he had established some kind of record like breaking the most ribs of the opposing team in a season.

"Hi ya, Tim. How are you?" But we were never good friends. I wondered why was he looking for me?

"Just fine, Marty. Couldn't be better. And I bet things must be great with you, too. Even us jocks get down and listen to a little rock 'n roll on occasion. As a matter of fact, I've been following your career for years. And man, I just love your stuff!"

I found it hard to believe he listened to my records.

"Marty, I'm gonna get right to the point. His finger was leveled at my head, which was at his own chest level. "I want to speak to you about a very serious investment."

Tim stood there beaming. I couldn't have asked for a better 'mark'.

"You know Tim, you just can't trust anyone." I said. "But I don't even want to know who told you about this incredible opportunity although I must say I have a pretty good idea." I wiggled my pelvis. He looked shocked. "So just keep it to yourself. But let me tell you Tim, it's gonna be like Texas and oil. There are so many places that are just dying for rock 'n roll ... like Africa for instance. Why, bootlegs of my old records sell for hundreds of dollars over there. I hear they're buying them with diamonds ... in Johannesburg."

Tim Carver had a puzzled look on his face. Was he just trying to concentrate? He said nothing. Maybe my sales pitch had been a little too grand too soon. "All I can say Tim, is that it's only the beginning but now is the time to get involved and I mean deeply because Marty May productions are ready to go all the way. Anywhere in the world. We're gonna fly the friendly skies." Wasn't this am airlines commercial?

"Marty May Productions?" Now he looked totally dumbfounded. He loosened his collar even more. "What the hell is that?"

"Why... that's the name of my ... uh... production company, of course. Its what you'd be investing in." Maybe he didn't like me taking all the glory with his hard earned money. After all, he was a pro football player and I suppose they have egos themselves. "But I don't really care what we call it, Tim. If you came on as a full partner then something like *Carver May Communications* would be just fine with me. I mean, we might as well tap into pro sports as much as show business eh? And it's your investment as much as mine." I looked at him confidently. I was sure I had him. I mean, sports were almost like show biz, right? So I was halfway there to begin with. And all the time me hating sports. Just goes to show you.

"My investment?" He held up his hands like he was waiting for a pass. "What the hell are you talking about? I want to talk to you about life insurance. I sell it off season."

"Life insurance?"

"Yeah, life insurance." He totally ignored everything I had said and went right into his own sales pitch. "You know, a big star like you, Marty, shouldn't be without life insurance and other kinds of insurance too. I mean what if you lost your hand in an accident? How would you play guitar? We've got coverage for that too as well as..." He went on and on but I wasn't listening. What a disaster. I was slowly backing away from Tim Carver just shaking my head.

Then just when I got out of his range someone tapped me on the back. I turned around and there stood before me a vision in Spandex, a large vision of a woman in a white disco like outfit, dripping in gold. But she was so heavy that she must have sewn two stretchy jumpsuits together. There was a cavalcade of bleached blond tresses rather uneasily surrounding her head which had to be a wig and her makeup was so severe it was scary it looked like she'd been done by every makeup artist in the Bloomingdale's cosmetics department one right on top of the other all trying to create the new Cleopatra. She smiled at me like a cat with a canary; the glare of her capped teeth was blinding.

"Marty, it's me! Betty Klein!"

Maybe so, but this was hardly my teen queen I remembered.

"Betty!" I gasped and without thinking: "What happened?"

"What do you mean, Marty?" she laughed in a cute, confused sort of way.

"Oh, I just meant that I was wondering where you were. I thought you might be greeting everyone at the door or something since you are the social chairman. You know, I've been here quite a while ... looking for you."

"Oh I know!" she said, "Everyone's been asking me where I've been. You see my youngest, Amy, has this phobia about baby sitters so she hid the remote control to the garage door to prevent us from leaving - isn't that cute! And I couldn't get a hold of Harry because he was doing an emergency root canal and well anyway, here I am!" She spread her arms with the confidence of a Playboy centerfold revealing some luscious package.

"Root canal?" I didn't understand. "I thought you married a doctor."

"What made you think that, Marty?" She put down her arms and tried to figure this out. "I mean Harry is a doctor but he's a dentist. Hey! They're doctors too, you know." This did make her laugh.

Then she just reached out and grabbed me and gave me a big and I do mean big, wet kiss. "I just can't believe it's actually you, Marty," she whispered in my ear. "I've missed you so much." I was barely surviving her perfume.

"Oh look what I did!" she giggled and tried to wipe her lipstick off my cheek. "We don't want to leave any telltale clues now do we, Marty." And than she stood back and held my hands and examined me. Like she was buying a dress.

"Marty, you look terrific. Just amazing. And look at that outfit! Just incredible!" She called to a woman of equal dimensions standing nearby. "Sylvia! Come over here, will ya? This is Marty."

"Hi ya, Marty," the other woman said flirtingly. She and Betty were dressed nearly the same except in different colors: tight spandex pants and flowing tops and lots of makeup and jewelry. I was sure that I remembered Betty doing the same things with her girlfriends in High School. One day they'd all wear kilts, and the next day they'd all wear culottes and then the next day...

"Will you look at this outfit, Sylvia!" said Betty as she opened my jacket and held it open. "And these scarves! Aren't they just amazing! Will you look at these scarves, Sylvia!"

"Beautiful!" agreed Sylvia. "Just beautiful! Makes you want to cry, they're so beautiful."

"Is he a rock star or what?" Betty said to Sylvia winking at me.
"Definitely!"
"Didn't I tell you?"
"Absolutely!"
"Isn't he gorgeous?"
"Unbelievable!"

"Look at those boots!" We were starting to gather attention and people around us were beginning to wonder what was going on.

"Oh my God!" Sylvia bent down and pulled up my pants leg. "It's snake.' They're made out of real snake. Makes me shiver!"

"Is he a rock star or what?" repeated Betty for the second time. I was beginning to feel like Miss America.

"Uh ... don't you girls want a drink or something? Why don't we cruise over to the bar?" I would have preferred to crawl over to the bar. They ignored me.

"Isn't he just the cutest thing?" said Betty as she pinched my cheek.

"Adorable!" Agreed Sylvia. "And those boots! Oh my God!"

"He was my first, you know," said Betty I couldn't believe she was saying this.

"I know, I know!" said Sylvia. "And we're not too far from the... scene of the crime? Are we, Marty?" This almost made her burst at the seams with laughter. And believe me, the fabric was stretched enough as is.

"My first..." Betty suddenly looked very seriously at me, "And my best!" Her lower lip hung low to reveal even more perfectly capped teeth. I think she was trying to be sexy.

"How about a drink!" I said loudly with more than a little bit of panic in my voice. But they wouldn't budge.

"Now you scoot!" Betty said to Sylvia, "And let me and Marty get reacquainted." She stared at me.

"Don't do anything I wouldn't do doll," said Sylvia provocatively as she left us. I couldn't imagine doing anything she would do. What did she do?"

"You haven't aged a day, Marty," said Betty quite seriously.

"Uh...yeah? Thanks. You haven't aged either, Betty."

"Oh, Marty! she fluttered. "You show biz people sure know how to turn a girl on. You remind me of John Davidson."

"John Davidson?"

"You have the same, shall we say, *savoir faire* with women." She did some kind of slow grind with her hips. It must have been subconscious; no one could do that and be aware of what they were doing, could they?

"Bet that's your limousine outside. I've never been in one..." she moved closer, " ... yet." I got the hint. She winked at me again or maybe her eyelid was just weakening from the weight of her false eyelashes.

"Well, it's not exactly mine completely but I guess it's mine tonight. After that it turns back into a pumpkin." I hoped the word *pumpkin* had not offended her. I was beginning to feel like a Cinderella whose grand ball turned out to be Bingo Night at the local Veterans hall.

"Now Marty," said Betty gravely. "You stay exactly where you are while I run to the little girls room. Don't you run away! We have to make some serious plans."

We? The plan *I* was seriously considering was a nonchalant trot out the doors followed by a headfirst dive into the limo and ending with a tire squealing exit out of the parking lot before Betty returned from the toilet. I could do that and forget this ever happened. Yes, I could do that but, as Richard Nixon once said, it would be wrong. But who cared?

And at that moment, just when I was about to escape the netherworld of suburbia, with great commotion the band marched in, lugging their equipment and trailing their girlfriends behind them. I couldn't help but watch them set up, it was a comforting touch of normalcy in this crazed atmosphere to see amps placed on chairs and cymbals set on stands. It seemed they were a simple four-piece outfit - two guitars, bass and drums - and the P.A. was already set up so it only took them a few minutes to set their gear on stage. That's the way to travel, I thought, mobile, although they probably had more equipment than the Beatles at their height. I walked over to the guy who appeared to be their leader, desperate for a little camaraderie.

"How ya doing man?" I asked.

"Fine. Sorry we're late. Our van broke down. Are you the guy who hired us?" He asked me. "The shrink?" He had on jeans and a flannel shirt but I had longer hair than he did.

"Hell no!" I said, a little drunk. "Do I look like the kind of guy who would hire you?"

He shrugged his shoulders.

"I'm Marty May."

"No! "

"In the flesh."

"Hey, Hank, get over here!" he called to the drummer in a black leather motorcycle jacket. "This is Marty May!"

"Nice to meet you, man," I said confidently.

"Who?" said the drummer.

"Marty May!" said the leader. "He had a lot of hits back in the Sixties. You're from around here, right? "

"Seventies!" I corrected him. "Gimme a break. Well, I was from around here but I've been living in New York and LA as long as I can remember. I'm bi..."

The both looked at me warily.

" ... coastal." I finished and they looked relieved.

"So you had some hits?" said the drummer haughtily "Tell you the truth, I never heard of you. See you later." He seemed to enjoy saying this and he went back to setting up his drums.

"He's got an attitude," said the leader." Too many drummer jokes, I suppose. So what are you doing here? We're supposed to play only oldies, songs that these people know. Are you gonna sing some of your old hits with us? That might be cool ... if we know them."

"Uh...no, I didn't plan on that. Actually, this is my class, I was a member of the class of sixty-seven and this is our reunion so I figure I'd come by for some laughs." I felt ridiculous explaining this.

"Oh yeah, cool. Whatever ... I'll see you later. Gotta tune up." And he left.

What the fuck. So what do a bunch of nineteen-year-old New Jersey kids who probably can't even tune their guitars properly know anyway? This was the last straw of humiliation for me. I was feeling drained, all used up, and more than a little bit drunk. And then Betty returned from the bathroom. She looked a little better. Maybe she had gained a few pounds, but at least she was trying to be something. And she appreciated me. Immediately she held me hand.

The band finally got it together and their first song was *Words,* an early hit by the pre-*Saturday Night Fever* Bee Gees. I think this was the theme song for my class and everybody started screaming and dancing and the next thing I knew Betty was pulling me onto the dance floor. *Its only words and words are all I have to take your heart away* sang the singer of the band while Betty sang along into my ear. Then she added "But I have more then words for you tonight, Marty." Punctuating her message with a slow grind into my pelvis while she squeezed my hand so tight I feared for my guitar playing. I took Betty's hand in both of my own to try and loosen her grip and when I did she whispered, "Oh, Marty, you have such a gentle touch." The dance floor was full and they had turned the awful cafeteria lights down and Betty was really grinding into me and I was feeling some kind of sexual excitement. Things were starting to come alive down below and now I was drunk enough not to care who from.

"Marty, I got to tell you something," She looked at me and fluttered her eyelashes so furiously that one of them became slightly unglued. For the first time I noticed the alcohol on Betty's breath and I suspected that she was as much in the can as I was. "I've been in love with you ever since that night."

This I couldn't believe. "But Betty, I don't think we really talked much after *that* night. I figured you just wanted to forget all about it. We were kind of in different crowds."

"Oh, I was just so shy, Marty. And you were always so cool, you know. You were such a loner and you didn't let anybody ever got too close to you. But all the girls thought you were so sexy." Well, this was news to me. Fifteen years ago, I would have done anything to dance with Betty Klein like this on a permanent basis and now that I *was* dancing with her all I could see were her loose eyelashes and the exit sign beckoning. But I didn't want to be alone either.

"Marty, I'm just dying for some excitement in my life. These suburbs are the pits. Believe me, you haven't missed anything," I had suspected for a moment that I had. But her honesty was surprising and honorable. And then she burped and giggled. "Sometimes I'd love to just leave it all and move into the city and live the artistic life like you do."

Her fantasy was so far from who I really was that I was feeling like an imposter. Now, I'm not saying that in some lonely motel room somewhere on the road, I haven't submitted to ladies of far fewer charms and less grace than Betty, but for once in my life this just seemed plain immoral. I was having enough problems with the failure of my own dreams and I couldn't take on hers as well. I knew I had to do something fast.

"Betty, I've got to tell you something too."

"Oh, not now, Marty don't rush things. All that can wait till later." She looked at me with dreamy, nearly tear-filled eyes and I realized sadly that she had as many false hopes and dreams about this night as I had.

"You don't seem to understand, Betty! It's about tonight!" I was starting to panic.

"Tonight?" she asked brightly. The band had stopped but she started to sing anyway, *Tonight's the night...* I stared at the ceiling until I heard her whisper: *Spread your wings and let me come inside.* And then I felt so sorry for her and for me and for Rod Stewart for what she had done to his song.

"Betty," I said, holding her at arms length by the shoulders. "There's nothing I'd rather do than ... complete what we started together so many years ago... but I don't know how to tell you this ... I've got to go. And right now, too."

"Got to go? What do you mean? It's only eleven o'clock. I thought ... She sounded tearful and she clutched at my arm, digging in her nails.

"You see, I have a meeting with Keith Richards! It's very important," I said. "This is the only time he'll meet with anyone."

"At this time of the night?" she said. "Who's Keith Richards?"

"Have you ever heard of *The Rolling Stones*?" I asked incredulously. "Well he's in it."

"I thought Mick Jagger was in The Rolling Stones?"

"Right, right, they're both in it for a while. And they want me to ... uh ... join, too. You know, the more the merrier! But I really got to run. I'm sorry but you know ... duty calls!" I tried to smile.

"But, Marty! We were just getting to know each other again! And there's so much more I want to know!" she pleaded.

I scribbled my number on a matchbook and handed it to her. "Call me next time you're in the city," I was starting to trot away from her backwards and I almost knocked over another dancing couple, and then a table of hors d'oeuvres.

"We'll have lunch!" I yelled back as I ran from the cafeteria.

Betty was just standing there motionless and then she opened her mouth to yell loudly: "SYLVIA!"

When I burst outside the cool night air was refreshing and sobering. And then I saw another shinier, newer, longer limousine pulling up next to mine. In the back was a man on the phone, a phone in the limo. My own driver had spotted me and gotten out to open the door for me. He didn't seem perturbed by the sight of the other limo, in back of his. Didn't even notice it. I guess limo drivers are the last ones to be impressed with things like this.

I lingered at the open door for a moment trying to figure out what was going on. Finally a small guy in a pinstriped suit and slicked back hair emerged from the other car. He immediately spotted me and walked right over.

"Marty May?" he said with a very assured voice

"Yeah? That's me."

"Al White here. How the hell are you buddy?"

I looked at him, his gold watch, his gold cufflinks, and his perfect silk tie. His stretch limousine, which I'm sure, was his (rented ones don't have phones). Betty had told me he was one of the other ones in our class who had *made it*; an armaments dealer selling guns, bombs, napalm. Anything he could, I was sure. And he was about to go inside and have everyone make a huge fuss over him and his success and the important people he counted as close friends. He didn't need a thing from those inside tonight; in fact, he probably thought he was doing them all a big favor by even attending. I'm sure he wouldn't stay for more than half an hour; then back to 21 for drinks with Henry Kissinger. His car was still running. And I just stood there looking at him, slightly swaying, and trying to focus. He could probably go back into his car make a few calls and get me an appointment tomorrow morning with the chairman of the board of Warner Bros. if I played my cards right. But that was something I rarely did.

"Murderer!" I said with crazed eyes. And I got in my car. "Take me home, James!" I told the driver though

I had no idea what his name was. Nor home anymore, for that matter, either.

Part Two
Blast From the Past
Amagansett, Long Island
1982

Chapter 1

The days following my aborted high school hustle were gruesome for my psyche and my soul to say the least. My self-image was tanking at the bottom of the hit parade and for maybe the first time in my male adult life I understood the moral axiom about the importance of being able to look at yourself in the mirror while shaving. Considering the questionable ethics of modern business I wondered if this accounted for the abundance of beards but more then that I wondered how would I look in a sharp goatee myself?

Wanting to get away, having nowhere to go and no cash to take me there, I searched through the pile of paperbacks stacked next to my bed looking to get into someone else's tragic fictional life and forget my own for a while. Out jumped *Women in Love* by D.H. Lawrence, which I remembered buying at an airport, somewhere in the Midwest, during a long, monotonous tour full of waiting and empty of women.

I can't say much about *Women in Love* but I do remember that in the very beginning two sisters were talking to each other about marriage and one asked the other if she was not tempted to get married as she herself was and she replied, no, she wasn't tempted to get married but she was tempted NOT to get married. It was more the temptation to be divorced, to be free, to be younger in some way again that split Barbara and me up. A temptation neither of us could resist.

What a word - divorce. Sounds like *execution* or *bankruptcy* or *circumcision* - one of those things its hard to do over once its done. Yet it's one of the more definite actions I've taken in my life so far and it must been a momentous one because I've been trying to figure out what it all meant ever since. Maybe if I was able to fully understand what happened to my brief marriage with Barbara then I might also be able to figure out what happened to my truncated career as a rock star too. And due to lack of funds for a proper psychiatrist I'm forced to perform my own analysis. *And so it goes* in the words of Kurt Vonnegut.

The problem is that now I have difficulty remembering much about the actual marriage itself; all that day-to-day living we did together as man and wife. What was our routine or did we have none? Did we lie in bed at night and watch television while eating

Chinese take-out? Did we ever have breakfast together and if so what did we eat? And most important, how often did we make love and for how long?

Barbara was a nice girl and I'm a nice guy, my high school reunion aside and I'm sure we loved each other at the time. But nice people, even in love, are hardly grounds for such a serious step as marriage in this age of non-commitment. Of course, we had gone the standard route first: living together, partying it up as much as we could and maybe we just started to think in the same terms when David Bowie sang *It's not the side effects of the cocaine - I'm thinking that it must be love!"* (Not that there weren't side effects of the cocaine, too.) But no, we didn't marry for love and I know that now. And it would be easy to say that we got married for all the same reasons that I so desperately wanted an American Express Card: respectability, legitimacy, all that crap. But that wasn't it either.

Now I'm pretty sure that we married out of nothing more serious than a sense of curiosity, a sense of going backwards to find the next thrill beyond music and drugs and late nights. Somehow, I got marriage confused with a great many other taboos that had intrigued me because at that time marriage was just another one of those things that my generation wasn't gonna do like our parents did. Besides, there's almost a perversity in getting married these days. I mean you don't really *have to* anymore do you? It's like rubbing your romance in the face of a rather unromantic society, like John Lennon and Yoko Ono did when they put a naked shot of the two of them on his album cover. And there is a tradition of marriage in rock 'n roll if you can believe it. Truth be told, we're a very traditional bunch. You might expect rock stars to be the last to give up their freedom when the reality is we all seem to have a craving for matrimony regardless of the consequences. I give you Jerry Lee Lewis as the finest example of what I'm talking about because when he married his fourteen-year old cousin it almost wrecked his career. People could accept him as a crazy man, drunk half the time, popping pills, getting in fights ... but marrying his cousin? It was the baddest thing he could do.

Back in the Sixties Abbie Hoffman and Jerry Rubin threw dollar bills onto the floor of the New York Stock Exchange just to see what would happen. That's exactly why I got married: to see what would happen. I was sure to be immune from the trap of domestic ennui so why not? We'll make it a teenage drama: rent a car drive to Delaware in the middle of the night (Las Vegas was too far!) wake up a Justice Of The Peace (whose wife plays the organ for a few dollars extra). Just like an Elvis Presley movie. Isn't that how you do it?

And when three months later I found myself in a suburban chapel outside of Pittsburgh with Barbara's father walking her down the aisle and my mother sitting in the first row crying and me in a rented cutaway with pants that itched like hell and a church full of people ready to give us wedding presents of *pre-selected pattern silverware*, I said ... Wait a minute? This isn't how Elvis would do it at all. Or Jerry Lee Lewis or John Lennon or Phil Spector or Bo Diddley. And nowhere in that whole ceremony were the words rock 'n roll even mentioned even though Barbara and I in these modern times had been allowed to write our own vows. We didn't change much though except she didn't have to *obey* me like a pet dog.   Thinking back, I wish I kept that in.

But at the time I said, forget it, I'm not going to let the whole thing get me down. I'd look at my marriage like an artist, like how Andy Warhol would look at a car accident or an electric chair. That silly ceremony wasn't really our marriage, that expensive reception with *petit fours* and California Champagne wasn't a celebration of anything I was a part of. I mean, our union would be something else entirely, something out of Scott and Zelda, Bogart and Bacall, Fairbanks and Pickford, Lennon and Ono. But ...jeez ... that's an awful lot of silverware ... we better start writing thank you notes.

Bad start. But I can't blame it on that. There have been worse, much worse, that survived. What it was really was *a false* start. Because, like I said, I was just curious to see what would happen if we did it, if any knot was really tied. And what happened was that while curiosity was drawing me to the alter; temptation was waiting in the wings to drag me us the nether world of divorce. That place where they try to make what once happened disappear. You can't dissolve your birth or your death or your high school graduation but divorce is the last bit of legal magic left. Back in the Middle Ages if you were rich enough you could pay for a place in heaven. With divorce you pay for a quick way out of hell.

The tipping point, came one day when Barbara just marched into the bathroom while I was shaving to announce that she was leaving. "Where are you going? I asked and kept shaving. "I mean I'm leaving you," she said. "I'm getting out of this marriage. I'm leaving in every way imaginable. And I just said, "OK. So where are you gonna go?" And she said, "Amagansett." And I said, "Have a nice time." I honestly thought she was kidding or testing me or pissed off about something. I don't know what I thought but when I received a pile of long very legal documents from our lawyer a few days later, I realized the joke was on me.

Amagansett is a resort town on the tip of Long Island next to East Hampton. We spent a summer there a few years before. A summer of beautiful weather in the heart of prime resort territory, where everybody from the sweltering city would have preferred to be. It was one of the most wrecked summers of my life.

I chose Amagansett from all the variously quaint towns out there because I liked its Indian name and because it was not full of as many society people as East Hampton.

The house we rented had been built back in the twenties by a robber baron who did not get out to the place till the depression was well under way and Roosevelt had built some kind of WPA Fish Factory just upwind from his mansion.

The rationalization for renting such an extravagant place was that it would be an inspirational setting for me to write songs for my next album. I think I wrote one and a half songs but I easily blamed my lack of output on how the salty sea air kept rusting the strings of my guitar. I bought a surfboard and kept it in the living room, hoping it would inspire me to write some Beach Boys style hits. After all, Brian Wilson had written many of their classics while letting his bare feet play in the sandbox he kept under his piano. But standing on the surfboard placed on top of the couch with my guitar strapped on didn't have the same effect on me.

Whenever we'd begin to get really relaxed I'd look at Barbara and tell her how nice it was and she'd tell me the same and the next thing we knew we'd be racing into the city to buy cocaine and go night-clubbing until after a few days of serious partying we'd crawl back to Amagansett and do something like buy a Badminton set out of guilt.

I remember once in Amagansett we had brought back a fairly large quantity of coke from the city and were up all night doing it. When the sun started to come up we made desperate attempts to block it out - throwing sheets up over the windows. It was really pathetic and I looked at Barbara and she at me and we could only make half *wired* smiles at each other. We didn't want the night to end even though we were incapable of having any more sex. As usual, we ended up taking *Quaaludes* or *Valiums* and sleeping the whole next day. When we awoke, we rarely spoke about the night before.

It all comes back to the unreal-ness of unearned money. Like most rock stars who reach my point of success, a few gold albums but no platinum ones, no mega dollars rolling in and you never earn your money in the traditional sense. You live off of advances because if you're doing at all well and showing promise of doing better it's not difficult to get your record company to constantly advance you large sums of money on future royalties. Of course, you give them something too: some interest in your publishing, another option for one more album, *pick of the litter* of your off spring ... anything you can.

Living off future money has a strange effect: You spend it faster; tomorrow's money today for the promise shown yesterday. But that summer was the apex of what was supposed to be the good life and Barbara and I had plenty of temptations to choose from. In a few years divorce was the only one left.

For a while after we split Barbara was kind of mad at me. She thought that I was responsible for making her waste three years of her life. She said that I started her on drugs. This wasn't true: she used more speed for cramming for exams at Sarah Lawrence than I could possibly imagine - she was primed. She blamed me for her unproductively during our marriage, too. I would say this wasn't true, that she was partly responsible for my achievements. This would infuriate her. I think this has something to do with what women's lib is about.

I was mad at her too. Toward the end I was throwing a lot of things around the apartment. I remember once I picked up Barbara's dollhouse. It was an old antique and had more to do with folk-art than childishness. She was screaming at me; calling my way of life disgusting, my records shit. I picked up this dollhouse very calmly brought it up over my head and smashed it to the ground. It made quite a crash and lay in a thousand splinters. We stood and stared at each other, wild-eyed, breathing hard. She ran out of the bedroom; when she returned she was holding my guitar, my 1959 Fender Telecaster. She had it over her head.

"No! Please No!" I screamed. And then for a moment I thought she was going to and then she put it down on the bed and sat down next to the guitar and started crying, sobbing uncontrollably and refused to let me comfort her. If it was me, I probably would have thrown that guitar out the window making the most violent theatre my demons could conjure up. But she didn't; she was beyond that and she knew that we were beyond anything at all.

Barbara's sense of control had brought her back to the point of departure when she'd first met me; back to teaching school, which is what she had always planned to do anyway, in a grammar school in Amagansett. It took her a number of trips to move her stuff out. And I was secretly pleased, when on her last pickup she asked me if she could take some of my own records. I'd lost a wife but not a fan.

There had been other women in my life since my divorce but nothing too serious. There was still a bit of Barbara left over; I still had the fractured remains of that dollhouse in a shopping bag somewhere.

I sat on my couch, looked at my guitar, and I could not help but say out loud "WHAT FOR?" what was I doing all this for? But I knew that it was really all for this hunk of wood and metal and tightly wound strings that's where my rock & roll love affair is. Not the music or the records or the fan worship but just for the electric guitar. And I don't have the slightest clue as to why that is.

It's like in that movie *Close Encounter of the Third Kind*; Richard Dreyfus plays this normal kind of suburban guy who one starry, starry night gets buzzed by low flying UFO's in his telephone repair truck. Their bright lights give his face half a sunburn, and it totally fucks his mind. Soon, without knowing why, he begins to build this model of some mountain with everything he touches; first it's at dinner with his mashed potatoes and eventually he puts together a large scale model mountain in his basement with mud and chicken wire and he just hasn't the faintest clue as to why he's doing this madness. But he's obsessed with this vision. What happened was that the UFO crew has put this image in his mind in some sneaky way like how they flash popcorn for a millisecond on a movie screen and the next thing you know you're standing at the refreshment stand ordering a large bucket of the stuff. Like a *top forty* record they have this image playing over and over and over BECAUSE that particular mountain is the place where they're planning to land and make contact.

And for me it's the same thing with this damn electric guitar; it represents something a lot bigger, a lot more important. It's just a model of something else. I don't know, do you think there's a colossal Fender Telecaster Guitar somewhere waiting for me up in space?

I sit here waiting for the phone to ring. And who am I waiting for? Do I really think that one day one of the music biz Moguls is going to call to say: "Marty, it's all been a huge mistake! You're supposed to be a major, major star! Your last record was NOT the bomb we thought; the computers made a mistake. There's even been an error in your age – you are not thirty-three! You're sixteen and you've still got years ahead of you to be a teenage idol!"

And what the fuck for? I'm not a complete idiot and it hardly requires genius to figure out what happens to rock 'n roll idols and demigods: They turn into burnt-out, ego consumed, dementedly hip, terminal teenagers. No one can stand being around them. And that's if they're lucky enough to live past thirty.

But the sad goddamn truth is that I'd say: "Well, let me think about it Mr. Record Mogul...YES! YES! YES! I'LL DO IT! I'LL DO WHATEVER IT TAKES! I'll sign anything away, including my slightly used soul, because I want IT so bad I can't stand it anymore! And I don't even know what IT is anymore. I don't believe in happy endings and I know that rock 'n roll doesn't either. So, just like Richard Dreyfus in *Close Encounters* they've put the rock 'n roll mountain in my mind and I keep piling on the mud and the chicken wire hoping to finally see it, the great truth, or at least a model of it. All I want is a little piece of history! That's not much to ask, is it? And then the phone rang.

"Hi mom," I said. "No, I'm fine," I said. "All I said was Hi?"

"How could I sound depressed?"

"Yeah, really everything's fine," I repeated.

"Well ... who ever has all the money they'd like? But I'm not starving."

"Come on, you don't have to do that. You can't afford to keep sending me checks. I'll be all right." I insisted.

"Hell, I don't know what to say, that's very generous of you mom. I'll accept it as a loan - nothing more.

"How's everything in Florida?" I asked.

"That's nice," I said.

"No, it's a little chilly up here," I said.

"Who's Rita?" I asked.

"Oh yeah, I remember you told me about her. She's a widow too, isn't she?"

"I'm glad you have a nice friend," I said.

"No, mom," I said slightly annoyed, "That does not mean I don't have friends. I got some friends ... I looked at my guitar, "Some very faithful friends, in fact."

"No, I haven't heard from her lately," I said.

"Of course I know she's my only sister. I've just been busy," I said defensively. "But she could call me too, you know."

"Oh...busy doing a lot of things. I went out to Pocahontas Heights last Friday."

"For my high school reunion" that's why." God, I didn't want to have to go through that all over again, on the phone.

"It ... it was very nice. Great."

"Yeah, some of them have followed my career."

"No.   No new recording contract, yet. I told you, I'm not in that big of a hurry. You know what they say, mom,
If you want to make a comeback, you got to go away for a while."

"Well, I'd love to come down to Orlando and visit you, too. Maybe in a couple of months, let me see what's going on." I said.

"I will," I insisted, "Don't worry, I know plenty of vegetables. And I'll drink some milk If I get too pale," I laughed; some things never change.

"Bye mom," I said. "I love you, too. And thanks for the check."

This was rock 'n roll history? My mother sending me a check for a few hundred bucks so she can sleep at night knowing her only son isn't starving? As David Bowie said, "This isn't rock 'n roll this is genocide" At a very late age.

I went out to the deli and bought a sandwich and a beer and I went to the newsstand and bought a paper and I came back home and twenty minutes later the sandwich, the beer, and the newspaper were finished and I was right back where I started. I began to panic, realizing that I didn't have any idea how to fill the empty hours of this day. I picked up the phone. And be it curiosity or temptation or romanticism or whatever, I don't know; but I quess Barbara went for it too. Because an hour later, I was out the door on my way to Penn Station to catch the Long Island Rail Road. To Amagansett.

Chapter 2

Three of the four walls of Dave Simmon's living room were covered with bursting shelves full *of albums. They were in plastic covers with numbers and codes on them; the symbols meaningless to anyone but him. He used to rate his records with A, B, C, D's and F's but then there was that time when he invited a whole band up to his apartment for an interview and they started pulling out records and demanding to know how he could do such a thing to music. So he made up his own code but it still was the same thing.*

On the fourth wall was a massive stereo system. It was capable of playing anything that had ever been recorded: records, of course, but also cassettes, eight tracks, and both half-track and quarter track reel-to-reels. There were two different sets of speakers, one large and one small. The smaller set was supposed to simulate the sound of car speakers. There wasn't much furniture to be seen, most of his decorating funds had gone into making the place as sound-proof as possible, but there was one large leather chair, not new, but ideally situated equidistant in front of the speakers for perfect stereo listening. That was where Dave at that moment, his eyes closed, rocking his head to the music.

> *"Now what Loretta?*
> *The doctor says that you're much better*
> *You can feeeel everything*
> *Burn yourself with a cigarette*
> *Oh girl that's gonna sting!"*

Following the chorus was a beautiful solo on an electric twelve-string guitar. It consisted of variations of one phrase, memorable and concise, played in higher and higher octaves, like a jet plane taking off and soaring into the sky. When the chorus returned it was full of luscious harmonies. Women's voices, choirlike, surrounded the somewhat nasal but not unpleasant male lead voice.

> *"Now what Loretta?*
> *Oh not Now what Loretta?"*
> *(Slow fade)*

Dave got up, picked the needle off the record, and said "Great." to himself. He picked up the phone and dialed while glancing at his legal pad full of notes in front of him.

"Hello, Marty? This is Dave Simmons, I saw you last week."

Marty was throwing some clothes into a suitcase. His Long hair was wet and brushed back and it showed where it was slightly receding.

"Oh ... Hi Dave." he said while trying to find a pair of socks that matched.

"Marty, do you have a minute? I'd like to run down a few things with you."

"Well ... I'm kind of in a hurry. I'm going away for the weekend. But ... will it take a long time?"

"No, not at all. It's just a brief bio sketch on you for this rock and blues book. Sometime later I'd like to do a longer interview but this is all I need for now."

"Okay," said Marty but he wasn't in the mood to be doing this now; he had other things on his mind. But he couldn't say that they were necessarily more important.

"Great, it will just take a few minutes and could be fun. To begin with, just let me run down some facts of your career and than you can correct me if something's wrong, okay?"

"Fine," said Marty. But he wasn't looking forward to this; hearing the facts of his career was not his idea of fun.

"Born March 5, 1949, Newark, New Jersey."

"Right," said Marty absentmindedly.

"You only have to correct me if I'm wrong," said Dave. "I think it will save time."

"Right."

"You grew up in Pocahontas Heights, New Jersey, Your father died when you were sixteen. You met Blind Red Rose at a college mixer and joined his backup band soon after."

"I was his backup band in the beginning," said Marty impatiently. "We'd pick up the rest of the musicians at the gigs, usually bass and drums. Red didn't start carrying a full band for about, oh ... a year and a half, I guess."

"Right," said Dave, not needing such detailed information. Marty May would be just a short entry in his book. Nothing compared with, say, Johnny Winter or Mike Bloomfield. "So, you stayed with Red Rose for five years, made two albums with him, and you did a tour of Europe. Then you left when you got an offer from VCI Records. You made one album as Marty May and the Maymen. You left VCI ... or did they drop you?" asked Dave.

"I left," Marty lied. But why shouldn't I lie, he thought, they were the losers on that one not me.

"Okay," continued Dave, "You signed with Premier Records. Your first album was Mayday. Kind of successful went gold. Your second album was called Burning, live album but new material. And that went gold, too?"

"Right," said Marty. "Over six hundred thousand." Even Marty was impressed when he said the number.

"Okay but one thing I'm confused about - both these albums sold well, so why did you leave Premier?"

"Oh, I don't know...the usual reasons. Greed, I guess, being the first. I was with a big management company and it was their idea to leave, get a better deal. Premier only had contract for these first two albums, some slipup by their lawyer, and we thought I could get a better deal and more money somewhere else. But they hadn't considered the price I'd pay in losing momentum and having to get to know a new company and all."

"What was the name of that management company?" asked Dave.

"Oh ... don't make me talk about managers, I'm depressed enough as is."

"Okay, I was just wondering for myself anyway. None of that will go into the book. So ..." Dave turned the page of his notes, "You signed with Windsor, you made two albums The Usual Place and This Time I Mean It. How did they do?"

"Not good." said Marty dryly.

"And you were dropped?" asked Dave.

"Yes, your honor. I confess."

"And that was about three years ago?"

"Something like that."

"Okay. I can get the rest of the information, titles of songs and names of musicians you worked with off the albums themselves."

"You have all my albums?" asked Marty surprised.

"Of course," replied Dave. "As a matter of fact, I was just listening to Mayday before I called you. That song "Now What Loretta" is great. Really a great song."

"Wow...thanks,"

"Oh, by the way. Did Ruby Rose get in touch with you? I gave her your number."

"Yeah, she did..."

"He played at Tramps you know. I thought you might come by and jam but I didn't see you there."

"No ... I had family obligations" said Marty. "How was the show?"

"Great. He could have used a guitar player like you but aside from that he was great. How could he be anything else but great? He's a legend."

"He couldn't, agreed Marty. "Ruby said that it would be his last tour, his health you know,"

"I don't know about that," said Dave. "These old blues guys always say that they're gonna retire. Suppose it helps the draw at the door."

"Yeah, that's true," said Marty. "I hope it's not his last. I'd sure like to get another chance to play with Red."

"That would be great."

"Yeah, it would have been." Dave didn't catch the past tense of Marty's statement.

"Hey man, thanks for your help.

It was a strange thing, thought Marty. It was like they had been talking about someone else.

Chapter 3

She looked good as I walked off the train. Her hair was the same sensible, short cut; a little lighter brown than I remembered. I guess the beach did that. She had on jeans, a cashmere sweater, and jogging shoes. Her figure looked a little fuller though she was by no means fat. I guess she had just matured; I wondered what I looked like to her had I matured?

"So, here you are." Barbara said pleasantly as I stepped off the train. "I thought you might have been just kidding me."

"Hi," I said. We shook hands awkwardly. I kissed her on the cheek. "No, I wasn't kidding. I was going crazy in the city. I feel better already." We walked to her car and got in.

Before she started the car she gave me a perplexed look. "God, you're pale, Marty. Don't you ever go outside?"'

"No, basically I just hang upside down in my closet waiting for it to get dark."

"I bet that's not far from the truth. But if I know you, your closet is probably too messy for you to fit anything in, even a vampire." She did know me.

"Well you look pretty healthy, I must say."

"I suppose," she said, "I feel pretty healthy. I jog on the beach."

"Jog?" I exclaimed. "You jog? Why, you never even wanted to walk, always took a taxi even if..."

"No cracks," she said that with enough seriousness that I did not continue.

"Well, I don't jog on the weekends," she added.

"Why not the weekends?"

"Too many city people."

"Am I one of the city people?" I asked defensively.

"No, of course not,"

"Why not?"

"Because you don't have their kind of money," she said.

We drove through the town of Amagansett. It wasn't very big. It had the usual suburban fixtures: supermarket, dry cleaner, and real estate offices advertising summer rentals. But the closest thing to fast food was a pizzeria.

Out of the town it became more rural. A few farms, lots of open spaces and pickup trucks with a few dirty faced kids and their dog hanging on in the back. But it was a little suburban as well; a few developments had sprung up.

"Pretty country," I said. "I hadn't remembered it as this nice."

"Well, when you were here last I don't think we left the house except to drive back to the city," She laughed.

"Oh, that's not true." But it almost was.

We drove to her house in her new looking *Volkswagen Rabbit*. "Nice car looks new." I was running out of things to say.

"Oh, yeah, Thanks." she said. "The teacher's union has a credit plan. I got it on time." She told me the details of her time payments. I told her about my dealings with American 'Express. Soon we were talking about the weather. That scared both of us; we didn't seem to know each other very well anymore. A few years can dissolve your conversational common ground without you suspecting it.

"Barbara, I want to tell you something," I finally said. "I want you to know how much I appreciate you letting me come out here for a few days. I really mean it; I needed it – believe me."

"Well I guess I felt sorry for you, Marty. That high school reunion you told me about sounded really depressing. My god, what made you go?"

"Depressing isn't the word, it was just awful. I can't even believe that I grew up there; it means nothing to me now. I don't know why I went."

"Well everybody grows up somewhere. Even rock stars." She smiled at me.

"You can use that term loosely these days."
She took a deep breath "How's the music been going?" she asked hesitantly. "Have you been playing around much?"

I didn't think that she really wanted to know.

"No, not too much lately. I was doing the local club circuit for a while but I found that after paying for some pickup musicians, which also meant that I had to get a rehearsal studio and then a roadie and a truck, well, I came home with about fifty cents."

"Well, I guess it's good to keep your name out there."

"Maybe I should find a couple of impostors so there could be two or three Marty Mays playing at once. Maybe I could make some money that way. I heard that Andy Warhol once sent an impersonator on a lecture tour for him.

"That would be impossible," said Barbara as she checked both ways to see that there was no cross traffic at the stop sign. "There's only one Marty May," she sighed.

"But let's not talk about me, Barbara. That's why I came out here; to get away from all that stuff for a while."

"Good," she said dryly. I didn't respond to this.

"God, I must sound like some obnoxious movie star who says 'But enough about *me,* what did *you* think of my last motion picture?'" This made her laugh.

"You're a funny guy, Marty." And I don't know why but I gave her a little kiss on the cheek right while she was driving. I think that shocked both of us because we drove on in silence for a while.

Finally she spoke. "Well ... aside from being so pale you look pretty good, Marty. You cut your hair a little, I see."

"Yeah, I was beginning to feel like a dinosaur."

"Have you been behaving yourself?"

"You mean now that I've lost my partner in crime?"

"You know what I mean." She gave me a half dirty look out of the corner of her eye.

"Can't afford not to," I said. "But really, I'm just not that interested in life in the fast lane anymore. It took its toll on me, on us, too." Something in me wanted to talk about us very badly. I don't think she would care to be as introspective, though.

"Yeah," she agreed wearily. "I know what you mean. All that craziness seems a long away from here. My life these days is rather sedate." she smiled and shrugged, "To tell you the truth I don't think I ever really was interested in the rock 'n roll life, I was just interested in you."

We reached her house and pulled into the driveway. It was newish in a rural suburban development; there was a potato field in back. The way her little green lawn was separated from the potato field struck me as rather funny and a border of chain link fence did the job of protecting her from potato attacks. It was ranch house style with no garage, surrounded by young, scrawny bushes. The dogs of the neighborhood started barking and I felt like I was entering enemy territory.

"You live here?"

"Yeah. With my husband and kids and dogs."

"What?"

"Just kidding, Marty." She laughed. "I saw you noticed the swings. Isn't that the setup you'd expect from someone who lives in a house like this in this kind of neighborhood?"

"Well...I don't know what to expect."

"I live with another girl who teaches at my school; we rent it. She's down in Mexico on holiday, she teaches Spanish. So I have the house all to myself."

"Is it expensive?" I asked as she let me in the front door.

"Not really" she said. "In the winter, it's quite cheap. The rent goes up in the summer but it all evens out okay for two working girls."

I was beginning to feel jealous. Compared to my own, her life seemed organized, purposeful; even a house and a car. It was hard to believe that I was the one who had supported her all those years. I followed her while she showed me around the house. But it was her I was looking at. She looked young but not like a teenager; a timeless quality. A few chunky wooden bracelets on her wrist made her fashionable enough; one step removed from preppie. She was too old for khaki pants. I felt strange in my black jeans and cowboy boots. I didn't fit in. For the first time I could recall I felt as if I was dressing too young. The order of her little house and life really got to me. Why hadn't I turned out like this? What was I doing wrong? Getting a weekly paycheck was totally foreign to me. When the money from my last record advance ran out about two years ago I had started to pick the bones of my career to make a living. In the beginning, my name was still current enough so that I could get a club date once a month and put five hundred to a thousand bucks in my pocket. And the publishing money would trickle in from time to time too; mostly from foreign collection, stuff that took years to get to you. A smart lawyer once told me that I should hold on to my publishing; it was the only thing I would ever have that resembled a pension plan. But even that had slowed down considerably. Once I had eight guitars, now I was down to two: my original Fender Telecaster and a Martin acoustic. If I sold either of those it would be difficult to still justify the title 'musician'.

"Now don't judge me by the furniture," said Barbara a little self-consciously, "We rent it furnished. By the way, what did you do with all of our furniture and stuff? Do you still have that bed?"

"Of course I still have the bed."

"You know those old brass beds have really gone up since we found that one in Woodstock, You should hold on to it. The mattress must have disintegrated by now. I remember the night you threw up all over it after that party for the Grammy Awards. We sprayed Lysol into it for a week, I thought I was going to die." We both laughed. It was the first time we seemed to be enjoying sharing a memory.

She led me into a small bedroom. "This is your room." I set my suitcase on the bed and we sat down fairly close to each other. I think it made her uptight.

"So ... you're leaving on Sunday?"

"What's the matter? Are you getting nervous already?

"Oh, no ... no, I'm not nervous, Marty." She paused. "Well, maybe I am, a little. You know a year ago I wouldn't have had you out here for a weekend. I wouldn't have felt strong enough."

"Strong enough?

"Strong enough in the emotional sense; strong enough to resist the ... past."

She smiled and just walked on back into the kitchen.

Lunch went easy; beer is the best tranquilizer I know. She told me anecdotes about her students, the people she knew. I filled her in on my high school reunion. She found it quite hysterical and suggested I write a song about it. Not a bad idea; I hoped I would remember it.

After lunch we took a bike ride; I rode her roommates. It was a girl's bike and I felt a bit silly with my cowboy boots but it was pleasant enough with the wind in my face and all.

That night as we sat and watched TV, Barbara suddenly turned to me and asked: "Where's your guitar? I just noticed you didn't bring it; it used to go with you everywhere, even on our honeymoon, if I remember correctly."

"It's back at the apartment, under my bed."

"Why didn't you bring it along?"

"My guitar and I both needed a little time alone, our relationship was getting stale." Barbara laughed.

That night we probably looked like any other suburban couple watching TV, drinking beer, and eating a few potato chips. Barbara said goodnight after Johnny Carson. Seemed to be her habit to retire at that time always - schoolteacher's hours. It was typical of us that I should stay up later; some things never change. I watched a rerun of "The Twilight Zone."

The next day we went out exploring in her car. I told her how much I envied her having a car and maybe I could get a loan somewhere and get one too. Gently, she reminded me that there was a prerequisite for getting a loan - namely a job.

"Details, details" I replied in mock exasperation.

"You could get a job, Marty. You're not that different are you?" Was there a trace of resentment in her voice?

"Oh yeah? What could I do? Sign autographs?" I sneered to hide my hurt at her suggestion.

"Seriously," she said. "You could teach guitar. Didn't you use to do that back in New Jersey?"

"Yeah, I did, but Barbara, I think I'm a little too old for that now. Christ, that was almost fifteen years ago. Could you imagine what it would be like? I can see it now: every kid would want to learn how to play "Stairway to Heaven" just like Jimmy Page of Led Zeppelin. Or worse they'd all be into the latest heavy metal and I couldn't take it.

"Well...then you can't have a car." She made a face at me. "So there!"

"I got it! Could you use an assistant teaching third grade? I could clean up after milk and cookies."

"I'm afraid I'd get you confused with my students."

"Now you watch it!"

"Sorry, Marty. It's just that you seem so much younger than me. And you're not; you're two years older. It's embarrassing."

"What can I say? That I got a portrait home in my closet that's really aging?"

"Dorian Gray May. I almost believe it."

"Maybe I'm just a professional teenager." I immediately regretted saying that.

"Well, maybe the 'Professional Teenagers Union" has a credit plan," said Barbara. "And you can get a car after all." One for her.

"Naw, I don't think so. All that union does is supply us with cute college girls." One for me, too.

We drove all the way out to Montauk Point. We came near to where the mansion that we once rented was, but neither of us suggested going to visit it. Let sleeping mansions lie. She pointed out the interesting spots to me like where Nazi saboteurs had come ashore on the beach from a submarine. They were caught on the Long Island Railroad.

"Like most commuters." I observed. I was feeling relaxed and tranquil. Long drives tend to do that to me. I was meant for life on the road. It was never the driving that bothered me, as a matter of fact, I would always prefer to drive at night for eight hours between gigs than take a plane the next day. I could feel some continuity between concerts that way; watch the countryside change. When you fly you're just up in the air. When we reached Montauk Point Barbara pulled into a parking lot by the harbor where all the fishing boats came in. We got out of the car. It was disgustingly picturesque. But seagulls don't do a thing for me. I'll take one black raven over a whole flock of them anytime.

She pointed to a bar near the dock. It had neon beer advertisements in the window and pickup trucks pulled outside.

"You want to go have a drink? This is one of my hangouts. All the fisherman hang out here...its kind of cozy."

"Yeah, but is it safe? Aren't they like rednecks out here?" *Easy Rider* had been one of my more impressive cultural references.

"For Christ's sake, Marty! It's not nineteen sixty-seven! Most of these guys have longer hair than you ever did and smoke more pot in a day of fishing than you put away during the whole *summer of love!*"

We walked in and there was a Grateful Dead song on the jukebox and a picture of Bruce Springsteen over the bar. And a bunch of guys with long hair and plaid jackets hanging out. It was almost a time warp. Barbara said Hi to a few as we went in. I felt jealous.

"You seem to know these guys, eh? You get around Barbara," I said not looking at her.

"Well, I do live here, Marty! It's been almost three years, you know. If I didn't know better, I'd say you sounded a bit jealous." She smiled at me; I had to look at her.

"ME? No" not at all. I just wondered how you knew them ... that's all." I let down my defenses. "Has it really been three years? It just doesn't seem that long ago."

"To me it does. It seems like light years ago."

"I guess that's because you moved out of the city," I said accusingly like she was some kind of a deserter. We slid into a booth facing each other.

"That's not it at all, Marty. I mean, I have a whole new life now. But for you nothing has really changed." She added condescendingly: "And it probably never will."

"What do you mean? Everything's changed for me, you know that."

"Oh, I know Marty. I know that you've been going through hard times. I mean, I don't hassle you about any of the money you owe me) do I?"

"Not money..." I said with emphasis. "Alimony."

"Well whatever you want to call it. All I'm saying is that you're the same person you ever always were. You're still a rock 'n roller. But me, I've changed. I'm not a groupie anymore."

I had my mouth open ready to say something I might regret about groupies and alimony when the bartender came to our table to take our order. He returned with two beers.

"You haven't changed that much, Barbara. You still drink Heineken." And I added charitably, "You were never a groupie either.

"Well, I was either your groupie, Marty or your cheerleader..." This made me think of Betty Klein. The thought made me wince. "...Whatever you want to call it."

"I think I prefer groupie to cheerleader," I said with a giggle. "They stay thinner."

"And now I just feel like..." She searched for a word.

"Like an adult?" I suggested.

"Yeah," she said. "Like an adult. And I like it too," she added defensively. "I feel more in control of my life and the things that happen to me. I don't just believe in fate or the whims of the music business. I don't know which is more fickle. I couldn't argue with her there.

"You really don't think I've changed?"

"Marty, I don't think you'll ever really change. I think that rock 'n roll has stunted your growth." Before I could retaliate she put up her hands in a defensive manner: "But I mean that in a good way, I really do." I noticed her slim wrists; I always liked them.

"I don't know, Barbara, maybe a little change would do me good. I'm losing my taste for this adolescent anxiety."

"Well if you did change, Marty, if you really wanted to live a … uh … I guess normal' is" the only word … a normal life, and if you were really serious about it, well, maybe we could try to work a few things out." Before I could say anything or even think of what I would say, one of the guys who had been standing at the bar came over to the table. I told myself not to get jealous. Not now, not after what she had almost said.

"You're Marty May aren't you?" he said to my surprise.

"Uh...yeah. Why?"

He grinned from ear to ear. He had a full beard and looked like a big bear. "Hey man! How yaw doing?" He grabbed my hand and shook it enthusiastically. "I used to be one of your biggest fans!"

"Oh yeah? Uh...that's nice. Thanks, thanks a lot." Just what I needed.

"For sure, man! I saw lots of your shows years ago and I bought a few of your albums still listen to them too!" Then he beaded his eyebrows in consternation and leaned close) putting both hands on the table. "What happened man? Why'd you stop making records?" he asked perplexedly. "Couldn't stand the disco?

What did he mean by that? That my artistic integrity wouldn't permit me to record in a world that allowed disco music to flourish? Or that disco had shoved me out of the recording business? Could there be any truth to that? After all, disco had closed the gap a little where rock fit in. Precariously, in my case.

Maybe, I should just be straight with him and tell the guy the truth: Why am I not active? Because no one will give me a fucking recording contract, you turkey! That's why! But instead I said "Oh man, I'm just taking it easy you know … I'll put another one out one of these days." I looked at Barbara. She didn't appear happy about this intrusion; it was her turf. "But thanks for coming over and saying hello."

"Sure man, my pleasure, stay cool." Luckily he was one of those fans who sincerely just want to say hello and express their appreciation and that's all. And there's nothing wrong with that, I love it. But in the past I've had people come over to me and just stand there and expect you to entertain them without a guitar, I'm hardly capable of.

But I still felt embarrassed. It had something to do with Barbara being there. It was like the classic TV drama where the overworked executive is being hassled by his ignored wife that he's spending too much time with his business and not enough with her and in the middle of his promises to change all that, he gets a call from his boss and has to run out to a meeting. The ridiculous thing was that something like this had not happened to me in a very, very long time. Why now?

"That was nice," said Barbara with zero enthusiasm. "It's nice knowing that people appreciate you, that you mean something to them."

"I guess so," I said sheepishly.

"You guess so? What do you mean?" There was a trace of hostility in her voice. "You really meant something to him. Most people never experience that. If you think I get that kind of hero-worship from my students you're crazy,"

"Don't get mad about it."

She went and lit a cigarette; it was the wrong end. She angrily snuffed it into the ashtray.

"Who's mad?" But then she realized she was raising her voice and she added more gently "It's just nice, that's all." "I know ... I know...but I never know what to say to them. I know they mean well but when someone asks me why I'm not making records lately I feel like I'm letting them down in some way."

"Marty, that's ridiculous. You don't owe anything to anybody...except yourself."

"Well I'm an American. What do you expect? I feel guilty if I'm not producing something."

"I don't know about that. I mean, I don't really produce anything...I guess you're more of an American than I am."

"The pure products of America go crazy,"

"Who said that?"

"Uh...I forget."

"You're not so pure. You're just...uh...quintessential." She smiled. "Pretty big word for a little school teacher, eh?"

"Sure is. But I know what it means; they're always using it in record reviews, at least the ones in *Rolling Stone*, so I looked it up one time: doesn't it mean something like the purest or most perfect of a kind?" I felt dumb explaining a word to her. After all, she was the college graduate, the teacher.

"You got it. And that's you all the way. I meant where else but America would there be a Marty May? Supposedly normal suburban boy meets electric guitar at the age of seventeen and..."

"Fourteen," I corrected her.

Chapter 4

It's amazing what a few good beers on a beautiful day in a rustic setting can do. Amazing but hardly unique. It makes you very horny. Of course, it helps if you're with someone who is an immediate sexual possibility.

It was hot in the bar; after a few beers, she took off her sweater. Underneath was a white man-tailored shirt. As she lifted her arms over her head to get the sweater off, her shirt strained against the bra she wore underneath which strained against her breasts. I could see her nipples. Nipples that I had seen a thousand times naked, at all times of day, in all positions. But they had never turned me on like this before. Forbidden fruit is the obvious phrase that pops to mind. She tied the sweater around her neck, put the collars of her shirt up and continued talking as if nothing had happened. My face did not register any change; below the belt there certainly was a different story arising. I wanted nothing more than to reach across the table and fondle her breasts, perhaps undo a button or two of her blouse. This wasn't about fucking. It was about something else, some kind of fantasy not totally separate from Betty Klein in her cheerleading days. I'm sure that Barbara in her jogging shoes and pastel sweater would never in her wildest dreams realize that for me, for my libido, she was a sex symbol, a sexual object, sometimes nothing more than a pin-up with her knee socks replacing stockings and garters.
Be it true or just vanity I pictured myself as a bad boy. And I wanted to fuck 'good' girls, and make them bad. It's no coincidence that one of my major sexual fantasies, that with Barbara Klein, had taken place on school grounds because I met Barbara in a school too. Her school.

I believe it had been my first solo tour; mostly clubs and colleges. Actually not quite solo, I was *Marty May and the Maymen*. Our album was not doing that hot but it did seem to appeal to college kids. It was what they used to call boogie music basically just a speeded up version of what Blind Red Rose used to call a "shuffle". These kids used to go crazy for it in the early seventies they'd dance like mad and I'd play as many notes as I could as fast as I could, similar to what Alvin Lee did with Ten Years After. Except instead of learning my chops from old records in London I had a real stamp of authenticity from my years with Red Rose.

Back then, I got a real charge out of playing college concerts. It was an ego thing. After all, these kids would be nearly my age, but they were still in school, taking the bullshit that I'd stopped putting up with years ago. Of course, I was taking a different form of bullshit in the way of A&R men telling me what kind of songs I should be writing according to their latest survey of teenage tastes. But the point was that I felt like a man of the world; I had seen places and done things in my five years with Blind Red Rose that they wouldn't ever do. I had made love to black women ten years older than me, I had stayed up all night on speed playing my guitar in the back of a van, I ate pig's feet and chitlins (though I didn't really like them). Hell for all comparative speaking I was *black* compared to these kids. Though whatever 'color' I had picked up from Ruby and Red seemed to have washed off like water paint since I left them. After all, Red Rose had neither credit cards, divorces nor alimony and certainly no class reunions to attend - that was all *white bread*.

Playing a college is different from clubs or concert halls. Although it's a smaller event for you, the performer, it's a much bigger event for them, the concert committee, than it would ever be for a jaded professional promoter and his staff that watch new bands come in and out of their venues every week. A college might have only two concerts all year so for these kids it really was a big deal. These kids on the concert committee would spend weeks *planning a* show, debating on whether the deli platter as outlined in the group's rider should have more roast beef or turkey; rye or whole wheat.

At a *real* concert, maybe there would be one or two people assigned to your group from the promoter's *organization.* Often they don't assign anyone, they just tell you when to go on and they send someone around to give you your money at the end of the night. But at these college gigs, chances are that you'll have six or seven of these little buggers at arms length at any given time. I would use my position to my utmost advantage and really rub in WHO I was and WHAT they were, whenever I could. I think I just instinctively knew that some day one of these kids would grow up to work in the collection department of American Express.

-I think at this particular college gig, something had not been done correctly and I was sitting in my dressing room pouting. Maybe they had brought us domestic beer. And that was another thing that bugged me about these schools: They always gave you a locker room for a dressing room and I'd feel pretty damn silly changing into my satin pants with the smell of jockstraps and knee pads in the air.

So ... I was sitting in the locker room and in walks this very cute coed with cutoff shorts, an alligator shirt, no bra, and a big smile. I was probably doing my rock star best with sunglasses and acting very stoned. She's carrying this big round deli platter full of roast beef and ham and cheese and she very nicely announces that she is Barbara and she is in charge of the catering. At virtually the same moment, someone walked in from the sound company to tell me that the concert committee had misinformed them. They thought this was an acoustic concert and they had not set up enough equipment to properly amplify a band like mine and show time would be delayed at least an hour.

"WHAT?!" I yelled. And then I say nothing. I just sit there and there's silence and gradually the locker room is filling up with various members of the concert committee and they're all holding their breaths and looking at me in my satin and shades and they're wondering what I'm gonna do. I know they're scared.

I let the tension build and then I stand up and scream: "Can't you fucking morons do anything right?" And than I looked at the girl named Barbara and her platter of cold cuts and she doesn't seem as intimidated as the rest. "What's this SHIT? 'You were supposed to give us a HOT MEAL! After the show! Not this crap now!" And I grab the deli platter and I threw the whole fucking thing into the showers where it made quite a disgusting mess. Everyone is stunned and I'm elated.

After my flying deli platter stunt I sat down. "I want all of you to get out of here and leave me alone! Now!" And they all did. The rest of my band were on stage at the time, which was lucky for me, as I doubt they would have controlled their laughter. But when I looked up I noticed that the girl who had brought in the deli platter was still there. She was looking at the ceiling shaking her head. And I was thinking that, gee whiz, this girl really did have a nice set of tits, maybe I should have picked on someone else. And her legs weren't bad either. I was tempted to ask her to turn around so I could see the whole package.

"You're an asshole," she said dryly. "Now you're gonna have to settle for pizza. And if I have anything to do with it you'll settle for cold pizza." She turned to see if anyone else was in the room. I could just barely see her ass peeking out of her cutoffs. "And if you think that I'm gonna clean up the fucking mess you can take your guitar and shove it!" She turned to walk away and as she rounded the corner of the row of lockers she had one last remark: "And don't think that I don't know that you're staring at my ass. Enjoy the view, Marty May, because it's as close as you'll ever get!" And she was gone and I fell in love.

The concert went well; most did back in those days. The problem with the sound company was minor. I think they were ready before I was. In a situation like this I would usually keep a keen eye out for possible *later-ons*, keeping track of all available hopefully adoring females within my eyesight. After all, Sarah Lawrence College was not far from Manhattan, it was a progressive school they must have coed dorms. But my usual *modus operandi* was not in effect this particular evening, as I couldn't get the deli platter girl off my mind.

After the show there was a small reception for my band and me in some faculty lounge. My bad behavior before the show had apparently been erased by the two encores we got. I'm sure it had been written off to artistic temperament or preshow nerves. And there was hot food waiting for us which as usual we ignored moving instead to the cold beer. I spotted the girl, Barbara, standing by herself. Unfortunately she had changed out of her cutoffs and was wearing a skirt. I approached her with less apprehension than I should have: I was ego propelled.

"You changed?" was my first question. I smiled, she didn't.

"Yeah. It was cold." And so was she.

"You called me an asshole before," I said without shame.

"Right." She nodded her head in agreement like she was addressing a moron.

"Well ... that's hardly any way for the head of the catering committee to act," I said haughtily.

"Well that's hardly any way for Marty May to act," she mimicked. "I put a lot of time and effort trying to make things nice for you. And you were... an asshole!" I think she was slightly hurt.

"There you go again"' I said jokingly. "Listen, I'm sorry I threw your platter. It was stupid ... and childish. I just wanted the concert to go right, that's all."

"Don't give me that shit," she said loudly. "You weren't upset at all. You just wanted everyone to know what a big bad rock star Marty May was and I was your victim. You know, we're not as stupid as you might think. I've seen your attitude before."

"What do you mean? I had a lot of problems at that particular moment. There wasn't any *attitude* involved."

"Yes there was. I bet you never went to college, I bet you were kind of outside the *in-group* in high school, and whether you know it or not you resent it. It's typical for a guy like you."

"Who are you? Dr. Joyce Brothers? You don't know anything about me." But she did.

"Hey, I don't care. You can go through life with a big chip on your shoulder if you want to but you're much too talented and ... attractive a guy to have that bogging you down." Now she smiled. I liked the way she said attractive.

"You may have a point.

"I do," she replied.

"How about ... we kiss and make up?" I suggested.

"I got a better idea." Softly, she put her hand on my shoulder and whispered in my ear: "Let's fuck...and make up."

"What...?" I was astonished. This had never happened to me before.

"Don't pretend you didn't hear me."

"Here?"

"Of course not." She looked up with exasperation. I would eventually come to know that expression well. "We'll go to my room." She took my hand. "I think you need a good fuck, Marty May." She said loud enough so that anyone who wanted to could have heard.

"You're the doctor."

Her room was nicer than I expected. She said since she was a senior she could live alone. She seemed to have a way to turn the lights down low down pat. I mumbled something about if she was on the pill or any other precautions. She didn't even bother to answer. We got undressed; I was glad that she had left enough light on so that I could see her. She had a wonderful body firm and athletic but just soft enough to the touch. She led the way. I wasn't surprised when she got on top but I was surprised to find myself moaning in a way I had never done before.

It didn't take long; within an hour we were back at the reception smiling slyly at each other like coconspirators. And holding hands. Something wonderful was happening, something that seemed to mesh perfectly with my career at the time. I had a lot of confidence; I knew I would make it. I could play the guitar as well as anybody; it was part of my body, it was as easy to talk on it, as it was to make words come out of my mouth. And I was serious about it too. I think this was what most turned on the writers and the critics at the time.

And she, Barbara, was serious too. She didn't joke around much; she didn't laugh easily. And when later that night we talked about my future and my career and what I wanted to do she would nod her head slowly in agreement as if always to say: "Yes, you can do it, it can work out just like that if you want it to." Her belief in me seemed to strengthen and reconfirm my own.

I started to call her regularly from the road. Her full name was Barbara Harris; she wanted to be a teacher. She was from a suburb of Pittsburgh, Sewickley, and her father was an executive with a steel company. She began coming down to the city regularly to stay with me on weekends after my tour was finished. We'd stay up late talking about my career; she seemed as interested in it as I was. We didn't take any drugs back then aside from an occasional joint but I didn't like the distance that even that would put between us and how it would lessen our seriousness. And we sure didn't need it for sex.

I'd take her to rock clubs and introduce her to the luminaries that I knew. She was never overly impressed; not like some groupie on the road who, after we were finished fucking, would ask me if I ever met Rod Stewart and then squeal with delight when I would lie and say, 'of course.'

Soon *Marty May and the Maymen* broke up and I left the record company we were with. It was ambiguous as to whether they dropped me or not. I was working at the time with a manager lawyer who was great at getting big record deals. He said that it was legally vague whether they could hold on to me as a solo act once the band broke up and the label didn't really care about me that much to fight it. For their own ego they sent us a notice saying I was dropped. He encouraged me to go on my own and switch record companies and I took his advice. And after we made a nice deal with another company he told me that as long as I didn't get into cocaine that I had nothing to worry about. I ignored this part of his advice, probably the only sound advice he ever gave me.

Things were happening so fast. My first real solo *album Mayday* seemed to be a hit right out of the box like everyone was just waiting for it and no one was surprised but me. I found that I wanted Barbara with me all the time. I'd even bring her to meetings with my manager or my record company When I spoke, more often than not, it was with her words. The main thing she use to say to me was "This business is fucked."

After she graduated from Sarah Lawrence she moved in with me in the city. It was an easy decision for her. Back in Pittsburgh her parents were contemplating a divorce and she wanted to stay far away from that. She said that she was going to put off becoming a teacher for a little while. She wanted to see the world.

And she did; she came with me on the road. I think that I gave some of the best performances of my life. I didn't have to worry about who I was going to fuck later that night. Since I was a 'solo' now there wasn't as much need for the camaraderie that holds a normal band together. I could let my backup band go their own way while Barbara and I went ours. And for a while our way was only up.

Aside from seeing the world, Barbara also got to see a few New York apartments. We moved around fairly often in those days; the minute I could afford something better, we got something better, till we finally moved into the place where I still live. We got married about a year after. I had another successful album and tour and then I switched labels. I'm not sure why. It was kind of like moving apartments.

My new label pressured me into going to L.A. and make a country rock album. Well, it didn't take much pressure really, they just offered a few weeks in a Hollywood hotel and a good per-diem with a rental car and I said sure, why not. I guess they envisioned me as the new Glen Campbell or something. They were certainly giving me enough money so I did what they wanted. We went to L.A. and lived there for a few months in the Sunset Marquis Hotel. We did an awful lot of cocaine, we were awfully bored, and the album, although completed, was never released. I came back to New York and did a quickie rock album instead. It sounded like a quickie, too. If things moved too fast for me on the way up they went at supersonic speed on the way down. The quickie New York album did not do too well, far below their expectations after what they had paid to sign me. The next album did even worse. I was dropped from the label and remained in that spot where they dropped me. And here was Barbara, back to her original plan of teaching school. She and I and rock 'n roll was just a little awkward detour off her predestined path of respectability. To think of our beginnings and how we met and all was easy, but to try and think about most of the time in between the beginnings and the end was difficult. Our marriage resembled a speed-reading courses you only concentrate on the first and last sentence.

The beginnings are always so much more clearly defined. Like when you're doing a concert there is no other moment like when you first hit the stage, when the anticipation of the audience merges with your own stage fright to form a jet stream of energy. But the truth is that life–seems to be just a series of events with clear starts and then the clarity fades as time goes on; the ripples move further from the center of the pond. Or maybe that's just the music business. I mean, the favorite way to end a three-minute single is to have the chorus repeat over and over again while it slowly fades away. Records fade, careers fade … like a bright red t-shirt fading in the wash...

I was thinking of this as I sat with Barbara. Her teeth were white and bright; they hadn't faded at all.

"The water out here must be better in some way," I said. "Your teeth are incredibly white, whiter than how I remember them."

"That's because you were always wearing sunglasses," she said jokingly.

"Well, I could put a pair on now if you'd feel more at home," I retorted, I looked around the bar; it was filling up with fisherman types. "Maybe we should both put on shades, it would be good for our image." I suggested sarcastically.

"Image?"   She laughed. "That's a funny word. I don't know what it means, maybe because I don't have any image that I know of."

"Are you kidding? Judging by the looks you've been getting, I'd say that you're the reigning sex symbol of Montauk Point."

"Oh Marty." This embarrassed her. I think she blushed. "The way you think...we really are two different types of people."

"What's different?"

"Well, to begin with ... I'm a day person."

Had I missed something? I was expecting a far heavier answer. "You know you used to sleep all day and stay up all night. I swear, there were times when our schedules were in synch for only a few hours. I mean, my dinner was your breakfast"

"That reminds me of something Lou Reed said in an interview," I interjected. "He said that his week beat most people's year."

"So what does that have to do with me being a day person? And why do you prefer the nightlife? I never really understood this about you."

"I don't know. The night always seemed to hold more ... possibilities."

"Possibilities of what?" she asked suspiciously.

"I don't know, I guess the usual excitement, romance, the unexpected, the hope tomorrow that will never come."

"Well ... I don't think the night holds many possibilities for marriage. That's a daytime sport."

"Maybe you're right," I said passively. "So ... have you come up with any possibilities?"

"For what?" she asked surprised.

"For marriage," I said. "Have you found anyone else?"

"No.   I'm not looking." I strangely felt relieved.

"Why not?" I should have quit while I was ahead.

"Well ... because I've been involved with this man for a while, not that seriously. He's married." She didn't look at me while she said this. "It's kind of a strange relationship."

"Who is he?" I felt a lump in my throat.

"He's an artist," she replied as if that explained everything.

"A musician?"

"No, of course not! He's a painter – a real artist."

"Ouch," I said softly.

Chapter 5

We soon left the bar and took a long walk along the docks and watched the fishing boats come in followed by seagulls - the usual postcard stuff. We didn't say much'. I think for the first time since I had arrived we were both trying to seriously consider how we had fit into each other's lives. The sun would be setting soon and something about that seemed to relieve some pressure from me. I thought about what Barbara had said about her being a *day person* and me the opposite. Could it have been as simple as that?

I did remember, toward the end of our marriage, that our lives had gotten ridiculously out of synch. There had been a time, somewhere around the era of the rented mansion that we were pretty together; lived as ones got up and went to bed together. But it had been my game she was playing and that was a turning point. After that summer Barbara slowly started to retreat from me back into the more disciplined and routine life she had been brought up with while I marched deeper into the rock in roll canyons. It was a gradual thing; she stopped going out with me at night to clubs and concerts but I was hanging out with more musicians so I didn't feel alone. I never screwed around. I guess that would be the standard pattern for a breakup but Barbara would always take care of me sexually even if sometimes she made it seem like a chore. Still, it was one of the last things in our relationship to die.

She had begun talking about going back to school; to get whatever was needed so that she could teach if she wanted to. I guess I wasn't listening very carefully for in her own way she was certainly telling me that it was over. She wasn't interested in doing cocaine anymore and I still was though it was barely as much fun without her. And the long talks we use to have about my career seemed to bore her. The music business had not turned out to fit within her personal guidelines of how a business should be run. It was too unlike her father's steel business and she resented this and started calling the people I was dealing with crass and in her more disgusted moments, idiots and pigs.

I would awake around three or four in the *afternoon* and Barbara would already have been to school *and back*. My nightlife had reached ludicrous proportions~ but this seems to be what happens when a musician such as myself isn't making records or touring sporadically. I remember when I met John *Lennon on* the stairs of a rock club *in* the Village. I was with the owner who introduced us. I was so nervous at meeting Lennon that I didn't really know what to say to find common ground between a Beatle and myself.

"So ... uh, what are you doing these days?" I asked John Lennon.

"What else do you do, when you're not making music?" he said in his unmistakable accent. "You're out getting fucked up."

This came as a shock. I thought that there could be few things in the world as exciting as being John Lennon, ex-Beatle. But I guess he really meant it because not long after this he went into his self-imposed exile and became a househusband.

"What did you think of John Lennon's death?" I asked Barbara. We were standing at the end of a dock watching some fisherman clean fish.

"It made me glad not to be living in the city anymore," Barbara said coldly. "It really is a jungle."

This made me mad. How could she say this? I think I would have yelled at her but I wouldn't have known where to begin. I wasn't asking about the crime, I don't give a damn about the crime; I was asking about the loss. That was the important part. I still wasn't sure how we were going to get over it; if we could get over it. Could just the few years difference in our age mean that much that John Lennon would lose his significance for her? Or was it something else? The essential difference between us that was perhaps always missing; the faith and the belief in something that went far beyond some teenage fad.

Since John Lennon's death, I must say that I had not felt quite as desperate to resume my climb to stardom. At least sometimes I felt this way. If he could end up like that, what hope was there for me? Where was the pot of gold? But these thoughts only occurred to me in my darker moments, but for the most part, I went on living like most people, stopped thinking about John Lennon being gone or nuclear war... things like that.

"I still can't believe it happened," I said calmly, ignoring her comment as best I could. "I remember I was sitting home listening to the radio, it was WNEWFM and the song that had been playing finished and Vince Scelsa came on and said that a man tentatively identified as John Lennon had been shot in front of the Dakota. He had no other details, there was nothing else to do but put on another record and wait. The thought that what did happen was going to happen was unthinkable to anyone, I think."

I felt sad remembering that day and my eyes were filling up but Barbara was looking out to the harbor and couldn't see this.

"I got on my knees and started praying that he wouldn't die."

She turned around and looked at me. "You prayed, Marty? I didn't think you were religious."

"I'm not. It didn't matter. But as I was praying I had an awful feeling it was too late and then Vince Scelsa came back on and said John Lennon was dead. You could hear the tears in his voice and I was crying too just standing there alone in my apartment. I guess a lot of people were. And I'll tell you something, Barbara, ever since that night it just hasn't meant the same thing to me."

"What hasn't meant the same thing?" she asked. She really didn't understand.

"Rock 'n roll."

But my days in Amagansett with Barbara that weekend were free of rock In roll and the music business and I felt like I was playing hooky from something; like being back in my apartment, waiting for the phone to ring was part of my job. For better or worse, I belonged to something.

Gradually, Barbara began to fill me in with the facts about her affair with the painter. His name was Garcia Ortega and he was very famous within the world of modern art. She told me he had been noticed during the Fifties, had been an important founding member of the 'abstract Expressionist school of painting, and had been best friends with Jackson Pollock who was perhaps the most famous member of that movement. She explained that Garcia Ortega and Jackson Pollock and their clique were like rock stars at the time. Like wild beatniks, they drank too much and they were womanizers and many of them, like many rock stars, were now dead. Fool that I am, I asked her why she knew so much about them.

"Because I majored in art at Sarah Lawrence and I teach art now, Marty." She looked up with that familiar exasperated expression. "That's what I was studying all that time! You know, the problem with musicians is that you have no memories!"

"You know a famous producer once said the exact same thing to me," I said cheerfully. "He said it was because we only learned how to count to four."

She laughed. "Who said that to you?"

"Uh...I can't remember." This made her laugh. At her house Barbara took out some art books and shoved me some of Garcia Ortega work along with that of Jackson Pollack and other abstract expressionists. It looked like Beatnik art to me; mostly just bright colors arranged in very abstract (obviously) designs. They didn't really draw anything you might recognize a bird...a face, or a tree. I was highly suspicious of it. But this probably had more to do with Garcia Ortega's dalliance with my ex-wife than his efforts on canvas.

"Does Jackson Pollock live out here too?" I asked innocently.

"He did until he died many years ago," said Barbara, being a bit of a wise-ass. I always suspected her of holding her education over me a bit. "He's buried in a real interesting grave. Maybe we'll go see it sometime," she suggested enthusiastically. It hardly sounded like a fun time to me.

Later that night Barbara got a phone call and when she came back to the living room where I was watching the news. She asked me bluntly "Do you want to go visit Garcia Ortega tomorrow?"

"Sure," I said brightly. It was good acting.

"Okay." And then she went back to the phone. It must have been him.

"What about his wife?" I asked her when she returned. "She doesn't mind you dropping in?"

"Oh, they don't live together. Not for a long time."

"So why don't you two live together?"

"Well ... for two reasons. First of all, Garcia needs his privacy, he needs solitude for his work." She was quite serious. I couldn't remember her ever mentioning anything about my need for solitude for my 'work'.

"And secondly, our relationship is not monogamous.

There are other women in his life besides me." She looked away as she said this, then walked into the kitchen and began doing dishes.

The old pervert, I thought. Probably got a slew of young chicks out here. I didn't sleep well that night thinking about tomorrow's 'culture day'.

On the way to Ortega's place, Barbara stopped to show me Jackson Pollock's grave though I had hardly requested the tour. WP drove to the back of a small country cemetery and got out of the car. Barbara pointed into the woods behind the gravestones.

"There he is," she said excitedly. "Isn't that the most beautiful grave you ever saw? It's so...natural. Look there," she said and pointed. There was a small plaque fastened to the boulder. It was so tarnished and covered with fungus I had missed it but as I looked now closely I could see the writing: it said Jackson Pollock.

"It's like a signature," I said.

"It is. It's his. Isn't it perfect?"

I was about to say something sarcastic but then I thought, she didn't understand what John Lennon meant to me and now I couldn't understand what Jackson Pollock meant to her. Maybe we're even. But in my heart of hearts I must admit there was no comparison.

"He was in a car crash along these road around here. It was nineteen fifty-six. Today his *paintings sell* for a lot of money - fortunes!" This excited her.

"It's funny how that doesn't happen in rock 'n roll. Take a guy like Jim Hendrix, his record still sell for

The same amount if not less. It doesn't seem fair in a way; like these guys, these painters, all they got to do is think about selling their stuff to one person one buyer, and I have to think about selling my stuff to millions of people. I'm supposed to do something everybody's gonna like right now - do you think that's fair?"

"It's different," was all she said. I don't think she appreciated the analogy. This world was holy to her now and I shouldn't tread on it with the dirty boots of rock 'n roll.

We got back in the car. I think my reaction to Jackson Pollock's grave had disappointed her like I was supposed to see the light or something. What light I wondered?

★

At Garcia Ortega's house, Barbara didn't bother ringing a bell, we just walked in and she softly yelled, "Garcia?" The familiarity bothered me immediately.

Garcia Ortega was sitting in his living room that was immense. He stood up when we entered. He had a full head of gray hair, sort of longish; his face was weather beaten and full of lines. He almost looked like an Indian. He was shorter than either Barbara or I, and he wore a paint-splattered white overalls. There was even some paint sprinkled throughout his hair. He wore wire-rimmed glasses not unlike John Lennon used to wear. I bet he had copied his look and I would be sure to bring this up to Barbara later,

Barbara kissed him on the cheek and he smiled at me and offered his hand. We shook hands before anything was said. I thought this was somehow significant; a gesture of peace.

"Garcia, I want you to meet Marty May we used to be married."

"Hi," he said and then he sat back down. It was hardly an enthusiastic greeting.

"How are you, Garcia?" asked Barbara a little too stiffly I thought.

"Oh fine," said Ortega. "A little tired. Joyce and her sister came over last night. They were doing some cocaine so I stayed up a little too late. But we had fun."

I was shocked.   I tried to catch Barbara's eye but I couldn't. She would look only at him. What did he mean that they "had fun"?

 I concentrated on keeping a rising rage down. Garcia seemed to be greatly engrossed in the television show he was watching. And that's what we did that Sunday afternoon: watch TV. I couldn't believe it. Here I was, with this world-famous artist, a virtual walking money machine, and he just sat there and watched television. It was a BIG television and he had a remote control in his hand. I liked when he turned off the sound whenever a commercial would come on. Barbara asked me if I wanted a drink. "Vodka Tonic," I said though I usually only drank beer. On Sundays, I move on to the harder stuff - you have to. Then a commercial came on and Barbara was in the kitchen or somewhere fixing drinks and I was sitting there with Garcia Ortega in silence.

"I don't know too much about art," I said.

Maybe he was hard of hearing.

"I said that I don't know too much about art," I repeated louder. "But Barbara showed me some of your paintings in a book and I liked them very much." Though I really didn't like them or dislike them, I just looked at them. They didn't inspire much of an emotional reaction. The commercial seemed to go on forever.

"I'm kind of an artist myself," I said, immediately feeling stupid.

"Oh, so you paint?"

"Well no, not that kind of artist. I'm a musician."

"And what do you play?"

"Guitar, electric guitar, you know, rock 'n roll, blues, things like that. I write songs too." I felt like I was bragging, like it was important to put us both on an equal creative level.

"Oh, that's nice." For the first time he smiled at me. Maybe he was nervous too; I never think of that. "I don't get a chance to listen to much music anymore." He spoke with a slight accent. "When I lived in New York I used to like to go to hear some jazz. Sometimes Charlie Parker or Thelonious Monk used to play back then. There was a club called the Five Spot. It was a fine place and we all went there. I'd be please to hear some of your music sometime."

"Well, I'm sure Barbara has a few of my old records lying around she could bring them over."

"That would be nice. I do look forward to that." Then Garcia turned the TV back on and Barbara returned with the drinks.

Trying to figure out the relationship between Barbara and Garcia was not easy. They hardly spoke; I saw no signs of affection between them. And after her experiences with me I was appalled that Barbara would even associate with someone who did cocaine not to mention sleep with him. I could think of no other reason for their affair other than that she idolized him. Maybe she had not changed as much as she thought.

After a few hours of TV and drinks we left Garcia Ortego, I supposed to sisters with cocaine who would take our places on the couch   later on. But Barbara said that he went to bed fairly early these days though she assured me that he had been quite a hell raiser in his prime.

"What do you mean early?" I asked as we were getting into the car. "Didn't he say that just last night he was up doing coke?"

"Oh, he doesn't really do any. Maybe just a hit or two to make him feel young." She smiled.

"It didn't sound like a few hits to me." I said. We were in the car. "I'm surprised you'd be attracted to someone into that after all we went through.

She turned to face me with disapproving eyes. "I told you he is NOT into that. And for your information, I haven't done any cocaine in years." She started the car. "I think you're just jealous Marty," she said softly.

"Jealous?"   I said, amazedly. "Are you kidding? Of that old coot?" But she just smiled.

We went to a bar called Stephen Talkhouse for a nightcap. It was right in the town of Amagansett. A friendly bar, woody and warm and the smell of whiskey and beer in the walls. Barbara pointed out a framed poster of one of Garcia Ortego's shows at the Whitney; it was signed. He was a real local hero, not such a bad thing to be, I guess. Barbara seemed to be drinking a lot more than I remembered. I asked her and she replied that it was part of the life out here. Everybody drank.

"Like required reading at school?" I suggested sarcastically. My image of her as the innocent little schoolteacher who had run away from the big bad world of rock 'n roll was quickly fading.

I took down a couple of vodka tonics much too fast before I asked her the question I had been wanting to ask all day: "Do you really fuck that old man?"

She didn't let this get to her. "He is not an old man," she said drily. "He's a great artist and, yes, I do sleep with him on occasion. You know we are not married anymore, Marty: you really shouldn't be so jealous.

"Who's jealous?" I lied. "I just can't imagine you two together rolling in the hay, that's all. When did it start?"

"About six months ago. I met him at a parent's night at school. I teach one of his kids."

"He has kids? That hardly looked like the kind of place where kids live. Isn't he afraid that they'll crash their skateboards into his pre-Columbian art?" I found this funny and couldn't help but laugh.

She didn't. "They don't live with him. They live with their mother, his wife, not far away."

"That's funny that you met him in school;"

"Why is that funny?"

"Because you met me in a school, too. I guess that's just your modus operandi, eh?"

"You're being obnoxious, Marty," she said and she was right. I wasn't drunk enough to use that as an excuse, yet.

"I'm sorry, you're right. Tell me about his kids. I sat back in my chair and tried to cool out.

"Oh, they're very nice, I think the little girl may have some talent, too. They love their father, he sees them a couple of times a week." She acted as if he had painted the perfect parental plan.

"That's pretty weird," I couldn't help saying it. I shouldn't judge other people's lives. But it didn't seem ... American.

"You don't know what you're talking about." Barbara snapped. "You never wanted to have kids. Have you forgotten about my two abortions?" She glared at me.

I had and I hadn't. Or at least I didn't think about them. The first one had been right at the beginning; we had only been living together a few months. Barbara didn't take the pill; she thought it dangerous and I didn't argue so she used a diaphragm most of the time and what we thought to be good timing the rest. What happened was bad timing all the way around; a horror to be sure. I think by this time abortions were fairly legal in New York but for some reason I took Barbara to see a doctor out in Pocahontas Heights. He was an old family doctor, my mother use to take my sister and me to him for things like flu shots. He was either always a bad doctor who never ran into a bad enough situation and that his incompetence became noticeable to his patients or else he was past his prime, senile, unaware of present-day abortion procedures, or else he was just crazy. I didn't go into the examination room with her; I hardly figured that this was it, that this was the abortion. When she came out I asked her what happened and all she said was: "He gave me some kind of a shot."

The odd thing was that the question of getting an abortion or not was never considered. I took it for granted that she wanted one; that for us to have a child was impossible. The term "right to life" had hardly been invented.

So he gave her a shot. And we thought that this was some prelude to the simple operation that would follow. When she told me that he had not mentioned any further procedure) we were both puzzled and we would call him the following day. That

121

night, we ended up at The Brasserie, an all-night restaurant. I liked the place a lot; it had a colorful crowd all the way from hookers to diplomats, sometimes together at the same table. We had just been seated; we were sitting across from each other. I told Barbara she looked a little pale, she said it was just the light. I had put my leather jacket on the back of my chair, it dropped off and I bent down to pick it up. And then I said to Barbara that I didn't remember her wearing red pantyhose and she said that she didn't know what I was talking about and I bent down under the table again and I touched her leg and it was wet. Something red was dripping onto the floor and it was her blood.

I told her what I saw; she said she was feeling faint. I picked her up out of her chair and carried her out of the restaurant and into a taxi. I don't know how I did it; she's nearly the same size as me. We went to New York University Hospital. Thank god the cab driver knew it to be the closest one. There was a great deal of blood on the floor of the taxi but Barbara said she felt all right; she was almost cheerful but she was deathly pale. Later, the doctor told me that she was probably in shock the whole time. He also told me that she didn't have a hell of a lot of blood left in her body by the time she reached the emergency room. He couldn't believe that any doctor would consciously try to induce a miscarriage when abortions were so simple these days; it was the kind of thing that doctor's who were close friends with a patient used to do years ago when abortion was illegal. He wanted to know the doctor's' name but I wouldn't tell him because I knew that Barbara didn't want her parents to find out and if there was any big commotion they might. They even thought she was living with a girlfriend.

So, she spent a few days in the hospital, I called up the doctor who had done this and called him a butcher and he hung up on me; and we didn't speak much about it afterwards. And Barbara and I promised each other that we would not forget again.

The second one was different, cleaner, colder. I wasn't even there; I was on the road. By this time she was back in school and she no longer accompanied me on my tours. She called me in Toronto; I was playing at a club there for three nights. I think the conversation went something like this:

"Hi."

"Hi."

"Guess what?"

"What?"

"I'm pregnant."

"Again?"

"I saw my gynecologist last week and he called me today to tell me the results. He says he can do it tomorrow."

"Do what?"

"An abortion! What did you think? Deliver the baby?"

"Don't yell at me! You're the one who got pregnant."

"That's right."

"So ... what do you want to do?"

"Is there a choice?"

"There's always a choice."

"Big choice."

"I guess you should do it ... if that's what you want."

"What do you want?"

"I don't think I want a baby. Not now."

"Yeah, we might as well wait till they go on sale. She laughed...a little.

"That's not funny."

So, I guess I'll do it tomorrow."

"Do you want me to come home? I can cancel the show and come home if you want."

"No, don't bother." This annoyed me.

"It's not a bother. After all, I'm the father."

"Now that's funny," she said and hung up. And when I tried to call back the operator said the phone was off the hook.

I didn't go home. I wish I had. In my weaker moments I even wish that she might have had the baby. In a way, this is the abortion that haunts me; not the gruesome first one. This is the one I feel guilty about, the one I feel confused about. The one that seems wasteful and uncaring and inhuman.

And I was alive and Barbara was alive and we were divorced and there were no children to make things messy. And I guess that's better or fair or something.

"No, I haven't forgotten about your two abortions," I lied.

I was beginning to suspect that the reason Barbara had invited me out here was just to show off, to see how great she was doing: her cute little house and car, her artist boyfriend, her cozy bars. To show me that she didn't need me anymore. I ordered more drinks, doubles for me. And as the Talkhouse bar seemed to be filling up with more people in down vests whom Barbara seemed to know I just kind of sat there and thought how much I didn't like anyone.

Garcia Ortego and his perfect artistic world went round and round my brain like a scratched record. It didn't seem right. I mean, rock 'n roll is the important art now, isn't it? Before, there were only canvas and paints for people to express themselves with but now we had electric guitars and recording studios; far more powerful tools. But guys like Garcia Ortego didn't have to worry about a program director at some secondary FM station in Oregon not liking his work. He could dictate to the world just what art was. And that was the way it should be for rock 'n roll too. Or at least that's the way it seemed it should be after my fifth vodka tonic.

He had everything I should have a good place to work, the acclaim, the love of my ex-wife ... did I still want that?

It was obvious I wanted to leave. I asked Barbara if I could drive. She said I was too drunk.

"So what? If it's good enough for old Jackson Pollock, it's good enough for me!" I said with more than a slight slur. "Let's go out in style sweetheart. Let's join the fuckin' world of art!" But still she refused to let me drive. On the way home I alternated between giving Barbara leering drunk grins and jealous dirty looks.

When we got back to her house she put the TV on as if by habit. And I resented that.

And I'm thinking to myself what the hell am I doing out here anyway? This is my ex-wife, not some new flame, there's no budding romance here. Divorced couples aren't supposed to get together on weekends. This is perverse. But maybe Barbara didn't invite me out here to show off, or even because she felt sorry for me. Maybe she wanted me to come out because she was lonely like me; her life was not as full as she made it sound. I couldn't believe that Ortego gave her all the attention she wanted.

Barbara went into the bedroom for a moment saying she wanted to put on something 'more comfortable. I was drunk as hell.

"I'm drunk, Barbara," I said smiling when she returned. She was wearing a robe and slippers.

"So am I ... I think, Marty," she said as she sat down on the couch not far from me but not that close either. "A little bit maybe, but it's nice to be here now, watching everything peaceful and quiet. She smiled back at me.

I leaned over and gave her a little kiss on the cheek. She didn't seem to mind.

"Who' s on TV?" she asked.

I didn't say anything. I gave her another kiss.

"Now come on, Marty," she said with a frown. "Who's on TV?" She reached for the TV Guide on the coffee table in front of the couch. As she leaned over, her robe opened and I could see her breasts a little.

"The hell with the TV," I said. "Let's fuck." In my drunkenness I thought a direct approach the coolest.

Her expression changed radically, she reached for the collar of her robe, closing it up completely. I think she had just sobered up real fast. She got up to change the channel and then sat down in another chair.

"Didn't you hear me, Barbara?" I slurred. "Do you wanna fuck..." I lowered my voice, "...make love?" She
continued to ignore me and all of a sudden I was full of rage.

"What's the matter? Should I say it in Spanish? Is that what Garcia asshole does? Or is he more refined than me? I think I was swaying even as I sat down.

Barbara stood up. "Marty, I'm going to bed. I think you should leave in the morning. There's a telephone number for a taxi on the bulletin board in the kitchen. And she started to walk out.

I'd like to say I don't know why I did what I did, but I do know. I wanted to hurt her, I wanted to punish her in some way for leaving me, for everything that had happened to me and had not happened to me. At that moment it was all her fault. And I was drunk enough to mistake my vengeance for lust. I was sorry the moment myself that it was just the booze. It happened and I tried to convince

As she stood up to leave, I guess I kind of dived for her and I tackled her and she was on the floor underneath me. Her robe was fully open; I was grabbing at her breasts and trying to kiss her, but she was swinging her head so wildly that I couldn't.

"Barbara!   I want you so bad," I yelled down at her. "Can't you feel it too ... you're the only one ... the only one!" The words didn't even sound true as they came out of my mouth.

"What the hell do you think you're doing, Marty?" she screamed. "Get off of me! Get off of me right now! I mean it! GET THE HELL OFF OF ME!"

Then Barbara hit me really hard, somewhere in the stomach. I didn't think that I felt it but it did something to my strength, zapped it all away and I rolled off of her. She got out from under me and stood over me. Her face was livid and she was screaming and she tried to kick me but missed. I was ' trying to catch my breath and I guess she could tell that I wasn't capable of any more of an attack.

She ran out of the bedroom and I kind of crawled back over the couch. And then she walked right back into the living room. She had more to say.

"You want to know why I sleep with Garcia Ortego?" she screamed. "I'll tell you why - because he's an artist Marty! A real artist. Something you'll never be. Once I thought you were but you're not, you're shit. You and your rock and roll world, its all shit! IT'S SHIT! SHIT! SHIT!" She was starting to cry. "It almost ruined my life and I think it has ruined yours! Because you're never gonna grow up and you'll never be a success and you'll probably end up dead with a needle in your arm like the rest of your heroes!" And then she ran out of the room.

"Hitler was a painter too." I yelled meekly after her, still trying to catch my breath. I thought I heard her door lock.

I don't know how long I lay there, maybe an hour. At first my head was *spinning so* badly that I thought I might throw up, but I didn't. I just tried to concentrate on the TV, thinking of nothing else, but that was impossible. What had I just done? Was I really that kind of monster? I wondered if I could leave that night, if there'd be a train or maybe I could just wait at the station. I didn't want to chance having to face Barbara in the morning. Or myself, out here in alien territory. One thing, all of this physical exercise, had sobered me up way too much.

I heard her door unlock and Barbara walked back in and sat down. Her eyes were red and swollen.

"Are you all right?" she asked. "I didn't mean to really hurt you."

"Yeah, I'm okay...I'm really sorry ... I can't believe I actually did...that." I couldn't look her in the eye.

"I know. I can't believe you did it either. And I can't believe I said what I did ... I didn't mean it, Marty. I really didn't. I'm sorry. You know I think you're great. No one's ever been a bigger Marty May fan than me."

I looked up and she was smiling and there were tears rolling down her cheeks.

"The crazy thing ... is that I wanted to make love to you tonight anyway. You didn't have to do that." And this made her cry even more.

"You did?" I didn't know what else to say.

"Come on." She stood up and took my hand and we went to her bedroom, not unlike the first time. But when we tried to make love it was awkward and I couldn't come and I'm sure she was feeling the same nothingness. And this had more to do with the end of a marriage than the Xeroxed divorce proclamation that my lawyer had sent to each of us in the mail, a few years ago.

I left the next day feeling twisted and hung-over...

Part Three
Cold and Electric
Los Angeles
1983

Chapter 1

I was staying at the Sunset Marquis Hotel in L.A., a block off the Strip. It's a hollow hotel. By that I mean it has a swimming pool in a courtyard, all surrounded by the rooms. I've never been in the swimming pool for a couple of reasons. First of all, having grown up in the Fifties, I have a fear of public pools; somehow I always associate them with polio. I don't know why; it's one of those memories that you're certain of for a long time and then one day you don't know if it was ever real at all. That's what happens to memories and history. Time turns everything to fiction.

The other reason I don't go in the pool at the Sunset Marquis is because I had once heard that the actor Van Heflin had died in that very pool one morning of a heart attack or something and that he had floated there all afternoon before anyone realized what had happened. I guess he didn't look much different from the lifeless crew lounging on the deck chairs. But, I don't know if this is really true. Still, it's not disgust that keeps me out of the pool or any sort of squeamishness; it's respect. I wouldn't have a picnic on Marilyn Monroe's grave either.

This isn't the first time I've been to L.A. I've been out here lots of times. I've played gigs out here and recorded out here too. I like L.A. I like saying "I like L.A." because Keith Carradine once said it in a movie about L.A. It really rolls off the tongue nicely.

Once I was here for a record company convention. It was my last label, we had signed a big deal (a lot of money) and I, Marty May, was destined to be their "next big thing". Unfortunately, destiny rarely follows orders. The convention was held in one of the newer big hotels, in a recently built development, in what once was some big motion picture studios back lot. Judging by the leftover karma, they had probably filmed *Gone With The Wind* there. Things started out really swell: I had a chauffeured limousine at my disposal and a big suite with three very large color television sets. Everyone treated me like I was some legendary artist like Salvador Dali or someone, except I don't think they would have offered Dali so much cocaine at his age. I should have known better at the times nothing begins this good.

Every night there was a gala *dinner and* show and speeches by the executives of the company and the 'parent company (who really had the cash). I don't know whether or not there was a grandparent company. Maybe the U.S. government. I sat through two nights at a large banquet table with my manager, his wife and a few *music biz* biggies. The third night, some disco act was going to perform and the chairman of the board was going to speak.

Never having been much of a sports fan, I was getting sick of hearing rock 'n roll talked about like it was major league baseball. Each night I would hear how we were all a "team" and we had an awful lot of "heavy hitters" coming out with some real hardball product, not to mention all the promising "rookies" (I guess I was one) who were waiting in the "dugout" for their chance "at bat." I was starting to get jock itch. So that night, I was rather heavily fortifying myself for the "Wide World of Sports And Disco" to follow in the hotel's cocktail lounge where I struck up a wonderful conversation with a young waitress who thought that Marty May was the best thing since Mickey Mouse (probably her last big hero).

How was I to know that, while I was upstairs in my suite doing my duty for this Californian beauty and making the earth move or at least the bed rattle, the chairman of the board was talking about their most promising new artist Marty May? To make a long, sad, story short, when the spotlight shone on where I was supposed to be sitting after what I was told was the biggest send up in the history of the music business, I was nowhere to be seen. The chairman, I heard, considered my "promise" broken.

I guess it was my own horny fault not to mention that I was married at the time and should not have been seducing highly impressionable but awfully cute blond waitresses, but, as poetic justice would have it, the record company did to me just what I'd done to that wonderful waitress though with none of my loving touch. And without so much as pulling off my brass buttons and breaking my saber in half, I was very unceremoniously dropped from the label a few years later when my last album shipped gold and returned platinum.

My mother has always told me that a bitter man is a defeated man so how can I complain? I had my kicks and a few hit records, and every so often, something amazing happens like on the flight over here, when the stewardess recognized my name off my boarding pass, said she was my biggest fan and invited me into the restroom during the movie for my initiation into the "mile high" club. I told her thanks but I didn't smoke grass anymore.

She smiled and said this had nothing to do with drugs. So...like any good passenger, I dutifully followed.

Tom Dunn is an executive of a fairly young and hip record label on the West Coast. They have a limited artist roster; they never seriously got into disco; and their double knit suit percentage was the lowest in the last *Billboard* poll. Some would refer to his as a 'boutique" label. You can't win: just when the athletic side of records is starting to finally go away, in walks the garment industry! From softball teams to fashion shows...

I've known Tom Dunn forever. During the sixties, he was a pot dealer in the East Village. I met him at The Fillmore East (a true rock In roll palace if there ever was one) during a show with Blind Red Rose. It was one of the best gigs I ever played with Red Rose, a time when rock interest in blues was at its peak. Tom met me in the dressing room and turned me on to something "strong". The next day the music critic of the Village Voice had named me "Miracle" May. So, I considered Tom Dunn to be good luck and got him a job as a roadie (who picks up equipment) with Red Rose and eventually as a road manager (who yells at the ones picking up the equipment) when I went solo. I always seemed to get along better with roadies and road managers then I do with other musicians, and Tom and I spent a great deal of time together both on and off the road. He was a laidback kind of guy (usually stoned) who always used to put up with my temperamental nature and didn't get upset when I'd call him at three in the morning to see if he knew where I could score. But once he hit California his mellow nature found its perfect resting place, he became a charter member of that lifestyle reserved a plot at Forest Lawn and there was no way he'd return to New York City. I think he quit in the middle of a tour or maybe the tour ended in L.A. He just said that East Village winters with no heat had lost their charm. He started out as the stage manager at the Roxy theatre and ended up with a beard (of course) and a good job with this record company and a house that slides into a canyon every couple of years.

When he called me in New York I played a little hard to get.

"Marty May, please," he said.

"Marty doesn't live here anymore," I said with finality.

You see, I've finally figured out that life is just a matter of watching the percentages and lowering your odds, and lately most of my calls before five o'clock were from bill collectors.

"Are you sure? This sounds an awful lot like Marty," said Tom suspiciously.

"Oh no, mister! I Mr. May houseboy! He gone on long tour of Japan. I don't know when he ever come back."

"Marty! For Christ's sake! This is Tom Dunn! Who the hell are you kidding?"

"Tom! How are you? I was ... uh... just practicing my accents ... thinking of going into acting." Sometimes I just amaze myself.

I've been trying to track you down for weeks, Marty," he said. "Finally, I called the musicians union there in New York. By the way, it seems you owe them a little money, past dues." Tom snickered.

Even the people I don't owe money to are reminding me of the ones I do. "Money? Past dues? Well...gee ... I don't know what they could possibly be talking about. They never mentioned anything to me and I'm down there all the time picking up checks..." I lied.

"Checks?"   Tom didn't buy this.

"Sure ... never mind. What's happening, Tom?"

"You're what's happening, Marty! I've got a gig for you. Did you ever hear of Eric Noise?"

"No, I can't say that I have, Tom."

"Well, he's the boy wonder New Wave producer. He discovered that kids from England with the shaved head and the squeaky voice. He's got three records on the charts right now. And he wants you!" said Tom excitedly.

"He wants me? What for? Do I owe him money too?"

"Here's the scoop, Marty. He's producing this group called the White Castles. They're very new wave. They all wear skinny ties and have short platinum blond hair. I signed them to the label myself but they didn't have a producer. Then I heard about Eric Noise over in England.

"He never even heard the group. He didn't even want to hear their demo tapes. His prime artistic, interests are royalty percentages and album budgets he can skim on and bonus checks for big sales and making sure he's never more then an hour away from a coke dealer." Eric Noise sounded like a great many other producers of genius that I had met.

"Rumor has it," continued Tom, "That before he became famous producer, he used to work for the telephone company as an operator no less. Anyway, we made a deal, and he's been producing the album for months; that is until he ran into a major problem."

"What's that?" I asked.

"That these kids can hardly play, that's what! And he desperately needs some hot guitar."

Hello! I thought loudly.

"So... " Tom said seductively, "Being your old buddy and all, I told Eric Noise that there's only one possible guitar doctor for this delicate operation and that's none other then Marty May. And what do you know? It turns out that he's a big fan of yours! Your first record rescued him from some kind of emotional breakdown or something. So, I said that maybe, just maybe, we could grab you from your busy schedule, and you could lay down a little guitar on the White Castles' album." There was a pause.

"So how is your busy schedule? Not counting your long trip to, where was it, Japan?" There was more then a hint of sarcasm in Tom's voice.

"Well ... busy is not really the word," I said softly.

"I can imagine. You're not exactly a household word these days, eh?" I think Tom meant this question, as they say, rhetorically.

"What are you trying to do? Get on my good side?" I was pissed off. Maybe Tom Dunn was trying to twist the knife a little; trying to get back at me for the days when he used to follow three paces behind me, carrying my guitar.

"Hey babe! I'm offering you a gig! I'm on your side. You know that I think you're the greatest, I'm just trying to convince everybody else." he said defensively.

"I'm sorry Tom. Yeah, you could say things are just a little rough lately, that's all. Just got back from visiting my ex-wife."

"Barbara? How's she doing?"

"Don't ask."

"That usually means better then you," he laughed.

"Listen, maybe we should end this conversation right now on such a high note." As usual I had a voracious appetite for the hand that feeds; an unhealthy interest in the dental work of gift horses.

"Listen to me, Marty. There's a ticket waiting for you at our New York office, and you're booked into the Sunset Marquis for a week."

"How about The Beverly Hills Hotel?" I asked, pushing my luck.

"Hey Marty, don't you read the *Wall Street Journal?* Those days are over - money's tight. Why do you think everyone is jumping on this New wave craze? You can sign these groups for close to nothing and make these albums for peanuts. And these kids haven't yet picked up all the expensive habits of your generation of stars. You see, the business has finally found a way to go below the common denominator of taste and quality and that point was pretty low to begin with." He laughed. "So anyway, maybe even practice the guitar a little bit before you come out, okay?"

"Hey Tom! Don't forget who you're talking to, this is 'Miracle May'! Allstate Insurance couldn't put you in better hands! I looked at the tips of my fingers as I said this. My calluses had almost disappeared; I was afraid to pick up my Telecaster. The strings were so rusty I might get tetanus.

Now, I may be broke, and I may owe everybody, but the one account I've always kept in the black is Manny's Music Store. I've been shopping there since I was fourteen years old, when my father somewhat reluctantly bought me my first electric guitar. My mother gave him hell for this, said it would ruin my schoolwork (which it did) and I can still hear my father's voice yelling: "Turn that goddamn thing down!" but I don't think he was ever sorry he did it. Till the day he died he was convinced it "Kept me out of trouble." Hah!

From that day onward I have loved Manny's. Whenever I go in there I'm reminded of the thrill of getting that first guitar. And it has a very soothing effect on me, too. Something about the newness and shine of all the guitars and other equipment. I guess other people might feel the same way about walking into a Ferrari showroom. Dressing rooms may be dumps, clubs may be clip joints, and the big auditoriums may sound like garbage cans, but Manny's is class.

I bought strings, cords and picks; then I picked out some of the new electronic effects pedals like phases (kind of a soaring jet plane effect) and digital delays (echo). I thought these might come in handy in sounding New Wave enough for Eric Noise and the White Castles. I walked out feeling proud to be an American with a charge account somewhere.

The flight to L.A. was great, thanks to that stewardess, but I must say that I was disappointed that Tom hadn't sent me a first-class ticket. As a friend of mine who has risen to a high position in the biz once said: "You gotta fly first class because what if the plane goes down? You want to be listed as those who died in Economy Class?" Pure executive thinking.

I had barely checked into the Sunset Marquis when Tom Dunn called to tell me we were all going to meet that night at Dan Tana's restaurant for a little pre production party.

A limousine picked me up and I was the only one in it. It seems that Eric Noise had his own limousine, the White Castles had their own limousine, and Tom Dunn would be buzzing between the two of them, so I rode in style by myself. I put on some classical music and helped myself to the bottle of white wine Tom had left me. I didn't have the nerve to put up the partition between the driver and myself. He looked about the same age as me.

Tom had said that the golden days of the music biz were over. I guess in those days I would have had two limousines in case of a breakdown and, of course, champagne instead of Blue Nun. The only people I know who don't like limousines are those who can't afford them. I like them and I'm not ashamed. It was about a half a mile from my hotel to Dan Tana's but I told the driver to take the long way there. Like via San Francisco.

Dan Tana's has been the main watering hole of the L.A. music scene for as long as I can remember. It reminds me of the restaurant that Efrem Zimbalist Jr. used to hang out in 1177 Sunset Strip. They serve Italian food and have red and white-checkered tablecloths. It's the kind of place you might expect Gloria Swanson to walk out of a scene from *Sunset Boulevard*. Funny that it seems to do such a great job of impersonating all this Sunset Strip and Boulevard stuff because it's on Santa Monica Boulevard. But I guess that's just Hollywood - things are never quite what they appear.

It was late and Tana's tables were filled with stars; at least they looked like stars. The bar was packed with people trying to pick each other up so they could drive into the L.A. canyons and hills together. Probably ending up in hot tubs or Jacuzzis though I don't really know the difference between those two water sports. Tom Dunn wasn't there yet. I had arrived before a record company executive; this was no way for a rock star to act.

I looked around Tana's and noticed that hardly anyone was looking at the person he or she was with. Most everyone was looking at the front door to see who was coming in. The funny thing was, after the famous person everyone had watched entered sat down, he or she would do the same thing: look at the front door.

I had expected to see lots of familiar faces from the old days, but I didn't recognize a soul. They were obviously music biz types, but I guess these days, the places chance less quickly than the faces.

Then the White Castles walked in. I recognized them by their matching haircuts: spiked platinum blonds. They were dressed, how shall I says asymmetrically. They all had on shades. There were lots of girls with them and I gotta admit it, they all looked very young. Tom Dunn was chaperoning. Eric Noise followed. He looked like the kid everyone made fun of in high school. His glasses may have been just like Buddy Holly's, but the effect was just not the same. And his crew cut with splashes of lime green and Popsicle purple was a little forced.

Introductions between the White Castles and myself were brief. When Tom started to explain who I was to the drummer, he just interrupted saying: "I never listened to that music." And he walked away. What music was he referring to? But Tom just shrugged and looked a little embarrassed and I didn't really care. Maybe they were mad that an outsider had been brought in to work on their album. Maybe he really hadn't heard of me; although I'm always amazed if that is the case, I guess it's possible. Or maybe the guy just spent so much time getting his hair done that he didn't have any opportunity to listen to music or learn how to play it either. I've sure been introduced to lots of guys I didn't know from a hole in the center of a record, but I always faked my way through. Just to be polite. Either New Wave groups don't subscribe to Amy Vanderbilt's book of etiquette or maybe they're more honest.

Anyway, we got a prestigious round table, and soon the conversation hit the speed of light, mainly because of the amount of cocaine Eric and the Castles had snorted. But at least Eric Noise seemed interested in Tom Dunn's history of him and myself and my music.

"One of those songs you cut back then has always stuck in my mind for some strange reason," Eric said to me raising his eyebrows in some vaguely pseudo aristocratic British way.

I didn't like the way he had emphasized back then but I answered laughing: "Maybe you liked it." Tom Dunn laughed too but only until he noticed that no one else was laughing. Then he turned his laugh into a cough.

"No, there was another reason," Eric Noise said. "It was the title. Something about pillows."

"Feather Pillow Fortunes?" I suggested. It had been a slow ballad. Sort of dreamlike slow Jimi Hendrix stuff, with guitar breaks. I had done my best to get the sound of that Fifties instrumental *Sleepwalk*.

Eric snapped his fingers very loudly, like he had been practicing. All eyes were on him.

"That's the one," he said loudly and strangely.

"Fortunes!" I waited for him to continue. He just smiled and stared at me as if we shared some secret together and continued top beat on the tabletop.

"And ... uh ... why did you like it?" I asked.

"I haven't the slightest idea." He stopped tapping and addressed the entire table. "I don't really know why I like *anything*. Actually, I don't much like anything." This made him laugh and so the others laughed too. "You see, I just dislike some things less than others. I guess I disliked that little ditty of yours the least compared to everything else." Again, Eric and his entourage found this hysterical. "I mean, there really wasn't much worth listening to back then was there?"

"Well, I don't know if you can say that. I mean what about..." I was speaking softly.

"Oh, I remember now!" He loudly interrupted, banging the table with his hand. "It was the title, after all. 'Feather Pillow Fortunes!" You see, I was just so depressed at the state of music back then I used to sleep all day. And your song with its title use to really put me to sleep. It was quite amazing actually."

Not as amazing as the way my fist slamming into his scrawny little jaw would have put him to sleep. There was a time when a comment like that might have sent my drink, if not my fist, right in his face. I've thrown a few punches in my day, though none of them were too effective except the one I threw at my gold record the day I received divorce papers from Barbara. That particular right hook cut an artery and blood shot about eight inches out of my wrist. But times change, and I didn't want to hurt anyone anymore, least of all myself and my big chance to break into the high art of New Wave. I kept my mouth shut.

Dinner was typical: Everyone ordered a big meal, and by the time it arrived, everyone was so coked up that they couldn't eat a kernel of wheat germ under threat of torture. Except me. I'd stopped using anything stronger than an occasional joint a few years ago. To me now, cocaine was a question of whether thirty seconds of exhilaration was worth hours of feeling wired and anxious. And besides, I could no longer afford to pass up a good meal at an expensive restaurant.

I was seated next to the White Castles' guitarist. He was about my height but about half my weight) possessing the now de rigueur rock star starvation look. Whatever happened to the Chubby Checkers and Fats Dominos? Everything about this guy was skinny: He had on a skinny little lapelled jacket made of some shiny material like Bobby Darin would have worn during his 'Mack The Knife' days and a skinny leather tie that would certainly come in handy when tying your girlfriend to a bedpost on one of those more adventurous nights modern couples have. And he chain-smoked these skinny little brightly colored cigarettes. Who I assumed to be his equally skinny girlfriend sat next to him though they hadn't exchanged anything more than slightly meaningful glances throughout the whole meal.

She had on a very, very short little polka dot dress like what Twiggy used to wear; purplish in color with matching tights. Her hair matched her boyfriend's platinum blond color and was arranged in the proper New Wave *I've just been abused* messy look. She appeared to have on no makeup other than tons of thick black eyeliner. If she was just a little less wasted looking she might have been attractive. Only Marianne Faithfull can look wasted and still turn me on.

I was drinking and the White Castles were snorting but nonetheless the guitarist and I and were both *pickers* so I tried to start a conversation with this guy: "What kind of guitar do you use?" A surefire hit question; I've known few guitarists who could not go on for a while about their gear.

"I don't know," he replied in-between drags of his skinny red cigarette.

I was amazed. "Oh... is it one of those custom jobs? No real brand name?" I asked.

He looked at his girlfriend and she looked at me like I was an orangutan.

"Well, then how could you not know?"

"I never looked, I don't care, and I think that talking about fuckin' electric guitars is the most boring thing in the world. Don't you?" He and his girlfriend stared at me, sort of in unison.

Maybe he was right; if you're not into it, any technical conversation like electric guitars is boring. So are conversations about the weather. So is sticking a key into a keyhole if you really want to get into the everyday ennui of life. But you gotta start from the outside if you want to get inside people and doors. I wasn't gonna let him get off that easily.

"Yeah, okay, but what do you think about the theory that electric guitars are really nothing more than phallic symbols and that lead guitarist are actually just masturbating for a living?" I could shock as well as the next guy, New Wave or not. I stared back at him and his girlfriend.

"I love to jerk off," he said matter-of-factly. "I do it every night, sometimes twice; sometimes as soon as I wake up." None of this seemed to faze his girlfriend who just continued to stare blankly at me. Maybe this was what New Wave was all about. I remember at the time of my last album, around 1977, it was the time of Punk, The Sex Pistols and all that, I was doing an interview with a writer I had known for years, kind of a conservative, scholarly type. But when he showed up for the interview, he had on a tattered old leather motorcycle jacket direct from the Salvation Army covered with chains and safety pins. All he wanted to talk about was Punk; he had asked me what I thought of it.

"Uh ... I think I like it though I haven't really heard that much, just *Anarchy In The U.K.* and a few other songs ...but I think it's good. It'll give this business a long deserved kick in the ass was my reply at the time. In retrospect I think I miscalculated exactly which side of this 'kick' I would end up on. But I could tell the writer was not convinced; he was looking for a fight. I think my clothes were too new or something.

"You don't really sound convinced," he had challenged me, "Is there something you don't like about Punk?" he asked like a KGB interrogator.

"Well ... I don't know...There is one thing that's lacking."

"What's that?" he had asked.

"Love," was my reply.

At first he didn't quite know how to react to this but then he said: "You better watch it Marty, you're getting sentimental." Wiseass journalist! But I knew I was right. All rock 'n roll is about love even The Rolling Stones if you listen between the lines.

"What's the matter?" the White Castles' guitarist asked me sharply. "Don't you jerk off?"

"Uh ... sure. As a matter of fact I was just on my way to the men's room." I looked down at my right hand: "Looks like its you and me tonight, sweetheart." My hand waved back, I laughed. They did not.

This was useless and pointless and depressing. I looked at this skinny couple: they weren't touching. I wondered if they ever held hands. I think Tom Dunn had once told me that the White Castles usually turned their backs on their audience when they performed. I wasn't surprised, mutants of the me generation. The only thing I could say in this guy's favor was that he didn't have to go through the age-old musician's hassle and quest of trying to get laid after the show.

When we said goodbye later that night, Eric Noise put his hand on my shoulder and said, "Marty make it pragmatic!" Then he jumped into his limo and split.

When you're a high school dropout like myself, you tend to be suspicious of people who use big words. I had a vague idea of what 'pragmatic' meant. I thought it had something to do with people who went right home after school and did their homework or the correct way to climb the corporate ladder. But I couldn't figure out what the hell it had to do with making a record even if it was New Wave.

Chapter 2

We began recording the next day at a very famous and expensive Hollywood recording studio. The place had produced hit records for years. Some time ago a well-known blond California female singer/songwriter had donated some of her own paintings to decorate the walls of the studio's reception area. I had been in this studio some years before and I remembered the paintings as being mostly of the sea and the beach and actually quite nice. But when I walked in) there were sheets hanging all over the place, held up by gaffers tape, covering the artwork. I thought maybe they were doing some kind of renovation; I asked the receptionist what was going on.

"Mr. Noise ordered all the paintings covered up," she said.

"Did he say why?" I asked surprised.

"Something about it not being pragmatic."

"Oh...I guess he's the boss." But I couldn't see the point, really, other than to intimidate this poor girl.

"Yeah, I guess so," said the receptionist, "But it's a drag for me having to sit out here with all these sheets. It looks like the place is being painted or something."

"I see what you mean."

"And I'm allergic to paint. I'm even starting to sneeze," she said and then she took out a Kleenex and did just that. "Definite paint vibes," she said.

On the door to the control booth was a large sign "KEEP OUT! PRIVATE SESSION!" What a joke. The only thing that signs like this accomplish is ensure that anyone who reads it will definitely find some excuse to open the door and peek in to check out what stars are in there.

I walked in very timidly so as not to disturb whatever work was going on but I could have been trailing a pet rhinoceros and I don't think anyone would have noticed. Private session   my   ass. It was like a party in there. The place was packed. Eric Noise had picked up quite an entourage of West Coast New Wave stars. I recognized some of the faces. Here was a guy with a shaved head and a long black cape that I think had made some hit records back in the early Sixties. They were almost novelty records all about spacemen and flying saucers but New Wavers considered him a founding father.

Also inside were other current New Wave stars from L.A. I thought it strange how a movement that perhaps had started in the lower-class slums of London, born out of a welfare state semi poverty and a sense of no future, had taken such a hold out here in California; the sun drenched cornucopia of the American Dream. But this was hardly a surfer crowd; there wasn't a tan face among them. Pallor and a look of total dissipation seemed to be a la mode.

The White Castles were their usual bubbly selves slumped into a corner with their girlfriends, not talking to each other like a pile of used puppets – Punch and Judy for *1984*. There were some rock writers too; the radical fringe who believed that to love a style of music is to look like its it was hard to tell them from the members of the group. I detected English accents other than Eric's. These were the most radical looking of all; I was sure they were two of London's most famous rock critics. One had taken the Keith Richards' look to such an extreme that compared to him the 'original' had the vibrancy of Jack LaLanne. And the other had gone to the ultimate measure of putting the quintessential safety pin through his cheek. But wasn't this a little old fashioned? Punk was passé, I'm sure New Wave required something a little more high-tech, perhaps a digital tattoo across the forehead. Of your social security number.

Eric Noise was playing some of his latest hits for everyone. At 2:00 an hour this hardly seemed 'pragmatic'. Its most recent was by an all girl group called Desperate whores; their hit was titled *"We're All Pink Upside Down."*

They sang off key, I think on purpose, and with zero emotion. Hardly the new Ronettes in my opinion. There were odd background noises, unpleasant screeches, high-pitched and animal like. Eric's hits all sounded, well, very 'noisy' to me. But I tried to look impressed and enthusiastic. It was difficult.

The White Castle's basic tracks had already been recorded so when it finally came time to begin work I went in to overdub by myself, leaving Eric and company staring at me through the glass partition. I was reminded of an old episode of The Twilight Zone where an astronaut was put behind a similar glass partition on an alien planet. I plugged in my Telecaster and waited for Eric's instructions to come over my headphones.

"Now listen, Marty darling," said Eric. "What I want here in this section is some real pragmatic electric guitar."

"Uh...does that mean like, uh, marching music?" I joked.

Eric ignored me. "Now Marty, make it as cold and electric as you possibly can. I want you to imagine Jimi Hendrix being brought back from the dead, hooked up to some electrodes and than made to play. Except without thinking. Thinking always got Hendrix into trouble." I couldn't believe what I was hearing. How could he say this? Eric Noise was older than me for sure; he had lived through Jimi Hendrix too. I felt like he was talking about my dead father. And there was something racist in it, too.

"In fact," Eric went on, "thinking always got Hendrix into trouble. Those ridiculous oh so psychedelic lyrics of his still make me laugh. It was probably him thinking too hard that killed him in the end the boy just didn't know his limits!" I could see Eric turn to face his entourage and I could hear them all laughing through my headphones. I wanted to control myself, just get the job done, and get out of here. I pulled off my headphones and placed them on my amp beside me. I pulled out a cigarette and pretended to look for a match. I could see that Eric Noise was trying to talk to me through the glass partition but I raised my hand and mouthed: "Just a minute."

A dozen years ago, somewhere backstage in New York. Maybe it was Madison Square Garden or The Fillmore East. Those were different times: maybe not so sophisticated as now but a lot more mythological. It was after I had left Blind Red Rose and I had my group, the Maymen. It was a semi solo thing. I just didn't have the confidence to really sing yet. We had made a hurried album that was lucky enough to be getting a lot of attention IT the press and within the industry. Concept albums were the thing; the last throes of Sergeant Pepper and all that; plenty of room for the long guitar solos which were my forte. Back in those days, I could play for an hour without repeating a riff. I don't know what happened to that kind of music.

The critics were making a few comparisons between Jimi Hendrix and myself. I think it had to do more with the sound of our guitar playing than anything else.

Like Hendrix I had used a Stratocaster on that album instead of my usual Telecaster and I was playing around with feedback and using the tremolo bar in the same ways he did.

Strangely, even though Hendrix was black, I think my own playing was more blues influenced. Someone in the publicity department of my record company thought it would be a nifty idea for Hendrix and I to meet and be photographed for Rolling Stone with some caption like 'Guitar Wizards Confer' for the Random Notes section. I certainly was not opposed to the idea; I still have that photo back home in my box of press clippings although thank god Rolling Stone had the good taste not to use that caption.

His dressing room was very quiet. Everybody was whispering and smoking hash in long pipes. I'll never forget his groupies. They were certainly a different, classier breed back then. Like a tribe of beautiful gypsies with strange powers. A stunning black girl with a pierced nose with a diamond in it was reading my palm when Jimi Hendrix walked in. I really don't think the rock world has seen anything like him since. He's the only one who has come close to unseating Mick Jagger as THE sex symbol of rock 'n roll. Things had come full circle from Presley and Jagger who began as talented white boys imitating their black idols to Hendrix who seemed to be at least lyrically mostly influenced by none other than Bob Dylan, the white, Jewish son of an appliance storeowner. And come to think of it, Dylan really had the first afro I remember ever seeing on a rock star. But that's the wonderful thing about rock. It matters far less who you are than who you *want* to be.

Hendrix was dressed in cascading colors; some kind of aqua military bandleader's jacket with his bare chest showing beneath, purple pants, high Indian boots with fringe, and lots and lots of scarves.

More than how he was dressed I remember his hands: very large and finely developed, full of muscles like Nureyev's legs. Our conversation was minimal. I could hardly think of anything to say but I had read that he'd been in the Army Airborne for a while so I asked him which was more difficult, playing a big concert like this or parachuting of a plane.

"Oh, you know, they both have their ups and downs." He said in that low, soft voice of his and smiled. Still gives me a chill...

★

I felt a tap on my shoulder. It was the engineer. Eric Noise wanted to talk to me; could I please put on my headphones. Eric sat in the booth stone-faced. I guess I had been daydreaming awhile.

"Gee, I'm sorry, 'Eric." I apologized, "I guess I went into the zone there for a minute.

"Zone on your own time, Marty," Eric said slowly and coldly. He did not look happy.

"Yeah ... sure ... uh ... but I'm not too certain if I know what you mean by this 'pragmatic' thing, Eric. I have a phase and a digital delay with me. If you'd like me to try either one of them on this track. I'm sure I can get some get some strange sounds out of them."

"I hate gadgets," he said crisply.

"Well, what kind of feeling are you looking for?" I asked.

"Feeling!"   Eric screamed so loud my ears hurt. "Who said anything about feelings? I hate feelings! I don't want any feelings at all! I want it COLD! I want it ELECTRIC! Do you hear me? COLD AND ELECTRIC!" He turned to the engineer: "Run the tape."

I tried playing along to the basic track a few times, but it was just not happening as far as Eric was concerned. He stopped the tape, said something to the engineer, and then said I could relax for a moment. I hardly wanted to go back into the control room and face, that crew, especially those two British writers, so I went into the men's room to get away.

When I walked back into the studio, the air conditioner was going full blast. It was hardly needed; it was a chilly night.

"Uh, Eric, it's a little cold in here. Do you think we really need the air conditioner?"

"Trust me, Marty," he whispered. "Just play."

So I did, and it got colder and colder, and my fingers were getting stiff, and I was making lots of mistakes, and it seemed the more mistakes I made, the more Eric liked it.

"Eric, please stop the tape," I finally said. "It's really freezing in here. Could you please turn down the air conditioner? I really don't need it."

"I know it's cold, Marty. But it's electric! It's cold and electric! This is the best I've ever heard you."

"I don't quite get it, 'Eric," I said.

"And what don't you get, Mr. May?" said Eric with as much condescension as he could muster.

"Well, to me, if it's electric, its hot. And if it's cold, well, then its dead. So if it's hot, it's got feeling and lots of it. At least that's what I've always thought.

"Marty, you're forgetting something, aren't you? I didn't bring you out of your *forced* retirement to think, now did I? I brought you here just like I would an old instrument, just for the sound you make. You have a certain sound that displeases me less than most sounds. So don't think at all and just play till I turn you off!" I could see him lean back in his chair and cross his arms. The voice of Ozymandias.

The last thing I wanted was a confrontation. I considered counting to ten but then I looked through that glass and I saw all those glaring faces and I felt like Clarence Darrow at the Scopes 'Monkey' trial. Like I had to defend something, something more important then whether or not I blew this gig. Like I had to do it to save rock In roll from these barbarians in there. I don't know, I probably should have counted to ten. But that's the problem with musicians, we can only count to four and then for better or worse, we start.

"Eric, you don't play anything do you? As a matter of fact, I heard that before your production career, you were a telephone operator." (Some of the faces in the control booth with him looked a little surprised to hear this. I'm sure it would be all over *Melody Maker* next week.) "Well maybe those are the sounds you're looking for: dial tones and busy signals. You can just get them right off that phone in there. You don't need me for that."

Eric stared at me for what seemed like a long, long time. I had to open my big mouth when he had all the numbers on his side: The number of hit records held produced the number of people in his entourage, the number of hits of cocaine held done.

Finally, he whispered something to the engineer, who got up and twisted a dial on the wall, and I could feel that the air conditioner had been turned off". "Lot's try it once more," Eric said sinisterly. Like he was ordering the juice to surge through the electric chair after two unsuccessful jolts.

I played my best, I really did, and I think that I hit it on a number of takes, too. I tried to give the song a sense of melody that the White Castles were incapable of. I figured something had to *swing* on this record on any record for that matter. It might as well be my guitar. But Eric didn't look happy. After each take I'd look up to him expectantly) but held just shake his head *and have* me do it over. He wasn't going to let me win this one. It was too late for that.

Finally, Eric stopped me in the middle of a take. "You're sounding a bit old tonight Marty. Let's try it again tomorrow." But I didn't believe there would be a tomorrow, He stood up and the whole Eric Noise show departed from the studio in record time. Everybody trying to get prime seats in the limos, I guess.

Chapter 3

Later that night, I sat in the living room of my Sunset Marquis suite staring into the kitchenettes *thinking* about pop art, Andy Warhol, the color of Andy's hair, *and* the color of the refrigerator. *Refrigerator white*, it would be a better name for a group than the White Castles. And why didn't they capitalize the T in *the*? That seemed awfully pretentious to me. After leaving the studio I had stopped to pick up a bottle of Russian Vodka. I was drinking it straight and cold.

The Beatles' movie HELP! was on T.V. The first time I'd seen it was in a theatre somewhere along the New Jersey shore. I must have been about fourteen or fifteen. Hot nights at the movies in resort towns are the stuff of real adolescent vacation memories - a blooming sensuality of things to come much later. The theatre had been crowded with teenage girls, and every time The Beatles sang, the girls screamed. I'd mainly been interested in seeing what kind of guitars they were playing - they used all the top brands Rickenbacker, Gretsch, Gibson - kind of like the Cadillacs and Lincolns of rock 'n roll gear and it was the most important thing in the world to me back then.

On TV there were no screaming girls but HELP was interrupted far too often by commercials; one of which was about the joys of long-distance telephone calls to grandmothers and other loved ones. I don't know if it was that commercial or the title of the movie itself that pushed me to pick up the phone. Probably it was neither. Probably it was the Vodka.

"Barbara, is that you?" I knew it was. The connection was very good, and her voice very sleepy.

"Marty? Is everything all right?" It was always her first question. She wouldn't want to start yelling at me for disturbing her at this hour and find that I was in the hospital or jail.

Yeah, everything's fine. I'm in L.A" and there's nothing good on TV." Two lies out of three. Then suddenly, I remembered my disastrous visit to her in detail and I felt a panicked need to create an excuse for this call. I couldn't come crawling to her after what happened.

"I was just wondering if I left my address book out at your place. I can't seem to find it, and you know, there are some numbers I could use while I'm out here."

"You just realized it was gone?"

"I guess so," I lied

"No," she replied innocently. "I haven't seen it, Marty."

"Probably just left it home. You know, I've never been such a great packer." I laughed nervously - glad that was over. "I'm... sorry that my visit out there ended on kind of a sour note. I don't know what got into me."

"Forget it, Marty. I'm sorry too. I guess it just wasn't such a good idea." She sounded annoyed and automatically I wondered if she was referring to our sex? Had it been as unsatisfying for her, too? Made her feel empty like it had me? "You know it's three o'clock in the morning, Marty."

"I'm sorry, I was just wondering about my address book. Did I wake you?" I didn't want to hang up.

"It's all right. I'll smoke a cigarette." I heard her light up. She always did smoke in the middle of the night" just one cigarette and then back to sleep. It made me smile.

"So. What are you doing in L.A.?"

"I'm out here doing some guitar work on an album by a new group. They're called the White Castles, and they're very ...New Wave." I said sarcastically.

"Oh yeah? New Wave...isn't that kind of like punk?" She had obviously stopped reading *Rolling Stone*.

"Yeah, a little bit, but not so violent. It's simpler than *my* kind of music, not so technical. Some say it's progress but I'm beginning to think it's a giant step backward. The songs tend to be very simple in the lyrics and very fast and it's kind of...cold, and ... well I don't really know how to describe it, really. I don't get a hell of a lot from it personally. This group, the White Castles, they're on Tom Dunn's label."

"Are you getting paid for this?"

"Yeah, sure ... but I'm not exactly sure how much yet." I said, bracing myself for the blow.

"Well, maybe you can send me some of that alimony that you promised but I never received. You know, the only reason I haven't hauled you into court is because I guess there's something in me that doesn't want to tarnish the name of Marty May."

"By the way,"   I said, wanting to change the subject, "Tom Dunn asked about you. He hadn't heard about our divorce. He's the one who got me the gig out here. Can you believe it? After all these years, he thought of we."

"Well, one thing I must say about Marty May fans, they sure are loyal." Was she softening up? I couldn't tell. I was surprised she had stayed on the phone this long. Maybe she had that same feeling of something terribly unfinished that was nagging me. "How is Tom?"

"Oh, fine. Really doing great. He likes L.A. a lot and you can't blame him. This town has been good to him, and he's gone for the whole program. You know, Hawaiian shirts with the collar out over his sports jacket." I laughed. "He's even got a hot tub!"

"Terrific."   She sounded like she was falling asleep.

"Hey Barbara, guess where I'm staying?"

"San Simeon…the Hearst Castle?" she yawned. "Disneyland?"

"Come on, be serious!" I said playfully. "Marty, it's a little too late for knock-knock jokes." "You're not gonna believe it. I'm at the S and M!"

"What's that? A massage parlor?" she asked sleepily.

"Oh, come on! You know! The Sunset Marquis! How can you not remember? We lived here for three months while I made that awful country rock album that never came out. We all used to call it the S&M. You gotta remember, Barbara."

"I remember all right." She hardly shared my enthusiasm.

"Those were good days, weren't they, Barbara?"

"Good for you maybe," she said accusingly.

I thought that a fight might at least keep her on the phone for a while. I didn't want to go back to watching TV, by myself, in this room. Not right now.

"Good for me? What's that supposed to mean?" I knew the answer. Why was I doing this?

"It's supposed to mean that here in the almost real world of Amagansett, it's three o'clock in the morning and this is your very happily divorced ex-wife you're speaking to, and most of the 'good old days' at the S&M, as far as I'm concerned, I was either very bored or too stoned and usually feeling like an unwelcome addition to everyone's overcrowded expense account." I hear her take a long drag from her cigarette. I didn't know what to say. She was right about the nonexistence of a rock 'n roll wife. I don't know how any of them stand it; no wonder most take more drugs than their star husbands.

"I mean, Marty, I thought you saw that when you came out here. This is the kind of life that I always really wanted, that I was really meant for. The years I was with you... it just wasn't really me. It was like some crazy dare I took."

"Well, I don't know. I'm sorry you feel that way." I don't know why I went on to say the things I did. After that weekend I felt that I had learned some lessons about myself and about her too; they were sad lessons to be sure. But now, out in L.A. unable to fit into what should be my own turf, I was unsure of everything again.

"Maybe that wasn't me back then either"" I said. "Not really me. And maybe it's a different me and a different you now ... maybe things could work out differently this time. Things aren't as crazy anymore, you know."

"Oh come on, Marty, what for?"

"Because ... I gotta admit that sitting next to you and watching "The Tonight Show" out there in suburbia and listening to the dogs barking across the street didn't feel bad ... it felt like what *normal* should feel like. Maybe I could get used to it and maybe it would be different. And better for both of us."

"And what's really gonna be so different, Marty." She obviously wasn't buying this.

Only a real fool lies on his application to get into Heaven but I went right ahead. "Well, I'll tell you, Barbara, I'm thinking of getting out of the music business, 'For one thing." A long silence followed.

"Have you been drinking, Marty?" she asked suspiciously.

"No," I lied.

"Then don't say something stupid like that. Not at this hour."

"Why? Au contraire, as the French say, what's so stupid? I think it might be one of the first smart things I've done in quite a while. My star isn't exactly ascending these days, ya know."

"Now you listen to me," she said forcefully. "You getting out of the music business would be like you changing your name or something; changing your whole identity. I mean you've been doing this your whole life - it IS your life. And you gotta accept that. Because what else are you gonna do? You've got no education; for Christ's sake you didn't even Graduate from high school. What would you do?"

Admittedly, I was unprepared for this question because I wasn't really thinking of getting out of music at all. As far as I was concerned, I WAS out of it. But when tempted by the past, one almost always wants to crawl back into its falsely remembered warm cocoon somehow. Especially after you've had a few drinks.

"I don't know what I'd do, Barbara, but if it meant you and me getting back together and really starting a new life, I think I could do anything. I just need some... normalcy, some security. Tomorrow is too big a mystery these days. I'll tell you what, I could drive a limo." I thought of my youthful driver earlier. Only problem was that I'd lost my license for recklessness.

"Sure, go ahead and drive a limo. And everyone will want to interview the brilliant Marty May for the amazing way he whips those doors open for his passengers. Who are you kidding? You couldn't stand to be anonymous and you know it."

"Hey Barbara, I'm trying to tell you that I still love you, if you can believe that." And for just that moment maybe I did mean it. But the words began to sour almost immediately.

"Well, I can't believe it. This is getting ridiculous, you must be drunk. Goodnight Marty."

"Wait! Barbara!" I felt panic. "Please, just tell me one thing. What went wrong? Can someone explain that to me? Please?"

I thought she might hand up on me. She had done it before. This was not a totally original conversation. During the first year or so following our split there had been other three AM calls though I didn't want to admit it to myself.

Finally she spoke. "Nothing went wrong, Marty."

"How can you say that? Look at us! Our marriage went down faster then the Titanic. And with fewer lifeboats."

"You know something, Marty, you're a pain in the ass," she said almost affectionately.

"Thanks a lot."

"No ... what I mean is that, you know, for you, it's okay. That's what you're meant to be. You're a rock star and you're supposed to be arrogant and self-centered and impossible to live with. I mean, isn't that what kids want?"

"I don't know. I never consciously tried to be like that."

"But that's what happens," she said. "I don't think you can have both Marty; you can't expect to be happily married AND have the sixteen year old girls dying for you. Listen to me, just do what you're good at and let me get some sleep, okay?"

"But that's just it, Barbara. I can't do it anymore. I'm thirty-two years old; it's all different now. It's not even my kind of music anymore. And I can't fake it - I could never fake it. It was always real to me. I can only feel it and I'll tell you something, feeling just isn't *in* anymore! And when the accountants and lawyers figure out that I can't relate to those kids who buy all these records any better than they can, then I'm really through." (But I think they had figured this out already.)

"Now listen to me, Marty," she said sternly" "You know what you have to do if that's really the case? You have to join them. Get a job in a record company or become a producer or a manager. Teach some other nineteen year old up and comer to turn on those kids like you used to."

"I don't know if I can do that either!" (At the very least it would mean growing a beard and moving to LA.)

"You'll be surprised what you can do if you're broke enough. Speaking of which, I gotta get up in 'four hours and go teach finger painting. You may bitch a lot, Marty, but no one knows better than I do what a hustler you are. You'll get by. Goodnight!"

"Wait Barbara. Don't hang up! Just one more thing, please."

"It better be good, Marty." She did sound exhausted.

"Please ... that night at your house ... which I'm really sorry for..."

"I told you to forget it, Marty."

"I know ... but I can't forget what you said ... about me not being an artist ... and that rock 'n roll is shit ... did you really mean that stuff, Barbara?" She took a deep breath.

"No ... I didn't mean it Marty. But how could you try and force yourself on me? That was really disgusting!" I should have left well enough alone. Now she was getting mad.

"If I say I was drunk is that enough of an excuse?"

"I guess sot at this time of the morning anyway."

"Thank so Barbara." My eyes were welling up. "I needed that."

But this was too corny for her to stand. "Oh God you're too much! Goodnight Marty." And she hung up.

Well, after all, we tragic heroes do need our daily fix of emotional display. "Show me a hero and I'll show you a tragedy. Who said that? Shakespeare? F. Scott Fitzgerald? Chuck Berry? I don't know. Maybe Barbara hadn't given me all the sympathy I had craved after my ordeal in the studio, but it was better than none at all. If she had shed a few tears in memory of our dear, departed marriage, I might have shed a few with her. I'm not opposed to crying as long as somebody else starts first. And I had wanted to cry about something: me, her, rock 'n roll, New Wave...something!

The phone rang. My heart jumped; maybe it was Barbara, and she'd had second thoughts about a real reconciliation. The what the hell would I do?

"Hello!" I said much too enthusiastically.

It was the hotel reception. "While you were on long distance, a Mr. Tom Dunn called. He wants you to meet him at Dan Tana's restaurant in half an hour. Do you know where that is?"

"I think so. Listen, can you tell me how much that long distance call just cost me while I've got you here?"

"Hold on...Uh, Fifty One Seventy."

"Wow! I should have called collect."

"That's what I was thinking too, Mr. May."

It was late, and Tana's was packed. The scene hadn't really changed, though I had a feeling mine was about to. I squeezed in at the bar. I overheard a fat guy with a beard say, "That's Marty May. He use to be somebody." His date who looked fifteen even in her high heels, said: "Oh yeah? Who did he use to be?"

I felt like Brando in On the Waterfront. All the checkered tablecloths reminded me of that plaid lumberjack he work in that movie. I wanted to go over to the guy and scream: "You were my brother!" You should have looked out for me!" But the guy wasn't my brother and I wasn't a fighter who was forced to take a dive; I'd jumped with no one pushing me at all. But I wasn't upset, the important thing was to be recognized...even as a has-been.

"Hey Marty baby! How you feeling!" I turned around and there was Tom Dunn. He smiled and gave me an earnest look.

"How am I feeling?" I repeated. "Well, I guess I'm feeling a little too much, Tom."

"What do you mean?"

"I mean that Eric Noise didn't seem to think that my guitar leads were cold enough. Whatever that means."

"Yeah, I know. Eric called me at home. I take it the session didn't go too smoothly."

"What else did Eric say?" I hate waiting for bad news.

"Well, actually, I've got some unpleasant business, Marty. Eric has decided - and it's his prerogative as the producer of this project - that he wants to try a different approach."

"You mean I'm fired, Tom?" He half grimaced.

"Well, I guess...but it doesn't really fully explain what Eric has decided to do. Actually I can assure you it has nothing to do with you. Eric still feels that you are nothing less than a brilliant musician. But as I said, he has decided to use a different approach to finish this album. He might even use the guitar player in the group." Tom shrugged his shoulders. I knew that the praise was his, not Eric's.

"That moron? Does Eric Noise have a death wish on top of all his other problems?" My back was up. "That kid has enough trouble walking not to mention playing the guitar!"

"Well, I know what you mean," Tom said conspiratorially. "Between me and you, they're not really the hottest bunch of players around, are they? Well, Eric also mentioned that he might bring in this New Wave guitar genius from England who only has three fingers or something like that. I'm sorry it didn't work out. I guess it was just a personality conflict."

Tom Dunn smiled. He had been almost cheerful in the way that he had fired me. He had given his little speech, and now he was off work. He ordered a vodka martini, me too.

"Hey, come on buddy," I said. "For once in your life, why don't you try telling the truth? Maybe you'll like it. "

"What the hell is that supposed to mean?" he glowered.

"Tom, tell me something. How much are you making now as director of ... what do they call it now? ... Contemporary Artist Development or something like that?"

"You want to know, I'll tell you! About sixty grand a year and a king-sized expense account, and what the hell business is it of yours?"

"Well, you might remember the first job you ever had in this racket, when you were just another hippie from the East Village with hair down to your ass who took too much LSD."

"Marty, so what ...? So you gave me my first job in this business. What do you want? A finder's fee or something? I'm sorry it didn't work out with you and Eric. And if you want to take it out on me, well, go right ahead. That's what friends are for. But believe me, I feel like hell about it too.' I'm just the bearer of bad tidings. What are you trying to do?"

"Tom, you don't understand. I don't want you to feel like hell. And I'm glad you've got a nice cushy job. Believe me, when it comes to people who work for record labels, you're a diamond in a sea of costume jewelry! And I *do* appreciate the fact that you tried to get me this gig God knows I need the work. But what I really need is for someone to tell me the truth."

"What truth, for Christ's sake, Marty?"

"The truth about me! The truth about why I can't get arrested anymore in this business. I used to turn down dinner invitations every night. Now no one returns my phone calls. No one will listen to my demos. I'm a forgotten man, Tom. And if you're really my friend you'll tell me why I'm a has-been, Tom! And I'm getting paranoid too. I worry that there's some kind of blacklist going around with my name on top of it. I can't take much more Tom!"

I surprised myself with this outburst. Some people heard and stared at us; most were too busy watching the door. Tom sat back and finished his martini. I guess I was speaking a bit too loudly because a few people at the bar had moved away. They could see the next morning's headlines in the L.A. Times:

Bezerk Rock Star Kills All At Dan Tana's
Blames Record industry Indifference

"What can I tell you, Marty?" Tom lost his corporate jive and spoke with the voice of an old man. "There's no black list that I know of ... It's just changing.

You sense it from the outside, and believe me, I know it from the inside. It's changing, and I don't know why or how. And when I tell you that every day I'm flying this sixty grand job strictly by the seat of my pants, I'm not kidding. I don't know what these kids want to hear anymore I don't even know if they want to hear anything! Every year it's different: Heavy Metal, Glitter Rock, Southern Rock, Punk Rock, New Wave, Power Pop, and Disco - my god we killed them with Disco - and it makes no sense to me because if it's good it's good no matter what the fuck they call it and if it's bad, well, I let someone else sign it. And more times than I'd like to think of, the bad stuff is a hit. And I'll tell you something else; you think Eric Noise knows any better than we do? He's just running as fast as he can to stay ahead of the wolf pack at his heels so he doesn't end up back at the phone company looking up numbers."

"So why the fuck did you sign the White Castles?" I challenged Tom.

"Because all the good stuff I signed had bombed so badly that I thought I'd better try the really rotten stuff." We sat in silence and drank.

"The truth can hurt; it can also make you very thirsty.

"You know something, Marty," said Tom after ordering another round. "You don't know what a lucky son of a bitch you are for making it when you did. These days you don't have to wait ten years to become a has-been. It can happen to you in six months. Did you notice that kid with the noisy group of parasites that I said hello to when I walked in? Over at the corner table?"

I looked over. A guy who looked like a younger Kenny Rogers was carrying on with a full table of merry makers. He was dressed in expensive pseudo cowboy duds. I also noticed a few bottles of champagne on the table.

"Well, anyway," Tom continued, "a little over a year ago, I saw him play at The Palomino and I signed him to the label. He's a hell of a singer, and his songs ain't bad either. Real commercial but not bad, very list-enable. He's one of these California singer/songwriters. You know, they all kind of sound like Ricky Nelson, who I have always loved, by the way. So I took a shot. And he had a medium sized hit..." Tom mentioned the title. I thought I'd heard it; maybe I'd even seen the guy perform it on Merv Griffin. "We managed to get it barely in the top fifty but things are looking good when he starts to go out with this horror film actress and he gets his picture all over *People.* So we're happening and I'm a hero right? Wrong! He doesn't know it yet but when his option comes up in a few months we're actually dropping the guy. And I don't know what I'm gonna tell him because I don't really know why. Maybe one of the accountants who runs the company didn't like his last show or his new manager or his new haircut, who the fuck knows? But the corporate guys sent the word down that if he's in the red - and who isn't on their first album? And if he's not making as much money as one of our parking lots, get rid of him." Tom shook his head sadly. "So the best I can do is sign some other bright new face and let him be a star for fifteen minutes, too."

"You know something, Tom, said. "Sometimes I think that the present is all people can deal with nowadays. The minute someone becomes a memory it's just too painful. And it don't take too long to become a memory anymore, either. Hell, they announce 'golden oldies' on the radio that were hits less than a year ago. We've OD'd on memories, like I can't take seeing those films of John Kennedy in Dallas I don't want to think about it because it makes me think of too many other losses. So, we just let the past drift away further and faster every year. The current's just too swift. Too goddamn swift You just can't beat against it, Tom!" I don't know if I was making any sense. I did know I was pretty drunk and messing up the last paragraph of *The Great Gatsby*.

"But I'll tell you what the future is," I said softly.

"From the mouth of Marty May? I'm listening." Tom bent close.

"It's cold and electric." I whispered wide-eyed.

"Are they from England?" asked Tom seriously.

"No, no, Tom, from nowhere at all!" I laughed loudly. I don't know why. We drank together for a while and talked about the good old days like two crusty old gold prospectors who had struck it rich once many, many years ago but had now lost the map to their mountain of gold.

"Listen, Marty," Tom said drunkenly as we got up to leave, "I'm gonna work out the dough with old Eric Noise. He can't just cut you off like that after flying you all the way the fuck out here. I promise you, you'll fly home with at least a grand in your pocket." He winked at me.

"A grand?" I slurred. "You better make that a baby grand, Tom ol' buddy. I don't wanna have to pay for no extra luggage." I was drunk and silly and I didn't care.

Tom laughed. "That's the spirit, babe! Don't let them get you down. This ball game ain't all wrapped up yet."

I couldn't believe it! Another jock disguised as a record company executive! But Tom's all right, though I wish he wouldn't call me babe so much. He did pull through with the thousand bucks and told me not to hurry home because the hotel was already paid. I spent the rest of the week hanging around the swimming pool of the Sunset Marquis, wondering if Van Heflin had been on a raft when he died, or if held floated on the water. And if he'd gotten a sunburn.

Part Four
Eat a Peach
Times Square, NYC
1983

Chapter 1

Returning to New York was not as depressing or traumatic as I worried it might be. The unsettling circumstances of my California adventure had ironically given my New York life a sense of security. In fact, the Eric Noise, White Castles, Tom Dunn experience allowed me to take a renewed glimpse into a world I hadn't really been close to in quite a while: the craziness and ego-mania of recently arrived superstars, the boredom of listening to their stoned conversations. Yes, I had conveniently replaced all of that nonsense with only glamour, celebrity, and endless fun nights. I had tasted the good life once too, and now the taste had grown bitter. I didn't envy Eric Noise or The White Castles because I knew their own rainy season was quickly approaching. And they were burning their bridges with the enthusiasm of General Tecumseh Sherman's march through Georgia.

And here I was entering my apartment a thousand dollars richer. Even the cockroaches looked excited to see me again as they scurried out of possible harm's way. They needn't worry; I wasn't in a killing mood. And while I was gone it seemed that my superintendent had installed a smoke-detecting device on my kitchen ceiling. This made me feel well protected and cared for even if I was sure my landlord had acted only under penalty of law. You see, it doesn't take much to arouse my homing instinct and as I inspected the curious new device I sang what I could remember of 'Keep the Home Fires Burning.'

In my kitchenette was a calendar, a rock star calendar that was sent to me by Circus magazine. I guess I was still on their mailing list. Thank god this month was through and I could flip the page over. There had been a grotesque picture of some Satanist heavy metal band, each member holding a human skull. Where they 'dug up' all these skulls I can't imagine; perhaps they were made out of plaster of Paris, as unreal as the group's supposed black magic image. The lead singer was also holding a dove in one hand with his mouth poised to bite its head off. I can't figure out why kids go in for all this kind of crap. Maybe it's from being brought up on Dracula and Frankenstein movies. Little Richard meets the Wolfman was never far off. There was a circled Monday towards the end of last month, it was while I was in L.A. and I couldn't remember what it was for. When I turned the calendar to the current month I found myself facing Sainthood, another heavy metal group whose image ran more toward a sexual gospel approach. The lead singer, Paul Saint, was dressed in flowing white robes and some lighting effect had put a halo over his head. In the background were a few scantily clothed beauties strumming large golden harps. Sure beat the hell out of skulls and the thought of raw dove for dinner.

And then I remembered what that circled Monday had been. A black Monday to be sure for it was to be my day of reckoning with American Express. But the day had passed and I had no threatening letter from them waiting in my mailbox. It was typical of big corporations; they make you believe that your little debt is the most pressing matter of concern to them when in reality you're just another number who they'll get to when the computer says it's time. I supposed I should call them, these things always get worse when you ignore them, but for some reason the card, MY card, was losing its importance to me. Before it had been a symbol of all that I'd lost but lately I've been face to face with many of my real losses and I didn't need the card to remind me. Besides, I couldn't use it anymore so just holding on to it was not as fun as I thought it would be. It was like dating a beautiful girl with a chastity belt on.

"Mr. Moore, please."

"Account number." It was difficult to ascertain whether I was speaking to a man or machine. I dug my credit card out of my wallet where it waited with useless business cards from record company executives who would meet me drunk or stoned late at night and tell me to call them in the morning and then not pick up my calls. I read the embossed code as best I could but my card was scratched and beat up, probably from chopping up too much coke.

"Yes, Mr. May. How can I be of service to you?" said the all too familiar voice of American Express - Mr. Moore. He seemed so calm and congenial perhaps he had forgotten about me. Damn, I shouldn't have called.

"Hi! How are you?" I said cheerfully as if greeting my best friend.

"Oh, why I'm just fine, Mr. May. So…nice of you to ask," he added sarcastically. "I'm just sitting here patiently awaiting your arrival to our offices. I believe you're a little tardy Mr. May, as a matter of fact, I believe you're a great deal tardy. Over two weeks, exactly seventeen days late. I was just sitting here trying to schedule a court date that I hoped wouldn't inconvenience you.

Now he was pissing me off. How the hell could he schedule a court date? He as no judge. "Yeah ... well, that's what I wanted to speak to you about. Uh ... I was just wondering if we could make an adjustment to the that schedule."

"Why certainly Mr. May, for a good customer like you we go to any lengths to please. Why don't we all fly down to the Bahamas and you can write a check over cocktails? Would that be more to your liking?" And then that obnoxious high-pitched laugh of his.

But after Eric Noise he hardly intimidated me anymore. "Hey listen Mr. Moore, I don't need this crap okay? I'm not as naive as you might think. And I know and you know that all a guy in my position has to do is hire one of these lawyers who advertise in the back of the New York Post and declare bankruptcy and you'll be lucky if you end up with ten cents on the dollar from me. Compendia? And don't give me that jive about scheduling a court date because I know that these things can take years before they reach a judge, and no judge has put his schedule in your hands." Not bad, I thought. "So, if you want to listen to what I've got to say, fine, and if not ... well, that's up to you." And then I added emphatically: "It's no skin off my ass!" And if he didn't approve of my language I'd hang right up on him and sell my card to some black marketer. If only I knew one.

He got the message. "What did you have in mind?" he said evenly.

"I'll send you a hundred bucks, and I'll try to keep doing that every month. As far as the card goes, for all I care you can come over right now with your own pair of scissors and cut it in as many pieces as you'd like. It's lost its nostalgia value for me." And that was true.

"One hundred dollars? That's hardly a dent."

"Well then let's forget it. I can use the hundred myself and..."

"All right. Send us your hundred dollars."

"And no legal action," I added firmly.

"All right, no legal action. At least not for the time being," he added ominously.

So I sent him a hundred bucks and how long I could keep this up was anyone's guess. But it was worth it just to have him stop; interrupting my early morning REM sleep with his phone calls and I was running out of disguises for my voice.

Besides the thousand bucks, the other nice thing Tom Dunn did for me, his former employer, was to call a producer who was working in New York on my behalf. Tom knew the guy well, assured me that he was not from the Eric Noise School of production. The point being that this guy might listen to my demo tapes and if he liked what he heard perhaps get involved and rejuvenate my fading career; even submit me and my demo tapes to Tom's label for consideration. This seemed ass backwards to me; why couldn't Tom listen to my tapes himself and if he dug them go to bat for me within his company? But Tom explained that these days you need outside juice to make things happen. Within the record company itself any enthusiasm for signing an artist is highly suspect. It's taken for granted to be a favor for somebody or even worse evidence that you're on the take. I had heard stories about A&R men who were willing to give you a record deal if you consented to remit a substantial portion of your advance money back to them in cash. Unfortunately, I knew no such A&R man or I certainly would be recording at this very moment.

Times Square is named after *The New York Times* but I think the times have changed. It's no longer the cradle of journalism. I don't go down to Times Square too often; and when I do I guess I'm just another tourist with my head in the sky trying to figure out how the hell they get the guy to blow smoke rings out of the immense Marlboro billboard overhead. I was on my way to the Record Plant. It's a recording studio a few blocks west of Times Square and it's where the famous producer that Tom Dunn had turned me on to was to be found. Still producer shy, it had taken me a few days to call the guy but when I did he was very cordial and said that, yes, Tom had called him and, of course, he had heard of me, and certainly, he would be thrilled to listen to my tapes. I tried to make a specific appointment with him but he said just come down to The Record Plant any time and he'd be there. This seemed rather flippant and a little bit inconsiderate considering the travel involved but in reality it was a pretty safe bet. It's not uncommon for a producer to be in a studio from noon to six in the morning when he's working on anything intense and I guess he figured that since I was a musician there was little chance that I'd show up at nine in the he morning unless I had been up doing coke the whole night before and in that case no one would want to speak to me anyway.

The Record Plant was located on the ground floor of a fairly mundane looking office building. The only clue to its secret identity was a California styled redwood door stolen from some Log Cabin and the RECORD PLANT lettered in high-hippy psychedelic style. Like most doors in New York it was locked. I buzzed, I was interrogated on the intercom, and I was admitted. Once semi inside, I was again questioned as to the nature of my visit by a very businesslike receptionist.

She told me to come in, have a seat; he'd be with me shortly. His name was George Peter Humboldt. Many producers seemed to prefer three-part handles such as this; maybe they're into numerology. Or they figure it gives them a larger credit on the album. George was quite famous, he worked mostly with stars, and he liked getting them together in a real work like atmosphere. He preferred studios in the Caribbean or on yachts.

It was comfortable inside the lobby of The Record Plant. There was a Fifties looking jukebox filled with hit singles that had been recorded there, a large color TV mounted high up on the wall and a coke machine that didn't require money. The walls were covered with brightly colored Velour and strips of rustic wood paneling. With a recording studio as diverse as The Record Plant it's important not to limit your decor to just please one type of clientele; it's kind of like the way they decorate airplanes. Watching the ball game on TV were a few studio musicians probably waiting to be called back into their sessions to double their parts or do a harmony or change the whole damn thing.

A studio of the top quality of The Record Plant smells of money. They charge over two hundred bucks an hour and they can certainly afford the loss on the Heineken beers that they put into the coke machine for fifty cents a shot. The place is immaculate and the equipment is serviced with the same care and attention given Boeing 747s like your life depended on it. You're encouraged to good work by the influence of the professionalism surrounding you. I'm appalled when I hear of super-groups who will book such a studio for days on end at over twenty grand a week and then not bother to even show up. Ah, the price of fame. But maybe this is why the equipment is in such good shape.

George Peter Humboldt appeared in about a half an hour. I was starting to get into the ball game; this was a bad sign. Our meeting took about a minute and a half. George Peter must have taken a speed-talking course.

"Marty baby! How ya doin'? You look great you look beautiful. How do you do it? Look at me, like death warmed over."

Warmed over? No, but run over perhaps. George was dressed (except for his sunglasses, which had his initials on the corner of the pink lens in rhinestones. How did he know I looked so great? I'd never met him before.

"You know it's a real pleasure," he said real fast, "It's guys like you who make this business great, make it something we can all be proud of." He shook my hand enthusiastically and like a moron I stood there smiling and just kept nodding my head as he continued. "And that Tom Dunn, one hell of a guy, great guy - one of THE greats!" George P. put his hand on my arm, lowered his voice and continued his rapid-fire delivery: "He called me from L.A. and filled me in on what was happening and asked me to take a listen to you. And you know what I told Tom Dunn? I told him Tom, if I can't find a few quiet moments in my schedule to sit down and listen to a tape of someone with the credentials and integrity of a Marty May then I didn't deserve to be in this business. That's exactly what I told him. And you know what Tom Dunn said?"

I opened my mouth to reply but he beat me to the punch.

"He said, G.P.H. I respect you for that. And you know something Marty? From a guy like Tom Dunn that's worth more than all the platinum records that line my walls at home. Because at the end of the day if you don't have any respect from your peers in the industry, you know what you got?"

More money than everyone else? I thought.

"You got *gotz*, you got *guano,* and you got *zip*! You know what I'm saying?"

I shook my head in sincere agreement with him like we had been through some war together.

And then he stopped talking so abruptly that I was caught completely off guard. This was my chance to speak but my voice came out in a high-pitched squeak. I cleared my throat.

"...Uh...right, right, I couldn't agree with you more, it's uh, integrity that has the... lasting power, that's what Tom Dunn is all about." I said hesitantly but to be honest I was unsure of what my own pitch should be; self-promotion has never been my strongest talent so I tossed the ball back to him to give me time to think. "What are you recording now, George?"

"Legends, Marty, that's all I can say: LEGENDS!"

Was I supposed to know what he meant? A rock opera of Tom Sawyer? "Really?" I said.

"You bet," he answered seriously. "You know how sometimes you just know when you're making a hit? You know, that gut feeling you get in the pit of your stomach that says BAM this is it! I've got it! You know that feeling, Marty?"

What else could I say? "Sure do!"

"Well that's the feeling I've got now, Marty. You see, I can already visualize this record at the top of all three freakin' charts pop, soul, and disco. And that's the key, Marty - visualize your success!" (Did this have something to do with the rhinestone initials on his glasses? "You're not gonna believe whose playing on this, I swear you gotta keep smelling salts on the console to keep my engineer from fainting when one of them walks in." (But I bet he preferred a different nasal ingredient. "Can you keep a secret, Marty?" (Of course this meant in music biz jargon to tell everyone I knew.) "Elton's gonna lay down some wild eighty-eight's as only he can do, ok and Mick and Keith have promised to sing backups as a personal favor to me. My motto is use nothing but the best - don't settle for less."

"You mean they're all in there now?" I said amazed peering around the corner.

"Oh no, no, of course not. I'm just laying down some basic tracks. Who knows when one of these monsters will blow into town? But if they do, you can take my word for it - they'll be on this record!"

I had absolutely no idea what record he was talking about. I've heard other producers hype a project beyond belief and it ends up sounding like The Muppets go Calypso.

"I wish I could give you more info, Marty, but I just can't. You know how it is, when the boys at the top tell you that if word goes out on the street you're dead!"

"I know what you mean," I said lamely. "About my tapes, I want you to know that they're kinda old and I have some newer songs if ... But he wasn't listening, he was just checking his watch.

"I can tell you one thing though, Marty, don't be at all surprised if when you hear this record you don't say to yourself isn't that the KING himself singing?" He smiled wildly.

"Elvis...? But..."

"The man may be dead, I grant you that. But the voice lives on." He leaned closer. "The Colonel called me, he said he's got some tapes of Elvis singing background in every possible key and tempo - it's just a question of speeding up the tape a little here and there. Fuckin' Elvis! Can you believe it?" Well, I couldn't, sorry.

"Listen, Marty, I gotta run, time's money in our racket. But listen babe, the pleasure is strictly mine. So don't be shy!" He gave me a friendly pat on the back. "Stay in touch!" He gave me the thumbs up sign, clapped his hands, winked his eye, shook my hand with both of his and started to jog back to where he came from. I wondered if all that had been some secret Masonic signal?

I yelled after him: "But my tapes! You forgot my Demo tapes" They were still in my hand.

Again he clapped his hands but keep moving. "Right Marty! That's what I like to see, an artist who takes care of business - I can respect that!" He gave me another thumbs up sign from down the hall. "Leave them with the receptionist - I'll call you when I get back from the Bahamas."

"The Bahamas?" I cried.

"A man's gotta work AND play, Marty. Don't forget that!" And then he disappeared behind the door that said 'Studio A', back into that *mondo* expensive fantasyland; a multi-million dollar rattle for thirty five year old babies. But I'll tell you something; he didn't seem as crazy as Eric Noise. At least his ego was nurtured by talking about the biggest stars in the business and not himself. I figured that I had about as good a chance of receiving a grant from the Daughters of the American Revolution as I did from hearing from George Peter Humboldt. Walking down the street I made up a little blues:

Hey Mr. Producer - In your expensive studio
Hey Mr. Producer Tell me 'bout all the stars you know
I'm just a poor boy with no good place to go
So gimme a contract - Cause I sure could use the dough!

I sang it to the tune of "I'm a Man" by Muddy Waters. Stolen riff with bad rhymes, no wonder I wasn't getting a recording contract.

Burlesque is a two-sided word: a little naughty - a little funny. Strippers and comedians; they say that New York was full of the finest Burlesque theaters in the country until Mayor Fiorello LaGuardia closed them down in the thirties. He was the mayor who followed Jimmy Walker who was good looking but corrupt. LaGuardia was ugly and honest; you can't have everything. Walker was famous for giving away the keys to the city to heroes like Charles Lindbergh, unfortunately he gave away a lot of the city to people with less heroic aspirations, too. He was forced to resign from office. LaGuardia, on the other hand, smashed slot machines and when there was a newspaper strike he went on the radio himself to read the funny papers to the kids. But he closed down Burlesque and he made striptease illegal - He let comics strip but not women. (Sorry for that.)

Now there are all sorts of places around Times Square where you can watch girls shed their clothing but not one place where you're going to find a comedian like George Burns or W.C. Fields both of whom started in Burlesque. It all backfired on the spunky little mayor who read the comics. Personally I must say that I'd prefer Jimmy Walker; comic strips make me nauseous, always have. I wouldn't have minded to be around New York City during the Twenties, who knows, I might have been a comedian with a guitar. After all, look what Jack Benny did with a violin.

Today, Burlesque is dingy little theaters where girls dance to recorded music for dirty old men with raincoats on their laps. I passed lots of them on my way through Times Square, walking home from The Record Plant. Standing in front of one, *The Follies*, I couldn't imagine anyone going inside on such a clear and bright afternoon. It seemed too perverse. So, I paid a few bucks and walked in - maybe it would help my song writing. At the door, a big black guy in a U.S. Marines T-shirt, sun visor, and purple reflector shades took my money and informed me that the show would start in a few minutes. A Vet, no doubt. It was in between sets; no girls were to be seen. From the enormity of the brightly lit (even in daytime) sign outside announcing: "GIRLS GIRLS GIRLS FOLLIES" I had expected a larger theatre but there were only about a hundred seats, divided by a runway. There were about twenty of us perverts in there; we kept a polite distance from each other. To my horror, one of the dirtier old men who had been sitting a good five or six seats away from me slid over just one seat between us.

"You know, this ain't the original Follies," he said.   I smiled and gave him a good look: unshaven, greasy balding hair, sallow complexion, and yes, of course, a raincoat. He was smiling at me through rotten teeth. "Uh...no kidding?"

"Naw! The original was some place; let me tell ya, that Flo Ziegfeld could really put together a show. Why, these girls is shit compared to Ziegfeld's girls."
Ziegfeld's Follies? "This guy had to be close to eighty if he really remembered that. I looked at him again; maybe he didn't look so bad for his age.

"A real class show. But you know something? That Ziegfeld died broke."

"No.? "

"Sure did, he was a real chump, penny wise and pound foolish, you can learn a lesson from the guy."

"Oh yeah?"

"Sure.' You're too young to remember the crash."

"Thanks for noticing," I said. He ignored me.
"It was called Black Monday, everything hit bottom and Flo had all his fuckin', money in the market, like everyone else, so Flo you see, when it came to little things he was a cheap son of a bitch and on Black Monday he was in court fightin' over a fifty dollar tab he owed a sign painter. So da guy who handled his stocks couldn't get a hold of him to tell him to sell everything before it was too late and he lost everything. Can you believe that?"

"Unbelievable,   I agreed.

"So the old' bastard died broke!" The guy cackled. "Just goes to show you."

"Sure does." This only reconfirmed the wisdom of staying out of court with American Express; who knows what might have happened. The lights started to go down.

"And I'll tell ya something else," said the old man as he stood up to move back to his seat.

"What's that?"

"I was that sign-painter." He howled with laughter as he moved back to his place. Impossible but I believed him; it was more fun that way. And then the voice of Ratso Rizzo announced: "Ladies and Gentlemen," (What ladies?) "Would you please give a warm round of applause to former Vegas showgirl Inger Peach!"

Most of the hands were in laps, under coats; the applause was warm but muffled. A moment later I thought I was dying and my life was flashing in front of me. The lights dimmed, the music rose and a tall buxom blond came out of the wings to the opening chords of ... MY SONG!

I slumped down in my chair and tried to hide my face. It was like meeting my mother in this dump. I don't know why I was hiding, I'm sure there weren't any critics from Rolling Stone among the audience but then again. The song they were playing was from my album MAYDAY and it was called "Lingering, Lately In Love" I had written it about Barbara. It was one of my few Top One Hundred singles, although it died somewhere in the low twenties and I was sure at the time it was because it wasn't danceable. How wrong I was because ex-Vegas showgirl Inger Peach was dancing, prancing, shaking, caressing, undressing, vibrating, and mouthing the words in addition to doing a number of other movements that defied the laws of gravity. Far from undanceable, "Lingering, Lately, in Love" was nothing less than pure locomotion. And in her bright yellow, feathered boa and gold G-string she was dressed for speed. A matching gold top soon came off to reveal two tasseled pasties that she was very adept at spinning in opposite directions. And she did all of this on ultrahigh heels, not less then five inches high that most girls would find dizzying just to stand up in.

To my utter disbelief, my songs went on and on, one following another as it all came off: bra, pasties, G-string, mini G-string. I couldn't have picked a more tasteful selection myself. I sat paralyzed in the front row. The peak of her presentation came when she went back into the wings and reemerged with a shaggy gold rug. "The rest of my little show will be of a slightly more vertical nature, gentlemen." The slow "Feather Pillow Fortunes" that had been so helpful in putting Eric Noise into dreamland accompanied her.

And vertical it was, the smaller G-string came off and well ... everything turned pink. The lighting was somewhat subdued, which kept it from being too stark a lesson in female anatomy. My own view, in the front row was nothing short of confrontational. What she was arousing in me the Supreme Court refers to as 'prurient interests' and I called a hard-on. As I leaned forward to discreetly adjust my zipper and relieve some pressure our eyes met. She was resting on her elbows, lying on her back, with her legs high in the air. She bolted upright and her legs dropped to the floor with a thud.

"Marty May!' she yelled loudly. She quickly shifted to her hands and knees and crawled to the edge of the runway. We were but inches apart. "You're Marty May!" she exclaimed with glee.

I was mortified. My fellow perverts looked shocked and upset. The old guy who said he was Ziegfeld's sign painter gave me a disapproving glance; I shrugged my shoulders at him in a futile gesture of innocence. The big black guy in the Marines T-shirt was jogging down the aisle towards me; he had taken off his shades and he had 'I am dangerous' written all over him.

"Jus' what the hell is going, on here, Inger?" he asked jutting his chin out at me.

"This is Marty May!" She told him as if that said it all. I said nothing, but I instinctively went to shake his hand.
A known trouble maker eh?" The bouncer sneered at me. "Don't ya worry, honey, I jus' love taking care of guys like him!" And instead of shaking my hand he started to twist my arm behind my back and force me out of my seat. I was not resisting. This naked blond in front of me had zapped all my strength.

"Stop that, you big hulk," she yelled and punched him in the shoulder. He let go of my arm. "This is Marty May, he's a rock star! Why he's the greatest rock star there ever was. She smiled at me. I was doing nothing but staring in horror. "Leave him alone!"

"Okay, okay Inger! I thought he was bothering you, all right? How the hell am I supposed to know?" He put his reflector shades back on as if to signify all's cool on the western front and smiled at me. "Nice to meet you Marty - it's a pleasure to have you visit our emporium. He seemed pleased with himself for using that word. He shook my hand and walked away, filling in a few other customers as to who I was on his way out. I felt like Frank Sinatra.

Inger Peach grabbed me by the hand and said: "Come on with me, sugar," and sort of pulled me onto the stage. I had no choice but to follow her lead. She was totally naked except for her high-heels. "No one is gonna mess with you around here while you're with me," she said reassuringly. She took my hand and led me down the runway like some puppy dog. In those shoes she was a good head taller then me and we walked down the runway to the amazed glares of the all male audience. I couldn't imagine what they thought must be happening; they probably figured I paid a lot extra. One of them had the nerve to boo.

"What's the matter? Didn't you get enough Pussy?" Inger yelled at him. "Try this!" And she flung her gold jewel encrusted G-string right at him. It almost knocked the guy off his seat. She winked at me. "It was falling apart anyway," she whispered.

The dressing room was right off the stage, one large room for all the girls who danced at the Follies. I always imagined that men wouldn't be allowed in such a place but none of the girls lounging around in various states of undress seemed to give me a second glance as they smoked cigarettes and read Cosmopolitan. Each girl had a separate dressing table with a mirror surrounded by bare light bulbs. Inger gestured for me to sit down in front of hers and grabbed an kimono robe from a hook and put it on. She pulled up a chair and sat down across from me. She was putting a cigarette in a holder or maybe it was just one of those gadgets to help you cut down nicotine and took a deep breath. "Well if this ain't rich!" and she lit her cigarette and blew out a big puff of smoke. For a few moments she just sat there, smoking, shaking her head and smiling and making little exclamations like "Jesus H. Christ!" and "God damn! I gotta pinch myself again!" until finally she stuck out her hand and shook mine heartily. "I'm Inger Peach!" she said in a very sexy Southern drawl. She smiled. As opposed to the sign-maker sitting next to me she had great white shiny teeth.

"How do you do, uh, Ms. Peach?" I said lamely. "I'm Marty May."

"Ain't that the truth!" She kept smiling at me. She grabbed a little bottle of perfume off her dressing table and started dabbing it on herself all over. When she put at little touch between her legs, she winked at me.

"You know this is real funny, Marty." As she leaned forward to put the perfume back on the table she rested her hand on my leg. "But I just had a feeling that we'd meet some day and I knew that it would be in the big apple tool I guess you could call it women's intuition."

"Well...I guess you'd have plenty of that," I was trying not to watch where her robe was coming undone. "You're quite a woman."

She laughed. "You want a beer, sugar?" I liked the way she called me sugar. "Sure, I said."

"Don't go away." She winked and got up and walked out of the dressing room. The other girls didn't seem to take too much notice of me. They were undressing all around me, getting into their costumes. It was impossible for me not to look. One of them walked in looking like a pretty young schoolteacher; I thought of Barbara. She had on a little gray flannel skirt and jacket and a white blouse with a black grosgrain ribbon bow and scholarly tortoise shell glasses. She undressed completely and proceeded to put on black stocking and garter belt and a black leather bra. Then black leather bracelets with studs and a matching dog collar. The last thing to come off were her tortoise shell glasses. She could have been one of a hundred girls you might see browsing around Bloomingdale's little would you guess. Inger returned with a couple of beers. She handed me mine, we both drank out of the bottle, and watching her hold that green bottle to her lips really turned me on. We made small talk: what was I doing there. ("Just by accidents" I said) and how long she'd been working there ("Seems like forever, sugar" she said). I felt shy like a little boy around her. She seemed so much more in control than I, like the way she had thrown her G-string at that guy in the audience and the way she had kept the bouncer off of me. It was a take-charge quality I had never seen in any of the girls I've known. I'm sure hers was a tougher world than mine and she seemed right on top of it. And that turned me on, too.

Now I know that people don't want to believe that any girl who makes her living shaking her tits and lying on her back spreading her legs while lonely old men jerk off in the audience could be truly beautiful, but she was. Her skin was smooth and white like porcelain, her eyes were large and blue and sparkling, her hair long and blond and silky and her mouth was, well, just luscious. She was a big girl, almost six feet tall and her body was certainly voluptuous but all in proportion to her size. Nothing about her seemed decadent or used up like you might expect. Maybe her hair was bleached but that's okay so was Marilyn Monroe's. She was very fair with reddish pubic hair and pale pink nipples though once we reached the dressing room she was modest and covered her.

She sat there and smiled at me like I was a Teddy Bear. I tried to speak; I think I had been staring at her all over. But she didn't seem to mind.

"I was surprised to hear my music in here," I said.

"Really?" she said giggling. "I can imagine it must Have been quite a shock. Kind of like 'what's a nice song like you doing in a place like this'?" (God, I loved her Southern accent.)

"Yeah," I said. "Kinda like that."

"Well, I'm the one who plays you, sugar. It's got nothing to do with this hole in the ground, believe me. Why, if it was up to them, they'd have us shaking our ass to disco. Can you imagine?" That this would be beneath her dignity seemed perfectly reasonable. "So all us girls got together and jus' told the boss that we want to pick our own records. I mean, what could he say? This is hardly a place for music lovers. But you know, picking your own stuff, it helps make things a little more bearable, if you know what I mean, sugar. You can kinda build your own world around it."

"What made you choose my records?" I asked figuring she had found them in a bargain basement somewhere.

" 'Cause I ain't hardly listened to nothin' else since I'm this high." She gestured with her hand measuring about two feet off the floor. Of course she was exaggerating; girls like Inger are born totally grownup aren't they? It was hard to imagine her in toddler's clothes.

"And you are just the cutest thing I ever laid eyes on, sugar!" She stood up, kinda lifted me up with her, put her arms around me, let her robe fall wide open, pressed her breasts against me, and gave me the warmest, most dizzying, kiss I'd ever had. She wasn't shy. Later, I learned that she had been waiting for this kiss quite some time. About five or six years ago I was kind of between records or labels and not doing much except wasting myself nightly. So when my booking agency called and asked if I wanted to open some shows for Electric Light Orchestra down south, I figured why not. It would be good for my health, anyway. But not in my wildest dreams would I have imagined what that tour would do for my sex life six years later for among the twenty thousand faces at the Omni auditorium in Atlanta, Georgia, was a sixteen year old girl named Margaret Ludlum who would grow up into Inger Peach.

Chapter 2

He told his friends to be quiet, keep it down, don't light no reefers or flash no beer cans - her parents were really strict. How the hell should he know why but for Christ's sake, they kept the poor girl grounded for the last two months and that was just for being a half-hour late one school night after saying she was going to the library.

"If I had a piece of ass like that for a daughter, I'd more then likely lock her in the cellar myself," said one of his friends in the back seat. They all guffawed loudly.

"Shut the fuck up! If her old man thinks anything funny is going on, he won't let her out. And Margaret's a nice girl!" This made his friends laugh even louder but when he clamped his fist and grimaced at them they shut up. It was his car.

He tucked in his plaid cowboy shirt and smoothed his long hair back with his hand as he walked up the path to the front door. It was a nice house, recently built, with a big front lawn. Good thing too, he thought, so her parents won't see his car full of jokers.

He couldn't find the doorbell so he tapped the little brass knocker three times. He could hear her inside saying, "I'll get it, daddy," and then another voice, much deeper, saying, "Now you sit down, young lady, so I can meet this boy and see what he's up to." The door opened and there stood her father. He was a big man; he still had on his tie and white shirt from his day at work. Her family was rich for this Atlanta suburb, real estate or something.

"Good evening, sir. I'm Michael ... uh... I'm here for Margaret." Her father just stood there not saying anything and Michael thought, shit, this guy's gonna give me a hard time, I just know it. Shit. "Ya all know we're going to see the concert tonight? At the Omni, sir?" The boy didn't know what else to say.

Finally her father spoke. "Why don't you come inside and meet the rest of Margaret's family, son." But there was something threatening in the way he said it.

"Why, thank you, sir." 'Their house was nicer then his own, the furniture all seemed to match, like it was all bought at the same time in some ritzy department store. There was a well stocked bar in the corner. The father pointed to the couch.

"Thank you, sir," said the boy again and sat down. The father sat across from him in a black leatherette recliner. It looked like the father's usual chair. And throne.

"What did you say your name was, son?"

"Uh ... Michael Katz...sir."

"Katz? Is that a Jewish name son?" He frowned.

"No, it isn't, sir...just a Georgia name as far as I know. My family's been her for years. Before the Civil War, I suspect." The boy smiled the father didn't. Prejudiced son of a bitch, thought the boy. In his fancy house and clothes he's no different from any Georgia cracker.

"Where are you taking my daughter tonight, son?" The father leaned forward. "And more importantly, what time are you bringing her home?"

"Uh ... we're going to the ELO concert at the ...

"Now what the hell is an 'ELO' son?" The father took a long slurp of his Scotch.

"It's a group, sir, a band - an English band. The full name is Electric Light Orchestra but everyone just calls them ELO. It's a little easier on the tongue, you know?"

"Well all this acid-rock sounds the same to me. Not much point in it as far as I can see. So when are you bringing my Margaret home?"

A good-looking fortyish woman entered the room. She had on slacks and a sweater. Nice body, thought the boy; that's where Margaret got hers. He stood up.

"Hello, I'm Margaret's mother."

"Hello, I'm Michael ... Michael Katz." The woman sat in another chair near her husband's. Neither of them smiled. It would be easier getting gold out of Fort Knox; he knew he still had to answer that question.

"Well, the concert starts at eight o'clock sir. I think there's another band that goes on first someone called Marty May - I don't really know too much about him.

This worried the mother. "Dear, I think he's black, this Marty May. Those Negro concerts can be dangerous - they go crazy when they hear that music." She directed all this to her husband but had confused the name with Marvin Gaye.

Michael said: "No, I don't think so ma'am, I saw his picture on the poster - just as white as you or me. He's supposed to be a real good guitar player, kinda like Eric Clapton."

"I just wouldn't want Margaret going to any Negro concerts. Not that I have anything against the black people, ya know, but sometimes they tend to get a little carried away - it's in their blood."

179

''*Son, I've asked you two times when you're bringing Margaret home.*" *The father frowned at him.* "*I'm not going to ask you again.*"

"*Yes sir, Mr. Ludlum. Like I was saying, sir, this Marty May, goes on about eight or so and I guess ELO will be getting' it on about nine-thirty or ten so I figure with encores and stuff ... The boy looked hard at the ceiling and counted on his fingers.* "*We should be getting home sometime around one or one-thirty.*" *This didn't seem too extravagant; it was Friday night.*

"*Well, you can get home whenever the hell you want son but I want my Margaret home by midnight!*"'

Oh shit!

"*Well ... of course, if you say so, sir, but that will mean leaving the show early.*"

"*Well I can't see where that would make much difference,*" *said the father.* "*It all sounds pretty much the same, anyway.*"

"*I just hope we can get out of the barking lot while the shows still on...*" *The boy was desperately trying to think of some excuse. These tickets had cost him twenty bucks; he deserved a chance to try for a little 'action' after the show. What's the harm? All the girls he knew were on birth control pills anyway.*

"*Margaret,*" *the father just interrupted him and yelled back into the house.* "*There's a young man here for you.*"

She appeared instantaneously probably listening the whole time. She had on hip-hugger pants and a paisley halter-top. God, she looked good enough to eat, thought the boy. Her old man wasn't so crazy after all - he knew what a prize he had.

"*Hi ya, Michael. We better get going, I guess, or we'll be late.*" *She obviously wanted to get out of the house as fast as possible.*

"*Now hold on there a minute, young lady,*" *said her father.* "*Sit down right over there.*" *He pointed to the opposite end of the couch.* "*I have informed Michael here that he better have you home by midnight ... or else I'll come looking for you.*" *Michael laughed but then he realized her old man wasn't kidding.* "*Understood?*"

"*Midnight? Oh daddy! The show won't even be over by then!*" *she pleaded with him.*

"*It's midnight or nothing at all,*" *he said.* "*Take your pick - makes no difference to me.*"

"*And you remember what happened when you were late last time, don't you dear?*" *said the mother with a smile. Up-tight bitch, thought Michael.*

"Don't worry, sir. I'll have her home by midnight." He knew it was useless to argue with these two monsters.

As they were almost out the front door, the father said: "And son, one other thing."

"Yes sir?" What the fuck now thought the boy.

"If you want to take my daughter out again, you better get yourself a haircut."

"Daddy!" said Margaret almost in tears.

When they reached the safety of the car Margaret said: "I'm sorry, Michael, I'm sorry you had to go through all that crap. They do it to every guy I date!" she wailed, "I can't stand them. When I'm eighteen I'm getting my ass out of here for good."

"Ah that's all right. You know Sammy and Jeff?" He pointed into the back seat and took off down the block.

"Sure do, Howdy boys!" she said. She was smiling now, she felt free. They drove a few blocks and then she said, "Michael, honey, could you pull over for a second - I gotta do something." So he did. "Now, none of you boys peak, ya hear!" Naturally all three boys wouldn't take their eyes off her now. She quickly undid her halter-top and lifted it up so she could get to her bra, reaching behind her back she quickly undid it and took off. For a second or two nothing covered her large breasts except the stares of three totally bedazzled teenage southern boys. Then, she redid her halter-top and held the bra out in front of her like a dead fish.

"I don't know what's wrong with my mother," she said. "She just refuses to buy me a bra that fits. Why hell, I'm a thirty-six D and she buys me a thirty-four C and expects me to wear it." She giggled, "I think she's just jealous if you want to know the truth."

The boys were speechless until Michael said, "I'm sure glad you asked me to pull over, Margaret, I might cracked up otherwise." They all laughed.

Margaret and Michael only stayed long enough at the concert to see the opening act, Marty May. She liked him a lot and thought he was sexy, sophisticated - dressed in black leather pants and a ruffled shirt, not like these Georgia boys in their plaid shirts and Frye boots. He seemed to sing all of his songs about girls, almost from their point of view, like he could read a girls mined. There was one called "Now What Loretta" that especially moved her. It was about a girl who was trapped somewhere, maybe an institution like a mental hospital. Margaret felt trapped herself; but she knew there was going to be a lot more to her life then this so she kept her cool, biding her time until she was able to make her move.

So, when Michael suggested they leave before ELO went on and told his friends to find a ride home, she didn't mind. She'd remember this Marty May and see if he had any albums out. There was something about him she really liked. Maybe someday she'd even get to shake his hand or something.

Michael didn't mind leaving either because after what had happened in his car on the way there all he could think about was getting his hands on those huge tits of hers. And he knew that he better get her home on time or her old man was really likely to come looking for him and with a daughter like this, he just might be carrying a gun. She did let him caress her breasts and kiss her nipples and she even held on to his cock for him a little bit when they parked not too far fro her house. But the whole time she was thinking about Marty May. There was just something about him. Something much grander then this horny little Georgia boy had to offer.

Margaret found his records and they were some of the things she brought with her when she left home early one morning about two months later, boarding an Atlanta bus bound for New Orleans.

Chapter 3

Like most beautiful, southern girls Inger loved to talk, especially to a captivated male listener such as myself. Call it the Scarlett O'Hara syndrome. Seeing as I couldn't really hang around The Follies all night until she got off (not that I really would have objected) she told me to meet her at midnight at P.J. Clarke's on Third Avenue; said she just loved their cheeseburgers. I got there early. It's an old-fashioned bar wedged between the skyscrapers around it they had refused to sell out, probably figuring they had a civic duty to remain standing and serve the populous. By the crowd that was there that night they may have been right. It was three deep at the bar in front. I slowly threaded my way through to get back to the dining room where a virtual siege was taking place: about twenty peoples mostly couples, were wedged in a small hallway with the ladies room on one side and the open-faced kitchen on the other. They were all vying for the attention of Frankie, the nonchalant maitre'd, who stood with a bowed head and a pad full of names telling everyone it would be at least forty-five minutes for a table, I thought perhaps Inger might have to find a different favorite cheeseburger this evening. But then, there she was, pushing her way through the crowd, taller than everybody else, a pink little fur jacket over her shoulders, and calling: "Oh Marty! Yoo-hoo! Marty May!" in that gorgeous accent of hers. Before I had a chance to tell her about the wait for a table she gave me a quick kiss and zoomed right over to Frankie who put his pad and pencil down on the kitchen counter and greeted her with a big hug. She gave him a BIG kiss, and nearly picked him right up off of his feet. She had to be a good foot and a half taller than him.

"How ya doin'? Frankie Darling'!" she said and gave him another kiss right on top of his head. "Ya know you're New York's sexiest host?"

"Just terrific, Inger 'I got your reservation right over here." And Inger with her terrific reach grabbed me and we all headed to a prime table right by a window that had a suspicious looking RESERVED sign on it, which Frankie grabbed and stuck in his jacket pocket. "Enjoy yourselves," he said and walked away.

"God that's great Inger!" I didn't think we'd be able to even get a table. He told me at least forty-five minutes. I didn't think they took reservations here."

"They don't, sugar."

"Well then, how did you ... ?"

"Only permanent reservations darling!" She gave me a sly wink.

We ordered drinks, more beer for me, and a champagne cocktail for her. It was quite a contrast to see her outside of The Follies. She appeared as an elegant though perhaps slightly shady lady with lots of ready cash. Inside her dyed fur jacket she was dressed fairly conservatively: one of those slinky silky dresses that fastened down the front and look as though they'd come wide open with the pull of a string. They seem to be favored by young, attractive woman executives: practical yet sexy.

"You know something, sugar? On the way over here I started to get real mad at you." She shook a finger at me.

"What for?"

"Because you never answered any of my fan letters! That's what for! I must have sent you at least a dozen from various parts of the country." She faked a frown.

"Fan letters?" I said guiltily. "I must have never got them, did you sent them to my record company?"

"That's right and one time I even called and talked to some little secretary in publicity who assured me that you got all your mail."

"I don't know Inger. Sometimes they can be pretty lax in forwarding you mail, especially after you've left and moved on to another label." But this was a lie. I'd gotten quite a bit of fan mail forwarded to me over the years. And the fact is that I barely opened any of it and I don't think I ever answered a single letter. I don't know why; I guess I thought it wasn't my job, that I should be above all that, or something. And Barbara had thought it was silly too when I asked her to be head of my fan club. That's right, I'll blame it on her.

The main thing we talked about at Clarke's was Inger's job, 'Exotic Dancing', as she euphemistically called it.

I didn't know how touchy she'd be about it but she wasn't; she wasn't ashamed. If anything she was proud; it had gotten her to where she wanted to be able to buy beers and cheeseburgers at a chic East-side bar for her hero Marty May.

I don't know why she gave me all the credit for helping her run away from home and "stop sitting on my ass and start shaking it as she put it. She told me that she had left Georgia shortly after my concert at The Omni, and that she'd never gone back in all the years since.

"Things were just going from dismal to disastrous with my parents," she said. "Any day, I was expecting my daddy to build a tower in the backyard and stick me up in it and turn me into the Rapunzel of Atlanta. I really could never figure out what they were so scared of. I guess it was sex, that I'd get pregnant or something and run off with one of the local losers. They should have known better. I'd had my eyes set on better things for a long, long time. Marty, did ya ever see that movie Gypsy?"

"Yeah, I think so, about the stripper and...

"Gypsy Rose Lee."

"Yeah, and who was that women who played her mother? With the really big voice?"

"Ethyl Merman," she answered with authority.

"Yeah, right, she was the mother. God, do you know that Ethyl Merman made a disco album?" I had nothing personal against the woman but this was a prime example of the level the record industry had sunk to. "So what about Gypsy?" I asked, failing to make the obvious connection.

"Well, I can remember it like it just happened yesterday. I was home after school, I couldn't have been more than fourteen, and I saw that movie on TV. And I just knew."

"Knew what?"

"Jeez! You're not such a quick study, are you sugar?" she said well naturedly, but correctly. I always seemed to just miss the obvious though real quick on the obtuse.

"Oh, I get it. You mean you saw Gypsy and you knew that's what you wanted to do, be a stripper." I smiled but I was confused. "You mean at fourteen you knew that?"
"Sugar, most of the me that you see right now was with me back then too." She cupped her hands under her breasts.

"God, that's great," I said. "I mean ... about the movie. You know, it's funny but I guess I was about fourteen too when I found out what it was that I wanted to do, too. That's about when I got my first electric guitar."

"Well, we're the lucky ones I guess sugar. The ones who get a calling early on in life. Most folks spend their whole life searching for it and rarely do find it, you know? That's just *soooo* sad, I think."

But there was something in what she said that bothered me, like we were on an equal level. I didn't say anything though.

"So what happened? When you left Georgia?"

"Well, I headed down for New Orleans. I heard that there were lots of strip joints down there; some of the boys I knew had been down to the Sugar Bowl, and they gave me glowing reports. But it was actually pretty gruesome, you know? Like most of the places were real tourist traps where the girls would dance on top of your table for five bucks. And during Mardi Gras, whew! Just forget it! What a zoo!" She laughed.

"But, did it bother you in the beginning? Taking off your clothes in front of a lot of strangers?" I suppose this would be a typical question for a man; I wonder if woman would ask it?

"Never gave it a second thought, Marty. It was as easy as rolling off a log. First of all, you don't got that much on in the first place to take off, so there ain't much work to it. And secondly, I could never figure out why some skin was okay to show and other areas you're supposed to keep covered. It never made a hell of a whole lot of sense to me. She winked. "But I sure am glad that that's the way it is! Suits me just fine."

"I'm surprised for girls to do what you do but they just did it for the money. As a temporary emergency measure or something." I didn't want to offend her. "I always figured that it was difficult ... work."

"Temporary? Are you kiddin', sugar? I've been doing this since I'm seventeen, over five years, and I don't plan to quit till my tits are falling down and my bank account is full up!" She took a big bite of her cheeseburger. "Why, does it bother you being on stage in front of a lot a of strangers? It sure didn't look that way down at The Omni." She was good at speaking with her mouth full, like she was always eating in a hurry.

"Well ... what I do is a little different. I try and keep my clothes on, ya know." I laughed.

"Maybe so, sweetheart, but you bare a lot more of your private areas than I do. No one know what I'm thinking when I'm up there."

I didn't want to talk about this. It seemed presumptuous to keep comparing the two of us. The only common point we had as far as I could see what that we both did find out calling at an early age.

But maybe that was a lot more to her than I gave her credit for. I don't know, maybe if my career wasn't down and hers wasn't up, I could be a little more magnanimous. Though I didn't exactly consider The Follies the peak of one's career until she told me that she usually walked out of there with at least two hundred dollars in cash. Each night. And that was just an average day's work. There were always those occasions when some drunken out-of-town conventioneer would stuff a fifty or hundred dollar bill down her G-string.

"So you came to New York directly from New Orleans?" I reached over and lit her cigarette for her, chivalry not being dead when the lady is buying.

"Oh, not I've been all over the country and I've done it all: stripping, go-go dancing, topless waitressing though I didn't care for that much, the guys would always grab my boobs when I'd be serving them drinks. Before coming to New York, I was in Vegas."

"Really?" I said. "Were you a dancer?"

"I was a showgirl," she added proudly.

"What's the difference?"

"No, you gotta learn the nomenclature, Marty." This made her smile; she liked pulling out that big word. "A showgirl is the one who does simple steps with her boobs pushing out of some flashy outfit and a headdress two feet high while the dancers run around and make it look like we're all dancing. You see, when you got a pair as big as mine or some of the other showgirls it really is not as sexy as you might think if we let these things swing into our faces, which is what would happen if we really danced."

"Oh," I said embarrassed and feeling naive.

"But I had to get out of Vegas.

"Why's that?"

"Well, you see, the casino I was working in was part of one of the big hotels down there and one of the owners of the hotel one night decided he just had to have me and I told that shrimp to just get and it turned out he was the wrong person to say that to. He was very 'connected' as they say out there. He finally gave me an ultimatum: either I put out for him or I wouldn't be able to work in any casino in Vegas or Atlantic City for that matter. You see, these boys are all very tight with each other. So really I had no choice and I split."

"He was that bad, huh?"

"No, he was okay looking, actually kind of cute. But he was the kind of guy who you didn't want to be lying in bed with some night when a few of his 'partners' would burst into the room with machine-guns. That kind of stuff still goes on out there, ya know. Although you never hear about it." This seemed to still bother her and for a moment she seemed glum.

"Were you sorry to go?" I asked stupidly.

"Well, sure I was sorry," she said impatiently. "The money was great. And I had reached the top of my field, in a way. And it just wasn't fair! I mean, I was damn good at what I did! But you can't cry over spilt milk, sugar." Her good nature returned fast. "And what the hell," she leaned forward and whispered: "I stole my Vegas costume and now I'm the star of The Follies and believe me, there's a lot of truth in that old saying about how it's just fine being a big frog in a small pond."

"Has the boss from Vegas ever tried to contact you here?" I was paranoid I was moving in on some mobster's obsession.

"Oh, no. I don't think he could really care less about me, if you want to know the truth. He was just on some kind of a power trip; you know how some guys are. Couldn't take no for an answer."

"And you really like working at The Follies?"

"Yeah, it's fine ... the money's not bad and they keep anybody nasty from grabbing me. And the people who own the place are nice guys." She took a compact from her pocketbook and checked for food in her teeth.

"Nice guys?" I was surprised. "I thought all these places were owned by gangsters."

"Oh, no," she said, "That's just what you see on TV, the guys at 'he Follies just got to look tough so they can keep the customers in line. You know that big black guy at the door? Horace?" Why, he's just a big pussycat. Wouldn't hurt a fly. And he's a philatelic, too!"

"Philatelic?" I exclaimed. "Is that like a child molester?"

"Marty! Hell no! It means he collects stamps!" This made her laugh big time. Me too.

"And the owners are a couple of accountants from Queens, nice guys." she added. "It's a good investment, they say.

"How do you feel about the customers?" I asked snobbishly, forgetting for a moment that that is exactly what I was a few hours ago.

"They're fine as long as they adhere to the 'look-but-don't touch" thing. And the ones who come in day after day, night after night, well, I gotta admit I feel kind of sorry for them. There's somebody living inside each of those bodies, ya know."

Her compassion surprised me, I figured strippers to be cold and hard. But than again didn't anyone who loved my music as much as she did have to have a lot of heart? Just kidding. Then she started to rub her foot up and down my leg under the table. I think I blushed.

"But enough about me, sugar, let's get into you." She crinkled up her nose and winked.

"Uh ... what about me?" It was hard to think with her foot going up and down my leg. She must have taken off her shoe and she kept going higher and higher up my leg. She had amazing muscle control. "You know, Inger, I'm not such a big star, anymore. It's been a long time since I played gigs like the Omni." My God, now how'd she get her foot all the way up there?

"Marty, you'll always be a big star as far as I'm concerned. When I saw you down there in Atlanta you seemed different from the rest ... you seemed to care about what you were singing. You know when I was in Vegas I took a night off to go see you play in L.A. at the Roxy."

"You went all the way to L.A.? Just to see me?"

"Sure sugar! I'd walk a mile for my Marty!" She threw me a kiss across the table. "You want another beer, honey?"

She signaled for the waiter before I had a chance to answer, "And you jus' gotta have some of their deep-dish Cherry pie, it's out of this world. And remember that this check belongs to me understand?"

I swear, her kindness made my eyes start to fill up. Or else it was her foot rubbing my thigh. "Thanks ... really, you can't imagine how much I appreciate all of this Inger. I've been having a rough time lately."

"Don't tell me you haven't eaten in a while?" She looked concerned.

"No, not just the meal, Inger, I mean meeting you and talking to you and ... well, no girl has made me feel this good and this wanted in a long, long time."

"You just wait and see how good I can make you feel, Marty," she whispered. "Now you hurry with your dessert so we can go on home to my place. For some real dessert." She licked her lips.

Inger Peach, the former Margaret Ludlum of the Atlanta suburbs, lived in a high-rise apartment not far from Clarke's on the upper east side of Manhattan. She said that she didn't really care that much for the neighborhood, too many doctors, lawyers, and Gucci pocketbooks for her taste, but when she had first come to New York she was scared of the well-publicized crime rate and she wanted some place safe. Her building had a uniformed doorman who greeted her by name and stood next to two closed-circuit TV monitoring systems, one for the laundry and one for the service entrance in back. The lobby was immense and immensely ugly. Inger could 'detect my distaste as we walked through it and made a face and said: "Kinda makes you want to hate Pablo Picasso, don't it?" Although I didn't notice anything really bearing Picasso's stamp. But I knew what she meant; him being the father of some vague concept of modernism that should have been relegated solely to those horrible looking sculptures of unpainted steel that large American corporations seem to just love to put in front of their headquarters. But maybe there's a method to their corporate madness, maybe these horrible sculptures are used to scare people away and not go inside and find the true ugliness buried in the books and ledgers!

All the way up the elevator and until we reached the door to her apartment (which was on the top floor) Inger continued to apologize for living in this high-rise. She blamed it all on the bad rap that New York gets from the rest of the country: it's crime and violence and uncaring people. She told me a funny story: "You know, when I first got here I had heard just how unfriendly New Yorkers were, ya know, and one day, I don't know how it happened, but I got off the subway at 42nd Street. I sure as hell wouldn't do that now, and all the guys along the street were yelling, 'Hey Baby!' and I thought, hell, New Yorkers aren't unfriendly at all. But I'll tell you something, Marty, this may be a rough town but as far as I can see it's a pretty square deal here, you get what you pay for. At least in this city if someone pulls a gun or a knife on you, you can pretty well figure it's because they want your money. Out in California they'll kill you if you ain't the right astrological sign. And New Orleans? Well, the only thing that keeps their murder rate down is that most of the time everybody's too drunk to shoot straight."

I agreed with her. New York is a city for people who want the best and expect the worst; or as Lou Reed was once quoted: "Even paranoids have enemies." But I was surprised at how Inger seemed ashamed of her building; this seemed uncharacteristic of her and her self-assured stance. Perhaps it was because, in her heart, she felt that she was sacrificing some of her dignity or pride or self-respect or whatever you want to call it by working as she did even if the money was great, but she was willing to accept this sordid ordeal as long as she could fill in the pieces of the rest of her world with total freedom and control. And in this building there was nothing she could do about how badly unmatched the wallpaper and the carpeting was in the hallways. But entering her apartment was another story, another land; like walking into another century. She switched on the lights and told me grinning: "High Bordello was my decorating scheme." And she wasn't kidding. It resembled something that Kitty of Gunsmoke fame might have called home. A personal Gaslight Club. The walls were covered I with a textured scarlet wallpaper, velvety to the touch; underneath my feet, thick oriental carpet, probably imitation, made me want to take off my shoes. There was a crystal chandelier overhead which Inger set at a slow burn level; it used those little orange flickering bulbs that resemble candles.' The furniture was antique looking, some real, some copies; a red velvet chaises lounge, a large straw chair meant for a south Pacific native king that rose in a large arc overhead, a Victrola with a decal of a little white dog, an early cone shaped speaker, and

something about 'His Masters Voice' written on it. The only modern touch seemed to be a low glass coffee table in front of a Victorian couch. On either side of the couch were large oriental vases full of silk flowers. Heavy curtains that blocked out the sunniest day. In short My kinda place.

"All's you need here, Inger, is a professor"" I said.

"A teacher? What for?"

"No, no," I explained. "That's what they called the black piano player in the whore houses of New Orleans.

Like Jelly Roll Morton or Professor Long Hair." She was impressed by my knowledge although it came directly from Blind Red Rose. He told me once that he played in one of these Bordellos, with Jelly Roll Morton, said it was the original House of the Rising Sun right outside the French Quarter. But Ruby started to say that was impossible and he started pouting and wouldn't say anything further.

"Now you make yourself comfortable, Marty, while I change into something more ... sociable," said Inger provocatively. She disappeared into the bedroom. I first sat on the couch but then nervously stood to examine the small, framed photos on the wall. They were sepia toned, all of nude women, Victorian looking even in their nakedness. More voluptuous bodies than today's girls; Rubenesque, I think they call it. One had a shawl around her shoulders while unashamedly displaying her breasts with a demure smile kinda like Mona Lisa. Maybe Mona was actually posing naked too and old' Leonardo just covered her up for the sake of society. Maybe that's the reason for her mysterious smile. There was another photograph of a grinning young girl, naked also, not older than sixteen or seventeen, lying on her side. Her eyes were closed in some sort of faked reverie and she had one leg crossed and was modestly covering her crotch. And another of a dark beauty with piercing eyes sitting on a window sill with a brass bed behind her; and a girl in a chair holding a glass with a bottle of 'Raleigh Rye' on the table beside her, wearing widely striped stockings and little sandals. She looked a little tipsy and was staring dreamily at the glass in her hand, her hair piled on top of her head like women of that time did. There were photos of other naked girls whose facial features had strangely been scratched out, making their nakedness look obscene and inhuman.

"Admiring my Bellocqs, sugar?" asked Inger as she walked from the bedroom.

"Yeah, I guess so, what's a Bellocq?" I turned around; she was wearing a long white dressing gown and little shoes with puffs of feathers on them.

"Did you ever see that movie Pretty Baby? The one where Brooke Shields played the little whore?"

"Yeah, was Keith Carradine in it?"

"Yeah, he played Bellocq ... or someone like him."

"Right. He was a photographer, that's right, always taking all the hooker's pictures. I didn't know it was a true story."

"Well, I don't know if the movie was true. But it was kinda based on this guy Bellocq, though I doubt he looked much like Keith Carradine. He had something wrong with him; he was a 'waterhead' or something. I found out about him when I was living down in New Orleans, that's where I found these prints though I didn't have them framed till a year or so ago. They're not originals because there are no originals. They say his brother destroyed them."

"His brother?" This intrigued me.

"Yeah, he was a priest. They say he's the one who scratched out all the girl's faces like that one there."

She pointed to one   of a girl in black stockings whose head was missing. "Can you believe that? Scratching out that poor girl's head? That's the kind of thing they'd do down in Atlanta." She seemed to take this personally.

"So what happened to Bellocq?"

"Nothing.   He   just   went   on   being   a   commercial photographer, I think. He never got famous, but now he is. They compare him to Toulouse Lautrec, you know that short little French guy. Did you ever see that movie Moulin Rouge with Jose Ferrer?"

Her movie knowledge surprised me. "How'd you learn all about this stuff?"

"Oh, you know, when you're mostly working at night you watch a lot of daytime TV. I can't stand those soap operas but I watched a lot of movies. You can learn a lot of history, ya know."

"So this Bellocq never got rich and famous, huh?" This depressed me.

"Oh, no. Died in poverty, I think, In his wildest dreams I bet he never imagined they'd make a movie about him and little old' girls like me would have his photographs on my wall. You just can't tell, can ya?" She put her arm around me. "You should remember this, Marty. You can't ever tell how its all gonna turn out in the end."

But I didn't like to think about things like this. I can't imagine anyone who figures themselves to be any kind of an artist gets much solace from the thought that they'll be recognized for their achievements fifty years after all the lights go out. Neither Garcia

Ortega nor Blind Red Rose either and everyone else in-between. And surely not Eric Noise and the White Castles (that's a laugh), and just as surely not me.

"It's funny about these pictures," I said, "All these girls are smiling. You wouldn't imagine what their occupations were from looking at them."

"Well hell, why shouldn't they be smiling, Marty? Maybe they were having a good time, ya know," she said surprised.

"But they were prostitutes," I insisted. "They couldn't have been happy."

"Well, I guess that's what they teach us in school and church," said Inger. "Sex and rock 'n roll will take you straight to hell every time." This made her laugh.

"I guess my middle class is showing," I confessed.

"So what do you think, Marty? Do you think ol' Bellocq would have wanted to take my picture?" She stepped back and stood under the chandelier and slowly took off her robe. She was wearing a pink corset and opaque white stockings. She had a string of pearls around her neck, and pink open backed high-heeled bedroom slippers with little puffs of pink Marabou feathers on them. She had on no panties, just a little V shaped patch of reddish pubic hair. It was lighter in color then I had noticed at The Follies. As a matter of fact, I couldn't quite relate her to the same girl I had seen lying on her back and spreading her legs. She looked very off work now; maybe attitude's everything.

I let out a deep breath. "I'm sure he would have."

"As a matter of fact, if you got a Polaroid around I could try to make up for Bellocq's absence." I said leering at her.

"You naughty thing! Now you just hold your horses and tell me what you wanna drink." She seemed totally at ease in her half undressed state. I shouldn't have been surprised.

"Oh...beer, I guess, if you got one." I certainly could of thought OIL something more exotic like Brandy or Amaretto or some other strange liqueur but I had been drinking beer all night at Clarke's and I didn't want to ruin what looked to be a very promising evening by getting nauseous. Besides, Paul Newman drinks beer.

She went into her kitchen and closed the doors behind her so the fluorescent lighting wouldn't interfere with the ambiance. I think it was one of the damn most considerate things I had ever seen anyone do.

"Why don't you just follow me, sugar?" she said as she emerged with my beer. And I did. Into her bedroom.

Her bedroom was more of the same except somewhat softer and more private; more pink then red. An imposing brass bed, covered with little pillows, dominated the room and we eventually sat down on it. She had a small stereo, which she switched on to the FM radio. "I don't want to have to be thinking about changing records."

Our small talk got even smaller as we sat and I drank my beer while she smoked too many cigarettes, which I admonished her for and then felt silly I guess we were nervous, I knew I was. Her corset exaggerated her already large breasts and I was having trouble keeping my mind on the line of conversation as she told me little bits of her life in New Orleans and Vegas and the stops in between. I was telling her something about myself, about my career or my marriage when I almost absent-mindedly stroked the top of one of her breasts. She took the beer out of my hand and said, "Let me give you a hand with those boots, cowboy." And she pulled them off but she didn't stop there and she took off my socks and undid my zipper and with my help pulled off my jeans. I took my shirt off myself. I was naked.

"Now you just sit tight," she said and got up and adjusted the door so that the full-length mirror on it was directly facing the bed. She got on her hands and knees in front of me and licked her lips and the view from the mirror was just ... perfect.

"I don't want you to miss a thing, sugar." And she leaned forward and took me very gently and very completely into her mouth.

Chapter 4

Like most musicians and actors I'm superstitious. We never say good luck and we don't wear green on stage except if we're playing Peter Pan. Still, one black cat can ruin my whole day. But I suspect this is a byproduct of hard times (like Voodoo in Haiti?) because I must admit that when things were going my way I was perfectly willing to take all the credit; luck was something I could manufacture at my will. But when more difficult times showed up I was always ready to put the blame on God, luck, karma, the stars, the ozone layer being eaten away by my aerosol shaving cream cans, and the fact that I once smashed a mirror in a dressing room by throwing a bag of stale M&Ms at it. But when I woke up in Inger Peach's brass bed that next morning and beheld this vision in long legs talking on an antique looking telephone and blowing kisses at me, I found myself searching for some reason to explain how I had stumbled into such good fortune. The only 'good deed' I'd done lately had been sending American Express a hundred bucks. Although I'm not sure that counts.

"Good morning, sugar!" Inger leaned over and gave me a kiss after hanging up the phone. I couldn't help but give her pubic hair a playful pat. "You naughty boy," she gently slapped my hand. "The least you could do is have a little coffee, first." (And maybe brush my teeth too, I thought gallantly.) She told me to stay put; she would serve me the coffee in bed and asked me how I liked it.

"With a little bit of everything. Just like last night." I smirked.

"Now, didn't anyone ever tell you not to kiss and tell?" she reproached me, putting on her robe and going to make coffee, leaving me with alone with my thoughts ... and erection. I don't think I ever had a sexual encounter quite like the night before. Maybe it was just because I was more sober than during my usual 'rolls in the hay.' I came twice; I don't remember that having happened in years. When Inger made love she seemed to have a plan, the same way she knew what order things came off when she was stripping. We weren't both rushing toward an inevitable climax; each step was meant to be savored. And she knew how to hold me back, when one too many strokes and it would have been all over. I admit that I was mostly following her lead but it wasn't like she was dominating me. And what if she was? If anything, she made me work harder at my own performance, using my imagination to make a smooth transition from one level of foreplay to another like a sturdy male ballet dancer whose strength makes it possible for his butterfly partner to drop into his arms. He'd always be there.

There had been other girls between Barbara and Inger, Christ, there had been other girls during Barbara, but I don't remember ever having felt as turned on as I had with Inger. It seemed A all her efforts were just to make me feel good with not much thought to her own pleasure and this just made me want to satisfy her even more. With Barbara our lovemaking was so... intellectual, we knew each other too well. Barbara rarely denied me but when we'd be having sex there was an unmistakable feeling on my part that she was doing it out of some sense of duty; almost to the point of martyrdom and this kind of just made me want to get it over with. Towards the end she almost always gave me a blowjob and that was all and that was enough. I don't know why she felt this way, maybe it had something to do with her being away at a girls preschools most of her adolescence. She seemed to get off more on talking about sex than doing it, which, I imagine, is what went on in those schools most of the time. In a way Inger regarded the sexual areas of her body as other entities, places not overly familiar and to be treated with a little formality. When she offered her breasts for me to suck her nipples she held them with care, like they belonged to someone else. Barbara regarded her body with the clinical objectivity of a gynecologist and she didn't seem to care in what unflattering light I might see her. No matter what she was doing, she always left the bathroom door open. To Inger this would be unthinkable.

And the girls on the road, well, then I'd usually just be so concerned that I was THE Marty May that they had seen and heard of, I'd usually be too inhibited to freely tell them my wants and needs and likes and dislikes. Sometimes I'd even fake an orgasm and then go into the bathroom and jerk off.

I'd gone out with a few nice girls after Barbara. There was a small dark girl I met in my local delicatessen that I got to know after many shy "hellos". She was part Seminole Indian and had a giving and loving nature but I think I was so concerned with all my immediate problems at the time and still tapering off from the rock star life that I hardly even gave it a chance. And then there were the girls that I would meet at four in the morning at an after-hours club, drunk and coked up and I'd leave their apartments the next day feeling wasted and useless and without sleep. I had stopped doing that after one occasion when I was so wasted that I couldn't even get it up so I was just trying to do my best for the girl I was with whose name I can't now remember and wouldn't you know it, the radio was softly playing and on came one of my songs. I felt awful and I turned it off and then later I considered hearing my song at such a time terrible bad luck.

But the most different thing about having sex with Inger was that I didn't feel the need to fantasize about any other girls the whole time. In the past my libido had required a cast of characters ranging from high school sweethearts, to movie stars, to the playmate of the month to bring it all home. Those were crowded beds.

Inger returned with the coffee on a white wicker serving tray. I wanted to ask her if last night had been as special and as great for her too; I wanted to ask her in a way that people who meet in singles bars don't.

"You're beautiful." I said seriously.

"You're pretty cute yourself, sugar," she joked.

"No, really, I mean ... in all ways. Last night was just..." I searched vainly for a meaningful adjective.

"Just as good for you as it was for me?" she suggested shyly. She held the white china coffee cup with both hands as she sipped.

"Yeah, exactly...that's what I wanted to say.

After we finished coffee we made love again. Finally, I was getting the object of my horny teenage desires. And that wasn't just lust. I remember once in seventh grade having an argument with another boy over whether he would rather forcibly make our mutual heart throb at the time strip for him or just passionately make out with her. He chose stripping and I chose kissing. Now, I'm not saying that he grew up to be a rapist or I a virgin with ideals of platonic love, but even back then my sexual desires were mixed with something else, something fleeting but strong, something that you could remember long after you forgot the physical. Inger was perhaps a long overdue sexual object for me but she was my sex symbol with a soul and I don't know if that's all bad, maybe we were indulging in mutual fantasies and isn't that the way it should be? I was the rock star of her dreams who was in some way connected with her desire to escape her hometown and she was the suffocating provincial my living color centerfold fantasy, who truly had a fine mind of her own and never wanted to say "no". If she had been a playmate, her data sheet would have listed me as her favorite activity, sport, and turn-on After we finished we lay in bed in each other's arms. Inger suggested that we stay in bed all day which was fine with me, I had nowhere to go, and that night she worked a later shift at the Follies which didn't begin till nine. Actually, to be truthful, you'd have to say that I lay in her arms because even without her heels she was a few inches taller than me. But that's okay when it comes to things like this I'm a totally liberated male, though I doubt if most feminists would agree that Inger was the model of a liberated woman. Or maybe they would; maybe that was only my own chauvinism talking.

"So what do you think about women's lib, Inger? Are you fer it or agin it?" I mimicked her Southern accent.

"You kidding' me, sugar? I am it! But I don't think some of the hotheads who run that show would agree with me. God, we had a funny scene at the Follies one night!" She started laughing and shyly she'd hold her hands to her mouth like Japanese girls do. I laughed too without even knowing the story.

"Well, have you ever heard of this group 'The Porno Front'?"

"Yeah, I think so, isn't it a group of women against pornography? They say it encourages rape or something? They're the ones who splashed paint all over that billboard The Rolling Stones had out in L.A. for their *Black And Blue* album, the one that showed the girl all tied up and bruised. They wrote "THIS INSULTS WOMEN!" or something on it, didn't they? I could see their point but if they really wanted to talk about ads that insulted women, why didn't they start with those commercials on TV where housewives compare laundry detergent like absolute morons. Why pick on the Rolling Stones?

"Yeah, they're the ones. But they've done some good stuff too – you know what 'snuff' films are?

"Yeah, I co."

"Well, they helped bring some of the animals who bring those films in from South America to be tried and punished. So I got to give them credit, but I think sometimes they get a little carried away or else they just don't have a lot to do with their time." She lit a cigarette like a pro storyteller who knew the importance of the dramatic pause. "So I think it must have been a Saturday night or maybe a Friday, I can't remember, but the Follies was packed, full of conventioneers – you know those funny ones who wear those little hats with the tassels on them?"

"Shriners?"

"Yeah, those are the guys." Funny how Inger called all men 'guys' and I called all women 'girls'. Maybe we did have a lot in common. "So the place was full and I, the star attraction, was going on just around midnight." In a gesture of mock conceit she rubbed her fingernails across her ample chest. "So I started dancing and ... "

"To my music?" I asked hopefully.

"Sugar, I don't dance to any other So, I hit the stage and I thought I noticed something funny, some of the men had their hats pulled too low, and no guys wear a hat on their heads in the Follies - they all put them in their laps so they can fiddle around with themselves underneath. Anyway, I was afraid maybe they were cops or something. You know, every once in a while when the politics of the day call for some action we get raided - its never anything serious. But there I was in the middle of my show and about to lay my rug down on the floor when these 'guys' jump on stage, take off their hats and long coats, and they're women! I was mortified, sugar, absolutely mortified." Inger started laughing so hard she could hardly talk.

"My God! So what happened? Were they from the Porno Front"? I asked.

"You bet they were and underneath their coats they had on gorilla costumes, without the head of course, and big dildos strapped between their legs! They were carrying on and screaming at the customers and calling them animals and pigs and one of them threw a few cream pies out into the audience."

"What did they do to you?"

"Well, first of all, I didn't really stick around too long once I saw what was going on. Horace, the bouncer, gave me the high sign to skid-addle and that's what I did. But they didn't seem to be directing their wrath at me. It was a good thing too because I would have decked the first one who said anything to me. Finally, it was just too funny, those women jumping around that stage in their gorilla costumes holding their dildos and screaming at the old men who were trying to cover their faces and get the hell out of there. And I thought what they were doing was far more insulting to women than anything I could have ever dreamed of! Finally the cops came and took them away. I still don't know what their point was. I mean, if anything I figure that what I do helps keep these guys off the street - they ain't gonna attack anyone in The Follies, that's for sure."

It was a confusing issue. My radicalism left over from the sixties appreciated The Porno Front's point. But the realist in me had to say that Inger was probably right, I've, never heard of a big rape problem in countries like Sweden or Denmark where pornography was legal long before it was in the U.S.

"And the funniest damn thing"" said Inger. "Was that the whole thing backfired on them. Their little 'raid' gave the Follies so much publicity that business was just booming for a while. Everyone thought that we had the

dirtiest show in town and that's not true at all places in this city where the girls let the guys touch them anywhere they want for just a few dollars and will pick up bills without using their hands, if you get my meaning. I would never do anything like that - I mean, after all, a girl does have to have her standards, sugar!" She put her hands on her hips defiantly.

"Long live The Follies!" I said heroically

"Well, maybe not as long as you'd think," she said excitedly. "That was my agent on the phone before."

"Your agent?" I was surprised. "I didn't know that ... exotic dancers had agents."

"Why, sure we do. I mean, it's show biz ain't it? A lot of these agents are just full of sugar honey iced tea but..."

"Sugar honey iced tea?"

"Oh Marty! You're just gonna have to learn how to speak Southern if we're gonna communicate at all! Now down in Georgia, young belles like myself are strictly forbidden to use any gutter talk so we gotta use our own ... euphemisms!"

"I don't get it."

"Oh! You Northerners! Try putting the initials together?"

"Sugar ... honey ... Iced...I get it! SHIT! Right? Most of these agents are full of shit. Is that what you're saying?"

"Well, I guess you just won the doll!"   She kissed me.

"Anyway, this guy I was speaking to is pretty well connected with some of the big hotels down in Atlantic City. He's trying to get me a job in one. It would be great if it came through - a lot of money. And who knows? Maybe some big Hollywood producer would spot me on stage and make me a star!" She half closed her eyes and puckered her lips and pushed up her hair in a Monroe-ish pose. "You want to be in the movies?"

"Have you ever met a pretty girl who didn't?" I liked her honesty.

And I loved how she never got dressed or at least not completely. Barbara used to always be wearing some ripped extra large T-shirt or some other piece of Goodwill Industry fashion that probably passed as very hip up in the Sarah Lawrence dorms but to me was nothing except extremely unsexy But I guess in Inger's case it was a different story. She probably considered dressing and undressing a chore, a part of work. Later on, Inger asked me if I'd like to take a shower with her. How could a gentleman such as myself decline her offer? We took turns washing each other and I stood back as she shampooed her hair.

"So. Would you move down to Atlantic City if you got the job?" I asked.

"Ouch! Oh ... Sugar Honey Iced Teat I got shampoo in my eye!" She let the water run in her face. "What'd you say sugar? You know, I do that every time!"

"I wondered if you got that gig down in Atlantic City if you'd move down there ... to live."

"Oh, I don't think so. Not permanently. Sometimes you can arrange it so that you work in shifts, ya know? Like ten days on and ten days off. They let you stay in the hotels. Why do you ask? You wanna move to Atlantic City with me? We'd make a pretty sight promenading along the boardwalk." I doubted if she was serious but just the hint of a suggestion terrified me. "Well ... ... I don't know ... I mean, I have a career here and everything. And back to New Jersey? I don't think I could stand it. I'm from there, ya know, and I went to my high school reunion a couple of weeks ago and it scared the hell out of me."

I switched places with her and shampooed my own hair. Luckily she had some stuff labeled 'Organic* - I was picky.

"Scared?" she said as she got out of the shower.

"What do you have to be scared of? I don't picture you as the kind of guy who gets scared, Marty." Did she mean this or was this Inger's own form of therapy.

"Well I don't know ... scared of being pulled back there, I guess, after trying so hard to get away from it." It was the first time I'd analyzed these feelings myself. I stepped out of the shower and Inger dried me off. All her makeup was off now and she looked much younger and very pretty in an innocent sort of way, It was possible now to picture her as Margaret Ludlum, the heartbreaker of Atlanta's suburbs.

"You'd be miserable out in the sticks, Marty. You're like me - you wanna play in the super-bowl of life even if it does mean sitting on the bench for a while."

"Don't tell me you're into sports?" I asked with horror.

"No, not really, not those you can't do in bed."

She gently dried my private parts with a towel. "But down in Georgia, you gotta learn to talk a little bit about sports if you wanna talk to the boys down there about anything at all! But what I was saying was that out there in the sticks you feel like absolutely nothing is going on. I remember sometimes I'd just stand on the street in front of my house waiting for something to happen - nothing ever would though."

"Yeah? I used to do the same thing, just watch the traffic moving."

"Well at least here in New York, you know something's going' on somewhere, even if you feel out of it personally." Inger put her hair up in a towel, I used my own towel and patted her breasts dry. She finally politely mentioned that she thought I'd gotten all the water off her about five minutes ago. "Yeah, I know what you mean. But New York City can sometimes make you feel that if you're not riding around in a limousine partying all night there's something wrong with you."

"Well there's nothing wrong with you, Marty," she said playfully. "I checked personally!" We moved out of the steamy bathroom back into the bedroom.

"So when will you find out?" I asked.

"Oh, he said any day now they'd give him the final word. A couple of their talent scouts came and saw me at The Follies. I was expecting it to be a couple of horny ol' gangsters but it turned out to be two women - both former showgirls themselves. Now THAT'S what I call women's lib!"

"Good thing they didn't show up on Gorilla night."

"You're telling me!" This made her laugh. "Can you imagine? But if I do get the gig, first they bring you down there for 'bout a month before ya' can go on the shift schedule, ya know, sort of a try-out period." I fiddled with the knobs of her radio trying to find WNEW-FM, the only station that played me anymore.

"You can stay here while I'm gone if this comes through, sugar," she said. "It would be a good place to work. It's pretty soundproof. I never could figure out how a rock In roll musician can practice in an apartment without the neighbors raising hell."

"But Inger ... isn't this a little sudden? You sure you want to let me stay here? It would almost be like me moving in or something."

She came over and sat down next to me on the bed. "Look Marty, there's one thing you gotta understand about me. I'll wait for anything - but once I got a hold of it, I hold on tight." She squeezed my hand. "I waited a long time to get out of Atlanta. Hell, I knew that place was the pits when I was fourteen, and I waited a while to get out of that sweaty joint down in New Orleans until a better offer came along and ... I didn't like waiting all these years to meet Marty May. But I believe things happen for a reason, ya know? My motto is 'things work out for the best - IF YOU LET THEM!" You know what I mean?"

"Well I guess so. I'm a bit of a fatalist myself." But I tend to blame fate rather than to just go with it.

"I mean, sugar, you can't tell me that it wasn't fate that sent you into The Follies yesterday afternoon. I mean, sugar-honey-iced-tea, if it was the day before I would have been off, you see what I'm saying? Just don't go looking a gift thoroughbred in the mouth." And she opened her mouth wide and sensually. Good teeth.

"Well, I get your point."

"But it's up to you, sweetheart. Inger stood up and put her hands on her hips; it made her breasts giggle along as she talked. She was totally naked except for
the towel on her head and the high-heeled slippers.

"As far as I'm concerned, you can move in here with me today. You say you got some money problems so why should we be paying two rents, ya know?" She wasn't at all playing hard to get, but it didn't matter because she was impossible not to want. "Tell me, Mister Marty May: Do you or don't you like what you see?"

"Well ... I do. I doll I said much more emphatically than when I A used those same words at my wedding.

"Well then - let's just go with the flow!" she said so I pulled her back into bed and she gave a little yelp. If we kept going on like this I'm sure there would be a place for us in the Guinness Book of Records. Living with Inger Peach was like being on vacation. I spent almost all of my time with her or at her apartment while she was working. One night, after ',"he Follies, she came home with one of those mini-amplifiers you use to play electric guitar through headphones. She said it was an anniversary present - our one-week anniversary. I guess I must have told her about Manny's Music Store which wasn't far from The Follies.
Inger should have been the perfect girl for me. She kept the same hours, thought mornings were for sleeping, that kitchens were just a place to make ice, and that bed was the logical place for a loving couple to spend spare time. But something was bothering me; sometimes I felt pangs of jealousy that she could earn so much got money doing what she did while I barely got by. But I tried to put that out of my mind and just go with the flow.

And then sometimes I'd think about Barbara. And I'd wonder what she would think of me living off a topless and bottomless dancer. Would she be ashamed of me? Then I'd get really mad at myself for thinking of her at all. What the hell should I care what Barbara thinks? She'd never contributed a dime to help support us and here was Inger, unmarried, with no commitment from me, feeding me, buying me gifts, and offering to let me move in with her, rent-free. And I wondered why I punished myself with destructive thoughts like I should have just been concerned with the bottom line, which was that living with Inger was doing amazing things for my guitar playing and singing. She loved nothing better then for m to just sit around and play guitar and sing my old songs and play little blues riffs while she stayed naked in bed and read Cosmopolitan and drank coffee. When I lived with Barbara she used to move into a different room whenever I'd pick up my guitar and then after a few minutes I'd find myself putting down my guitar and following her. Inger would even make comments like: "That sounds good!" or "You sure can play that thing, sugar." or "Why don't you write a song around that riff?" Every once in a while she would start talking to me about my career,

"You know something, Marty, I jus' can't figure you out sometimes."

"What's to figure out?" I asked. "I'm a normal, healthy, broke American boy of thirty-two, living with the finest piece of ass ever to leave Atlanta, Georgia." I jiggled my eyebrows and faked holding a cigar a la Groucho Marx: "So how's about a little Southern cooking?"

"Now be nice! I know you're healthy, believe me, but I can't figure out why you decided to give up rock 'n roll.   You're   so good."

"Give it up? Are you crazy? Rock In roll gave me up, sweetheart, not the other way around." Her naïveté peeved me a little. "Believe me, it wasn't my idea."

"Well ... I know that's what you keep saying, but I just don't buy it, sugar," she said softly.

"Don't buy it? What's not to buy?" I put down my guitar.

"It's a sad and simple story: Once upon a time, I had a nice record contract and I made a few albums and everybody expected them to be real successful like the ones I had made before. But they weren't, so I was dropped and no one else was interested in picking me up. Period!"

This wasn't my favorite topic of conversation, it was embarrassing and failure was not the image I wanted to project with Inger. It might mess up our sex life.

"And why wasn't anyone else interested in signing you Marty, honey?" It was a good thing she called me honey or I'd really get pissed off. This was private turf like a cemetery plot.

"I don't know, Inger ... they thought I was too old, that I'd had my chance already ... not up to date. They left me behind in the rock In roll scrap heap. I wasn't even good for spare parts." It was strange because I would almost cherish a conversation like this with Barbara but with Inger I didn't want to talk about my failures and past disappointments."

"Do you want to know what I think?" asked Inger gingerly.

"Go on, tell me," I said not really meaning it.

"Do you promise not to get mad at me?"

"I promise...I won't get mad at you," I said childlike.

"And you'll remember that I love you?" Although she now said this to me fairly often I had yet to really say it to her outside of moments of passion, the easy times say it.

"I'll remember," I said softly, preparing myself.

"Well..." she took a deep breath. "I think you deserted. I think you went over to the enemy at the first
opportunity."

"The enemy? What enemy?"

"The enemy of rock In roll - the straights, the squares, the corporate types, all that bullshit ... you preppie little wife!"

"Barbara? She loved rock In roll."

"Like SUGAR HONEY ICED TEA she did Marty! That little bitch may have loved the idea of it, from some little Ivy league tower but she had as much an idea as to what it was all about as a Chinaman! Maybe less!"

Now I was sorry that I had told her about my marriage. "You shouldn't say that, Inger. It's a hell of a lot more complicated than that."

"Well it seems to me sugar, that you started going downhill ever since you left Blind Red Rose."

"Downhill? What do you mean? You saw me at the Onmi and you loved me or so you say. And my solo albums did and you a hundred times better than anything Blind Red Rose ever recorded his whole life."

"Oh Marty, you don't understand. I did love you at the Omni - you were wonderful. Sometimes I have trouble saying what I mean, but it seems like what you was riding on was the 'soul' that you had saved up from working with Red Rose. And then one day - it just ran out. And I think you started getting more and more interested in all the things that you could charge with your American Express Card and all the swanky restaurants that you could be seen in. Hell, you acted more like an executive in one of those record companies than an artist. That little wifey of yours would have been perfect married to a junior Vice President but she didn't know the first damn thing to do with someone like you!"

And I couldn't help but remember that Barbara had suggested that I get a job in a record company when I had called her from L.A.

"Oh I don't know I think Barbara's too much of a groupie for that."

"Well there are corporate groupies too, Marty." I couldn't deny this. I had seen plenty of them at that convention I had gone to. Even groupies looked for a little security these days.

"There's only one thing you gotta be thinking about Marty and that's rock In roll - playing it and living it. And don't give me no sugar-honey-iced-tea about you being too old - look at Jerry Lee Lewis or Chuck Berry or even Mick Jagger! None of them are kids anymore. Hell, even Blind Red Rose is still playing you told me!"

She had a point to be sure. As a matter of facts I don't know when this teenage idol business took hold of rock In roll. I meant Chuck Berry didn't write his best songs till he was way past being a teenager. And Bill Haley was almost forty when "Rock around /he Clock" came out. And the old bluesmen that were imitated by bands like the Rolling Stones were all well into their forties and fifties before they were ever even recorded. I put the blame on the pre-Beatles era of Fabian and Frankie Avalon - hardly the golden age-of rock In roll. But I think the music-businessmen found these kids' easier to handle.

"I don't think you really have ever truly accepted yourself for what you are, Marty. Inger was almost pleading with me. "And I think that's the same thing that's holding you back now, I think you probably imagine you'd be better off as an ... insurance salesman or something. And sugar, you don't know how wrong you are."

"I don't know, Inger, guess I'm just too middle-class."

"Marty, you must have been sleeping during American history class. There's only two classes here, rich and poor. And those in the middle basically kid themselves they're on the way to the top while they're scared shitless they're gonna fall to the bottom."

When I was playing with Red Rose I could care less about things like middle-class values. Didn't even know what they were; I belonged more in the *if it feels good do it* class. I don't know when all this got a hold of me. Maybe it did have something to do with getting Barbara credit cards, wanting *things*. When the hell did I start being ashamed of being a rock 'n roller?

"It all just seems a long way away now Inger..."I said, starting to feel sorry for myself but then I just cut the shit. "But I'll tell you one thing, these weeks with you have been ... well, just unbelievable. I'm starting to feel like my old self, like I was sixteen again!"

"God help me," whispered Inger.

Chapter 5

"*Let me see that map, Marty,*" snapped Ruby from the driver's seat. *Marty handed her the tattered road map. He hadn't shaved that morning but it hardly mattered because even at twenty his beard was still sparse. He wore sunglasses and a wide-brimmed fedora like a pimp.*

They were stopped at a light. As she took the map from him she glanced at his hand. "*Where'd you get that rings Marty? I never saw that ring before.*"

"*Uh ... Sheila gave it to me.*"

"*Who the hell's Sheila?*" *she asked frowning.*

"*You know...Sheila,*" *he said shyly.*

"*No, I don't know Sheila.*"

"*You knows the waitress at the Whiskey in L.A. She gave it to me last night. It was her old boyfriend's or something.*" *He examined the ring; Ruby did too.*

"*But those ain't even your initials,*" *she said.* "*What the hell good is a ring with someone else's initials on it? I swears sometimes Marty I jus' don't know what's going on in your mind. I hope you didn't pay her nothing for that ring. I doubt if that's even real gold. Looks gold-plated to me.*" *She made a face.*

In the back seat of the station wagon sat Red Rose in his pork pie hat and dark sunglasses. He looked asleep but he wasn't.

"*Stop pickin' on da boy Ruby!*" *he said yawning.* "*Can't you see what's happening? Ol Marty here's what ya call a stud. Pretty soon he'll have dese lil' white girls payin' him fo' it.*" *The old man cackled.*

"*I'm not a stud,*" *Marty protested.* "*Its just that it was a man's ring. What was she gonna do with a man's ring? She was a nice girl, that's all.*" *He covered the ring with his other hand though he loved looking at it.*

"*I ain't pickin' on no one 'cept you, Daddy! You been sittin' in that back seat cutting' farts the whole way from L.A. I told you to stay away from those beans and rice. Who eats that for breakfast anyway?*"

The old man just laughed. "*Ah, you jus' jealous Ruby that Marty an' me is gettin' all the action - that's all.*"

"*What kinda action you been gettin?*" *she asked in a high shrill.* "*Besides gas!*"

"*I got my piece of da pie too,*" *he said.* "*Ya all 'member dat cute maid at the motel?*"

"*At the Tropicana?*" *asked his daughter.* "*There was no cute maids there of any kind at all and how the hell would you know if there was one! There was one old woman that's all.*"

"*She wasn't so old,*" *said her father.* "*And besides, you shouldn't be so uppity, a woman like dat is like som' fine wine - she get a whole lot better wit' age. Jus' like me. Ain't dat right, Marty? Mary will tell ya, Ruby. He knows all about women - he's a stud.*" *The old man emphasized the 'stud'.*
"*I'm not a stud.*"

"*Well I wish one of you studs could tell me jus' where the hell we are,*" *said Ruby.*

"*Why don't ya let me drive?*" *said the blind man in the back seat. He howled with laughter.* "*I betcha I do as good as you lill' girl!*"

"*Oh Daddy! Why don't you just shut up and stop cuttin' those mean farts! We gotta gig tonight.*" *She tried to concentrate on the map.*

"*Where we playing?*" *asked Marty.*

"*The Boarding House,*" *said Ruby.* "*And if this here is Market Street it's gotta be just a few blocks away. Damn these one-way streets!*" *The light changed, she handed the map back to Marty and drove on. The old man in the back started singing:*

> "*Gonna tell you a story*
> *Bout da stud called Marty May*
> *Breakin' da hearts of da waitress*
> *He steal her ol' mans ring right away.*"

"*Ah come on, Red, gimme a break will ya?*" *said Marty. The old man laughed and laughed. Marty blushed.*

"*Who's backing us up?*" *Marty asked wanting to change the subject off of his sex life.*

"*Those same characters as at the Whiskey,*" *said Ruby.* "*What'd you think of them?*"

"*Ah, they were all right. Actually the bass player was pretty good, the drummer slowed down at times. When are they getting here?*"

"*They left last night. They both live here in San Francisco or nearby, maybe Oakland.*"

"*You let dem two get away?*" *asked Blind Red Rose loudly.* "*What makes ya so damn sure that they'll show up tonight?*"

"*Because they don't get paid till tonight! That's why!*" *said Ruby emphatically.*

"*The old man said nothing and appeared to go back to sleep. Shortly thereafter they found the gig, the club called The Boarding House. It was a nice old building and Ruby Rose was glad to see that there was a large poster outside announcing her daddy's engagement.*

"*When did you start adding that?*" asked Marty when he noticed that Featuring Marty May had been added to Blind Red Rose's name.

"*Well, I figured the better known you are the more famous Red is,*" said Ruby. "*Besides, maybe you'll attract a few honkies.*"

"*Or a few of dem waitresses!*" cackled Red.

Inside, the drummer and the bass player who were both black had already arrived and set up. They were on the stage jamming with each other. Marty wheeled his Fender Super Reverb amplifier up to the stage and set up. It didn't take him long and he had his guitar out and strapped on in a few minutes.

Red sat down while Ruby went to get him some bourbon and to find the soundman. This wasn't the first time Red Rose had played the Boarding House.

"*Hi ya Ruby,*" said the soundman.

"*Hey, Paul, how you doing baby?*" Ruby asked nicely.

She was always very cordial to the man who ran the sound because she knew so much depended on them putting out for you.

"*Pretty good, can't complain, been a couple of years, hasn't it?*"

"*Yeah, yeah, I guess it has. We got an additional member.*"

"*Yeah, I saw it on the poster,*" said Paul. "*Who is he? One of Red's buddies? From Chicago?*"

"*No, no, he's a kid, that's him on stage.*" She pointed to the young man in the fedora bending over his amplifier and adjusting the dials. "*Name's Marty May, good guitar player.*"

"*Oh yeah? Where's he from?*"

"*Oh...Texas I think.*" She figured Texas had more blues roots then New Jersey."

"*Well, we better do a sound check,*" said Paul. "*We open the doors in an hour.*"

Ruby helped her father on to the stage, set up a Stool for him to sit on and adjusted his microphone. She took his National Steel Guitar out of the case and handed it to him. He didn't jam with the other musicians. It was rare that he played when he wasn't getting paid for it.

The soundman was at the back of the hall by the mixing board. "*Okay, you might as well go into a number. I'll just do the sound as you go along.*"

Ruby got off the stage and went and stood by the soundman. Blind Red Rose just held up his hand and the other musicians stopped playing. Then he pounded his foot on the ground four times to count off. By the first verse Paul had the sound down. He'd worked with Red before and he knew how he, or rather Ruby, liked it. Very dry and natural - no echo or anything. He and Ruby stood looking up at the stage judging the sound.

"He ain't bad," said the soundman.

"Well, shit, he's been playing the blues for fifty years,"   said Ruby. "Whada ya expect?"

"No, not Red, the kid. He's really pretty good. Reminds me of early Eric Clapton when he was with The Yardbirds or John Mayall."

"Yeah, he does," agreed Ruby though she had only a faint idea of what these groups sounded like. She didn't listen to a lot of white music. Especially white blues. Why should she, when her daddy was the real thing? And she resented the money that the white groups made playing second-hand blues.

"Wow, he's really good!" said Paul after Marty finished a lead.

"He's okay," said Ruby. "He's got a ways to go."

But this was just her way of talking and avoiding being let down further down the road disappointment for she knew that he was very special and that she probably wouldn't be able to hold on to him forever.

After the sound check, Ruby went up on stage to help her father.

"How did it sound?" asked Marty. "I'm putting some more treble on my amp - did I cut through?"

"Sounds fine," said Ruby. "But there's one problem."

"What's that?" asked Marty.

"That cheap tin ring you wearing. It shines too much - you better take it off during the show so it don't distract the audience." She laughed. "Find a waitress with a finer collection of men's jewelry."

But Marty didn't take it off and by the time he left Ruby and Red Rose a few years later he was wearing four or five rings every time he played. Just like Ringo Starr.

Chapter 6

On weekend nights, Inger asked me to come down to the Follies with her and do a little crowd baiting. She'd stand at the edge of the runway and I'd come out of the audience with a stack of dollar bills that she'd given me before the show and stick them in her G-string and in her bra or stockings depending on what she was wearing or rather, left wearing. It's an old scheme in her trade and it works - other guys would follow my lead and stock bills in her outfit too, and sometimes using five ten or even twenty-dollar bills.

At first it all just seemed like good clean fun, as Inger was so fond of describing her work. And hanging out at The Follies was new for me and I'd go to the movies on Broadway when I wanted to get out of there for a while. I'd hang out in the dressing room and I saw more tits and ass than I had in my whole life and I'd ask myself why this couldn't have happened when I was fifteen or sixteen and desperately needed this course in female anatomy - I would have saved a fortune on Playboys.

There were all types of girls working at The Follies.

The only prerequisite was a fairly nice body though the stage-lights could certainly hide a load of imperfection. There's really no such thing as a perfect body. For some of the girls it was a good thing too, for they would have tracks on their arms that needed to be camouflaged by the stage lights. But Inger said girls with those problems didn't last too long. Most of the regulars were girls like Inger, career strippers, some with kids, who appreciated the good money and had no desire to be secretaries. Mostly girls from out of town, the South or Midwest, who had dreams of being a part of the nightlife in this great city. And The Follies realized these dreams, just barely. In the beginning this was all new and titillating and fun for me but then I could feel it starting to change after a few weeks. I started to resent the customers; if one got too fresh with Inger when he was sticking money in her G-string I wanted to belt him, though I never would. And when she was totally naked except for her high-heels and boa and would take out her gold rug and announce   the "vertical portion of the show" it got so that I would have to leave and go sit in the dressing room until was over or maybe even leave the premises altogether and go sit in a movie. I didn't want to see Inger with her legs spread wide apart while the men in the audience whistled and cheered her on.

One late Saturday night, in the cab coming home, after an especially wild night, I couldn't hide my feelings anymore. "You know, Inger, I don't know how much more of this I can take."

She misunderstood me. "I know what you mean, sugar, I got so many singles up there in my bra tonight that I felt like a money tree when I came off stage! Where were all the big spenders with twenties and fifties?" And she laughed some more.

"No, no ... I mean I don't think I want to come to The Follies with you anymore. I don't want to play Judas-goat and I don't want to hang around there all the time ... and I don't want to watch you undressing for other men anymore either"

"Oh," she seemed a little taken back. "Well... I know it can get boring for you, sugar. Believe me, I get bored too. It's just for the money, you know, really the result is like any other job." She sounded defensive. "Why don't you stay away a while and I'll think up a few new twists to my act so that you'll see something different next time you come." I couldn't imagine what new tricks she could come up with; it seemed pretty cut and dried to me. But I didn't say anything else.

She told the driver to pull up at a twenty-four-hour McDonald's. Inger virtually lived on cheeseburgers and from the shape her body was in she was living proof that any prejudice against junk food was totally unfounded.

We were sitting on her brass bed watching TV when it started nagging me again. I just couldn't seem to let it go.

"You know, what I was saying before, Inger ... it's not your show being boring or anything...it's just watching you watching THEM watching you. It's just really starting to bother me. I didn't think it would, but it does," I said.

She was digging into a packet of large fries and scratching something off a little card McDonald's gave her to see if she had won anything. "Sugar-Honey-Iced-Tea!" she said when her card revealed a blank. She turned to met "Don't you let it bother you, sugar, it doesn't mean anything. I don't hurt no one and no one hurts me...and I make enough money to afford gourmet meals like this for the two of us." She laughed. "As far as I'm concerned, it's just..."

"... Good, clean fun? Well not for me it isn't. I

don't know', it just doesn't seem right. Especially when you're lying on that rug just spreading your legs for everyone to see ... it bothers me just to think of it. It just... isn't right ... it's immoral or something."

She stopped eating and pointed an accusing finger at me. "I do believe we've found a member of the moral majority right here in our midst!"

"I'm no puritan," I said, "It's just that now ... I care about you ... it's different now." I shrugged. "I don't want to get in over my head ... not be able to handle this. I don't know, sometimes it just seems so weird...that's all." I decided not to push the point but I guess I had pushed a few buttons in Inger already.

"You're just jealous! You wish that you could be up there instead me! I remember when I saw you down in Atlanta - you use to shake your ass pretty good trying
to turn those little girls on. And those leather pants were tight enough not to leave much to the imagination either!"

"At least I had my clothes on."

"Well not everyone's born with the talent you have, Marty. Some of us have to get by the best we can!"

She was crying and I never saw that before and I felt like shit. Who the hell was I to start passing judgment on her life? Here she had been feeding me for the last couple of weeks, and I had been almost living at her apartment, was a hell of a lot more comfortable than my own. And for the first time in a long time a woman had been making me feel like a real man. Whatever that is...

"I'm sorry, Inger." I tried to put my arm around her
but she pushed me away. Her own words came back to me: I realized that there was a person living inside her body too, like she had said about the customers at The Follies. Someone whose self-respect floated on a lot more unstable craft than I had imagine. And I had done my best to swamp it.

"I'm really sorry ... I don't know what got into me. You're right, I am just frustrated about my own career ... I'm so sorry. Can we just forget about it?"

But she was still weeping.

"Listen, I don't know what I was thinking. Its just that I think I...I love you," I finally said.

"Well, it took you long enough to say it," she said still whimpering.

"I do, Inger, I really do, you know I do. I'm a jerk. Say its OK?" I begged. "I promise not to mention your work again." I kissed her softly on the cheek where an ash-colored tear had run down and left a track just like the Smoky Robinson song.

What I had been about to say to her and didn't was that I was starting to have these dreams, that I didn't understand and that were worrying me when I would awake. Sexual dreams, but uncomfortable ones, filled with frustration. Sometimes she'd be in them and sometimes she wouldn't but when she was it was always in her Follies outfit. We'd be making love on a motorcycle and then I'd realize how fast we were traveling and that we were gonna crash, and in one dream I was back at my high school reunion, with Inger in a G-string and I was trying to cover her up and there were snakes outside and ... it was awful. Before I'd always had a wonderful dream life regardless what was going on during my waking hours. But now I was waking up anxious and no longer with a hard-on. And I had been doing that as long as I could remember. As a matter of fact, it used to be quite embarrassing when I would share a room with another musician while on the road.

But I could hardly make Inger understand that she was disturbing my deep sleep. I don't think that to a girl like her, who had left home with nothing and scratched her way to her position of independence and freedom that a few bad dreams would constitute any great sacrifice.

"I forgive you, Marty. But I don't understand you, I really don't." She shook her head sadly.

"You're not alone ... I don't understand myself, either."

"I mean, you were telling me about that horrible high school reunion you went to, and how you never wanted to turn out like those people and all. And in a way you were telling me that you were better than all of them."

"I never did say that, I never said I was better than them, I just..."

"Well you didn't have to say it, Marty, but it's how you felt. You gotta admit it! When you saw what had happened to that cheerleader ... "

"Betty Klein?"

"Yeah, her. And you told me how she had really let herself go to hell getting all fat and suburban looking and everything. Well, what you were really saying was that could never happen to you because you're so...'Classless and Free!"

"That's by John Lennon!" I said amazed.

"Damn straight it's by John Lennon. I'm not as ignorant as you think, Marty. I had a few records other then yours, you know."

"I never said you were ignorant!"

"I know a lot of John Lennon songs! How could anyone who cares enough about rock 'n roll to take in a mongrel like you NOT know a few John Lennon songs? And you know how the rest of that line goes Marty? *But You're all fucking peasants as far as I can see*! It was the first time I had heard her say 'fuck'. She said it with a vengeance She had stopped crying and started fixing her face. "Because you know something Marty? I think you picked up all the same bullshit values as the rest of your classmates! You may have the heart of a rock 'n roller - but you're square!"

"Square! I am not!"

"You sure are, Marty! You can take the boy out of suburbia but you can't take the...lawn-care program out of the boy! You're still worrying what the neighbors are gonna think!"

"That's ridiculous," I said. Or was it?

Inger stood up and faced me. She was still holding a French fry in her hand, which she jabbed at me.

"And since you're getting your conscience clean, I got something I want to say about you and your square
marriage that you've never gotten over."

"Of course I've gotten over it!"

"Bullshit!   You just took that ring off your finger and
put it around your mind! You still don't want to admit the truth about your little preppie bitch, Marty. She was just slumming, and you didn't know it because you were imagining yourself to be something you never were and never will be."

"And what's that?" I said angrily.

"Respectable!" she said with finality. "And better
than everyone else and entitled to more of the good life.
And you know something? In your own way, you were slumming too, because you think you're cooler then everybody else!"

"I DO NOT think I'm cooler than everyone else!"

"Well, that's the same reason why all of a sudden
you can't take me shaking my tits and ass in front of all
the old men at The Follies - because you don't want to think that
those guys might have their needs and wants and dreams too or
are you the only one who's entitled to a piece of the American
dream?"

"That's got nothing to do with it. It's just that ... I love you,
Inger ... and I don't want to share you with anybody." I took her
hand. "That's all," I said softly.

"Oh Marty, I love you too, sugar. And if we love each other
there ain't anybody who can take any of that away if we don't let
them. I got a job to do and you got a job to do too. You gotta start
rocking' again!" She sat back down next to me, put her arms
around me, and gave me a kiss. One thing I had to say about
Inger, she didn't hold a grudge. "But I'm serious when I tell you
that you. Better start getting to know yourself, Marty, or else
you're gonna spend your whole life living alone, with a stranger."

"Well ... who am I?"

"You're a rock star who's not exactly enjoying the best of
times lately. But all you gotta do, sugar, is expand your audience
and get some more fans, because you got one big one already."

"Thanks,"   I said.

"But things could be worse, couldn't they?" She put her hand
on my leg.

"They sure could, Inger ... they could be a hell of a whole lot
worse," I said hoping her hand would move a little higher up my
leg.

"Now eat your Big Mac before it gets cold!" she said
and continued to dig into her French-fries.

Part Five
Sainthood
New York City
1983

Chapter 1

Inger got her job in Atlantic City. In a way, I was glad because as much as I tried I could not stop these weird dreams completely, though they were occurring less frequently with less distressing aftermath. But I was sure that they were caused by her work at The Follies, and her job in Atlantic City was hardly of the same ilk; she'd be showing her tits and nothing more. It was almost like she was becoming a nun.

As she had warned me, her training for joining a bevy of beautiful breasts would take a couple of weeks to learn the steps. And then a few more weeks working on probation; a little over a month in all. Of course, I was not happy that she was going away, I would miss her terribly, but she reminded me in her usual optimistic fashion that soon I'd be going out on tour and we had to get used to being apart.

I knew of no such tour: the girl sure had faith. Also, she said that I better make up my mind if I was going to move in with her or not; she didn't seem to want a halfway affair. I knew I could easily get out of my present lease; the landlord would relish the opportunity to raise the rent but I was frightened of taking such a step. Inger was a wonderful girl and I truly believed I loved her but the last girl I had shared an apartment with had been Barbara. And looked what happened

Then Inger asked me some telling questions about if I thought I'd ever get married again and this really shook me, I gotta admit. But I told her I'd make up my mind (and I guess she could change her own if she wanted to) by the time she returned from Atlantic City. I think what she was really getting at was that she would hardly want to be commuting back and forth to Atlantic City every ten days if there was really no reason for her to be in New York. The most deciding feature in her life to date had been her practicality. So I had to decide whether or not I had the guts to become her reason. And she mine. Our parting was sad; how else could it be? We had found each other like two survivors of a tornado and we both feared that the wind would once again pick up and deposit each of us at distant ports. She left me the keys to her apartment and gave me a few hundred dollars to eat on which I said I couldn't possibly accept but finally did after she said that she'd start crying if I didn't.

Hotel bars are lucky for me. Or maybe they just make me feel lucky: like the Oak Bar at the Plaza with its large mural of the Pulitzer fountains or The Polo Lounge at The Beverly Hills Hotel with its unreal talk of enormous movie deals that probably end up as TV movies. These hotel bars probably made me feel lucky because usually someone else was picking up the check on a company expense account. There was no bar at The Sunset Marquis; maybe that's why things turned out so rotten out there.

But hotel bars are usually full of movement and travel and strange languages. People drink more when they travel; it starts on the plane. And survival instinct makes travelers more perceptive to their surroundings than in their hometown taverns so everybody's antennae are out and the air is charged. New York bars are especially full of foreign language the rest of the city. From the Arab sheiks to the South American cocaine smugglers, the only people with no money in this town are the ones who speak English.

A famous philosopher once said that it was very important not to confuse movement with action. Or was that Dear Abby? Maybe there's a relationship between these words and hotel bars. Where does all the loud talk and overzealous laughter end up? In the flash of a credit card and a hangover next morning? But forgoing that philosophic advice, I have gone to hotel bars looking for nothing but action on occasion and once, I believe it was in Milwaukee the night desk clerk called me and my new found travel-mate up in the wee hours saying that the chandelier in the room below was moving, what the hell were we doing? Tap Dancing, I replied.

So perhaps action can lead to movement after all. And given the immensity of the universe, who is to say that a swaying chandelier is less significant than a trip to a far off galaxy? So much for philosophy. And speaking of hotels I'll take the Ritz up in Boston. Strange, you say, for a rock In roller such as myself? Wouldn't I rather prefer someplace more conducive to dropping TVs out the window, naked girls running down the halls holding bottles of Champagne to cover themselves, than the staid Ritz, home of blue-blooded and blue-haired old ladies?

No, because it's the opposites in life that attract me, the juxtaposition of flaming youth (that once was me) and staid conservatism. To be truthful, I've only stayed at The Ritz on two occasions and always by myself and both times on promotional visits to Boston and the nearby suburbs to visit radio stations and do ID's which are, "Hello out there! This is Marty May and you're listening to the rockin' sounds of radio station ... " And more importantly, to eat lunch with the program director and then do three or four interviews with fresh-faced college reporters changing my bio for each one so as not to die from terminal boredom. One might be surprised to know that in a business renowned for its nightlife, most of the real business goes on during the day. This is when promotion men make daily pilgrimages to the world of FM and AM radio and try to make believers out of infidels, a world of constant religious fervor and quickly changing idols.

So my nights at The Ritz were my own. It was all on the company tab so I really had a ball. I would eat in the dining room by myself, drinking fine wine and casting flirtatious glances toward the blue-haired Brahmins who I knew could support me in a style I could grow accustomed to if only given the chance. I would sit at the bar and make small talk with the bartender who I think thought I was gay judging by the length of my hair which just goes to show how out of it he was. Everyone knows that gays have short hair and straights long. Once I sat in the breakfast room and spotted Lillian Hellman also eating alone but mostly chain smoking and oh, how I wanted to approach her and ask her about her days with Dashiell Hammet who wrote *The Thin Man*. But I decided, no, here was a woman who had gone through it all, been forced to take a job at Macy's under an assumed name during the 'Scoundrel Days' of Senator Joe McCarthy and if nothing else she had a right to be alone with her thoughts and memories of good friends and lovers now done, I suppose. There was a sense of dignity about her that I have never forgotten, a sense of survival, totally unpretentious but full of class and realism and a large dose of sadness. I wondered what she must have thought of Jane Fonda's portrayal of her in the film Julia. That must be strange. I do hope I live to see The Marty May Story come to screen. I'd like to see Brando in the title role, of course.

One shining afternoon I was having a drink in the lounge of The Gramercy Park Hotel with an old friend who had finally made it big. He had struggled for years in bar bands up in Boston before his group finally got a record contract. He visited me during one of my stays at The Ritz and was awed and depressed at the heights of my grandeur; he being in a rush to go play six sets in a Cambridge college bar that night. But this was well behind him now, for his group's debut album had gone platinum (over a million copies sold) with virtually no promotion from their record company at all, Wow the world was theirs. I had heard that he was in New York to record his new album and when I mentioned this to Inger before she split, she suggested that I should certainly call him and see if I could get some studio work. She was always encouraging me to start hanging out with more musicians and less accountants, though I was not really hanging out with either a great deal. She said that no one ever wrote a song about a lawyer.

So I called my friend but had no luck as far as studio work was concerned. He did say that he'd take me out for a drink on his newly acquired American Express card like I had done for him years before; which reminded me that time was running out. If I didn't send them some more money soon, Karl Malden was gonna come after, I'm sure. But I seemed to care less and less. After all, even our newly elected president had warned us all against the horrors of credit.

Outside The Gramercy Park Hotel were parked two tour busses with darkened windows and PRIVATE written in front. I don't know why this was necessary - I couldn't imagine any commuter mistaking them for public transportation. On the sides of these tour buses were decoratively painted titles like HITSVILLE EXPRESS or MOJO MOVER or STAR COMFORT II (I hate to imagine the fate of COMFORT I) These grand vehicles were a concept co-opted from country music stars who had been traveling in this fashion from state fair to amusement park and then back to the Grand Ol' Opry since the days of Hank Williams. Actually, Hank Williams traveled in a Cadillac where he OD in the back seat on new years day thus giving him semi-rock star status. But most country music performers used these buses to get to the people' because more often than not there was no airport within fifty miles. That rock In rollers are using the same mode of transportation can mean nothing else except a true clue as to what 'the peoples, choice in music is today.

The Gramercy Park Hotel had become a haven for visiting rock 'n rollers because of its proximity to halls like Madison Square Garden, The Palladium, and The Ritz. Also, the uptown hotels seemed to have reserved all their rooms and adjusted their prices to suit visiting members of OPEC. In Gramercy Park itself, which is right outside the entrance to the hotel, is a statue of Edwin Booth, great actor and brother of John Wilkes Booth. I suppose this homage to a member of the Booth family must have seemed right damn neighborly, to any of the number of Southern rock bands who have reached preeminence lately and have the occasion to stay at the hotel.

The bar in The Gramercy Park Hotel has no special name except 'The Lounge' and I know this because in the lobby was one of those little sign-boards with white movable letters and a black background that said "APPEARING IN THE LOUNGE" And it was funny that in this bar, full of mostly rock musicians, should be this over-the-top pop singer sitting behind a piano wailing out *I am a lineman for the county* with an emotional investment that would have driven Glen Campbell bankrupt.

That lounge was full of rockers of all shapes and sizes: New Wave, Heavy-Metal, a few dinosaurs (like me), and one or two strange hair-colored commercial punk rockers. I do emphasize the word 'commercial' because from what I read is happening in L.A. these days which oddly enough has become the bastion of PUNK, and even managed to produce a unique California evolutionary form of SURF PUNKS who are even more violent than the original to release a true PUNK in a civilized hotel would probably be akin to releasing a school of Piranha in the YMCA swimming pool on a crowded summer Saturday. If this sounds reactionary from a counter-culture hero such as myself ... well, obviously someone shifted the rules of conduct necessary for a Rebel Without a Cause life-style back into the Cro-Magnon period when I wasn't looking or was too stoned too notice But I shouldn't refer to myself as a dinosaur; Inger tells me that I'm always putting myself down and that if I didn't watch my ass I won't get laid for a week. The girl put the fear of God into me.

But now Inger was gone to the cultural hopes and aspirations of all New Jersey: Atlantic City, and I was sitting in the lounge by myself. The girl sitting at the piano was singing *Do you know the way to San Jose* and I wished only wished I had Burt

Bacharach's phone number so I could call him and let him know someone was murdering his songs.

"Hey Marty!" someone shouted at me from across the lounge. I waved and he came over loaded with the *accoutrements* of rock stardom: styled hair, expensive-looking-leather-jacket, and the latest digital-watch. And most importantly a set of Sony Walkman earphones casually gracing his neck.

"How ya doin' man! Great to see you!" he said as he reached the table. I got up to shake his hand - nervousness always brings the formality in out in me. "Sit down," he said patting my shoulder. Take a load off them expensive cowboy boots!" I was glad he noticed my Ostrich Tony Lama's because they were one of the few things I had to show for my American Express excess.

"Hi ya, Johnny," I said. "You sure look healthy, wealthy and wise...well, at least the second two!" I noticed the dark circles under his eyes. But in "our crowd" pallor is a true sign of affluence.

"Been partying a little too heavy and I guess it shows but I can't complain, Marty. And yourself? How ya doin?" He asked brightly, searching for the waitress.

"Not bad, not bad." I searched for something to brag about. "I got a new girlfriend," I said. "A real looker as they say."

"Oh yeah? That's great. It's about time you got laid," said Johnny jokingly. "What does she do?"

"A ... dancer, she's a real dancer," I replied. I was about to make up some story about the Joffrey Ballet. I don't know why. Worried about the neighbors? "Well actually... she's a stripper - an exotic dancer...she's pretty hot!" I smiled. I felt proud of myself. It was the first time I had told someone I knew about Inger and it didn't feel bad. I didn't want to betray Inger.

"Well all right!" said Johnny. "Who would have believed that an old man like you could handle that kind of action! I'll drink to that!" And we did - a couple of times.

"So tell me, Johnny," I asked later after a few drinks loosened us up. "What's the biggest difference?"

"Well, Marty, I'd say that the biggest difference is that you seem to drink a lot more - and a lot faster than I remember." he said sarcastically. "But that's okay - so do I. You know how it is, the pressure and all!" He laughed. The diamond in his ear caught the light and sparkled.

"No, no...not the biggest difference in me! I'm talking about the biggest difference in you - you finally made it. You're a big star now! So, how does it feel?"

'What are you asking me for? Marty May was a household name for years while I was still playing Sam and Dave tunes for fraternity parties up in Beantown. You know what it's like, Marty," he said a bit impatiently.

"Yeah, yeah, I know...but things change in this business and this business changes everyone in a different way too. It makes some people find religion after years of hell raising and for others, they can lose all traces of any beliefs at all. I mean...like take me, I'll always remember when I first kind of made it or got my first big advance or something. I remember how shocked I was at not having to take the subway anymore 'cause I could finally afford taxis. Although these days I'm back on the Lexington Avenue Local again.

Johnny laughed but I should have picked up that something in him was uncomfortable with this discussion. It was all a little too new to him to begin this kind of analyzing.

"Well sure, you're right, Marty. It's a whole new world for me now - no doubt about it. I mean, I don't even tune my own guitar anymore - my roadie does it! And, let's see, what else? Well, I can walk into a music store and charge anything I want now and before I use to have to hustle for a new set of strings."

"Your wardrobe has improved considerably, too," I said.   "I remember when you came to see me at The Ritz - they almost wouldn't let you come up.'" I laughed and he did too but I think I was patronizing him and he was aware of it.

"Yeah, yeah ... I never could figure out why you stayed in that place, it's full of ol' ladies. We prefer The Sheraton Towers. It's more exclusive." Point made. "But it's funny ... " He stopped talking.

"What's funny?" I wanted him to go on. I was getting vicarious thrills. It made me think back to better days.

"Well ... it's funny ... but Marty, I gotta say that it makes me kind of uncomfortable to talk about it, ya know? Like, I think if I talk too much about it or think too much about everything that's happened ... that it will all just disappear like it did to you." I said nothing. "That I'll be back in that broken down Econo-line Van full of amps, drums and empty beer cans and heading out to some dump to play six sets of Led Zeppelin covers." He smiled. "You know, you could start playing the bars up there now, Marty." I hope he meant this as a joke. "There's a big void since we became too famous."

"I don't have a Van." I said bitterly.

"But also," Johnny went on. "And this is really strange, but I never used to worry about money and now I think about it all the time. Before I never had any so I didn't care but now I'm paranoid that someone might be ripping me off in some way. I swear, we spend more time with our accountants than we do with our girlfriends." He took a sip of his drink and looked at me sheepishly. "I guess all I'm saying, Marty, is that I didn't expect to see this much so soon."

I had forced him into this position of clarifying our respective places on the pecking order. But I didn't like it, I wanted to get back on the same level. I was noticing that he didn't look entirely comfortable with his new found fame and fortune; he was looking at his fancy watch too often - and he didn't seem too at ease in his silky looking suit. And his ear looked a little red around the diamond stud. It was all new to him and he was touchy about it. It was natural I guess; I don't suppose I had been much different - I don't suppose anyone really is. It's hard to face those who knew you way back when. Maybe that's the reason I stayed away from Ruby and Red Rose all those years. I tried a 'big-brother' approach.

"Well, you know Johnny, when you make it on your first album its all gravy. There's no monstrous recording costs of the two or three albums that came before and went nowhere to pay back. I know a singer who after five stiffs finally went platinum. He didn't made one dime in royalties because he owed his label so much money! And he didn't write his own songs so he was really screwed - no publishing royalties either. So, consider yourself lucky. Besides, at your age you BETTER make it fast!" I laughed; I was at least two or three years older than Johnny.

"Oh yeah? Look who I 's talking. They're gonna cart you off to the guitarists nursing home any day now!" he said in thinly disguised fun. "But seriously, I know what you're talking about: our first album cost about twenty-five thousand bucks for everything. And I bet we've spent almost that much so far, including hotels and plane tickets, on the next one already and we haven't even finished laying down the basic tracks."

Well, let me give you one piece of advice, Johnny."
I pointed my finger at him for emphasis. "Don't worry so much about what others are ripping you off for - worry about yourself. Hold off on the expensive apartments and the little foreign cars and the fancy restaurants - it will all still be there when you retire and have the time to appreciate it. And let the 'nose candy' wait forever." Too late, I knew what an asshole I must sound like.

Johnny gave me a long sarcastic look as he shook his head, finally saying: "Some people never change. Gee whiz, thanks a lot for telling me all this, Ol' buddy, but have no fear. You see, while I was scraping by all those years up in Boston and living on fuckin' Big Macs and sometimes having to get a job as a dishwasher or a messenger or some shit, I had this friend...sort of... of," He said, emphasizing the *sort of*. "I mean, not that he really did a hell of a lot for me when he was up there acting like King Tut, but he was always nice enough to me in his own sort of way, you know, held give me tickets to his shows and copies of his records, shit like that. He didn't ever let me play on any of his records or audition for his band, though, because he only wanted real pros, ya know?"

"I didn't say a word and glanced away.

"So, anyway, when the rainy season finally came...well, he still hasn't dried off. But his old friends buy him a drink once in a while cause he's a good guy and a damn good guitar player. So don't worry, I'm not gonna let history repeat itself. It won't happen to me."

We drank in silence for a while. And then Johnny said that he had to get to the studio and even though my, "Oh yeah? Which one?" was highly enthusiastic, he didn't invite me along.

Now that Inger was gone I didn't have a hell of a lot to do. I thought of phone calls to make; I called George Peter Humboldt at The Record Plant and when he wasn't there I left Inger's number so he could call me back, although I doubted he would ever call. I called Tom Dunn to tell him thanks again and he told me about the latest 'Surf Punk' riots in Hollywood. He didn't seem concerned, just called it the latest fad to hit LA though more and more of these kids seemed to be dying from OD's then he remembered happening back in the Sixties He said it's more 'hard-ball' now. Surf Punks - Hard Ball - the whole world is turning jock

Must mean a war is coming. Because of the little cash Inger had left me, and what was left of my session money from L.A., even after I paid my rent and phone and electricity and American Express, I had a lot more spending money than usual. So, I could do a lot more hanging out. After all, Inger had encouraged me to be with musicians so I didn't feel too guilty when I strolled into TRAX around midnight one weekday night when it would not be too crowded and I would be sure to get in for free. Just when I was walking down the stairs to TRAX basement location, I saw a familiar face coming the other way. And he saw me too. He seemed to be alone.

"Marty May! How's my favorite star!"

"Hey Joe!" I yelled back.

"You just coming in?" he asked.

"Yeah..."

"Well, hell! Let's have a drink - I could use a little company." He turned around and we headed down the stairs.

Joe Lippell was one of the most famous and successful managers in rock In roll. He'd come up the long way - I think he started off as a roadie for the Beatles on their first American tour. After that, he had gone on to become a booking agent and then A&R director for a major label. But he found that being an A&R director had less to do with 'Artist & Repertoire and more to do with costs and budgets and company politics so he quit. Finally, he started his own management company. It seemed to be successful almost from day one.

He now managed SAINTHOOD, the all blond heavy-metal band whose angelic poses were at this very moment gracing the circus magazine calendar hanging in my kitchen. Their latest album had sold over three million copies - more than all of mine, and a lot of other people's, combined. I think SAINTHOOD was from the Midwest somewhere. Lately this seems to be where most giant American rock bands come from. I guess the word that the American rock 'n roll dream was over hadn't reached them yet. Kind of like The Battle of New Orleans being still fought when the war of 1812 was already over. I had known and respected Joe Lippell for years. He was one of that rare breed in the business end of rock that really liked to go out at night and be with music and the people who made it. You'd be surprised how many of these guys are at home in front of the TV come six o'clock. And, probably forbid their kids to play The Sex Pistols. All record execs say they admire the "ears" of John Hammond who discovered Billy Holiday and Bob Dylan but nobody spends the time in the studio or hangs out in the clubs like he did. My last album had been with the same company that Joe Lippell was A&R director of and after my album didn't go to number one with a bullet but rather to number one-sixteen with an anchor, they decided to drop me. Or at least that's one of the reasons I guess, notwithstanding my missing appearance in the spotlight at their convention a year or so before. When Joe heard I was to be dropped he had really gone to the wall for me but it was useless. They dropped me anyway. But he proved to be one of the few people I know in this business who ever put his job on the line for something he believed in. Too bad it was me. He looked like a rich manager should: he was balding, he had a beard, he had a gold Rolex watch and a gold chain with a gold and diamond musical note hanging from it around his neck. I was surprised he had on designer jeans I didn't think they made them that large. From the look of his waistline he didn't appear to be eating too badly. We sat at the bar at TRAX. He ordered a Martini and I followed his lead and had one myself, which is what I usually do when I can't think of what to drink. I felt good to be sitting next to one of the real 'heavies' in the biz. I hoped people would notice it. We small talked quickly and Joe drank down his Martini in a few gulps. I sensed he was preoccupied.

"Joe, did I ever thank you for that studio work you gave me with that girl singer of yours? I really appreciated it." (In fact, I knew that I had called him afterwards but maybe if I mentioned it again he would come up with something else. It had been over a year ago.) But he didn't seem to hear what I said. "Uh ... did anything ever happen to that demo of hers?" I tried to get his attention. "She was pretty good, I thought. A New Wave Linda Ronstadt."

"What Marty?" He looked up. "Excuse me, I was thinking about something else. What did you say? Demo? Whose demo?" He smiled and tried to concentrate and appear interested but I could tell he wasn't.

"That girl ... uh ... Judy something, the one that I played with about six months ago," I reminded him. "Her demo?"

Oh, her No, nothing happened I had to drop her," he said sadly.

"Oh, that's too bad ... I thought she had a good energy. What happened? Couldn't get a label interested?" I was surprised; with her talent and his clout I had figured it to be a sure thing.

"Oh no, that wasn't the problem Marty. There was
a lot of interest. I turned her on to another manager - a friend of mine. I heard that she just started recording an album out on the coast either for EMI or Capital. She's gonna go places - talented girl - lots of ambition."

I didn't understand. "Than why did you drop her?"

"Marty I just didn't have the time...or the concentration for that matter. I got my hands full with Paul. Believe me - he's a full-time job. Twenty-four hours a day." He rolled his eyeballs, none too happily. "A full time job," he repeated slowly for emphasis.

Paul was, of course, Paul Saint, the lead singer, songwriter and 'image' of Sainthood. He was a major star. The gossip columns treated his life as a continuing romantic saga; he had been rumored to be dating every blond of the year since Farrah Fawcett.

He was the only member of Sainthood whose name was at all publicized; I think there were only a few original members of the group left. Not that it mattered, for Paul Saint wrote all the songs, sang all the songs, and got all the paternity suits which, by the way, I just read he had taken out insurance against - with Lloyds of London no less! For all intents and purposes it was a solo act. Paul was known for his outrageous costumes and makeup: on one album cover he wore the outfit of a priest and had his face up made up like Brigitte Bardot. His look had gone anywhere from Charles Chaplin to Adolph Hitler depending upon the theme of his latest album. His Hitler phase was not greatly appreciated by B'nai Brith so he did a benefit concert to raise money for planting trees in Israel. He came on stage dressed as Moses.

For the last three years Sainthood albums had gone straight to the top of the charts. Their ascent and my descent intersected somewhere. It wasn't really my kind of music - it was real pop - heavy metal meant for young kids. The layers of guitar, drums and voices on their albums was so dense and thick that I could never grasp any real personality or musical point of view. But for what it was, I had to admit that they did it well. Once, I had even found myself humming one of their hits in the shower without realizing what the song was. When it finally came to me I was shocked - I didn't think I knew one of their songs! Now, that "So how's Paul Saint doing?" I asked Joe innocently.

"Oh great, Marty! Just great! He'll leave a nice amount of cash when he dies," Joe said sarcastically.

"When he dies? Is he sick or something?"

"He's sick all right, Marty - sick in the head. He just enjoys being miserable and fucked up all the time. Joe shook his head sadly. "And there ain't a fuckin' thing I can do,"

"What's wrong with him?" I was full of jealousy.

"Is he having trouble spending his money? Wasn't his last album a smash?"

"Sure, it was a smash," said Joe. "And so were the Mercedes and the Jaguar the week it went to number one. He gulped again on his Martini; it seemed to calm him down. "I'm sorry I'm getting so carried away, Marty, it's just that it breaks my heart seeing him do all this to himself after how hard we've both worked. I just came from his lawyer and we were trying to untangle his latest 'problem'," Joe said cryptically

"Drugs?"

Joe nodded. "They found some shit when he crashed the Jaguar. We're getting the bust reduced to driving while under the influence."

"I didn't know he had a problem," I said. "He must keep it pretty quiet." I was having trouble feeling sorry for Paul Saint. "All I ever read about is his latest blond."

"Oh, you know that's all bullshit, Marty. Me and his press agent just drag him to some party long enough for him to get his picture taken. Whatever story goes with that picture is pure fiction. He doesn't have time for romance. You wouldn't believe it, the way he carries on - he spends more money on cocaine than it takes to put a kid through college - and I know! I just went over his personal finances last week - we're talking over a grand a week! And then he gets so wired on coke, that after staying up for days on end he's got to drop about three Quaaludes so he can sleep for twenty-four hours. And then when he wakes up the cycle just begins all over again." Joe went on. "And I gotta tell you, when I first started managing Sainthood just before the first album, he was the straightest guy in the world. All he wanted to do was work his ass off and learn all he could about this business. He figured that being a hick from the Midwest he had to try twice as hard as everybody else - and he did. And now I need some kind of a stoned interpreter to get him to even speak to me about anything serious."

Joe had his head in his hands with both elbows resting on the bar. He look defeated. "And the thing is, Marty, I just know ... that some night ... God forbid," His eyes looked upward in that Italian Catholic way and he crossed himself. I'm gonna get that phone call to come pick up the pieces after he finally goes too far. I know it's gonna happen and I'm just dreading it, Marty. I've worked too damn hard in this fuckin' business to have that be my legacy. It's just not fair - not to him or to me. I can't sleep nights thinking about what he's out there doing to himself."

I knew that Joe Lippell's concern had little to do with business or money. He was not the stereotypical greedy rock In roll manager or some kind of heartless monster. He took pride in what he did; in his success. He smiled at me and put his hand on my shoulder.

"Well anyway, enough of my tale of woe - I talk too much. It's great to see you Marty. You look good. You know, I give you a lot of credit for keeping yourself together the last couple of years since you were dropped. (Together? The compliment shocked me.)

"You know, speaking of Paul Saint," said Joe. "Did you know that he really admired you, Marty? He was the one who recommended you for that studio work if you want to know the truth. If things had worked out, he was gonna produce that girl. But he wasn't even at the studio during the demo. See what I mean? But anyway, he really thinks you got talent. I thought you'd like to know."

"No ... I didn't know that, Joe. I didn't think he knew me from Adam." Our music was so dissimilar it was hard for me to imagine he thought of me at all. But suddenly I was overcome with waves of sympathy for this suffering superstar with impeccable taste.

"Oh believe me, Marty, Paul knows his music. He wanted to be successful in the worst way and he's made Sainthood for just that purpose. I mean, he thought up the whole act with the makeup and costumes and everything, and he had the talent musically to know what's commercial and what's not. And the fuckin' guy was born with a feeling for publicity like P.T. Barnum. You gotta understand that he's a different kind of artist from you, you're much more ... organic, I think what you do just comes from the heart, you don't think about it. But Paul Saint is ... well, he's more synthetic, man-made, I guess. He was a smart kid from Dayton, Ohio who took a careful look at the market and what was out there and where he could fit in and he designed something that would work...perfectly." I couldn't argue with this.

"After the car wrecks, I talked Paul into coming down to the Bahamas with me. Just the two of us, so he could cool out. All he brought with him was an acoustic guitar. Well, it took him a few days to get straight and he drank a little heavily to make up for it but that's All right because strangely enough he can handle booze, it's mild compared to his usual diet - but then he started writing some new songs and they were just great. Just what we need to move sainthood into a little more legitimate category and not so much of a gimmick band with the makeup and all. We were both really excited, I thought held turned over a new leaf, and he wanted to get back to New York right away and start recording the next Sainthood album. But I tell you, he wasn't back here for an hour or so before one of the parasites that leech on him turned him on and he was at it again.

"I didn't even hear from him for a week. That's the real problem all these drug dealers that he hangs around with, he thinks they're his friends." Joe stared into his empty glass. "And when I finally did hear from him he could hardly remember the names of the songs he had written. I can see it now on the six o'clock news - after Paul OD's on something. I should hire a hit man to blow them all away but there's too many. The city's crawling with them, like cockroaches" he said darkly.

I didn't know what to say, maybe I'd tell him about my troubles. Or maybe I should tell him about meeting Inger Peach - that might cheer him up. Or the scam I tried to pull out at my reunion. But before I could say a word he started to look at me very strangely and tapping his finger to his temple while he began to smile.

"Marty, I've got an idea!"

"I wouldn't make a very good hired killer if that's

what you're thinking - my hands shake."

He laughed. He seemed to be formulating some kind of plan. "I got an idea that could help Paul, help me, and help you too, Marty. And I think you're just the guy for the job."

Joe leaned close to me and whispered but I don't know why; the confidential part of our conversation was over. Rona Barrett could be singing Paul Saint's troubles to the world at this very moment if the bartender at TRAX was one of her sources.

"Paul is scheduled to do a short tour in a couple of weeks. It's just East Coast and it ends with one night at Madison Square Garden - it's only about ten dates in all. The reason I booked this tour is to get Paul and the rest of the band in shape for recording. Now tell me something, Marty do you still play around? Don't I see you advertised in the club section of The Voice every once in a while?"

"Well ... I do an occasional gig when I sense that the public is really starved for some culture," I said haughtily.

"So you can throw together some backup musicians when you need to?" asked Joe. "You know where to find them?"

"Know where to find them? Are you kidding? All
I have to do is go down to the Unemployment Office - that's where the best players in all of New York seem to hang out."

Joe whispered even softer: "So how would you like The Marty May Band to open for Sainthood on this little tour coming up?"

"And play the Garden?" I said very loudly.

"Joe put a finger to his lips. "And play everywhere Sainthood plays, Marty. Where Paul Saint goes - so goes Marty May. That's the whole point. I want you to try to straighten him out a little and get him in shape for his next album. I know he really respects you - he might listen to you." Joe was excited. "Peer pressure, ya know!" He winked.

"Why would he listen to me? I'm hardly the model of success."

"Yeah, but success isn't what Paul is looking for anymore* Marty. He's got that already. If anything, he's got too much of it. He needs something to believe in again. And whether you know it or not Marty, you're the real thing. You got something to do with the dreams he had, the dreams that he believed in. And you know what they say: there's only one thing worse than your dreams 'not coming true."

"I know," I said. "When your dreams do come true." But I hardly believed this.

"You got to help me put the fear of God into him,"
said Joe. "Make him start taking all this seriously once again."

"The only fear I know Joe, is that of The American Express Company."

"Listen, if you can start off by just keeping the drug dealers away from him, that will be a major accomplishment in itself. I know you'd be a good influence Marty." Joe seemed convinced.

"A good influence? No one ever called me that before. But how could I be the opening act for Sainthood? No one will know who the hell I am. I haven't been on a tour like this for years - and you know when my last album was out."

"Don't worry, Marty. Lippell Management has quite a strong arm of hype; we'll do a real bang-up job of refreshing everybody's memories. Hey! This could be a whole new beginning for you. We'll think of some good angles - didn't you used to open for Jimi Hendrix?"

"No ... not really ... I didn't open for him. But I did meet him once!" Some things I can't lie about.

"Uh ... Joe ... there's one thing I got to ask you about this tour ... if it happens ... I hate to bring this up but ..."

"Don't worry, Marty." Joe read my mind. "You'll be paid very well - you'll probably be making more money that you have in a long time. Unless you've been dealing drugs on the side."

"Only a little smack from time to time." I smiled but I could tell Joe didn't think this was funny.

"If you need it you can even take an advance," said Joe.

"I don't want to be Paul's roadie," I said.

"Everybody will treat you like the star we all know that you should have been, Marty."

What a guy!

Chapter 2

When Inger Peach called me from Atlantic City I was like a proud schoolboy who just gotten an *A*. For those who might question this relationship between a thirty-two year old musician and a twenty two year old stripper I can only say, well ... Freud can be fun, too.

"How did you know I was gonna go out on tour?" I asked her.

"What are you talking about, sugar? What tour?" she said Inger surprised.

"When you left for Atlantic City you said that we had to get used to being separated because soon I'd be going out on tour. You remember? Well it happened."

"Oh sugar! I just had a feeling that the wheel of fate was coming 'round to your part of the cosmos again! Tell me all about it."

"Have you ever heard of Sainthood?"

"Yeah - aren't they the ones with all those costumes and makeup? And all the hits?"

"Yeah, that's them. Well last night, I ran into Joe Lippell, he's their manager. He use to be head of A&R for my last label. We're still friendly after all that time. We had a few drinks down at TRAX."

"Some friend," she said. "Didn't they drop you?"

"Yeah ... but Joe didn't really have anything to do with it. It was the accountants and the lawyers and... well, anyway, he wants me to throw a band together and go out with Sainthood as the opening act for a couple of weeks!"

"Oh sugar! That's terrific!" Then the businesswoman came out. "You're getting paid, aren't you?" she asked suspiciously.

"Sure I'm getting paid. You don't think I'd do it for free, do you?" (Though I might.) "He's giving me five hundred a week."

"He's not giving you anything, Marty. You're earning it. I'm sure you're worth every penny. They're gonna love you, probably more than that ol' Sainthood. I bet you'll steal the show, sugar!" She was giggling gleefully.

"Well, I don't know about that. Sainthood has a real loyal following. I just hope they like me. But it sure is a good break and Joe Lippell is even gonna give me an advance of a thousand bucks."

"Where are you going to?" she asked a little worried.

"All up and down the East Coast: The Boston Gardens, The Spectrum in Philadelphia, two dates in Canada- Toronto Maple Leaf Gardens and another huge hockey rink in Montreal, and then ... you're not gonna believe it - I'm playing the Omni in Atlanta!"

"Oh no!" she exclaimed. "What if there's another lil' Inger Peach in the audience?"

"Oh, don't worry. I'm as faithful as an old hound dog." And I would be. And that was odd because I never was with Barbara; maybe the bonds were tighter with Inger. I owed her. "Then we do three dates in Florida: Jacksonville, Lakeland, and Miami or actually Hollywood, where there's this huge Sportatorium surrounded by palm trees and alligators.

And oh yeah, two dates in New York - we start at The Nassau Coliseum and we finish up with a night at The Garden."

"Oh Marty, I'm so happy for you sugar! I know that things are gonna start going your way. But sugar, promise me that I won't ever hear about you and any of those groupies anywhere," she pleaded.

"Hear anything? Are you kidding me? Listen darling, it would be like drinking Ripple wine after a steady diet of Dom Perignon Champagne." I meant that, too ... I think.

"Oh sugar, you just wait till I get back? First, I'm gonna go buy a whole new outfit, maybe something in hot red, than I'm gonna get some of that sweet-smelling massage oil, then I'm gonna strip you naked as a jay-bird and rub..."

"Oh God, please stop Inger! I'm going through bad enough withdrawal without having to hear a commercial!" She laughed. "Well, then just use your imagination, sugar."

"So how's everything down there?" I asked.

"Oh, it's okay. It's only been a few days. It's a little bit more dancing than I figured but that's okay, it's good to get in shape." she was hardly unfit when she left. "Today, we started to get fit for costumes. The other girls are pretty nice and the people in the hotel are nice - not as seedy as in Vegas - I don't think that the boys' have things locked up quite as tight down here ... yet. But I'll tell you something, sugar - I do kinda miss the Follies."

"You miss The Follies? What the hell for?"

"Well, you know at The Follies I was queen bee, the star of the whole deal ... and down here ... well, I'm just another girl. But I suppose I'll get used to it. It all just seems a little too corporate as you always used to say, Marty."

I had to empathize with her. After all, she was an "artist" in her own way too - and none of us fit too comfortably into that scheme of things. But God knows, even though she was away from me and I really missed her, I sure was glad that she was out of The Follies with her gold rug and her "vertical portion of the show."

"Oh, don't worry honey. It will be all right. Once we're finished with this month of training then we'll be seeing each other a lot again. It'll all work out." I hoped. But it was funny because even though she was the girl who had left home at seventeen and been through all kinds of experiences that I could hardly imagine, I felt sorry for her down there all alone and I felt protective too.

"I know ... I know, sugar. Hold on," I heard her talking to someone in the background. "Oops, I gotta run baby - dancing class. Call you later. I love ya!"

"I love you too," I said easily. It was a nice new feeling for me to miss Inger so much. Because for a long time it seemed that I had been missing something terribly but not having any idea what the fuck it was. Excuse my French ...

When a manager with the clout of Joe Lippell starts the wheels turning, it doesn't take long for the trip to begin. Within a few days I had a band of good studio players together and unlimited time in an expensive rehearsal studio. And even a roadie to tune my guitar. If I was spiteful I would have called my friend Johnny to brag.

I still hadn't met Paul Saint. He was in L.A. getting fitted for new costumes. As a matter of fact, I was getting my own wardrobe together too: A new pair of Levi's a
black-leather best and a frilly white shirt - wash and wear. I even got my hair cut - cost thirty bucks!

I was at a rehearsal when Joe Lippell called. My musicians were getting my set down easily, some of them were already familiar with my stuff. I seemed to be making more mistakes than anyone but this was probably due to nervousness and besides singing and playing the important guitar leads, I had to be checking up on everyone else. But when Joe called to tell me that

Paul Saint was back in town and that I should drop by his offices to meet him, I really started goofing up. I knew that my baby-sitting would soon begin.

Joe Lippell Management was located on half a floor of one of those giant tombstone-shaped office buildings that line the Avenue of the Americas. On the Avenue are little round plaques celebrating Central and South American countries like Nicaragua and Argentina and you'd expect the street to be used for the headquarters of companies like *United Fruit* or *Anaconda Copper* who do a lot of "business" down there. But life is never arranged so systematically and more than anything else the businesses that predominate the avenue are entertainment and book publishing concerns, which for all I know could all be owned by the *Chiquita Banana Conglomerate.*

Security was tight in Joe's building but in my new Levi's and hardly resembling a Salvadorian rebel I gained access to the elevators rather easily. On the twenty-fifth floor were large veneered double doors with gold lettering that led into Lippell Management. Under that was listed a dozen other companies that I knew were created for tax reasons, Any more subsidiaries and Joe would have to get another set of doors.

My first impression was ho good looking the receptionist was. And being half a chauvinist, I wondered if Joe got it on with her. She sat behind a large console for the telephone that she would pick up every few seconds when it rang to say, "Lippell Management - can I help you?" She knew this line perfectly. And then she would push the appropriate button to switch the call. The amazing thing was that she could do all of this with her plum-colored nails that were almost an inch long and seemed to want to curl toward some center of gravity, somewhere - maybe Bloomingdales. She didn't smile when I entered; it would probably crack her make-up.

I told her my name and that I was here to see Joe. She spoke to someone over the intercom, and then told me to have a seat; he would be with me in a few minutes. The only magazines in the lobby as I sat there waiting were Billboard, Record World, and Cash Box. I rarely got a chance to look through these publications as they cost about three bucks apiece and my Billboard subscription had run out so I voraciously started whipping through the recent copies to see what I had missed. Nothing seemed to have changed much except that the Disco Chart was smaller and given only half a page. There were plenty of photos, of performers and executives, all smiling, taken at various shows. I used to have pictures like this of me. The only clue to the industry's sad state the last few years was the lack of full color ads for new albums. As usual, the charts were full of records I didn't like. Sainthood's last album, which had been out for over six months was still in the top ten.

A secretary came out to see me. She was pretty, like the receptionist, and also had very long painted nails I wondered if Joe Lippell had a fetish about getting scratch marks on his back. I got up when she called my name expecting that I was to go in with her but she said that Joe was still in a meeting and wanted to know if I'd like anything to drink while I was waiting - soda, coffee, or beer? Just to be difficult, I asked for orange juice. They had it. As I sat in the reception area, I watched the 'traffic' come in and out. There were a lot of road manager types all carrying those brightly colored aluminum brief cases covered with backstage passes. They'd wear nylons baseball jackets - most of them with SAINTHOOD printed boldly on the back and their own name written in thread-script over their breast. Without exception everyone had on jogging shoes and looked like they didn't get enough sleep. I tried to get the receptionist to smile back at me but she wouldn't until one of the roadies recognized me. We knew each other slightly, I think he used to work for ELO when I toured with them and he came over and asked me how I was, if I was recording, what I was doing? I told him I was going to open for Sainthood and he said great, he was working with them now, doing the lights, and he'd see me on the road. The receptionist heard all of this. Next time I looked at her she smiled. I didn't smile back. So it goes: Stardom.

Finally the same secretary came back to fetch me. We walked through a maze of offices before reaching Joe's own. There were at least a dozen other secretaries and most had long painted nails too - how did they type? The whole office was decorated early-Star Wars; stainless steel, high tech. The gold records clashed with the silver metallic wall covering; I must advise Joe. In the future only platinum records would do. But there were plenty of those, too.

When a band is as big as Sainthood it takes a big organization to handle all the ancillary businesses or rock super-stardom like song publishing and production companies and most importantly - T-shirts and posters to sell on tour. Like the popcorn in movie theaters, that's where the money is. The walls were also covered with framed posters: some of Sainthood, some just California-style graphics which made no sense to me like a 3D Rolls Royce grill or an empty glittering swimming pool. I guess so people in from the Coast would feel at home.

As I walked down the hall I started giggling because I had just imagined that I would walk into Joe's office and he too would have long painted nails. The secretary turned around and looked at me. I stopped laughing. Joe sat behind a large desk covered with legal papers and records. A massive stereo took up one-half of his office and a fish tank the other. As far as I could see there were no fish in the tank. Someone else was walking out as I was walking in an d Joe was yelling at this person whom I recognized as a record company executive. Joe was saying that if he reneged on his promise of tour support held have his job. The guy looked pale and convinced Joe had meant it. But as soon as I entered, Joe's voice switched to extreme-pleasant and he said hello and asked me all about how the rehearsals were going and if I needed anything. Yeah, I said, a million dollars. And Joe said don' t we all. Ha!

Joe showed me the prototype for the Sainthood Pinball machine that was like any other except that the back display plate was covered with cartoon-images of Paul Saint in various costumes. While I nervously shot a few balls, hardly scoring any points, someone came in to ask Joe about some other group that Joe also managed. I knew Joe handled other bands besides Sainthood - most of them in the same heavy-metal mold.

And then a secretary asked him if he was interested in returning a call from someone named Eric Noise who wanted to know if Joe was interested in handling a band called the White Castles and Joe said forget it, he'd seen the group and they were a piece of shit so tell this Noise character he was out of town. He who laughs last, I thought, but I kept quiet. I began realizing that Joe handled other bands who could easily have opened for Sainthood themselves and it made me really appreciate what he was doing for me. I could hardly begrudge him all the signs of success that surrounded him. What goes around comes around - with both Joe Lippell and Eric Noise. Then like a hurricane Paul

Saint arrived. He walked into Joe's office backwards, yelling orders at the secretaries and accountants and roadies who were following and taking notes behind him. All I could see was the back of his floor-length white fur cape and his curly shoulder length platinum-blond hair. It could have been Jean Harlow but for the deep voice.

"Sue ... call Keith for me ... I think he's staying at The Pierre if he hasn't been kicked out yet which means he might be at The Plaza ... And send over a case of Dom Perignon to wherever the hell he is ... And Bernie ... You're gonna get a call from Tiffany ... I sent a pretty girl over there whose name is ... Darla or Carla or something that I met on the plane to L.A .... I told her to pick herself up a little going away present ... but nothing over five hundred! ... She wasn't THAT great a traveling companion ... and Sue make an appointment at Klinger for me - scalp AND facial ... and get me on the guest list at The Ritz tonight and a table too up front too. I want to see The Pretenders - I like that sexy American girl who sings lead - Chrissie ... and try to get me backstage too ... and make that plus six ... and I'll need two limos ... and tell them to forget that Italian white wine they put in the cars - it gives me headaches ... I need champagne on ice in both cars ... but you better include some Yoo-hoo for my date ... she's rather young!" He laughed and in a sweep of white fur and laughter he turned around to face me, beaming. After all of Joe's tales of horror I expected something out of Night of The Living Dead. But Paul was tan and had very white teeth and striking blue eyes like Paul Newman. His hair was in perfect little curls across his forehead and down to his shoulders. For Christ's sake, he looked healthier then me. I wasn't totally surprised, though, because I have come to the conclusion that life in the fast lane doesn't age you - it just kills you. Eventually.

He threw his fur cape on the floor. He seemed to be dressed totally in silks - powder-blue silk sports jacket, a boldly striped silk shirt opened almost all the way down the front silky pants with some kind of a leopard pattern on them and little red silk sneakers (though probably made of rayon.) He gave Joe a big hug and a kiss on both cheeks. "How's my spiritual mentor?" he asked Joe.

"Paul ... you seem to have a little tell-tale evidence on your nose," Joe said to him softly but loud enough so I could hear.

"Oh?" said Paul. I noticed the white powder that he tried to rub off; must have taken a quick hit in the elevator for his grand entrance. "I must change my make-up man - he's awfully messy." He laughed unconvincingly.

"Right. Your make-up man," Joe said sarcastically. He pointed to me: "Paul, I want you to meet Marty May - your opening act."

"Marty May! How DO you DO!" We shook hands loosely. For some reason, rock stars tend to lack a firm grasp on hands and reality. But Paul Saint seemed genuinely excited to meet me. "Marty, I can't tell you how happy I am to have you on the tour. You know, I'm your biggest fan! Always have been! You know that album you did...a while back," he added politely. "I think there were a couple of girls on it, dressed like birds or something?"

"Yeah, it was called *May Wings*," I said. "But the cover wasn't my idea - I'm allergic to feathers."

"Yes, yes!" exclaimed Paul. "What a great album that was! I still listen to it on occasion - I have a cassette of it for traveling." He looked at me intently. "That was a true work of art, you know, not the kid stuff we're doing here."

He spoke with the authority of success, which allowed him to be self-deprecating. But as usual, I felt embarrassed when rock 'n roll and art are spoken of together. "Thanks a lot, Paul ... uh ... that album did real well, in South Dakota, they told me." Which was true. Apparently, there was a strategic Air Command base out there and I was a big seller at the PX. The title of the album, *May Wings*, was a combination of my last name, naturally, and one of the songs on the record - "Wings" - which was a real soaring kind of rocker; a little bit like "Eight Miles High" by the Byrds. And the airmen in South Dakota could relate, I guess.

I tried to be funny in returning the compliment; "I wish I could say that I listen to you all the time too Paul, but I don't have a stereo right now."

"What? You don't have a stereo? Are you kidding?"

"Well ... no ... you see, my ex-wife got it when we split up." God, I was afraid I just insulted him. "But I used to listen to your albums all the times" I lied. "And, of course, I still hear you on the radio all the time. I mean, Sainthood is almost like continual Muzak when you turn on any FM rock station ... if you know what I mean. Not that it's any way like Muzak ... just that it is played continuously ... you can't get away from it..." I was digging myself in deeper and deeper. I was gonna get kicked off this tour before it ever started. But Paul hadn't heard the rest.

"You really don't have a stereo, Marty? That's unbelievable," he repeated. "Do you believe that, Joe? MARTY MAY does not have a stereo!" (Was he making fun of me? I looked at Joe but he was blank.) "Well, not while I have anything to do with things around here!" said Paul with finality.

He shouted into the hall outside Joe's office: "Bernie! Come in here will ya?"

A chubby young man with aviator style glasses and a mustache scurried in. "Marty, this is Bernie. Bernie - Marty May. Bernie's my accountant."

"Uh ... hi," I said meekly not knowing what was happening.

Bernie just smiled. He looked up at Paul. "Yes, Mr. Saint?"

"Bernie, I want you to send somebody out to buy Marty May a stereo system. Go see my pal Burt at Crazy Eddie's and put it on my account. And make it a damn good one! Marty will give you his address for the delivery. And he wants it today!"

Bernie the accountant looked at Paul and then looked at Joe. Joe looked at Bernie and then at Paul. Paul looked at Joe and then added: "Spend about five to seven-fifty." Joe nodded his head in approval. "We don't want anything so ridiculous someone is gonna kill poor Marty here to rip it off." He smiled at me.

And that was that. I looked at Joe Lippell to see if this was a joke or not and then back at Paul who was beaming like a benevolent monarch. "You really don't have to do this, Paul...really, it's okay...I have this little clock radio that has FM and is just fine...I didn't mean to ... "

"Marty, darling," said Paul with his eyes closed and one extended palm blocking my embarrassed objections. "Just consider it a long overdue token of my appreciation of your extraordinary talent."

I felt like Queen for a Day. "Well ... I don't know quite what to say Paul...Thanks a lot...thank you very much indeed." I said with the experience of failure, gift horses overly examined, and all that other crap. And when I got home later that night the superintendent had accepted delivery of a brand new stereo in about six boxes which I hurriedly struggled to get it all into my apartment feeling like Tiny Tim on Christmas morning.

I was in the midst of instruction manuals and speaker wires when the phone rang. It was Barbara.

"Marty, where have you been? I've been trying to call you for days and you're never home." Obviously, because I spent most of my time at Inger's, and strangely I felt guilty, like I had been cheating on her.

"Oh? I'm sorry. I've been taking ... dancing lessons."

"Seriously?"

"No, not really. I've just been running around a lot, taking care of business since I got back from L.A." (Why couldn't I mention Inger?) "Uh ... what's ... what's up?" I asked surprised. Since our split, I had been the one who called - not her.

"Something really exciting, Marty. You remember Garcia Ortega? The artist I introduced you to when you were out here last month?"

"You mean your boyfriend? Sure, I remember him." I said coldly.

"Well, he's not my boyfriend...he's just a friend."

"Whatever...what about him?"

"Well apparently, you-made quite an impression on him."

"Why? Does he want to paint my picture? I'll send him my modeling rates."

"Why are you being so nasty, Marty?" Relax, I told myself. She can't take Inger from you.

"I'm sorry. What about Garcia? I hardly said two words to the guy."

"Well, don't ask me. But since he met you he pestered me to bring over your albums - which I did - and he loves them! He uses them to paint with."

"I knew he had good taste," I said.

"But listen - after he started listening to your music he started asking me a lot of questions about you...

"I hope you didn't discuss our sex life, Barbara!"

"Of course not. What's to discuss?" Touché. "So anyway, I was telling him what a hard time you've been having - being broke and without a record contract…"

"You shouldn't go telling everyone all about my personal problems, Barbara. Its none of his business," I said, annoyed.

"But Marty, he's offering you a job."

"A job?"

"As his assistant. It's a jack-of-all-trades type of thing. Buy supplies for him - take him into the city for shows - arrange interviews for him - all kinds of interesting stuff. He's a fascinating man once you get to know him."

I don't like fascinating men; fascinating women okay - but not men. That's how they describe central American dictators. Ruthless and fascinating.

"God Barbara, this is quite unexpected. I don't know. Where would I live? What would he pay me?" But mostly, I thought, what about Inger?

"I'm not sure, Marty, but he's a very generous man. He put his last assistant through art school. I suppose you could stay with me for a while. We'd have separate bedrooms ... till you made other arrangements. As long as you promised not to attack me when you get drunk."

I ignored that comment.

"When does he want me to start?" I asked.

"In about a month. That's when his current assistant goes away to Europe. If this works out, Marty, it could be a real career for you."

"Career? What do you mean? What about my music?"

"When you called me from L.A. you said you were considering trying something else," said Barbara impatiently. "Has something changed?"

"But you told me to forget it."

"Well ... it was three o'clock in the morning, Marty," She said timidly, she didn't like getting caught being hypocritical.

"I don't know, Barbara. It's a big decision, leaving the city and all. And some things are just starting to go my way again."

"Marty, you know how it always ends. Even if you get another recording contract, you'd be back in the same position three years from now."

"You don't know that." I was mad but in fact those were my own fears.

"Well, I'm certainly not begging you, Marty." But in her own way, she was. "Its a tremendous opportunity. Who knows what it could lead to? Why don't you think it over and call me back in a couple of weeks. Garcia doesn't need an answer right away."

"Okay," I said with an odd feeling of defeat. "See what you can find out about the money. It's a big move for me - in a lot of ways."

"I'll ask him but Marty, don't go kicking a dead-horse your whole life."

"Maybe the old nag is just sleeping - getting a second wind!" I countered.

"You know what I mean, you're not a kid anymore. I'm only thinking about what's best for you, that's all," She said sweetly.

That "what's best for you" line really pissed me off.

But I couldn't help but think about her offer and being back in my own apartment only made me consider it all the more seriously. Maybe she was right about that "dead-horse" thing, that I didn't know when to give up. And then there was Inger. I should have told Barbara all about her, no holds barred, and seen if the job offer still stood. My lack of integrity was depressing. But was Inger really my future or was she just a temporary pain-killer? And could I really live with and accept what she did and planned on keep doing in one sort or another? My bad dreams had stopped for now, but what would happen when she returned? In the words of another survivor who was trying to crawl from the wreckage of once-great-glory: "I won't think about any of this today - I'll think about it tomorrow!" Scarlett O'Hara said that, of course, but I bet Richard Nixon thought it too.

Chapter 3

Soon, all I was thinking about was Paul Saint. We were together nearly twenty-four hours a day. I spent more time at the Sainthood rehearsals than at my own; I was getting to know his set as well as him. He even had an extra cot brought into his hotel suite at The Plaza so that after a night of nightclubbing with him I could get him back safe and sound and just fall out myself. Joe suggested this, I think. Too many times, he had dropped Paul off at his hotel front t door thinking all was well and then Paul would think of one more club to go to or one phone number to call and Joe wouldn't hear from him for days. The cot wasn't overly comfortable but with the pace he kept, I could   have   used   a stretcher.

Not hard to see Paul Saint's problem: From the moment he would hit the streets of New York, the hangers-on would seem to come up out of the sewers. Everyone was his friend from "way back when". Paul told me this was his reason for staying in hotels. He had tried having apartments but there would always be so many people crashing there that he couldn't get any privacy. Not that I believed he really wanted a great deal of privacy; But sometimes Paul wouldn't know which coke spoon under his nose he should snort first. The man ingested an incredible amount of cocaine. And he smoked a lot of strong reefer, that new California kind without seeds - American technology does it again. And he drank a lot of Vodka. He wasn't sticking any needles into his arms as far as I knew. I'd think held be too vain for that. I don't know how he carried on, but he just did. I've known and heard about other rockers who also have the same strange ability; usually, they do just fine till they drop dead. In the beginning, Paul was always offering me hits of coke and I was always politely declining to the unbelieving stares of anyone else who might be around. Not many turn down cocaine in these circles, But I had been on that train once before in my life and I didn't like where it had let me off. In my mind cocaine was something that always started great and ended horribly. I forced myself to remember these awful wired nights when I would have slit my wrists to get to sleep; it made it easier turning the stuff down now. Paul seemed to be slightly amused by my abstaining and I was hoping that it might slow him down a little bit, too. He was lucky that this upcoming tour was only a repeat performance of his last one; not much new preparation was necessary. Sainthood's last album had been based around some vague concept of rock In roll pirates. Paul had gotten the idea from the latest fashion craze in London - 'New Romanticism'. His genius seemed to be in spotting the newest underground trend and then commercializing it within the Sainthood format for a mass audience. And it worked; the actual 'New Romantics' bands that London scene had produced failed to catch on in America except on a limited, cult basis but sainthood had another number one album out of it.

As expected, Paul's guise for this tour was that of a swashbuckling pirate a la Errol Flynn: thick-brass-buckled belt, britches and knee-socks, billowy blouses, a crimson coat with shiny buttons. And sometimes a patch over his eye. The rest of Sainthood were appropriately dressed as 'the crew'. I certainly was glad and relieved once the tour got underway. And more dogging around town with Paul Saint till all hours and I'd need a pair of those orthopedic shoes that lace up the side. And they're much too $new wave* for me. It's hard to describe all the workings of an arena-sized tour because as a performer I missed a great deal of the logistical aspects. I'd arrive to the gig around seven for my eight o'clock show but the guys who would set up the stage and the lights and the sound system had been there since noon after driving all night from the last gig. And they rarely saw the show because they were sleeping. Unlike a club, where a scheduled performance might start two hours later than planned, depending on the size of the crowd and the state of the band, these arena-sized dates would go off perfectly on schedule due to the fact that they were mostly union houses and an hour's delay would result in costly overtime.

Sainthood's draw was so huge that they played few arenas with a capacity of less than fifteen or twenty thousand people. These were halls designed more for hockey or basketball or rodeos and needless to say, the acoustics were akin to playing in a giant oil drum. But the kids didn't seem to care if the sound bounced off the back wall and hit them again a half second later: The party was the thing.

Although this tour went from Canada to Florida$ I was amazed and bewildered by the sameness of the crowds, their dress their drugged state, their predictable reactions. It was safe for me to take a backstage pass and wander through the audience from time to time - no one would recognize me. There always seemed to be a skinny kid with a half grown moustache and his shirt tied around his waist nonchalantly offering you "Ludes - Mescaline - Black Beauties?" as you walked by. And the paramedics would always be shuffling stretchers backstage, usually filled with a passed out young girl and into an ambulance. The security checks at the front gates were systematic and had come to be expected by these kids, frisking and everything, I couldn't imagine an audience standing for the same Gestapo treatment back in the sixties. Soon I stopped wandering around the crowd - it was too depressing. I'd be the oldest person out there.

All the musicians and the tour managers traveled together by plane. On long tours Sainthood would lease a private jet but since this was only East Coast we flew by commercial airlines. There was me and my band, four in all, and our road manager whom Joe had assigned to us. There was Sainthood, which is four musicians plus Paul Saint; two of them brought their girlfriends - the rest preferred local talent. There was Sainthood's tour manager who always smiled and there was Ike; a large ex-green beret who rarely spoke and was "Security". We all had laminated ID badges that we wore at all times and reminded me of something you might show to gain access to a missile silo.

Below us by land, three semis and four station wagons made their own way. These were full of Sainthood's equipment and 'road' personnel: sound mixer, lighting designer monitor mixer, rigger (sets up the lights), stage manager, and individual roadies for each member of the group. Also four members from the lighting company who helped the rigger and than worked the four 'super-trooper' spotlights during the show. And there were others who just helped in general called *humpers* but the teamster union members at each venue only did the actual lifting of any equipment. And if anyone tried to lift an amp or even tune a guitar during their dinner break from six to seven PM ... well, there would be all hell to pay (plus a few union officials.) But certainly, the most important member of the tour was Bernie, the tour accountant$ who on more than one occasion had barricaded himself into a ticket office until a sheriff was summoned if he detected a bad ticket count. Ike, the ex-green beret would guard the door.

A grand tour like this soon takes on a routine after the first few dates that rarely varies: Because the tour manager is experienced and knows the sleeping habits of rock musicians he puts in three wake-up calls at fifteen minute intervals for each one of us. The first just gets you mad - the second opens the possibility you might have to get out of bed at this ungodly hour and by the third you accept your fate. If you're smart and have a hangover, you take a shower - than a mad dash for the airport. But seeing as we'd be holding up to twenty tickets, even if we were late they'd usually hold the plane. Then once on board you confess about your awful hangover and someone suggests the 'hair of the dog that bit you' cure so you have a quick Bloody Mary and an even worse hangover. Your flight resembles that of The High And The Mighty. The stewardess having heard of Sainthood but not Marty May so they get better service and you get another Bloody Mary. You finally check into a Holiday Inn identical to the one you just checked out of down to the same suspicious room clerk. You turn on the TV and take nap fully dressed.}

Too short a time later you go down to the arena for a sound-check which sounds awful and you can't hear yourself in the monitor speakers but the sound-man assures you that everything will be fine once the hall is full of people, You don't believe him for a minute; you know that he just wants to get out of there and go to dinner. You check out the food in your dressing room and you're reminded of what some amendment to the constitution says about 'cruel and unusual punishment'. Finally, some hours later, you do your show, you feel absolutely marvelous and it makes everything worthwhile. (Until your road manager tells you what time you must awake the following morning.)

Not that opening for Sainthood was food for the ego. When I would go on I usually was greeted with impatient demands for "SAINT-HOOD! SAINT-HOOD! SAINT-HOOD!" But I would proceed with determination and just try to ignore that half of the audience   still walking into the arena during my set and the other hall- squirming in their seats, trying to trade Quaaludes for joints.

I had made my set full of rockers; trying a tender ballad as the opening act would be the kiss of death. I even included Chuck

Berry's "Roll Over Beethoven" at the end, which was sure to get them. So with a lot of hard work (and a little begging), I usually managed to get off the stage with at least polite applause and even a few surprising whistles and shouts for more. And if anyone was still making just about any kind of noise resembling enthusiasm by the time I reached the side of the stage after my half-hour set was through, I would turn right around and do an encore. Usually something by Bo Diddley, just that beat alone was bound to get 'em.

Now when Sainthood came on it was quite a different story. There would be at east an hour break to allow the audience to reach a frenzied peak (encouraged by a few false start lowerings of the house-lights and endings of the recorded music that played during the intermission). The crowd's chants of "SAINT-HOOD! SAINT-HOOD!" were like something heard at the marine's training center at Paris Island. Finally the lights would be lowered once and for all and the music stopped and the roar of the crowd was nothing less than that given the Pope in Vatican City. This was it. This was what every kid who ever picked up an electric guitar dreamed about. It didn't get much bigger than this. And it had never really happened to me. Not on this level, not where you can count on it show after show after show.

I watched Sainthood's show every night; Joe Lippell had instructed me to do so. Though I couldn't see how a drug dealer would get to Paul up there. Their performance was well-rehearsed spontaneity; it never varied from night to night. First, the four other members of Sainthood would get on stage all in tattered pirate crew get-ups and launch into the loudest most over-wrought heavy metal anthem one could possibly imagine. It made the theme from Star Wars seem subtle. The reason for this was of a practical nature - it gave the band a chance to warm up and get into the spotlight a while before Paul came onstage and took over the show lock stock, and barrel. When they reached their crescendo Paul swung down from the side monitor-speakers on a rope. Actually, he was more lowered than swung there were three roadies on the other end of the rope. With his platinum blond hair and lurid make-up job and Captain Blood outfit he was quite a sight; I wondered who did the original Captain Kidd's make-up - was this part of the cabin boy's duties? I'm amazed that in Paul's usual stoned condition he didn't break a leg with this entrance but with the swirling spotlights it was made to appear far more spectacular than it really was. (Aside from a soft spot for babies and drunks, God also seems fond of heavy-metal lead singers.) Then Paul would run across the edge of the stage from side to side taunting and sneering at his fans - it drove them absolutely nuts! Girls would be trying to crawl on the stage with him and every once in a while (as pre-planned) one would get through the security guards at front of the stage and have to be dragged screaming from Paul's shaken torso by the gargantuan Ike. They only ones let the smaller girls get through the ones who could do no real damage. In my three years of relative inactivity I don't know what happened but this crowd was very, very young. I'd put the average age around fifteen. What happened? Did all the older rock fans move to Colorado? Paul's grand entrance was orchestrated by an ever-rising crescendo of a drum roll - something akin to what those natives in "King Kong" did to get their favorite monkey's attention. When it could get no louder Paul would roar into his microphone "GOOOOOOOOD EEEVVVEEENNNIIINNNGGG!!!" It was more an order than a greeting. "GOOOOOOOOOD EEEVVVEEENNNIIINNNGGG!!!" would roar back jailbait America. This was the standard Sainthood opening. Then every night regardless of how loud the crowd was, Paul would scream: "I CAN'T HEAR YOU!!!" So, "GOOOOD EVENING!!! They'd scream back even louder. This exchange would go back three or four times just like you might do with a hard-of-hearing grandfather. Finally when everyone in the audience should be hoarse from screaming Paul would take the microphone off its stand and rush back to the drum riser, jump up on it sometimes knocking over a cymbal which a scurrying roadie would re-stand, raise one tightly clenched fist high in the air black-power style which made me once again think of what Eldridge Cleaver once said about America's habit of a co-opting anything threatening, and ask the highly philosophic question: "DO YOU BELIEVE???" at the top of his lungs. The crowd would roar its affirmations with more intensity than anything ever heard at a Billy Graham mass rally. And on the drummer's count of four Sainthood would blast its way through their first song which was their first big hit and which was called (of course) "Do You Believe?" And then it was just nothing less than the expected pandemonium all the way through their two-hour performance.

Their songs were a crash course in what are supposed to be teenage emotions; they ran the gamut from "You're Okay - Your Just Like one of the Guys" to "All Day Sucker" to "I Could Kill You But I Won't" which Paul introduced as an anti-handgun song. The fans knew every song they played, and they would sing, clap, and stomp along.

If I really thought that I was doing this for my career I would have been discouraged; but the truth was that Joe Lippell had hired me to be a rock 'n roll nurse and I was making good money and everybody in Sainthood's crew was treating me like a real star, Joe must have given them the word, though, because usually the crew of a headliner like Sainthood would treat the opener like dirt - making up for their own time in that position.

After Paul Saint and the four other members of Sainthood I was next in line in the fame-game; something like where the secretary of state fits in order of succession after the President, Vice-President, and Speaker of The House. This rank entitled me to certain leftovers on the groupie buffet. But I just wasn't interested. The way these girls would do anything to get backstage - there were rumors that Ike the chief of security was charging a "Toll and then they'd just stand around till their chosen for the night would take them back to his hotel only to forget their name in the morning. It was just too meaningless. When I'd see these girls in their stretch-lame pants and too much makeup I Always felt like asking them if they shouldn't be home by now; won't their parents get worried. And I suppose you could say that I was being faithful to Inger too.

Paul was only half-interested in these girls himself. This caused a great deal of heartbreak and grief among these camp followers. But cocaine was his first love. He'd always be polite and talk to them a little but he'd soon disappear if one started getting her hooks into him. The start of the tour was full of energy and enthusiasm, much like the start of a war. I felt good myself; good to be working and out on the road and just good to be part of something that was moving. I was enjoying playing more than I had in years. Maybe because nothing was really riding on it and I could just do it for myself. And also it was reassuring that I could still get out there and shake my ass at thirty-two without pulling a muscle or having a stroke. There was life in this old boy yet.

And for the first couple of dates Paul too seemed to be really into it. Held drink a lot but, like Joe had said, he seemed to be able to handle that. But soon I started to get the feeling that he was just going through the motions and that he was getting itchy; maybe he had run out of cocaine. I had been the most loyal of Tontos - I was rarely away from his side and I could detect a change in his mood. After shows we'd sit in bars and I'd try to ask him questions and held just say, "Yeah, I guess so," or "I don't know, maybe" and tap his foot nervously all night long. He seemed to be waiting for something.

We were in Lakeville, Florida, and there was someone backstage who wasn't a member of the crew. He and Paul were very friendly and I overheard Paul ask him how his flight was and they snobbishly joked about the convenience of Lear Jets. Maybe I remembered this stranger from some night in New York out with Paul. I wasn't sure. I was getting suspicious; I caught Paul alone in his dressing room,

"How ya doing tonight?"

"Oh, hi ya Marty...great...just great," he said unconvincingly. He tried nonchalantly to put something into his jacket pocket. "How about yourself? You ready to knock them dead?" His Midwestern accent always amused me in contrast to his thundering voice of Thor on stage. He was starting to change into his pirate digs and he hung his jacket up.

"Oh yeah...sure! Gonna give it all I got. Uh ... Paul, I think your soundman wants to speak to you before you go on. He's at the side-of the stage by the monitor mixer," I lied.

"Oh yeah? Listens stay here and watch my stuff for me will ya?" He walked out the door.

I went into his jacket and pulled out a plastic baggie full of ... well, full of a little bit of everything. There was about a half an ounce of cocaine and maybe twenty Quaaludes and some opium and some other pills I didn't recognize and...just about everything except aspirin. I put it back before Paul returned.

"I couldn't find him, Marty. Are you sure he wanted to speak to me? There's no change in the show."

"Oh ... don't worry about it. I think he was just checking if you dropped your microphone or something. I'm sure it wasn't real important. I'll find him later and check it out for you. Uh...Paul, I was just wondering...don't I know that guy you were talking to? He looked real familiar."

"What guy was that, Marty?"

"Oh ... the guy in the cowboy hat and all the silver jewelry - didn't I meet him back in New York ... one night somewhere?"

"Oh him," said Paul matter-of-factly, "Sure, I think you did ... that's Tommy Moonshot. He's a real character... ol ' buddy of mine."

"Oh...yeah, sure, I remember him. What's he doing down here in Florida?" I asked with as much innocent interest as I could muster.

"Why ... uh ... I flew him down on a chartered plane. The poor guy works so hard that I thought he needed a little vacation, a little Florida sun. Don't you think he looks a little pale?" Paul laughed and continued dressing.

"What does he work at?" I knew I was pushing it.

"What's this, Marty? The third degree?" He was annoyed.

"No. No, not at all, Paul. I was just wondering because of I thought I knew him and ... uh...

He threw down his scarlet pirate coat and turned to face me. "Marty, I know exactly what you were wondering.

"Tommy Moonshot is a dealer, okay? And he brought me down that stash that you just took out of my jacket pocket a few moments ago. And for your information, my sound-man has not wanted to talk to me in years." He glared at me. Not as 007 as I imagined myself to be, I was completely taken by surprise. "I don't know what you means, Paul.

Someone wanted to talk to you and I was just looking for a cigarette, I hope you don't think that I would deliberately go ... "

"Marty, you know I don't smoke." He kept staring at me. Even without makeup he appeared deadly.

"Well, yeah. Oh right ... you don't smoke do you? I guess I ... uh ... forgot. I was just nervous about tonight's show - I get a little forgetful, I guess." Paul was not buying this.

"Listen, Marty, we've both been around far too long for this cat-and-mouse shit. I know what's going on. I know what Joe Lippell is trying to do and I know why you're on this tour and I don't much like having a babysitter at my age! If I didn't like you so much and if I didn't think that you deserved this break, I wouldn't have stood for this fucking game in the first place! And nobody, not even Joe Lippell, tells me what to do or what I shouldn't do because they know and I know that there is no fucking Sainthood show without Paul Saint!" The jig was up. "Comprende Amigo?!"

"Hey, I didn't like spying on you either, Paul. And to tell you the truth, if I didn't like you too and if I didn't think you had talent, I wouldn't give a shit. And even if I didn't like you, I still wouldn't want to see you destroying yourself and your career. And that's the bottom line as far as I'm concerned." I had not choice but to let it all out: "Paul, you know you have everything that I ever wanted? Everything that I ever dreamed about - and cam pretty fucking close to getting tool When I see you out on that stage and you've got twenty thousand kids going ape-shit over you...well ... how the fuck do you think that makes me feel? I want it so bad I can taste it! Sometimes as I stand by the side-fills watching the show I fantasize that I'm you! And then I think that I should be you too because I could do it better!"

(This wasn't true though.) "But I know that's bullshit because if I could do it better than it would be me out there. I'm not a dreamer anymore and I know that I have just about as good a chance of reaching your level in this business as I do of becoming a pro quarterback for the NFL. And it just kills me to see you throwing it all away! And what the hell for? Is success really so hard to handle? Well let me tell you something buddy, failure is a hell of a lot harder!" I was yelling before I even knew it. Either Paul felt sorry for me or he wanted me to stop yelling. "Marty, you'll get back up there...but I ... " But I wasn't gonna get down from my soapbox just yet - it had been a long time since I had such a captive audience for my tale of woe.

"Paul, when you're out there tonight you should take a good look at those kids. Because they think that you are no less than a god! You're everything they want to be you're talented and sexy and in control and most of all you're free! And maybe, somewhere, in those kids' heart of hearts they know that they're just a few years away from the starting gate for the rat race and then the rock In roll dreams soon die. You know when you're in this business you start taking all of this for granted but it's a big fucking deal for these kids - they don't have a lot of money and these tickets and these records aren't cheap. But they don't care because for now, you're their last grasp at freedom. You can't fuck up on them - they deserve better!"

"But Marty, it's bullshit!" Paul exclaimed. "I'm like a snake-oil salesman! It's all a mirage. If they think that I'm important to their lives they are sadly mistaken. I don't have a damn thing to do with their lives."

"Oh but you do Paul. Why do you think they buy millions of your records? It's because you're something bigger than their own boring lives. And they live for these concerts - I mean, what the fuck else do you think there is for them to do? Maybe play video games and get stoned and that's it! And if the people in your position stop caring - that will be IT! There's no more room for children anymore and society won't let them be adults yet so for a few years they get to bask in the fantasy and power of rock In roll. You know, you get more love, respect and just plain attention in two hours on that stage than most people get in a lifetime."

"What the hell are you talking about? They don't love me - and they don't respect me, either. Guys in my position fall by the wayside every five years after everything's been sucked out of them.'" He named a few examples; unfortunately I couldn't dispute it. "For Christ's sakes, Marty, they don't even know who the hell I am. And if they knew the real me, the real Paul Snadowsky,

they wouldn't bother coming!" His eyes were wild.

"Snadowsky?"

"Yeah." he said. "You didn't think Saint was my real name, did you?"

"Who cares if you changed your name? I did too - I used to be Marvin, so what? The real you is the one on that stage, Paul. You may not think so but ... "

"Oh yeah!" he interrupted. "You think they know me so well? Well, what about this? Do you think I'd still be a god if they knew about this?" And with that, Paul reached up and pulled at his hair and off came a wig of curly platinum blond. He threw it on a chair.

"Oh my God!" That he had changed his name was nothing but I was hardly expecting this. I was stunned. I made sure that the dressing room door was locked. "It ... uh ... my god, Paul ... it sure looked real ... that's amazing." I tried to smile. He had transformed into a fairly ordinary looking guy with a balding crew cut of mousy brown hair. I tried to lighten things up. "Well, I guess that's showbiz!" I said.

"It's just more bullshit," he said before sitting down in the chair, his wig in his lap.

"Well, at any rate, it sure is lifelike."

"Of course it's lifelike," said Paul wrapping one of the blond curls around his finger. "It's real fucking hair - I paid a fortune it and the three others that back it up." He pointed to a small black valise. "So they love ME, Marty? Take a look at my eyes - tell me what color they are." He beamed at me jutting his face forward.

"They're uh...blue?" I said. "Bright blue."

"No they're not, they aren't blue at all. They're a very non-descript brown that would hardly look so appealing on the cover of Sixteen magazine. These are contact lenses, Marty, and the bullshit just keeps on going from my capped teeth to my tanning lotion to my three-inch heels ... hell, I even stick a sock in my crotch! I mean even my voice isn't really MINE! You've heard all the echo and digital delay and that they throw on it out at the soundboard. Christ, if you had the right equipment you could sound like me:"

I sat in the chair next to him; searching for something comforting to say. And secretly wondering if I should have thought of all these gimmicks back in my own hey-day; maybe things would have been different. "But that's not... really the important thing, Paul. I mean, really what's the difference? Hair, teeth, and eyes ... we're all just dust-to-dust anyway. It's your talent that's real - that's really you. There's nothing phony about that."

Paul held his head in his hands and looked at me from the corner of his eye. "Talent? Tell me the truth, Marty. This isn't your kind of music and I know it and you know it - do you really think I'm so fucking talented?"

"Well, Paul, I'm not gonna lie to you. It's not exactly my kind of music true, but it's catchy and after watching your show so many times I find myself singing along. You just can't help but not. And really ... what I think is not so important. Haven't you ever heard the advice about 'not playing for the kitchen help'? 'Cause they're not the ones who pay good money to see you. And that's the proof of the fucking pudding. Those kids are the ones whose opinions really count - and they think you've got all the talent in the world - that's obvious. And they're the ones who ultimately decide what plays and what doesn't in this game."

"I don't know, Marty. Sometimes I get so confused. I don't even know what talent is anymore." He casually put his wig back on; smoothed it in place. I was relieved.

"Well, I'll tell you one thing, Paul - Joe Lippell knows what talent is and he thinks you got a hell of a lot. He told me that your new songs are the best you've ever written. He thinks this next album is gonna be the turning point gonna force the critics to sit up and take serious notice of you."

"Really?" He was surprised. "He really told you that?"

"Paul, he believes in you all the way! If he didn't held just take out a heavy life insurance policy on you and sit back and wait. Believe me, there are managers like that. And that's why I'm here, he doesn't want to see it all go down the drain." "But Marty, do you know what it's like? I mean all your life you work your ass off trying to make it and you're so depressed at not making it but you just keep pushing because you know that when you do you'll be ecstatic - you're just eating and breathing and existing for that day. And than - WHAM! You're the biggest thing since ... the last biggest thing - bigger than you ever imagined.

"And then ... you begin to realize that you're not getting off on it - it isn't what you expected. Like that song by Peggy Lee: "Is That All There Is?" But there's no place to go from there except back down. And that's terrifying." I could see the fear in his eyes. "And inevitable, tool"

"But Paul, maybe you just never gave it a chance to blossom. You went straight from starving artist to international pop superstar without stopping to collect any satisfaction. You just gotta slow down and let it become real again."

I don't know, maybe you're rights Marty. I tell you, I'm getting tired of all this anyhow. Maybe I should straighten out." He laughed. "At this point, it might be the only thing that will really get me off."

"Listen Paul, I got an idea: Give me that little bag of goodies and I'll go find Tommy Moonshot and tell him that we got the word that the law is after you down here for some ... paternity suit! So you don't want to be holding anything in case they grab you. And I'll send him back to New York. And then, after the show tonight, why don't we grab some beers and go back to the motel and play some guitar together. I'd love to hear your new songs."

For a long time he just seemed to be looking right through me and then he went over to his jacket and got out the bag and handed it to me, I was truly moved. "Oh, Paul, that's great! You're gonna start seeing what I was..."

"Get the fuck out of here before I change my mind and send you back to New York instead of Tommy Moonshot!"

I knew I was on thin ice. I wasn't sure if I had actually convinced him of anything at all or if he was just such a ham that he could not resist the maudlin sentimentality of playing along with me for this scene.

It wasn't hard getting rid of that Moonshot character. Once I mentioned 'the law' he made fast tracks. My show that night was a little lacking; I think I bad used up too much emotion with Paul. But his seemed to be better. At least he was trying again. He'd smile at me as I stood by the side of the stage and I'd give him the thumbs-up sign, which was admittedly corny but not had act so bad as if I'd given the V-for-victory sign. And with a case of beer trailing behind us (via roadie) we did go back to his hotel suite after the show. We most stature didn't play guitar together. Like most stars of his stature he carried his own portable stereo system that aluminum Anvil cases from hotel to hotel. He played me some rough tapes he had made down in the Bahamas of his new material. Joe was right - it was different from Sainthood's usual fare. The rhythms seemed to be a little more intricate than their standard jackhammer approach and there were some nice ballads, too.

"It's good stuff," I told Paul after the tape was over.   I   think it's just right; I think your fans will still go for it and I think the critics will have to admit that it's real growth. Shit, it's amazing what a few days of being straight will do for you!"

"Did you like that last one?" asked Paul shyly. "Somewhere there's a baby of mine... " He sang softly.

"Yeah," I said. "It's real pretty."

"It's about my kid," said Paul. "Do you think it's too obvious? I tried to make it sound like it's about a girl."

"Your kid? What kid?"

"My boy - Paul Jr. - that's what kid. He's a little over three years old." He smiled proudly.

"Oh my God! Who's the mother?" I wouldn't have been surprised if he didn't know her name.

"My wife Kate: that's the mother! Who'd you think?"

"I didn't know that you were married. How was I supposed to know? You never mentioned it."

"Well...we're separated, have been for a while. Kate couldn't take the lifestyle. She said New York was no place to raise a kid. I sent them back to Ohio - bought them a house in Shaker Heights. I couldn't really blame her."

"You're full of surprises, Paul."

"Now I really didn't know who he was. Heavy-metal demon or tortured family man?"

"Well, I don't publicize it. I don't think the sixteen year-old girls would dig it too much. The image* you knows and all that crap." He passed me another beer.

"Did your wife ever come on the road with you?" I asked.

"Oh ... a little bit. But she couldn't take it."

"Too wild, eh?"

"Wild? Are you kidding me? Too boring! What? Don't tell me you believe all that shit about me wrecking rooms and throwing TVs out the window? I've never done anything with a TV except turn it on and off; my publicity agent makes all that up."

"You've never thrown a TV out the window?" I was shocked. I thought all rock stars with money to burn did this kind of stuff for kicks. Personally, I could never afford it. Maybe I could have thrown a light bulb or two.

"Hell no!" said Paul.

"Well let's do it!" I exclaimed. "I've always wanted to!"

"What?'

"Come on! You're entitled to raise a little hell!"

"I raised my beer. "Chug-a-lug."

So we chugged a few more beers, wrestled with the TV - it was kind of screwed to it's base rock-star proof, I guess - and finally got it off. We did have the decorum to open the window first and check below that no one was passing underneath before we gave it the old heave-ho. Like two kids we watched it sail to the ground. Disappointingly, it didn't explode - it just sort of shattered. We were both still howling when the phone rang, It was the night desk clerk. I guess Paul Saint was the obvious suspect. Paul said that since it was my idea I had to answer the phone. So I told the screaming desk clerk that as members of the moral majority we could no longer sit idly by while Hollywood continued to present this filth and decadence on television. We'd done it for the youth of America - as a protest. And yes, of course, put it on the bill and send us up some Champagne.

The rest of the out-of-town dates went beautifully. Paul's shows were getting better and better, He was really putting out. And my own shows weren't doing too badly either. Afterwards, Paul and I would get drunk together and it even got to the point where I didn't mind when he took off his wig. Even tried it on once. Maybe blond hair was the answer? I was really looking forward to our final date at Madison square Garden. The critics would be shocked that I was playing The Garden - they'd have to take notice. Once again, my standing in the New York rock community would be assured. And Joe Lippell would have to congratulate me on a job well done. My mother would be proud.

Chapter 4

We returned to New York a few days before the Madison
Square Garden concert to give the crew and everybody a few days
to relax. Yours truly was hardly included in this mini-vacation
because I was back to baby-sitting Paul through his all-night
odysseys of the New York rock circuit. The bad news was that
Inger Peach would not be back from Atlantic City until after the
show and I was a little disappointed with this but then again I
knew there would be no way I could out-do my now mythological
performance at The Omni which had been the catalyst to send her
packing. She was making good money down there and the
management seemed to be 'straight' and they liked her a lot. They
had even offered to help her find an apartment or house in the
area if she wanted to work on a regular weekly basis rather than
ten days on and ten days off. She said that maybe this wasn't a
bad idea but I'm sure she told me all this so that I would make up
my own mind. Just hearing her voice on the phone was making
me incredibly horny.

"Do you miss met sugar?" she asked seductively.

"I sure do," I insisted. "I'm gonna be so out of shape by the
time you get back that you'll have to teach me all over again."

"Well, just remember even though I'm not coming back for
good - I'm coming back for fun! She giggled. I begged her to stop.

The night before the big show, Paul Saint and I were in
TRAX, that famous rock club on the west side, having a drink.
Paul had sworn to me that we'd make it an early night. As I went
into the men's room I thought I saw Tommy Moonshot walking
up to the bar where Paul was.

But a lot of guys wear cowboy hats. Later that night Paul
disappeared. He'd done this before; I wasn't too worried. Usually
he called me the next day to apologize and describe the raving
beauty, held just spent the night with.

He had been pretty cool concerning drugs lately too, just
smoking a little reefer and taking an occasional hit of coke.

Downright sensible! And besides, I figured that no one in
their right mind would jeopardize a show at Madison Square
Garden. But the next day I didn't hear from Paul like I thought I
would. I went about my business, getting ready for the night's
performance. I was in the shower when the phone rang.

"Paul! Paul! Wake up!"   I heard someone yelling.

"Hello ... Hello?"

"Marty? It's Joe Lippell. Where the hell were you?"

He sounded panic-stricken,

"What are you talking about? What's wrong?" I was afraid I already knew the answer. "Is it Paul?"

"Marty - you better get over here right away. I'm at The Plaza - room twenty-eleven." He hung up. I went out with wet hair and raced over to The Plaza, and up to the room. Joe opened the door. He looked drained.

"Well, I don't think he's gonna die!" he said.

"Die? What are you talking about? Where's Paul?"

"Take a look, Marty." And there was Paul. He looked awful. He was half lying on the bed with his knees on the floor and his head in his hands and his wig on crooked. The whole room smelled of vomit.

"What happened?"

"What happened? You tell me! You were supposed to be taking care of him so that nothing like this would accusingly. You tell me what happened!" Joe yelled.

"I was with him, Joe! But he disappeared, and I figured he picked up a girl. He was fine when I last saw him he was talking about how much he was looking forward to tonight's show!"

"That should have tipped you off," said Joe. "He never looks forward to a show!" He walked over to Paul, "Do you feel any better?" Paul's mumbled reply was not intelligible; didn't sound too positive, Joe sat next to him on the bed and shook his head.

"Well, I think Paul did some serious damage to the cocaine reserves of New York," he said to me, "And being the true artist that he is - he's expanding into new realm, heroin."

"Heroin?" I was shocked.

"Oh yeah! Haven't you heard?" said Joe sarcastically "It's the newest trend among the jet-set here." He pointed to Paul who said nothing. "I got most of the story out of him. He was up all night doing coke and he was getting so wired that he wanted something to bring him down. So one of his 'good friends' gave him a little heroin to snort and it was a lot stronger than superman here expected. It didn't really hit him until a few hours later." Joe looked at Paul not knowing whether to be mad or sad, "He called me about noon. He could barely get his room number out. I rushed right over here. Luckily the door was unlocked. He was throwing up everywhere and his eyes were rolling in his head. A few times he passed right out on me and I had to smack him right across the face." Joe looked at me like he felt guilty about this. "What else could I do? It was the first time I'd hit anybody in years." Joe started pacing the room. "This is fucking crazy! Look at him for Christ's sakes he's almost forty years old and I swear those thirteen-year-old kids who come to his concerts have more sense than he does!"

"Forty?"

"Sure! He's almost as old as me."

"I had no idea. Hell, he's eight years older than me," The weird thing was that I had always felt older than him.

When he told me about all those years of waiting to 'make it' he wasn't kidding. And the wife and the kid; I mean, I always considered myself to be masquerading as a teenager but Paul was really living a lie. None of this was making any sense. I looked around the suite with it's fireplace and antique furniture and beautiful view of Central Park and thick rugs and high ceilings with ornate molding and a king-sized bed ... it cost over two hundred and fifty bucks a day! And then I looked at Paul, with one shoe on and his sock down around his heel. His clothes were stained and his face looked dirty and unshaven - his dark whiskers contrasted grotesquely with his blond wig. Even his phony blue eyes had lost their luster and he had dark circles that looked like black eyes. His mouth was caked with dry vomit. Out on the street, he'd just be another bum. But he wasn't a bum - he was a superstar! His face had been on the cover of People magazine - they wrote make-believe gossip about him in The National Star. He was an industry too; he owned whole buildings of condominiums on the west coast of Florida. But as I looked at him I felt deceived like any one of his fans would have felt if they were in my place. And this was what I was tearing myself apart about? This was where I wanted to be? Would I be any different from him? Would it be me lying there stinking of puke?

All my professional life I'd hear rumors about the mega-stars of rock; about their drugs and their decadence, but for some reason I never really believed it. And then every couple of years one of them dies and I still don't believe it. I still have this image of Nirvana at the end of the rock rainbow. But as I sat there looking at Paul, I thought that I could just as easily have been looking at Brian Jones or Jimi Hendrix or Janis Joplin or Jim Morrison. Or even Elvis Presley - the King himself. And it just never seems to stop. I mean are Keith Moon and John Bonham really gone? I mean, where's the payoff? And then you think of someone who straightened out their act, was in love with a good woman, and a good father ... and there's John Lennon lying in the back of a policeman's car with five bullets in him and the cop asks him "Are you John Lennon?" and with all his strength he mumbles "Yeah ... " And I wondered if that cop would have asked him: "Are you glad that you're John Lennon?" what he would have said at that moment.

They say survival is the strongest human instinct. Reproduction is the second strongest, and if there's anything that's been pushing me all these years that it: Trying to reproduce that sense of grandeur that rock & roll had for me as a kid. But right now, as I looked at Paul Saint starting to throw up again when there was nothing left to come out, it was survival I was thinking about. My own. Was this really what I wanted? And I thought of Barbara's offer of a job with Garcia Ortega and a new life.

"Oh man!" I was surprised at my tears. "How could you do this to yourself? What for? You're playing goddamn Madison Square Garden tonight!"

"He sort of opened one eye to look at me and tried to smile but it only made him gag.

"Uh ... hello Marty ... I guess I ... fucked ... up." He could barely whisper

"He's so weak from throwing up that he can hardly walk," said Joe. "I don't know what the hell to do! In a few hours there will be twenty thousand kids waiting for his grand entrance - he just can't go on like this! It would ruin him!"

There was little I could think to do or say. Joe was right; Paul couldn't go on like this and yet it was too late to cancel the show. We sat on either side of Paul, not saying much.

"Listen ... let Marty do its" Paul mumbled.

"What?" said Joe. "What the hell are you talking about? Marty can't headline this show! This is serious! We're in trouble.'

"No ... no ... no," Paul whispered. "Marty can do it he knows all the songs - he told me ... he's seen the act over and over and over ... he knows it better than me. Everybody knows better..." He started to nod off. "Just wear this ... He tried to toss his wig at me, but it just fell to the floor.

Joe looked at me. "Is he serious? Could you really do it?"

"What are you talking about? There's no understudies in rock &roll!"

"But do you know the songs as well as he says?" asked Joe.

"Well, sure, I know the songs. I've been on tour with him for almost a month - and most of them are such huge hits that everybody knows them! After some of the shows I used to get him to play them for me on acoustic guitar so I could tell him what a good songwriter he was - like what you said I should do. And to tell you the truth, they're not bad...but what the hell are you talking about? I'm not Paul Saint!"

"Maybe 'Marty Saint' will do," said Joe. He picked up Paul's wig and put it on me. Paul was passed out cold by now.

"Not bad... said Joe quietly. "And I'm sure between the two of us we could get the makeup right. And his pirate outfit is right here in his trunk." Joe took another look at me in Paul's wig. "No, it's not bad." He said and smiled.

"Not bad? Are you out - of your mind? I can't ... " I took the wig and threw it on the floor.

"Shhh! Joe looked at me very seriously. Then he bent down and picked up the wig and put it back on my head. "Remember something, Marty, you had a job to do. I was depending on you."

"But I couldn't help it, Joe! It's not my fault he went and did this to himself! It's not..."

Joe covered my month with his hand with enough force that I knew he wasn't fooling. "Shhh! Just let Uncle Joe take care of everything," he said to me seriously.

He made me dress in all of Paul's stage gear; told me to stuff a sock down my pants. Everything fit pretty well except the shoes, so I kept on my own cowboy boots. Then Joe had me sit at the dressing table in the bedroom and he put makeup on me. "Where'd you learn to do that?" I asked.

"Sometimes Paul would be too out of it, and I'd have to take care of it," said Joe. "And in three years I have a pretty good idea of what he should look like, ya know."

Joe combined different parts of two or three pirate costumes; he said the more covered I was the better. I even wore the black eye patch used mainly in publicity pictures. The only thing that didn't really go were my cowboy boots with the knee britches and white knee socks but Joe assured me that no one would notice because of the monitor speakers on the floor. My condition at the time could be described as reluctant-catatonic. I knew what was happening though I dared not think of it.

Joe firmly fastened Paul's wig, The final touch was three-cornered hat with a large red ostrich plume,

"Now, go look at yourself in the mirror, said Joe with the understated assurance of Edith Head.

I think somewhere in the back of my mind I figured to play along with Joe until he saw the folly of his ways. But when I looked in the mirror - It was scary!

It was Paul Saint!

I was speechless and kept looking back and forth from the mirror to Joe and back to the mirror. "Now listen to met Marty," said Joe, "This is what we're gonna do..."

"What do you mean we?" I said weakly.

"Just listen," he continued. "We're gonna pack all this stuff up and you and I are going to the Garden and sleeping beauty is gonna stay here." Joe put his hand on my shoulder. "We're gonna have to cancel your part of the show."

"What?" I screamed. "Joe please! You can't do this to me! I've been waiting to play Madison square Garden my whole life! Please! Don't do this to me!" I pleaded. "This is probably the only chance I'll ever get!"

"Marty, we have no choice. You can't possibly do both shows - you'll be exhausted. And we can't do this changeover at The Garden - someone might see! We got to get together with the rest of the guys in Sainthood and tell them what happened - they won't want to blow this gig either - and you'll need at least an hour to go through the whole show with them. You just can't go out there cold, ya know." He spoke to me as if I was the unreasonable one!

"But Joe, it's The Garden!" I was almost crying.

"Marty, I swear I'll make it up to you," he said. "This is the way it's got to be. You got to understand something: Sainthood is a multimillion-dollar organization and an ongoing series of investments by the record company and just plain fucking banks tool And they're all gonna be there tonight - this is New York. Now, I've covered for Paul for a long, long time - a very long time and no one knows how fucked up he is but me. But, if he does a no-show tonight at The Garden, well, it will be the beginning of the end. You see, you can do anything you want in rock In roll as long as it doesn't affect the BUSINESS - and that's what this is - BUSINESS! If they start writing him off as a flake, an unsecured investment, then I'll be written off too. As a manager who isn't able to control his artist - that's what a manager's main job is supposed to be, ya know. And I've worked too dam hard to lose it all over him!" He pointed to Paul. "And no matter how crazy this scheme may be, I'd rather give it a try than just say fuck it and have to wake up tomorrow morning and face a whole new world."

There was no more argument. Joe was convinced this was the only possible way out of this mess. I hardly agreed but I accepted my fate. I looked forward to being laughed out of the music industry.

"All right Joe ... I'll do whatever you want. I needed an excuse to end this half-assed career of mine anyway. And I guess I owe it to you, because once you put your ass on the line for me and though it didn't work, I'll do the same for you. Though I know this ain't gonna work either." I could always change my name back to Marvin. Call up Betty Klein.

"No one outside of you and me and the band will ever knows Marty. You gotta understand that half the people in these arenas can't see much more than a moving speck with blond hair on the stage anyway. I'll speak to the sound-man - I'll tell him that Paul's voice isn't too strong tonight and he should really lay on the echo and all the other devices. And you just keep moving and jumping like the Saint here and shaking that hair of his and the band will pull you through." He seemed confident. "Just remember that the more fucked-up you act - the more they'll believe that it's Paul Saint!"

I did not share his confidence. "It will never work...it won't work ... it won't..." I pulled out my last ace: "Joe, isn't there a law against this? Isn't this fraud or something?"

"The only law that has anything to do with this is the one against first-degree murder, because that's what I'm gonna do to you if you don't shut up!" He said emphatically. The Italian in Joe was coming out. "So stop your moaning and groaning and listen to me: Now while you're on stage, I'm gonna come back here to

The Plaza and pick up wonder-boy who by that time will have had a few hours sleep and will be ready to face the world. I'll sneak him into The Garden so he'll\ be there when you get off. You'll turn back into Marty May and no one will be the wiser. He pointed at the sleeping figure on the bed. "And Paul Saint will still have a career."

I looked at Paul's pathetic figure. "What Paul has must be contagious," I said.

"What do you mean?" asked Joe.

"I mean I think I'm gonna throw up," I said.

Total recall has never been my strongest point. Like I've often said, I lost my memory somewhere back in the Sixties. What happened that night at Madison Square Garden comes back to me in bits and snatches. I remember sitting in the dressing room with the other members of Sainthood and Joe Lippell and hearing him explain to them what we were going to do. Although I had been counting on them to talk Joe out of it, the die was certainly cast when I walked into the dressing room and everyone greeted me as Paul. They were flabbergasted when Joe said that it was Marty - not Paul. And when he said that I was going to be filling in for Paul this night, they seemed to really get off on the idea; like it was something new and exciting to relieve the monotony of doing the same show night after night. For the next hour and a half while the audience was told that Marty May would not be appearing tonight due to a broken down truck somewhere (I didn't hear of anyone asking for a refund...damn!), and my band was told that I had food poisonings and sent home - we went through the Sainthood show from beginning to end. The songs with the most difficult arrangements were left out and the instrumental breaks in the other songs were expanded so I'd have more time just to jump around impersonating Paul instead of singing) which would be more difficult As we went over the show, I was surprised to see just how many songs I did, in fact, know. And most of the songs had long harmony sections like Queen or STYX so that all of the other guys would be singing too and if I forgot something I could just fake it. And besides, Oliver, the lead guitarist and Benny the drummer, the only original members of the group, said that I couldn't do much worse than Paul Saint himself on his more stoned-out nights.

As I stood by the side of the stage waiting to make my entrance, the band did their heavy-metal overture. I think I was shaking so much that I appeared a bit blurry. Joe stayed right next to me and made sure nobody talked to me. I compared the distance between myself and that center stage microphone to the *last mile* between a condemned man and the electric chair. A roadie fixed the rope that I would swing out on; I was to put my shoe in the loop and hold on to the rope with one hand while wildly waving and shouting. The moment came - I gave Joe Lippell one last desperate look - the three roadies on the other end of the rope pulled and I was swung out on the stage. The lights were flashing wildly and the crowd was just absolutely erupting. If anyone could have seen closely they would have known that my open-mouthed screams were actually screams of horror. Like a man being lowered into a cage of wild animals, deposited

center stage but when I went to step out of the loop the heel of my cowboy boot got caught and I fell down. Paul's little dancing shoes bad slid out easily, I thought the charade was up before it even started but as I lay there flat on my backs expecting to be lynched by this mob, I found that they were not booing. No, not they were screaming and cheering even morel This was something they would have loved to see Paul Saint do. Joe was right, the more fucked up I acted the more believable I would be! Oliver, the guitarist helped me get up and I staggered to the microphone in a faked-stoned stupor though the weakness in my knees did not make that too difficult. I sauntered across the front of the stage making faces and taunting the audience, as Paul would have done. Joe had them increase the amount of security so that none of the hysterical little girls in the front rows could crawl on stage but I couldn't have asked for more encouraging cheerleaders. They were screaming and crying and reaching out for me - one of them looked so beside herself that I lifted up the black patch and winked at her and played this drove all of them even more nuts. I mm= the stoned act to the hilt. When I couldn't think of anything else to do I'd just lean against the 'side monitors with a totally wrecked expression on my face and they loved it. Maybe I'm more of a 'trooper' than I give myself credit for more of a professional full of the old 'show must go on' bullshit; but whatever it was that was making my fear disappear and the 'ham' in me come out - something was happening! I was beginning to FEEL like Paul Saint it was like some kind of transformation.

There I was. In a way it was where I always wanted to be. I had come close but it was never like this. I looked out to a sea of cheering faces - and they were all looking at me, their eyes glued on nothing else - it was thrilling! And than I'd think, but it's not me - but it was! I moved around that stage just like Paul, camping it up to the hilt. Making faces and pretending I was screaming at them. Like some caged rock In roll beast. I swaggered up to the microphone. I had left my fear somewhere else. I wasn't Marty May anymore.

"GOODEEEVEEENNNIIINNNGGG!!!!!" I screamed in a Saint-like roar. There was so much echo on my voice that it kept reverberating for ten seconds.

"GOOOOOOOD EEEVVVEEENNNIIINNNGGG!!! They screamed back. They knew their part just like I knew mine. I repeated it a few times, and then I took the microphone off the stand and jumped onto the drum riser. Bennie, the drummer, gave me a wink and a smile and a thumbs-up sign but I didn't need it at this point. It was all real enough for me.

I put one fist in the air. "DO YOU BELIEVE?!" I beseeched the audience. And amazingly enough they did.

Because what they wanted was what I wanted. They wanted me to be a rock-god. And I screamed from Olympian heights. They wanted me to be everything that they imagined Paul Saint to be. And in a ways that was probably an easier job for me than for Paul himself - there was no conflict about what was real and what wasn't. Surprisingly, there was a little more heavy-metal soul in me than I ever would have imagined. I'm told that the show were very smoothly. Like I said, I don't remember too much; maybe it was a case of instant schizophrenia.

I do remember forgetting a line here or there and I don't think that I talked as much as Paul would have in between the songs. But the rest of Sainthood really pulled me through and Oliver would whisper hints into my ear like: "Do jumping jacks!" or "Twirl around in circles during the chorus!" or "Make your voice lower- growl morel" or "Don't smile so much - Paul was never happy!" And Joe Lippell was right - no one seemed to know the difference.

And then it was over. After one encore, Joe was back at the side of the stage and grabbed me (Personally, I would have done more encores!), threw a towel over my head, and whisked me back into the dressing room. The REAL Paul Saint was sitting there looking almost normal; looking just like me.

"You saved my life, Marty," he said faintly.

"Oh ... it was nothing." And I started to cry.

The next morning, I was awoken by a messenger from Joe Lippell. He handed me an envelope; in it was a review from that mornings New York Times:

SAINTHOOD ROCKS THE GARDEN

Although in the past this reviewer has found little to cheer about concerning the heavy-metal phenomena Sainthood, I must admit that after witnessing the five-member band's performance last night at Madison Square Gardens I was at least halfway turned around. Led by Paul Saint, the group's vivacious lead singer, the band did a set consisting of nearly all hit songs already familiar to their legions of fans. But what made this performance extraordinary was the amount of energy Mr. Saint exuded during his nearly two-hour performance. A combination of Captain Kidd (lately he has taken the new-romantics look so popular in London as his own trademark) and a crazed pied piper, the indefatigable Mr. Saint led both the audience and his own fellow band members through a rousing set. There wasn't that sense of over-rehearsed faked excitement which has marked some of their earlier performances - everything seemed fresh and new. Hopefully, this marks the beginning of a new era for Mr. Saint and his band Sainthood, for if this renewed sense of vitality could be combined with fresh original material, I feel that they could take their place with other first-rate rock bands who have also risen above their mundane and far too often gimmicky and uninteresting beginnings. This reviewer awaits hopefully that these wishes will be fulfilled when their new album is released in the months ahead.

Stapled to the review was a check for ten thousand dollars.

Part Six
Blind Red Rose
New York City
1983

Chapter 1

I called Inger down in Atlantic City. I told her about my temporary Sainthood and she got a real kick out of it; told me about a time down in Vegas when the same thing had happened to some famous stripper. It didn't seem like quite the same thing to me. I called Joe to say a very big thanks for the ten-grand. He said I deserved it and I couldn't argue with him. He also said, "Don't thank me - it's from Paul." Joe said that he was going to see what he could do to find me another recording contract. I wouldn't hold my breath on that one - money is one thing but miracles are quite another

And it seemed that even a little human progress might come about in the case of Paul Saint, too. Apparently, Joe had told him that this was the last straw and he could go find himself a new manager. This shook Paul up; he said that if Joe didn't manage him held quit the business. So, Joe said that there was only one condition under which held stay involved. And so ... probably at this very moment, Paul Saint is sitting in some shrink's office at this very ritzy drug rehabilitation clinic in Connecticut talking about his childhood traumas, probably with his makeup on.

But maybe I was the one who should have been lying on that couch for the whole experience left me ... well, confused. Whatever goals I had had now seemed totally muddled; that vision of rock super-stardom that I had always been wanting and living with was badly corrupted. Living on the edge loses its allure when one starts staring into the crevice below rather than making faces in the other direction at those afraid to come close.

And I was beginning to associate Inger with that *edgedom* syndrome too. Not that she took drugs, she didn't. But I just was feeling awfully tired of thumbing my nose IN at respectable society. Where they so much worse? Was there really any hypocrisy there that did not exist in the world of rock on roll? And eve while I lay in bed with horny thoughts of Inger, I also found myself thinking of Barbara, her job as school teacher, the way she had gotten out of the madness. And her offer of a job with Garcia Ortega. I was reading The Village Voice looking for a review of my Sainthood show. I had put the New York Times one in with my other press-book clippings - maybe it would be the last entry. An apt footnote to the professional life of Marty May -

pseudo rock-star. They didn't seem to have covered the show in The Voice. Instead the critic had done an extensive report on a "New Romantics" group that had played down in Soho for less than a hundred people. I guess the twenty thousand at the Garden didn't count.

But looking through The Voice I noticed with excited surprise that Blind Red Rose was making a return engagement at Tramps. It was billed as his 'Definite Final Performance, beginning tonight for two days. I called the club and found out that they were once again staying at The Chelsea Hotel. I called immediately and Ruby answered the phone.

"Marty! How ya doin'?" said Ruby Rose.

"I'm okay, Ruby, how about yourself? ' I asked.

"Oh, you know, I could complain but I'm too stubborn," she laughed. "I see that you and Red are back at Tramps."

"Well, yeah, when Red found out that he had to have this operation he wanted to do one more show first."

"What operation?"

"Oh, I don't know, Marty. These doctor's have explained it to me a thousand times and I still can't get it right. Something about Red's stomach lining - he's burning holes in it from all that Jack Daniels he's been putting away through the years. He's had to stop drinkin' for now - and it's driving him and me crazy!"

"I'll bet. That was sort of his diet staple, as they say."

"Well, he's a bit ornery but he'll survive. But listen, tell me how your high school reunion went - did they all make a big fuss out of you? I mean, imagine that: In your honor and all!"

I had forgotten all about it. Or at least I had tried my best to block it out. That's right, I told Ruby it was in my honor. I must have been crazy. It seemed a long, long time ago.

"Oh yeah ... well, you know how these things are, lots of old faces and drinking and all that. The best thing was that I got a limousine for the night." I didn't even lie.

"Oh, yeah? Well you must have impressed the shit out of 'em," said Ruby. She and Inger had the same warm southern drawl.

"Yeah, yeah ... but I'm just glad it's over now. And well, I'm just sorry that I missed playing with Red that night. Maybe I could make it up to you by coming down
to Tramps and jamming a little tonight?"

"Oh, Marty, that would be wonderful! You know, the last time we was here, Red was giving some interview to some guy who says that he's talked to you too ... I think his name is Dave something..."

"Yeah, I know him, he's doing some kind of a book about rock In roll and blues, I think."

"Yeah, yeah that's it. Anyway, Red was telling him that you was the best guitar player he ever had. He said that you was full of the white man's blues which in the long run were a lot more terrible for the soul." She laughed again

"I wouldn't argue with him on that," I said.

"Anyway, this writer was saying that it would be so great if you two ever got together again. I'll have to call him and tell him bout tonight!" she said excitedly.
"But tell me, how are things going with you?"

"Oh, I guess things are looking up," I said unconvincingly. "Best thing is I kind of have a new girlfriend."

"Where there's life, there's hope," said Ruby laughing.

"And where's there's hope - there's disappointment I added sarcastically.

"Red was right," said Ruby. "You do have the blues even worse than he does."

So how's Red doing, Ruby? Give it to me straight."

"Well ... he thinks he's doing fine, Marty. But the truth is that Red's performing days are over..."

"Oh come on, Ruby. That's what you told me last time."

"No, I'm serious, Marty. It's the God's honest truth. He's got to have this operation and then he's really got_ to find a place to settle down and ... go out to pasture, I'm afraid to say. The only problem is that there ain't a retirement plan for blues singers like my daddy, you know? If he had anything to fall back on, we would have called it quits years ago. We just couldn't afford to, that's all. These doctor's bills just keep coming in and Red ain't about to go on no welfare."

"No, he's too proud for that."

"Yeah, and too stupid! I told him, for God's sakes Daddy - you're almost seventy years old - slow down a little bit - and let this great country take care of you after all you've given in culture. But he won't listen to me. Besides he won't admit to being any older than sixty-two - and I'm almost forty-five myself!"

"Where are you thinking of settling down? Do you still have that little place outside of Detroit?"

"No, no ... God, it's been a long time since you was with us ... we had to give that up a while ago. But I heard that they're building some fancy new projects in Detroit
now.   You know they're trying to improve the city's image and all. It's these Ford people or something - ya know, they're always doing something for us po' colored." Her laughter was colored with bitterness.

"Projects? Can't you find an apartment or something?"

"Well ... I just mean for a little while, Marty," said Ruby. Unwittingly, I'd hurt her pride. "Then, after Red
gets over his operation, I guess I'll get a job or something as soon as I find someone to take care of him. I should says, someone who'd put up with him." But what she meant was someone who'd love him as only she did.

"Oh ... yeah. I see, well, I'm sure everything will turn out all right, Ruby," I said, but I knew better.

"Oh yeah, don't you worry, Marty! Red's got Lady Luck on his side - always has. You jus' come on down to Tramps tonight and bring your guitar. You still got one, don't cha?"

"Of course!"

"Just kiddin' you baby! I'll see you tonight and I know Red will jus' love to be playin' with his little pro-toe-jay!" She emphasized the word.

"Mozart May - on the way!" I said. Talk about what happens to the mega-stars like Paul
Saint, I had never really thought about what happens to guys like Blind Red Rose. Here, he goes through life blind and black and singing the blues, and I guess I just figured that there's a pot of gold somewhere at the end of his rainbow. Guys like Paul Saint end up ODing in hotel rooms; guys like Red Rose are lucky to have a room.

So that night, guitar in hand, I headed on down to Tramps. Since, Inger Peach was still in Atlantic City I was solo. When I walked in the place was more crowded than I expected. The tables were all full and there was a respectable sized crowd at the bar. Jerry Ryan, the owner, was sitting at the bar.

"Marty May! How the hell are you? Ruby said you was coming down - let me get you a Guinness." And he did. With an Irishman like Jerry, it was the only respectable drink' to have.

"I'm okay, Jerry. How about yourself?"

"Ah ... I can't complaint" he said. "How was your class reunion?" he asked with a bit of a snicker.

"Don't mention it. Disasterville."

"Those things always are, aren't they now?" said Jerry. "The girls get fat and your old pals get boring." He laughed. How come everybody knows this except me? "So what have you been doing since, Marty?" he asked.

"Oh, a little bit of everything. I went out to the Coast...and a few dates down South." I didn't want to go into details. "Mainly just trying to figure things out."

"Don't think too hard!" said Jerry jokingly. "You don't want to go burning out what brain cells you got left, now do you?"

"No, don't worry, Jerry. It's still a mystery to me and I think I'll keep it that way." Jerry and I were good at this kind of barroom talk about nothing in particular and everything in general.

"Not bad business, eh?" I said with raised eyebrows.

"No, no, not bad at all." agreed Jerry. "I think that Definitely Final Performance got to them. When someone gets to Red's age people tend to believe it more and more. It's not like when you write that about some punk band who everybody knows is gonna do another gig as soon as they need the bread."

"As soon as they need a fix," I added. "But you know it's still tough with these old blues guys. I bring some of them up here from Texas or out from Chicago or Detroit who are certified legends - these guys should be in fucking museums and maybe I get half a house. It's a shame too. These kids should have more respect for these guys, but no record company wants to record them anymore. Sometimes I think they forget where all this rock In roll came from. If it weren't for guys like Red Rose there wouldn't be guys like Mick Jagger."

"And there definitely wouldn't be guys like Marty May!" I laughed.

"That's right," said Jerry. "You got your first break with him."

"Definitely," I said. "Maybe my only real one, too."

"Well, it's just a shame that the blues ain't as popular anymore," said Jerry with resignation. "Years ago, I'd have lines around the block for a guy like Red Rose. All kids want is that heavy-metal shit, like that group that wears all the makeup...they were just at The Garden ... what's their name ... The Saints or something?"

"Something like that..." I said timidly. "You talking about Sainthood?"

"Yeah, that's it," said Jerry. "But I don't like to put anyone down - more power to them. A friend of mine got some free tickets and saw them at The Garden last time they came around. He said they actually weren't bad; said the lead singer has a lot of charisma."

"Well ... I heard that was one of his good nights," I said proudly. Where's Ruby?"

"Oh, she's right down in front, watching her old man." Jerry pointed toward the stage. "Everyone should be lucky enough to have a kid as faithful as that. She just sticks in there with him through thick and thin. And I think it's been pretty thin, lately."

"Tell me, Jerry, how's Red's shows these days?"

Jerry grimaced. "Not like it use to be, Marty."

"Has his stroke affected him?"

"Well ... I'd like to say that it hasn't ... but he's not quite as quick anymore, he relies on the other musicians for the energy, you know, and sometimes he forgets some of the words. But what can you expect? The man is ancient! He should be in an old folk's home - not on a stage."

"Yeah ... I know."

"But I gotta say too, that he still has his moments - there are still those times when it sounds like it's coming right out of a cotton-field in the Delta; that wailing ... you can't describe it, but nobody can do it like these original guys. And it's gonna die with them, I'm afraid to say." He shook his head. "It's just unbelievable that in this country they'll spend a fortune bringing over some mummy from Egypt and then they turn around and treat the real treasures, the real American treasures like Blind Red Rose, like they were just dirt."

"Well ... I guess that's why they call it the blues," I said. I weaved my way through the people at the bar and sitting at the tables and found Ruby Rose. She was sitting at the table closest to the stage, just like she always did. When I use to play with Red sometimes she'd stand so far out on the stage that people use to think she was part of the group - a backup singer or something. And she was never ashamed to clap and yell and hoot louder than anyone else in the audience.

"Marty May!" She spotted me and stood up and gave me a big old hug. She had-on a red dress and a large gold cross hanging between her formidable breasts.

I knew the low-cut dress she was wearing - it was her show dress. Her Afro seemed twice as big.

"Hi ya, Ruby. Well, I finally made it - guitar and all." She looked at the case I was holding.

"You know, I remember you holding some beat up ol' guitar case that first night I saw you play," said Ruby. "Some things never change."

"Unfortunately ... I gave my roadies the night off."

"And I suppose they're out partying with your limousine driver?" asked Ruby sarcastically.

"Right, you got it..." And then I looked up and saw Red Rose on stage. He was sitting on a straight-backed chair like he always did. And he was dressed in the same black suit that I always remembered him in and a white shirt with no tie and the top button fastened. If it wasn't for his straw porkpie hat and his dark sunglasses held look just like some Baptist preacher. He was in-between numbers and Ruby grabbed my hand and took me up to the stage.

"Daddy! Marty May has come down to say hello to you."

"Why, hello 'dere Marty, - he drawled. "How ya all doin' son?" He held out his hand.

"Hello, Red," I said. "I'm doing just fine." I still couldn't figure out if he was saying 'Marvin, or 'Marty'. I took his black hand into mine. It was so old it was like

looking at the hand of the first man or something. "And how about yourself, Red, how are you doing?" I asked slowly. Red always had trouble understanding my Northern accent.

"Oh, I guess I can't complain too much, Marty, though my daughter Ruby 'ere ain't lettin' me have enough bourbon to suit my tastes." He fiddled with his National Steel Guitar as he spoke. It was an amazing looking instrument - designed in the thirties as a louder acoustic guitar to be used in the big bands of that era, with a body made out of chromed steel. It looked more like a missing part of a fifty-seven Chevrolet than a musical instrument. But it was the only guitar I ever saw Red Rose play.

"Now, Daddy! You know what the doctor said!" Ruby shook her finger at him as if he could see her, "Not till after your operation. And then ... only a little bit on special occasions."

"Well, I don't know, Ruby," drawled Red Rose. Where I come from folks belie that a lil' bourbon never hurt no one - but no bourbon at all jus' might be the death of ol' Red Rose here. Ya unnderstan wha' I'm sayin' girl?"

"Daddy, you hush up about your bourbon!" With an audience full of blues fanatics waiting to see just what the hell was going on Red Rose was as oblivious to them as could be. "Marty May has come all the way down here to see you and all you can talk about is bourbon!" Ruby winked at me. "Marty's a big rock star now, daddy. Why, he's got fifteen-year old girls chasin' him everywhere he goes."

"Is dat so?" said Red. "Hows about loanin' me a few of your...disciples, Marty?" He laughed.

"Now you hush up, Daddy, and Marty's gonna play a little blues with ya."

"Well, that would be very nice indeed, certainly would," said Red nodding his head. "I guess you might even call this som' kinda special occasion, huh, Ruby?" He smiled.

"That's right, Daddy," said Ruby. "Very special."

"So...how's about a little bourbon then?" asked Red.

"Daddy, shut up and play!"

Red's regular guitar player stepped down and I plugged my Telecaster into his amp. Actually, these musicians weren't regular' at all. Guys like Red couldn't afford to keep bands together anymore so club owners like Jerry Ryan would supply a backup group as part of the agreement. In a way, it made the blues a very portable music - perhaps the most portable in all of America. No sheet music or rehearsals were necessary. With a few idiosyncrasies for each individual blues singer the chord progressions were all basic twelve-bar stuff.

Ruby spoke into the microphones "Ladies and Gentlemen...I'm pleased to announce that Blind Red Rose has a special guest who's gonna play a few numbers with him - Marty May!" I was surprised by the ripple of applause and even a few hoots This must be a very 'old, blues crowd, indeed. I noticed

Dave Simmons sitting off to the side at a table full of people. Red had a set way of beginning. He's just say "Ready?" And than if no one said anything and sometimes even if they did he's just stomp off four beats with his foot and begin:

"Sustuh come and toll me
On a black cat afternoon
The sky was raining bullfrogs
And the judgment comin' soon
I waz in da kitchen
Sneakin' whiskey from a jug
I said girl now don't you bother me
Jus' make sure my grave been dug
'Cause I'm a busy man Oh Lord! I got plans to make..."

And it felt so good and so natural and smooth as if I'd been playing with him every day for the last ten years; maybe I should have been. He sang as truthfully and as soulfully as any human being, ever. When I would answer him on guitar, it was as if he were speaking through me. I don't know where the blues comes from, I know there have been scholarly books written about their African influences; but I do know that standing next to and playing with Blind Red Rose was as close to the source as a middle-class white boy like me or maybe anybody would ever get. And if it was just blues-osmosis, well that was all right too. I did a few real extended solos - Red would give me a nod to go another twelve bars - and the crowd that was there would applaud after each break. God, it felt good!

I even played some slide guitar with a glass bottleneck, which I hadn't done in years. It all seemed to come back to me like it was-just in hibernation or something for all these years. During all my time as a solo every manager and every record company I ever had had discouraged me from doing any blues because they said that it just wasn't commercial. But here it was, still around, for over fifty years. When I'd switch my Telecaster to the lead pickup for that really screeching treble sound like an engine being revved too high and just hold that note for all it was worth, bending it up into uncharted territories, I found my recent events just racing from my mind down into my fingers. I'd make that guitar mad as hell at Barbara for leaving me, and sorry for Paul Saint, and lustful for Inger Peach with a little love thrown in too. I remember in my early days with Red, he always gave me the same advice over and over and over: "Jus' make that thing say something!" held say, meaning my guitar. "'Cause if you ain't sayin' anything then there's nothin' fo' people to unnderstan'." And after each song, I felt a little better, a little clearer, rid of a few devils. We did about six songs and took a break. The crowd didn't want to let us go but Ruby knew when it was time for her father to rest. She came up and took him by the arm and led him from the low stage. He walked real slow. It took him a long time to get down off that stage like he was almost doing it begrudgingly. Somewhere, somehow he knew, he sensed, that he wouldn't be getting back up on one for much longer.

"That felt good!" I said excitedly.

"Yeah..." said Red Rose.. "That rock 'n rollin' ain't ruined you ... completely."

Ruby and I laughed. "So where to from here?" I asked her.

"Oh, I guess we're going back to Detroit, Marty. We've got some friends there we've been staying with on and off. But we got to find a new place to stay soon. It's a little crowded where we are now and there are lots of kids so it's hard for Red to get some peace and quiet."

"I don't need no peace OR quiet!" exclaimed Red. "What I need is bourbon - I keep tellin' you dat!"

"Now once and for all, you hush up, Daddy! The only bourbon you're getting close to is the bourbon that I drink!" said Ruby with finality. She turned back to me, "Marty, I'll have to write you with an address after we get settled." She looked at Red, "And at this rate, we're never gonna get settled 'cause I ain't never gonna be able to get no job 'cause I ain't never gonna find someone to take care of you cause you is becoming more and more impossible every day!"

"How 'bout one of Marty's female followers?" Red suggested hopefully.

And the great thing was that I don't even think he was kidding. Why, he would have had a shot of Jack Daniels right then and there, ulcer or no ulcer, if Ruby would have let him. What Red Rose had taught me had more to do with life than just music and it had been an important lesson: Get it while you can. We sat and talked and I looked at the two of them together. They were an odd couple indeed. Blind Red Rose looking like the ancient relic he was, humming some tune to himself. If it weren't for the fact that he couldn't take a drink, I guess you'd have to say that he was a pretty contented soul; he sang away his troubles. Funny thing, for someone like Paul Saint, I don't think singing helped his problems at all - probably made them worse. But Ruby was a different story. She tried to keep up a front but she couldn't hide her anxiety about the future. She expected to hear nothing but bad news; and I knew the prospects weren't good. Red's peak was behind him. Things had been going downhill for a long time. And all Ruby seemed able to do lately was to try a I and slow down their descent as best she could by careful management of their meager resources. I've hear interviewers complain about guys like Blind Red Rose charging them for interviews, but they should understand that this was the end of the line, not like some twenty-year-old guitar wizard who thought (too often mistakenly), that after on hit it would be all smooth sailing. The big payoff had never come for Red and Ruby and it never would. But I don't think Red ever thought it would come; he never expected it. Maybe that's the difference between him and Paul Saint. No expectations - no disappointments. You see, Red's blues were not songs of disappointment really; they were songs of reality a harsh reality that only existed, had to be accepted, promised nothing. And we white boys, what do we sing about? Do we sing about our father's heart attacks? And our mothers growing old in a culture that loves nothing but youth and beauty in women? And divorce? And all the other inevitable No, not really. We sing about bogeying down some mythical highway with a six-pack in one hand and a sixteen-year-old blond in the other. There was a time when we started to sing about things more real but then we had the Vietnam War showing its bloody face every time you turned on the TV. Nowadays, you more likely to find reruns of 'Happy Days'. And songs about nothing at all on the Top Ten.

I wondered what Ruby would do without Red. Held been her life's work. She had long ago buried whatever dreams and aspirations she had for herself. Maybe it had been far more important for her to connect with a past father than a future lover. I hear that in black disappearing ghettos the incidence of disappearing fathers is a way of life, a way of survival. Us white people choose to keep up appearances - we prefer divorce; the illusion of a separated family that still is a family. I wondered how Ruby felt that day in that Bar-B-Cue shop when this old blind man in a black suit was led in and introduced to her as her father. What did that feel like? What kind of bond was made at that moment? And what would she do when he was gone. Would she be able to "unbury all those parts of herself she had denied all these years? I'd never seen her with another man) for all I knew she could still be a virgin though I seriously doubted it she knew far too much for that to still be true. I think, though, in a way. She was the most proper woman I ever knew, the most rigid and formalized. She had only one way of doing things; she took nothing but cold cash before a gig. Dave Simmons came over to the table and Ruby invited him to sit down. He seemed very excited. "God, that was just great! Why did you two ever break up?" I was embarrassed by this question; it was the one never brought up.

But Red said casually, "Oh, ya know, Marty had som' wild oats to sew - Lookin' for a lil' piece of da American dream - da fifteen year ol' female variety." And this made him howl with laughter and me too. If Inger was here and if only he could see her, maybe held have to admit that in the long run, I hadn't done too badly.

"Are you gonna play together tomorrow night?" Dave asked.

"That's up to Marty," said Ruby.

"Are you kidding? 'Wild, wild horses - couldn't drag me away!" I sang.

"Is dat one o' your songs?" asked Red.

"Oh, no it's by the Rolling Stones," I answered.

"Who?" asked Red.

Dave Simmons said that he wanted to do a big write-up in The Voice on Red and me. He said that he thought that there was going to be another blues revival. I disagreed with him; said only a war could bring that about. We did another set and it felt just as good if not better than the first. I left Tramps feeling great and looking forward to the next night. And maybe some nights after that, too.

Chapter 2

The siren of the ambulance was deafening. Pedestrians on the street corners held their hands over their ears as the orange and white van with 'ECNALUBMA' written across its grill tried to snake it's way through the traffic. Some people would try to peer in the windows as it slowed to pass through a tight spot and others just looked away, to the ground, anywhere. Those who wanted to see, saw a driver in a white uniform regarding the chaos and alarm he was causing with an efficient air of disregard. In the back was another attendant, also in white, looking down on an old black man with an oxygen mask over his face lying on a stretcher with his head raised. The attendant looked no more concerned than the driver. It was difficult to tell the feelings of the man on the stretcher, his eyes were closed and his face was covered by the green plastic oxygen mask but it was evident that the black woman next to him was very, very worried. She kept ringing her hands and her eyes were shadowed with grief.

The driver and the attendant spoke to each other in Spanish and this made Ruby nervous.

"Is he all right?" What's wrong with him?" she asked frantically.

"I don't know, lady," said the attendant in heavily accented English. "I'm not a doctor. I think he has a stroke but I can't say for sure. You just gotta wait, don't worry I get us there as fast as I can.

Ruby looked out the windows of the ambulance and saw the traffic bottling them in; she wanted to go outside and get the cars to move out of the way. To scream at them that this was her father and he must get to a hospital couldn't see they see that? So please move. For God's sakes, move!

"Should I get out and direct traffic?" she asked the attendant.

"No, no, no...Don't do that lady. We be moving soon. Don't worry, he got the oxygen on him now. He be okay."

"But he's not moving. Is his heart beating?"

The attendant took the stethoscope out of the front pocket on his smock. He hesitantly fastened it to his ears, as if he was uncertain how it worked. Haltingly, he moved the receptor around the man's chest over his white shirt. "Yeah ... yeah ... his heart is beating okay. I can hear it...it's not too strong but I can hear it. Don't worry lady, we be at the hospital soon."

"Oh god." She closed her eyes. She was praying.

"*Maybe it would be good if you tell me what happened said the attendant.*

"*I told you what happened she said impatiently.*

"*I knows lady, but I'm trying to get him out of the room and down the elevator and into the ambulance. And I'm putting the oxygen on him too. I don't hear everything you're saying.*

"*He was in the bathroom. I was watching the TV...actually he was watching the TV even though he's blind...*"

"*He's blind?*" *asked the attendant startled.*

"*Of course he's blind,*" *said Ruby.* "*So he had on this show, this public affairs show he was listening to about some canal in New Jersey that was real polluted - called Love Canal - he got a real laugh out of that. And then he said he had to go so I helped him into the bathroom. I could hear him in there, he was singing about this Love Canal, he was singing, 'Love Canal fulla hate for da hole human race'...*" *Then Ruby Rose started to cry. Sometimes she would cry when she was happy but she rarely cried when she was sad or scared like she was now. It embarrassed her and she was quick to wipe away her tears.*

"*You want a Kleenex, lady?*"

She just shook her head and quickly wiped away her tears with her hands. "*So, I was watching this show an I guess I was gettin' interested in it too, but thin after a while I noticed that he wasn't singing anymore and held been in there quite a long time, so I went in and he was just lying on the floor ... I guess he fell right off-the seat 'cause his pants were still down.*" *But than she was sorry she had said that, it hurt his pride. Hadn't heard any sound or anything - I would have heard him if he made a sound. And he was making strange noises as he was breathing.*" *And she added like it was very important,* "*And his glasses had come off - and cracked.*" *She held the broken sunglasses in her hand. She almost wanted to put them back on him as he lay in front of her.*

The ambulance finally broke through the traffic. Ruby and the attendant braced themselves as they sped along, swerving from lane to lane, but the man on the stretcher just rolled gently like a ship on the sea. The attendant took a clipboard with a form on it and a chewed-up pen out of his pocket. "*It will help if you can give me some information - things will go faster at the hospital.*" *Though, this was not really true. It would only help him - he wouldn't have to get all the information for his report from the nurse at Admissions.*

"*He ain't got no health care, if that's what you mean. But I think he's old enough for Medicare or Medicaid or something.*"

"Naw, I don't care about that. They take care of that shit at the hospital. I just need the facts. What's the guy's name?"

"Blind Red Rose."

"What?" said the attendant. "Are you kiddin' me? Is that his real name?"

"It is. It's his real name to me and I'm his daughter," she said proudly.

"Oh, I didn't know that, Lady. I'm sorry."

She didn't know why he was sorry now. "But I guess his real name as far as reports like the one you filling out is William Rose maybe William Rose, Jr.

"What's his date of birth?"

"I don't really know. Held tell me July fourth - he said that's why he's so independent." She had to control herself from crying. She didn't really know the year but she wanted to make him old enough for whatever benefits he might be able to get. "I think the year is Nineteen-Ten."

"Where was he born?"

"Mississippi...Tupelo, Mississippi." She didn't know if this was true either.

"Occupation?"

"Oh ... I guess you can put down ... Entertainer." Ruby remembered the one time her father had been to Europe and she had to fill in that same question on his immigration form. When she asked him he had told her to write in 'Eye Doctor'

"Where's he employed?"

"Well ... for right now, & club called Tramps."

"I never heard of it. Social Security number?"

"He don't have one."

"Lady, everybody got to have one of those. Everybody's got a social security number."

"Well not Blind Red Rose!" It was the first time she had felt mad.

"Okay, lady, okay." The attendant was finding it too hard to write. The ambulance was moving too quickly
now. "I finish it later."

Ruby took her father's hand in hers. It wasn't cold and she was afraid it might be. His eyes were closed and he didn't move. She bent down and whispered in his ear.

"Don't worry, Daddy, we be there soon. I'm here. Ruby's here - don't worry."

They reached Mother Cabrini hospital. When Ruby saw the name she said to the attendant: "But he's not Catholic - is that all right?"
"Don't worry, lady," said the driver who was now helping take the stretcher out of the ambulance at the
Emergency entrance. "They take anybody. We just go to the nearest hospital, that's all."
Two nurses and a doctor took over the stretcher at the door and ruby followed them in. The driver and the attendant just looked at each other and shrugged their shoulders and shook their heads. "You wanna get something to eat?" said the driver in Spanish.

Chapter 3

I was about to walk out the door of my apartment, guitar in hand, when Jerry Ryan called me from Tramps. He said that Red was in the hospital, held had a stroke, Ruby had just phoned him. I asked if it was serious, which was a stupid thing to ask, and he said it didn't look good. Not until I was sitting in the back of a cab did I realize the *pointlessness of* bringing my guitar with me it wouldn't be of much good where I was going. The hospital gave me the same feeling they always do - that of an outsider.

Mistakenly, I was asking what room Red was in but I should have known that held be in emergency; it had happened only a few hours ago. The nurse directed me to the intensive care unit. I walked down hallways of people with grim expressions of their faces, some in pajamas and robes. I had an aversion to hospitals ever since Barbara's abortion, her first one. But then again, who looks forward to visiting such places? The Intensive Care Unit was about twenty beds in one room, ten on either wall. Some were completely isolated by draping; many had electronic life-support devices by them. I tried not to look at any of the people in the beds. I spotted Ruby at the farthest bed on the left and smiled because I could think of no other expression. When I reached her, she put her arms around me tight. "Oh, Marty. I'm so glad you're here." She was crying. I had never seen her cry before.

"How is he?" I looked down at Red. He looked strange not dressed in his customary way; on the way there I had pictured him in a black suit on a white bed. But he was in hospital garb like all the others who lay in the beds. And he didn't have on his shades; his eyes were half open and the glistening cataracts over them made him look otherworldly.

"Can he talk?" I asked Ruby. "Does he know what's going on?"

"Just barely, Marty." She was gently rubbing his cheek but he made no sign. "Every once in a while he'll whisper something but I have to bend down real close to hear him. She told me what had happened: He seemed fine, normal, they were in the Chelsea Hotel and then she found him on the bathroom floor.

"What do the doctors say?" I asked.

"Well ... they say his condition has stabilized, whatever that means. They say that the next day or two will be real important. I don't know, Marty, everything they say just scares me so...I find it hard to concentrate when they talk to me." She looked at me with tears in her eyes. "Red don't belong in a place like this ... my daddy would hate to be in this kind of place. He told me he never once had been in a hospital before his last stroke. And then he just hated it. I had to force him to stay. Marty, he gets scared in places like this."' And then she just broke down.

I put my arms around her. "Don't worry Ruby ... there's nothing you can do. Everybody's gotta..." But I didn't finish my sentence. "Should I get a minister or something? Is Red religious?" I only asked because I knew of *nothing else* to say.

"No ... no, he wouldn't want someone down here he didn't know. He once told me that if anything... " And then I saw that Red's lips were moving.

"Ruby, he's trying to say something." She bent down and put her ear to his mouth. I couldn't hear him at all but she kept saying, "Yes, Daddy ... yes, Daddy." And then she said, "Yes Daddy, that's Marty, he's standing right next to me ... okay Daddy." she stood up. "What'd he say?" I asked.

"He knew you was here, Marty, he wants to talk to you. Here, take his hand and talk to him." She put his hand in mine. I bent forward. I had to put my ear right next to his mouth to hear him.

"Marty, is dat you, Marty?" He whispered very faintly. It was just the sound of his breath, not his voice.

"Marty, this train is leavin',"

"Red, you gotta stay here awhile, you can't go nowhere, just relax, and you'll be okay."

"No Marty, ya lissen to me. I'm dyin, I knows it ... Once girl ... I came and get her, ain't nobody hurt." And then he stopped, a slight grip on my hand. "Marty, are you there? Lissen to me boy, there's no time. I'm going...I came fo' Ruby ... she waz my baby and took her wid me ... I took care of her..."

I looked at Ruby but then I felt his hand tighten on mine and I put my ear back by his mouth.

"Yes, Red, I'm here I'm listening."

"Marty, I knew 'em all ... I knowed Robert Johnson ... he was a bad man wid da evil eye das what kilt him and Leadbelly...he waz a thief he stole one o' my songs ... but I don care, I had my rewards here on earth...ya unnerstan?"

"Yes, Red, I understand." But I didn't really. I couldn't.

"Marty lissen to me   you got da blues as bad as any of dem ever did ... I don know why ... yuz a white boy ... But it don matter blues is da music o' survival...everyone doin' it now black and white … we all slavin' now for the man."

I didn't know what to say. A dying man had never whispered in my ear before.

"Marty, I want ya to do a couple ' things fo' me now..."

"Sure, Red, sure."

"I'm dyin' Marty ... keep my songs alive foe me will ya ... and take good care o' Ruby too...I came to get her once but I gotta leave her now...

"Don't worry, Red, everything is gonna be okay...He squeezed my hand with a faint tremble but I knew it was all his strength.

"Promise me dat Marty ... take care o' Ruby an' keep my songs living so da next generation will know what the blues meant for all of us on dis earth..."

"Okay, I promise you, Red, don't worry, I promise you." My voice was shaking my eyes were watering. I didn't *know* if it was enough.

"Thanks Marty ... gimme Ruby ... where's Ruby?"

I moved back and Ruby talked to her father. I don't know where he was getting the strength. Finally his eyes closed and he appeared to be resting; Ruby stood up.

"What did he say?" I asked.

"He wanted me to bring him some bourbon." I hadn't even noticed that Red was hooked up to some machine until a high piercing buzzer went off and nurses and doctors ran over and told us to wait outside and pulled the curtain around his bed. We stood outside the swinging double doors to the intensive care unit and tried to look through the windows. There was nothing to see, his bed was completely surrounded by green drapes. Ruby and I said nothing to each other. I just stood there with my arm around her and then I put my jacket around her because she seemed to be shivering and then after what seemed like too long a time, a doctor dressed in green came out and just like in the movies shook his head and said, "I'm sorry, he's gone."

Ruby stopped shivering and let out a big breath. There were tears in my eyes. "Oh, Ruby..." was all I could say.

"You wait for me here, will ya Marty? I wanna go say goodbye." And she followed the doctor back into the room. I didn't know what was required of me now, what I should do, how I should act. The last death that I had witnessed was my own father's and then there was my mother, and relatives and friends who came to the house, sat with us, and took care of all the business that follows closely behind. I remember feeling somewhat in the way; death is something that adults do it's not a place for children. Ruby emerged ten minutes later. She was composed; maybe all cried out. She managed a slight smile. "I guess it's not really sad," she said. "Not for him at least. He'd lived his life exactly as he wanted - and outlived most of his cronies."

"Yeah," I could barely mutter.

"Tell me something, Marty, what was he speaking to you about?"

"Oh... just giving me some musical advice, you know..."

A nurse approached us from behind. "Miss Rose? Is there a funeral home you'd like us to call? To pick up the body?" This made me mad; it seemed abrupt, inappropriate, making room a little too fast.

"Oh God, I don't know, I hadn't thought about any of that. Funeral? Oh God." Ruby put a hand to her eyes but I could tell that she had decided that she didn't want to cry anymore. "I just don't know about any of that, yet. When do I gotta tell you?"

"Well, we'd appreciate it if you could advise us within twenty-four hours." The nurse said matter-of-factly. "We're awfully crowded," she added. This seemed unnecessary.

"All right, I will, I'll let you know as soon as I figure things out." Ruby turned to me. "Well, I guess Red can't argue against welfare anymore. I'm gonna have to go to some agency for some help. I don't got near enough money for a funeral. I'd never thought about it before. What do folks do when they gotta bury their daddy and they ain't got no money?" I don't think she really expected an answer out of me.

"Listen," I said. "Sit down here." I pointed to a waiting area. "While I make a phone call ... uh ...I got an idea."

"Who are you calling, Marty?" she asked.

"Now, you can't ask me any questions, Ruby. Please, I'll only be a minute." I hugged her and walked away to the phones. I don't know if this whole charade was necessary but it was the only thing I could think of at the time. I went through the yellow pages looking under funeral homes. I found one located just a block away from Tramps and I called. The funeral director I spoke to was agreeable and he had the correct sympathetic tone. Then I called Tramps. Jerry Ryan answered.

"Jerry, this is Marty May, Red Rose is dead."

"Oh Sweet Jesus," said Jerry. "I had feared the worst anyway. When did it happen?"

"Just a short time ago. His heart just stopped, he was through with living."

"How's Ruby?"   People always ask this, what can you say?

"Okay, I guess,"

I said. "But she's all alone now…I don't know if she's really thought it all through yet."

"Oh god,"   said Jerry. I heard a sniffle on the other end.

"Well ... what can you do."

"I'll tell you what we can do. I want to have Red's funeral at Tramps."

"What?" said Jerry. "How can you do that? Aren't there a lot of arrangements to be made and everything and

"Listen, its all taken care of. I even got someone to pay for it."

"Who's that?" asked Jerry shocked.

"Oh ... he's a real blues buff," I said. "If I can fix it all up, how about in two days - it would be a Friday."

Jerry agreed. The funeral parlor said it would be all right. I said that I'd come down and pay them tomorrow. And than they started asking me what kind of coffin I wanted.

And this one costs this much and that one costs that much and so on. I just told the guy that I wanted the best there is that five thousand dollars can buy. I wanted to have some money left over in case Ruby needed it. I went back to where she was sitting. "It's all set," I said.

"What's all set, Marty?"

"The funeral, everything. Is it all right with you if we have it at Tramps? In the spirit of the blues?"

"Marty, I toll you that I don't have any money for no funeral. I'm gonna have to go talk to those social service people and see -

"Don't worry, Ruby, it's all set. There's a guy, I can't tell you his name but he's a real blues fanatic... he was one of Red's biggest fans, and he's been... real lucky. He wants to pay for the whole thing. He said it's just his way of saying thank you."

"No? Really, Marty? I never heard of anything like this before. Are you serious?" she said unbelieving.

"Absolutely, Ruby. He won't have it any other way."

"I wished held been around when my daddy was alive," she wiped a tear from her eye. "Sob's it wouldn't have been so hard on him all these last years."

"Well he's probably sorry too."

"Marty, who is this man? I just can't believe it. Where'd he get this money to throw around?"

"Ruby, I told you, I couldn't tell you his name. He's very shy." I tried not to lie. "He kind of inherited his money, he's got something to do with The American Express Company, you know, that credit card company?"

"Yeah, I know," said Ruby. "Well I ain't gonna argue with him now. I guess I should thank him."

"Oh ... that's not necessary. He just wants to say he's sorry and he asked to remain anonymous."

Inger Peach returned the next day from Atlantic City. Things hadn't worked out. It seems that the same creep who had hassled her out in Vegas was now in Atlantic City and had spotted her just the day before. She couldn't believe it. He immediately took up where he had left off, only it seemed he had gained more power through the last years, he knew everyone down there. So she packed her bags and left. One thing I had to say about that girl, she had some serious convictions.

She had already called The Follies to see if she could get her old job back. No problem. I wasn't surprised. I doubted if they got girls of Inger's quality in there all the time. She was a star.

That night she and I went over to the Chelsea Hotel to see Ruby. Even in Ruby's bereaved state I could tell that these two women hit it off; there was some kind of immediate mutual respect. And when Inger went over and put her arm around Ruby and said, "I'm so sorry," it was with a tenderness that Ruby immediately responded to.

"Thank you darlin'," she said.

Inger insisted that we should all go out and get something to eat, that it was no good for Ruby just sitting there alone in her hotel room. So, we went to a place called Cajun a New Orleans styled restaurants not far from The Chelsea Hotel. They had a little Dixieland group on a bandstand and every once in a while they'd walk around the room playing their instruments except for the drummer who stayed put. It reminded me of what I heard New Orleans funerals were like so I didn't think it was in poor taste or anything for us to be there. When Inger went to the ladies room Ruby said to me, "Marty, I think you finally got yourself a real woman there."

And this made me feel real good about Inger, regardless of what she did or where she worked it was a stamp of approval from a woman who would know. The next day I got on the phone to prepare for the funeral. Jerry Ryan said hold do his best to spread the word too. It was his idea that I should play some of Red Rose's songs. It seemed the right thing to do.

I called Joe Lippell and asked him to come and bring Paul Saint if he could make it. I contacted Dave Simmons, the writer, but he already knew because he had shoved up at Tramps the next night. He said he had written the obituary for the Daily News. I didn't think that a loud backup band playing behind me would be right, so I decided to do it alone. I asked Ruby if I could use Red's guitar and she said of course. I cashed my check for ten thousand dollars; I think the man at the funeral parlor was quite surprised when I paid him in cash - all one hundred dollar bills. Red would have liked that. He said that they were putting Red in a lovely walnut casket, lined in white satin. I asked him if they could line it with blue satin and he said they could. I gave him the black suit and white shirt that Ruby had given me to drop off and when he asked for a tie I just said that, no, this was how we wanted it. And Ruby had given me an extra pair of Red's sunglasses too. The funeral was to be at seven o'clock at night.

When I showed up around six I was amazed that the place was filled with flowers - impressive wreaths of all shapes and sizes and from music people all over the country. I guess between Joe Lippell and Dave Simmons, the word had gotten out. There were flowers sent by B.B. King and Muddy Waters and even by some country performers like Kenny Rogers that you wouldn't expect it from. I don't think that anyone who is involved with popular music, be it rock 'n roll or New Wave or Heavy Metal could not help but be moved when someone like Blind Red Rose dies. Any loss to any endangered species reminds us all of our own transient Upstairs, in the dressing room, lying on a table was

Red's obituary from the Daily News- Jerry Ryan must have cut it out for me:

OLDTIMER OF COUNTRY BLUES, BLIND RED ROSE, DIES AT 69 - New York William (Blind Red) Rose, 69, a singer, songwriter and guitarist often described as one of the last of the old-time country bluesmen, died Saturday of complications following a massive stroke. A contemporary of such black blues artists as Muddy Waters, B.B. King and John Lee Hooker, Rose was one of the most respected blues artists of the 1940's and 1950's. Born in the rural northern Mississippi town of Tupelo in 1912, Rose entertained audiences throughout the world for more than 50 years with his loose guitar playing and his gutsy Southern blues style and his low-pitched voice. His songs were extremely personal, reflecting his social background. At age 7, he fashioned a guitar from a cigar box and screen wire and taught himself to play. A kick by a mule took away his sight soon after and Rose reportedly began to sing when he was the traveling companion of Robert Johnson, the legendary king of the Delta style blues singers, although there is no known existing recording of the two together. During his career, he made more than fifty records on about a dozen different labels. Many of them are collector's items though he received few royalties. He entertained on college campuses, in folk clubs and in the late 1960's during the blues revival peak he toured Europe. During this period Rose employed a backup band of both white and black musicians and is credited with discovering the white blues guitarist Marty May who went on to achieve moderate success as a rock performer. Rose acquired the name "Red, when he went to Chicago and formed a short-lived duo with Bukka White. Their aborted album was to be called "Red, White, and Blues". Apparently White insisted upon calling him Red due to the slight red tint of his hair. Red Rose is survived by his daughter and manager, Ruby Rose. A funeral will be held at TRAMPS on 15th Street on Friday Evening at 7pm. All those who appreciated Blind Red Rose's contribution to the Blues are invited to attend.

I was nervous upstairs in the dressing room. I just kept fiddling with Red's National Steel Guitar and waiting for Jerry to come up and get me. And when he did and when I walked downstairs, I couldn't believe it; the place was completely full. There were people standing everywhere. Naturally Jerry had kept the bar closed and there were people sitting all across it. And there were all kinds too, rich and poor, black and white. Somehow the word must have gotten out that this was some kind of an 'event' the place to be. Or maybe I shouldn't be so cynical; maybe they just all cared. Inger had come with Ruby, both ladies dressed in black, both looking elegant. The stage had been cleared of any instruments and Red lay in his coffin in his black suit and his shades. Jerry had lots of different blues records playing while the people continued to walk in, even a scratchy old recording made back in the thirties of Robert Johnson and Leadbelly. Jerry and I walked up to the stage next to Red's coffin where a microphone and a stool were set up. First Jerry spoke:

"I want to thank you all for coming tonight on behalf of Ruby Rose. We have gathered here together to give our last respects and to say goodbye to a legend of American history. Red Rose wasn't much of a talker himself and he could never understand my Irish brogue..."

There was a ripple of respectful laughter.

"...So we thought that instead of talking about Red Rose tonight, it might be nicer and more fitting, and I think Red would have like it better, if Marty May came up here and sang a few...blues."

I sat on the stool and adjusted the microphone. I saw Joe Lippell in the audience; Paul wasn't with him. I doubted he would be. But there were other people in the music industry there too. The producer Jerry Wexler who had started out by recording blues singers like Red and then had gone on to produce the finest soul singers ever heard like Aretha Franklin. And John Hammond was there too; he had discovered Billie Holiday and Bessie Smith and Bob Dylan

"Really, I don't know if Red would have liked this or not," I said. "If you had all paid an admission he might have liked it better," They laughed. "But I would like to try to sing some of Red's songs for you tonight, and maybe using his guitar here will help me do a better job," I smiled at Ruby who sat with Inger at a table right up front. "Red really never pronounced my name right, so I hope he'll allow whatever mistakes I make with his songs tonight ... but I just want to say that I owed an awful lot to this man we all do, really to Red Rose and other's like him and well, I better just sing." And I began. In the middle of the first song, Ruby started clapping along with me and then most everyone clapped along too; some even sang. We went on like that for over an hour. I sang songs of his that I was sure I would never remember, still could. And then after I was through, four dark but I did and I played blues licks that I didn't think I suited men from the funeral parlor came and closed Red's casket and took it out of Tramps to a waiting hearse while everybody stood and watched them file by with their heavy burden. Red would be buried tomorrow morning but Ruby a said that she just wanted to go to the burial alone and I respected and understood her wishes. After the casket was taken out, the crowd began to disperse and Joe Lippell came over to the table where I was sitting With Ruby, Inger and Jerry Ryan. "Marty, that was wonderful, I never knew you could sing blues so well...I thought all you did was rock 'n roll."

"Well, you know what they say – the Blues had a baby and called it rock 'n roll," I said smiling

"And you're that baby," said Joe thinking. "Maybe there's a concept there…"

"Joe, let me introduce you to Ruby Rose, Red's daughter."

"I'm so sorry," said Joe taking her hands into him own. "We all know what good care you took of your father for all those years."

"Thank you," said Ruby. "I appreciate you all coming down here tonight; my daddy would have like it." She was holding up amazingly well. I hadn't seen her shed a tear all night.

It was really a lovely idea to have Marty sing," said Joe.

"No. He's not too bad, ain't he," said Ruby as she smiled at me. "Musta had a good teacher along the way."

"Joe turned to me. "You know, Marty, I know a couple of guys who have this small specialty label, mainly jazz, but they do some blues too. They might be interested in an album of you doing Red Rose's songs. I could call them for you if you'd like. Would you be interested?"

"I don't know, Joe," I said. "Guess you gotta speak to my manager first."

"Your manager? Who's that?"

"Why, Ruby, Rose, of course."

"What?" asked Ruby. "I ain't yo' … "

"Well, you are now," I said.

Chapter 4

A few days later, I was in my apartment, packing things up moving to Inger's place. It wasn't too complicated a move; a few suitcases, the stereo system Paul Saint had given me, and, of course, that box full of my press. Maybe someday I'd seal it up and throw it into the Hudson but not yet. I didn't need to clean out completely though because Ruby Rose would be moving in soon. I'd talked her into staying in New York. Though, she really had no other place to go or to call home, home always being wherever her father was. And I convinced her that I honestly and truly wanted her to become my manager; she thought I was crazy. But I told her that I wanted to sing the blues for a while, get together a small backup band, see if she couldn't book some club dates. The label that Joe had mentioned was, in fact, interested. They thought an album of me doing Red's songs would have a good shot over in Europe. There wasn't much money involved but it was enough to put both Ruby and me a few months ahead of the game and if we fell behind I still had five grand left over to back us up. I even tried to get—Ruby to sign a contract with me; I thought it would make her feel more secure. But she wouldn't hear of it. It had to be the first time in history that a manager didn't want to sign an artist to a long-term contract; usually it was the other way around.

Once again, the gangster's had chased Inger Peach from her showgirl aspirations. Maybe it was fate; maybe she was needed more at The Follies where she could brighten the days and nights of the poor crew in the audience. I didn't know how I felt about it anymore. Maybe I'd try a little warm milk before sleeping they say this helps your dreams. So Inger was back at the Follies and I was back to the blues, back where I started. Maybe this time I'd do it differently. It's funny, but before, the blues always seemed a dead end, the same old clubs year after year, no real money; and rock On roll had seemed a world of endless possibilities eager to open up to the latest resident boy wonder who had the stamina to ride on through. But now, I don't know why, maybe something to do with watching Paul Saint, the end seemed fixed to me a highway with few exits. And if you missed the right one it would be miles and miles before the next. Maybe I was lucky I hadn't gone all that far. I could start over a lot easier than Paul Saint.

Cleaning up my apartment for Ruby, I came across that high school reunion invitation and I threw it out the window, as was my first instinct to do. I suppose Betty Klein was on the Pocahontas Heights Junior League Committee trying to raise money to send poor city kids to summer camp and give them free braces on their teeth or something. I wondered if *The White Castles* album ever came out? I couldn't guess a lot of albums are made that never do. I wished Tom Dunn luck in trying to lure Hollywood High nymphets into his hot tub. I knew where Paul Saint was although I had little faith that this 'cure' would last. But maybe he was rich enough to just keep getting cured, maybe that's the best anybody can hope for, for any malady of the soul or body. I did hope Joe Lippell was sleeping better at nights, he deserved to. And most of all I hoped Ruby Rose saw some future in her future without Red.

And Inger was back to spreading her legs for all to see, showing her shame and her treasure, but I thought I could live with it now. I wanted to survive and love was part of that survival so there was a small price to pay. Nothing's free; Red Rose use to say that. And at least now that I'm sharing Inger's apartment my rent would be cut in half. Take the good with the bad, I guess. I bet that Barbara was probably making love with Garcia Ortega on his paint-splattered bed. I didn't care. But I'll be damned if I was going to spend the rest of my days running errands for the great man himself. If I had taken him up on his offer I'm sure it would have ended horribly, anyway. I probably could have murdered both him and Barbara one windswept night at the beach while they rolled around the paint splattered sand - a combo of both *Psycho* and *From Here to Eternity*. I called Barbara and told her. I was short and to the point. She said I was making a big mistake. I told her I'd made only one big mistake in my life and that was marrying her. She hung up on me. I've started to think of Barbara as that 'Pretty little Preppie Bitch' as Inger is so fond of calling her. I know this isn't really all she is but I'm finding that simplifying people and situations helps clarify any decisions or plans I gotta make. There's a famous line from Chekhov. "And suddenly everything became clear to him." Well, that's how I feel, in a way. The only thing I'm not clear about is how I know that line from Chekhov.

Again, I've come to believe that rock 'n roll saved my life and that it's the most direct way to plug into the core of America's energy, its dark marrow, the source of all its awfulness and wonderfulness and its never-ending search for a soul. And the blues I'm playing now is kind of like, well, less affluent rock 'n roll; less luxury but a lot less stress. I'm sure I'll get back to it someday, to all its true glory and false promises but I'll try to stay on the outside and I'll treat it with a more respect, like a fine piece of china or a dangerous animal, you know, don't drop it or you buy it or it may bite. Something like that, next time...

I was about to shut off the lights on my final-trip out of my old apartment when the phone rang. I picked it up and a familiar voice hissed into my ear. "Mr. May, this is Mr. Moore from American Express." I held the phone at arms length and slowly brought it back to my ear.

"Oh ... I suppose you want to speak to Marty... this is ... " I held my breath and sought inspiration and found it on an empty breakfast cereal box in the garbage. "This is...Kellogg May, Yes, Kellogg. I'm Marty's brother." My voice deepened because certainly, if I did have a brother, and his name was indeed Kellogg his voice would be as low as Paul Robeson. Anyway, more dignified than my own rock 'n roll whine.

"I know who this is!" yelled Mr. Moore. "Don't take me for an idiot, Mr. May! I've had it!" He really did seem rather hysterical. The man certainly took his job more seriously then I took mine.

"I don't know who you are but if you'll keep your voice down I'll pass on any message to my younger brother, Marty when he gets back in town sometime ... next year,"

"Yes! You can give your 'younger brother' a message! You can tell him he's going to jail - that YOU'RE going to jail! You were supposed to send us a check weeks ago! You promised me! This is fraud!" The man was definitely breathing heavily.

"Fraud? Gee ... I can't imagine Marty doing anything like that. He may be a little frivolous at times ... but fraud? No, not Marty. He's an artist." and I added for my own satisfaction "And quite a famous musician, too!" My voice was so low I sounded like Orson Welles with laryngitis.

"You're crazy!" he yelled. "You can't get away with this! We're gonna get our money - I'm gonna get it! We'll take you to court."

"Uh...I don't think that would be possible. Hold on a second will you? Let me put someone else on who might be able to help better help you. And please, there's really no need to be so upset. After all, its only money!"

I held the phone a few feet away but I could still hear him scream: "ONLY MONEY???" I called out loudly: "Oh Hop? Could you come over here a minute - it's a call for Marty." It was hard not to laugh. I put my hand over the receiver and cleared my throat.

"Ah so. Hello? Is Mr. May's most honorable houseboy Hop Song. Master gone on long, long Asian tour. Maybe never come back! If you want talk to Mr. May you better fly Hong Kong!"

"Why you! I'll get you, I'll..."

I think I hung up on him first and I was laughing and he probably wasn't. So at least this time I won a small battle. And that's what it's all about. Isn't it?

62204791R00171

Made in the USA
Lexington, KY
01 April 2017